Vermilion

Also by Molly Tanzer:

A Pretty Mouth
Rumbullion and Other Liminal Libations
The Pleasure Merchant (forthcoming)

Vermilion

THE ADVENTURES OF
LOU MERRIWETHER, PSYCHOPOMP

Molly Tanzer

WORD HORDE
PETALUMA, CA

First Edition

ISBN: 978-1-939905-08-6

A Word Horde Book
http://www.WordHorde.com

for my father

Prologue

An owl hooted as the final sliver of orange sun disappeared below a range of jagged mountain peaks deep within the Colorado Rockies. Several stars were already shining sharply in the moonless sky, and as azure twilight darkened to ultramarine night, their fainter, silver-white cousins also winked awake. Starlight shimmered over black, snow-crusted pine branches and pale aspen boughs as a gust of wind shook the forest.

The owl was not the only creature in the pinewood that evening. After silently diving to clasp her talons around a thin marten bounding across a clearing, she winged her way over a handful of clapboard structures that squatted in the lee of the mountainside on a wide rock shelf just below the treeline. The accumulated snow on the rooftops and windowsills of the small sanatorium might have seemed cozy at yuletide, but it was late into February and thus it merely looked *cold,* especially when the shutters and doors shuddered in their frames and the torches illuminating the decks and walkways guttered in the wuthering wind.

Shuddering, as well, were a cluster of men and women dressed in white woolen hats, scarves, gloves, and matching uniforms as they attempted a sequence of deep knee-bends and toe-touches in something approximating unison.

"Briskly, briskly!" Undaunted by the elements, a woman with large eyes and larger teeth encouraged her class by demonstrating what she wanted

1

to see. "Down, hold, *up!* Down, hold, *up!* You can go a bit lower, Mr. Rutherford, can't you?"

A *yes, Miss Foxglove* was followed by a low groan as Mr. Rutherford redoubled his efforts.

"Better!" cried Miss Foxglove. "Yes, much better! I say, Mr. Gillis, that cough doesn't sound good. Rest yourself, but hurry back!"

Mr. Gillis was not the only one having difficulties. The air was so bitter that everyone panted in ragged, choking gasps; the exercise so vigorous that each sweaty face gleamed in the flickering torchlight. No one seemed to be enjoying the calisthenics, nor did they display much enthusiasm when Miss Foxglove clapped twice and announced cheerily that it was time for jumping jacks. After showing them the correct form, her white riding-skirt flapping as she leaped up and down, she bid her class imitate her, and began counting off sets of ten.

"This is terrible," whispered a pretty, auburn-haired girl to her neighbors. The older of the two only nodded his agreement, too winded to speak; the younger and leaner made a noise halfway between a laugh and a cough.

"I *hate* this shit," he muttered as they paused between sets. He wiped his dark brow with an almost skeletally-thin hand. "Feel like I'll have a heart attack any minute."

"Oh, Mr. Wong!" The young woman was extremely concerned. "If you're not feeling well…"

She trailed off, wincing when another volley of phlegmatic hacking emanated from the darkness several yards outside the exercise area.

"Poor Mr. Gillis," she murmured before noticing Miss Foxglove looking daggers at her.

"Miss Gorey, are you quite ready to continue?" Her tone made it clear there was only one correct answer.

Mr. Rutherford smiled briefly to himself as the young woman bowed her head in contrition, pleased that for once a rebuke was not aimed at him. He quickly sobered as they began another set, and his heavy gut began bouncing and rippling. His wife, also puffing from the effort, pushed a perspiration-soaked lock of greying hair from her damp forehead. When Miss Foxglove allowed everyone a longer break so she could check on the still-coughing Mr. Gillis, Mrs. Rutherford sighed in relief.

"I wish evening calisthenics wasn't required," she said faintly. "Just once

I'd like to go to dinner without feeling as though my bowels had been jolted out of my body."

"Given the fare, that's what they're after." Mr. Rutherford mopped his forehead with a handkerchief. "I asked the cook about supper. Salad, of course, and cabbage stew over baked beans."

This intelligence drew mutinous grumbles from the group. Hearing the ruckus as she returned, Miss Foxglove chirped that if they had breath enough for complaining, they had breath enough for more jumping jacks.

As they began another set, a round, yellow door set into the mountainside swung open, then shut quietly. Behind the group, a slender figure in a black frock coat and trousers seemed to glide through the night as he strolled along the smooth planks of the boardwalk, his white hands clasped behind his back. He carried no lantern to light his way, but did not stumble.

Miss Foxglove announced it was time for "limberness-enhancement." Busy with retrieving and unfurling their straw mats, none noticed they were observed. The man watched them from the shadows of a juniper thicket. A smile brightened his handsome face when the group sat down, extended their legs perpendicularly, attempting to fold at the waist and grab their toes. When Miss Foxglove reprimanded a nervous-looking woman with a large chest for wearing her corset under her exercise attire, a low chuckle escaped his throat.

"How do you expect to get a full range of motion wearing that *thing?*" Miss Foxglove shook her head in disbelief, her mouth puckered with prim disapproval. "Mrs. Grosvenor, as I have told you time and again, it is unacceptable to come to class wearing anything that constricts the breath. It may be the fashion outside this sanatorium to mold women's bodies so tightly they faint at the slightest exertion, but we are a *modern* facility, and as such, believe in healthy living for both sexes. It is 1870, after all, not 1770."

Mrs. Grosvenor opened her mouth, but at the sight of Miss Foxglove's unforgiving frown, she shut it.

"The notion that corsets are healthy for women is as harmful as it is outdated! Women can and *should* support themselves. It promotes self-confidence, and keeps the spine healthy." Miss Foxglove was really getting into her lecture, waggling her finger at the still-seated, now blue-lipped group. "I am shocked—really shocked! You should *all* know by now that a trim figure for women and men alike is the result of stimulating the blood by vigorously moving the body, and eating foods which promote optimum digestion and elimination." Miss Foxglove planted her hands on her own slender hips, perhaps to emphasize her point. "I shall suggest to Dr. Panacea that he make corseting the subject of one of his lectures. But for now, let's all lie down and stretch our spines! Roly-polys, everyone!"

The group drew their knees up into their chests and rolled gently from right to left. Miss Foxglove walked among them, praising excellent efforts and correcting when necessary. Unfortunately, the action sent Mr. Gillis into another coughing fit, and he excused himself, staggering away towards the door in the mountain. Though he passed the figure cloaked by the shadows of the juniper, he did not appear to see him.

Still beaming, the man watched Mr. Gillis until the door shut behind him, but when his eyes tracked back to the class his smile wavered. He counted the participants—one, two, three, four, five, six, and Miss Foxglove. Mr. Gillis would have made seven, had he stayed for the entire class, but there should have been an eighth. Concerned, the man shimmered over to where the group was now attempting to arrange their lower bodies into a cross-legged pose Miss Foxglove insisted was much-lauded by Oriental physicians for the purpose of "opening the hips."

"Oh! Good evening, Dr. Panacea!" Miss Foxglove finally noticed the visitor. "Everyone, look who's come!"

"Good evening—good evening to *all* of you," he replied in a pleasant voice with just a hint of southern drawl. "Ah, how I envy you! If there is anything more salubrious than taking exercise in the brisk air under the starlight I have not discovered it! But I see our class is a bit small tonight. Where is Mr. Woodworth?"

"Mr. Woodworth is unwell," said Miss Foxglove. "I checked on him before we came out, and he said his lungs felt too weak to bear the night air."

"This is the third time this week he's missed calisthenics," said Dr. Panacea, his worried frown every bit as charming as his smile. "I'll go check on him before we all assemble for dinner." He turned, and addressed the rest with such warmth they almost ceased to shiver. "Please, friends, do not allow Mr. Woodworth's indisposition to worry you! My patent medicine, when used in conjunction with cold- and hot-air treatments, is, as you know, the most modern, *scientific* solution for treating every complaint of body or mind." Dr. Panacea looked around at his acolytes. "It seems as though you have gotten enough *cold* air for the night... Miss Foxglove, what would you think of dismissing class a little early?"

"Certainly," she said. "Let's clean up, everyone, shall we?"

Stiff and sore, the class rose and began to tidy the exercise area. As they did so, Miss Foxglove stepped off to the side, leaning in for a private word with Dr. Panacea.

"Mr. Woodworth—will he be all right?"

"I fear his condition has continued to decline despite my best efforts." He patted Miss Foxglove on the shoulder. "Sometimes our best is not enough. Yet, lest I miss an opportunity to do some good..."

"Of course," she said.

Dr. Panacea bowed his farewells and retreated. Mrs. Grosvenor watched him go, admiring his figure as he strode purposefully back toward the mountain.

"For all the roughage and the nonsensical jumping about, I'm glad I came," she whispered to Mrs. Rutherford. "Aren't you?"

"Oh, yes," giggled Mrs. Rutherford, her eyes also on the doctor's slender waist and long legs. "He's such a... nice man."

"Nice?" barked Mr. Rutherford, his spirits improved enough that he gallantly took both his wife's mat and Mrs. Grosvenor's and set them in the crate. "Who cares about nice? Dr. P's a tremendous physician!"

"He's the best," said Miss Foxglove, noting the little bounce in Dr. Panacea's step as he ducked back inside the mountain. "There's no doctor in the world like him."

PART ONE

Chapter One

L ou Merriwether glanced up at the row of fancy, interchangeable townhouses half-shrouded by swirling clouds of chill San Francisco fog. A brass 5 glinted dully from above a doorway, and she was looking for 15. Just the next block up, should be, and thank goodness for that. She was eager to get in out of the rain, shed her wet things, and get warm.

Moisture dribbled down the back of her duster as she reached under the brim of her Stetson to scratch at her shaggy mop of short black hair. She squirmed and grumbled as the icy trickle soaked through her coat and shirt. It sure had turned into one hell of a shitty day. Lou had lived her whole life in the city, so February's fickleness didn't usually trick her... but that morning the weather had looked fine as cream gravy, so she'd walked, eager to stretch her legs after a long winter spent cooped up due to the constant freezing drizzle.

Fate always did enjoy laughing at Lou. Just before tackling her sixth, and final, and most remote assignment for the day, the puffy clouds had thickened and frigid showers began to piss down upon her. The drizzle had since turned to mist, but that wasn't much of an improvement.

Now thoroughly uncomfortable Lou quickened her pace, but before she stepped out into the cobblestoned cross street the first cab she'd seen in half an hour appeared to speed past her through a puddle, soiling her with a knee-high crashing wave of filth. Lou used her coat-sleeve to wipe the worst of the muck from the russet leather physician's bag gripped in her left hand, swearing quietly but creatively to herself.

By the time she arrived at Number 15 the wet had soaked through the edges of her boots, meaning her freezing feet were now also chapped; she wanted so badly to be home and taking a bath that she could almost smell hot soapy water. Lou pushed the thought away. A bath, she told herself sternly, would be her reward for a job well done—and to do her job well, she needed her mind anchored here, in the present.

She rapped her knuckles on the door, which flew open to reveal narrowed eyes in a florid, thickly mustached face. So fractious was the man's expression that Lou took a step back, her hand instinctively moving to grab either the contract in her inside breast pocket—or, should that prove an insufficient explanation for her presence, the LeMat revolver nestled snugly in her shoulder holster.

"Afternoon," she said. "I'm—"

"Lou Merriwether?"

"Yeah," she said. "I know I'm—"

"You're late." A great keg of a man, he filled the doorway, exuding self-importance and the lingering aroma of his lunch. Liver and onions, smelled like.

Lou took an instant dislike to him. "Sorry," she said, though she wasn't, not really. "It started to rain, and—"

"*Started to rain?*" he parroted. "Rain didn't stop us at the Battle of New Market! After the Grey Backs were sighted, we were ordered to be the skirmish line west of town. We got there by marching—through the driving rain! And we got there *on time.*"

Lou canted her head to the left. "Didn't the Union lose at New Market?"

The man glowered at Lou for a long moment—and broke into a hearty peal of laughter.

"Knew I liked you!" he boomed, and stood aside for her to enter.

The warmth of the foyer was such a pleasant change from the dreary chill that Lou's mood lifted immediately. Shedding her sodden overcoat she handed it over to the man. After hanging it and her hat on the rack by the door, he turned and extended his hand.

"Lieutenant Cyrus Siegert. It's a pleasure to meet you. Mr. Tisza said we'd get along just…"

He trailed off, peering at Lou in consternation. She knew he was taking in her round-cheeked face, thin lips, and narrow eyes. Hoping to forestall what she knew from experience could easily turn into a tense situation, she smiled at him wanly and grabbed his now-limp palm.

"I'm sure we'll get on fine, thanks," she reassured him.

He took back his hand, looking as though he'd like to wipe it on his pants. "No problem—no problem at all."

"Pardon?"

"As long as you can do what your partner said you could, Mr. Merriwether, everything'll be fine. Just fine."

Lou always let her clients assign her whatever sex they preferred, but she knew it wasn't her gender that bothered him.

"My, uh, people, we got a… *special knack* for this line of work," she said, hoping the lie would put him at ease. For good measure, she added, "Mystical mysteries of the Orient and all that. Always gotta be prepared, in China… you know… just in case some ghost tries to steal the Buddha off your family's shrine."

The worry-lines creasing Lt. Siegert's forehead relaxed, and Lou knew she'd said the right thing. But eager as she was to move the conversation away from asinine fabrications about her ancestry and toward the job she was there to do, the lieutenant's brows drew back together, heralding what Lou sensed would be another inane question.

"How would a ghost steal a Buddha?" he asked.

"Well now, the dead do have their weird ways, don't they?" she said, sidestepping the matter entirely. Regardless, the statement seemed to comfort the lieutenant. It was due to those "weird ways" that he'd hired Lou Merriwether in the first place.

"All right," he said. "Say, would you like a drink before you get started?"

"Yes, thanks." This gesture of hospitality considerably improved Lou's opinion of the man.

He led her into the ugliest parlor Lou had ever beheld. The edges of the plaid-upholstered armchairs looked like they'd been aligned to sit perfectly along the bands of the ugly tartan rug, and the war paraphernalia and china knick-knacks were set so deliberately on the mantelpiece Lou wondered if he'd arranged them using a chalk line. Despite the heat emanating from the pot-bellied stove in the corner, the room felt cold. Lou licked her chapped lips, eager for the warmth of whiskey sliding down her throat.

Lt. Siegert strode across the room toward the dry bar on the far wall. While his back was turned, Lou took what appeared to be a silver pocket watch out of her cinnamon-brown waistcoat and inspected it, nodded, and put it away again.

"This where she passed away?"

"The doctor said it was the best place to set up the birthing table." Lt. Siegert uncorked a bottle with a hollow pop and splashed some liquor into two glasses. "Damned nuisance. Had to move the rug."

He handed her the tumbler. After downing the contents in one gulp, Lou set the empty glass on a little pedestal table and wiped her mouth on her sleeve.

"All right, I'd better get down to it, huh?" She set down her satchel, crouching beside it to dig through the contents. "Got the gist of it from my partner—but I want to ask you a few additional questions about your wife's ghost. You're sure it's her?"

Lt. Siegert looked confused. "The spirit looks like her, talks like her..."

"Where does she appear?"

"Here."

"Anywhere else?"

"Never upstairs, but sometimes in the dining room."

Lou nodded, satisfied. "How long after she passed did she turn back up?"

"I got back from burying her, poured myself a drink, sat down on the sofa... and there she was, beside me," he said. "Looked me dead in the eye—so to speak—and... what's all that?"

"All what?" asked Lou, pausing as she withdrew a mechanical bee from her satchel.

"All that *stuff*," he said, nodding at what she'd already unpacked: a hinged, squat cylindrical tube of black leather about three inches in diameter and four inches long, a silver pitch pipe, a slim wooden box, the lid of which bore the carven image of a key, and a roll of yellow strips of paper covered in Chinese calligraphy done elegantly in shining blood-red ink.

Lou set down the bee and withdrew a leather pouch. "This?" she asked, loosening the tie to show him the contents. "White burley. Mind if I smoke in here? Or should I go outside?"

It had been a joke, but Lt. Siegert wasn't laughing. Instead, he was scowling the scowl of a man unused to being messed with. Lou's stomach sank as she sensed her day was going to get a lot worse, and quickly.

"I didn't know Orientals smoked tobacco," he said, confirming her suspicions. "Thought your kind preferred opium."

Before he'd even finished Lou was blushing and her heart was beating too fast. It never failed to sting when after doing her best to put clients at ease over the outrage of her being Chinese they still chose to be such assholes about it. She knew she should be used to this kind of bullshit by now, but the impotent anger she felt when people made ugly remarks about her heritage never failed to make her throat—and fists—tighten up. Not for the first time she wondered what it would be like to do her job without wondering if every little thing she did or said would provoke her clients.

Biting back the urge to tell the lieutenant where to go and what she hoped would happen to him there, Lou instead pretended to chuckle. There was no way she was going to give him the satisfaction of knowing how much he'd upset her.

"Yeah," she said, as lightly as she could, "but never on the clock."

"You sassing me?"

Lou's temper finally flared. "No, I'm just trying to do my job," she snapped, and instantly regretted her tone. The lieutenant looked twice as hot as a good bowl of Texas red and his face had gone about the same color, too. But Lou had an ace up her sleeve. "Look," she said more pleasantly, "the sooner I finish up, sooner I can file your compliance paperwork with the city. The city gives the haunted only a one-week grace period after a spirit shows itself to hire a psychopomp and get the problem taken care of." Lou gave him her most innocent smile. "Just how long did you say your wife's ghost has been materializing in your house?"

She knew she'd made her point, but she let the question hang in the air just the same. It also gave her a chance to get a handle on her emotions; she never did her best work when she was all riled up.

Eventually, when it became obvious that she wouldn't start working until he answered, the lieutenant shrugged. "Less than a week," he mumbled.

Hoping she could finally get on with what she needed to do, Lou turned back to her materials. She didn't believe him, but figured it couldn't have been all *that* long. Cyrus Siegert did not seem like the sort of man who'd willingly cohabitate with ghosts.

"Oh," said Lou, "by the bye, she ever say anything to you? The ghost, I mean."

"All the time."

"Can you understand it?"

"It's always pretty much the same. *Ohhhh, Cyyyyruussss, you did it the wrong way, Cyrus, ohhhhh Cyyyyyruuusssss, it's wrong, do it over, I hate roses, you should have knooowwwwwn.*"

Lou was jolted out of her mortification over Lt. Siegert's enthusiastic impression by the unusual post-script.

"Roses?"

"I told her when there's a thaw I'd replace them with azaleas. What else can I do?"

"Huh," Lou said.

"What?"

"Nothing—just a right strange reason for a haunting."

"She was always complaining. Women always find something to be unhappy about, don't they?"

"I reckon," said Lou, increasingly unimpressed by Lt. Siegert. "Well, I'll see if I can't get to the bottom of what she's mad about, just in case it's not really the roses. Sometimes the dead are more forthcoming with a stranger. One more thing—Vilhelm, I mean, Mr. Tisza, he mentioned a child had passed, too—do you ever see *his* ghost?"

"No," he muttered, and looked away. "Cyrus Jr...."

Lou stood, suddenly very interested in removing a few gewgaws from a low table in order to move the table itself off to a corner of the room. Then she scooched the couch a few feet to the left, and began to roll up the carpet, allowing Lt. Siegert some privacy to deal with his leaky eyes. She might not like her client much, but no psychopomp worth her salt ever mocked the grieving.

He did not speak until she began to chalk a circle on the now-bare floorboards. "Will that wash off?"

"Yup," said Lou, finishing up the first and beginning a second. "Don't worry. I clean up after myself."

"Do you... stand in the circle?"

"No. I gotta be able to walk around. Circle's for certain items I use that could mean mischief if a ghost got hold of them."

"What if ghost got hold of *you?*"

"Occupational hazard," said Lou, pleased when the lieutenant looked taken aback by her sangfroid. "But, see, that's the reason for the seven-day ordinance—there's less risk of a ghost attacking the living, or trying to possess them, if you take care of them quick-like. Dead souls rot over time, just like flesh, you know." It was obvious from Lt. Siegert's expression that he had not, in fact, known this. "Anyways, Lieutenant, I don't mind if you watch, but a nekuia is a complicated operation. I need to concentrate. And don't take this the wrong way, but I pride myself on rarely having to see a client a second time, if you catch my meaning."

"Of course," he said, and went over to do something with the coalscuttle.

Lou walked on her knees back over to her bag and reached inside, removing a pair of brown leather goggles with brass oculi but no lenses. Twisting open the leather tube, she shook out several circular vellum pouches, each protecting a glass lens. The pair she selected had an oily, blue sheen, and fitting them inside the brass sockets, Lou tightened them down with little thumb dials and fitted the entire apparatus over her head.

If the lieutenant had asked, Lou would have told him the odd hue was due to the glass having been treated with various proprietary chemical solutions, allowing her to see things usually invisible to the naked human eye—such as ghosts who weren't actively attempting to be noticed, some of her stranger tools, and the myriad doors to the spirit-world that were so important to her work. But he didn't ask, so Lou kept quiet as she looked around in all directions to see if there were any of those doors handy. There might be one on a ceiling of a room as easily as on the floor or the wall, but in this room she could locate no telltale green light.

Lou sighed softly. It was possible to create doors if one knew how—and had the proper equipment—but it was a time-consuming and tiring process. Too bad for her; it looked like she'd have to. Figured.

She decided on a convenient patch of bare floor and took a swaddled object out of her bag, gripping it firmly by the protruding ebony handle. Though it weighed little when obscured, it was incredibly heavy once she unwrapped it. Wielding it took almost all her strength.

"What's that?"

Lou pushed up her goggles onto her forehead and looked up to see Lt. Siegert eyeing her with alarm.

"It's a saw," she said. "I use it to… saw things," she finished lamely, not really wanting to take the time to explain.

"Like what?" he asked. When Lou hesitated, he said, "It's a bone saw, right? It looks funny, though, the blade..."

"Don't worry about it. I won't be sawing any bones. Blade's made of psuilver alloy which is why you can't get a good look at it. It's neither of this world nor the other."

Lt. Siegert looked mildly creeped out. Lou hoped this would stay his questioning and replaced her goggles. Saw in hand, she knee-walked close to the circles she'd chalked in the center of the room. Sweating a little from the effort she raised the tip of the shimmering blade and plunged it into the floorboards.

"What're you doing now?" he asked.

"Making a door in your floor," Lou said absently.

"What?"

Startled, Lou looked up. "Huh?"

"I didn't know you'd need to carve up my floor—that wasn't in the contract."

How Lou hated dealing with the living. The dead were so much easier to manage.

"I'm not making a hole in your floor," she said, trying to keep her tone as cheerfully neutral as possible, after all the earlier unpleasantness. "Well, I am—but you won't be able to see it. It's a spirit door, okay?" When he nodded, she forced a smile. "Glad we understand each other. But—look, I don't mean to be rude, but I *really* need to concentrate on this, and all these interruptions are making that hard. Maybe you want to take a stroll? Go have a drink, read the newspaper or something? I just don't want to screw this up. If I do, I'll have to return your deposit, and you'll have to go through the rigmarole of hiring a different psychopomp. And to be frank, not all of the agencies in this city are as understanding as I am of folks who might've let the grace period elapse."

"It's raining again," he said, glancing out the window. "I'll—I'll just go upstairs for a spell."

"Fine," said Lou. "That's fine. You might hear some weird shit going on down here, but rest assured it'll be all right in the end—and understand you *won't* be able to help. Best thing you can do is stay up there until I call you down."

Lou watched, relieved, as the lieutenant clomped upstairs. Renewing her efforts with the saw, she hewed slowly for a quarter of an hour. The only sounds in the house were her heavy breathing and a slight tinkling, like a wind chime, as the psuilver blade sliced through the barrier between the worlds of the living and the dead.

The results of her labor were three yard-long sides of a rectangle. Eldritch viridescent light seeped out around the edges, only visible with her enhanced vision.

Wiping the sweat from her brow with her shirt-sleeve, Lou reached for a pair of short tongs with psuilver tips and grabbed the edge of the rectangle. Slowly peeling back the flap, she uncovered endless, yawning, inky blackness, a sight she always found disconcerting though it was as routine as everything else about her job.

Door finished, Lou pulled off her goggles and replaced one blue lens with another, rose-hued one that enabled her to see active spiritual matter usually invisible to the naked eye. By using one of each Lou could observe the door and the ghost, whenever it arrived, though somewhat less clearly as with a matched set.

Ready for the next phase of the nekuia, Lou set a few tools inside the second circle she'd chalked on Lt. Siegert's floor, adjusted the variable pitch pipe to F#, and unbound the roll of yellow wards. She then took up the mechanical bee and wound it by the wings. It clicked a few times and began to emit a humming sound very similar to a real, living bee; she set it in the center of the first circle. Finally, Lou took out her revolver and checked it over, making sure the rain hadn't gotten into it, and ensuring the bullets were of the right kind.

Lou's LeMat fired two types of rounds: nine .44-caliber bullets from a smoothbore cylinder, and buckshot—or, her personal preference, a .60 ball—from a shorter shotgun barrel beneath the first. She could easily switch between them with a lever on the hammer that rotated the striking face. When walking around town she kept it loaded with regular shot, but for a nekuia she used special bullets. When casting these rounds, she mixed the lead with vermilion powder—not the brilliant "Chinese Red" used to lacquer bowls and shrines, but the real deal, made from pure ground cinnabar.

Vermilion had an unusual effect on undead: it immobilized them, or at least significantly slowed them down. Lou used her wards—the yellow papers marked with vermilion ink—to secure rooms against intruders, or when she was doing close-range work. The LeMat was handier when she wanted to keep her distance.

Lou replaced the gun in her holster, satisfied with its condition. That meant the only thing she had left to do was sit herself down in an armchair close to her workstation, and roll herself a cigarette. She lit it, striking a match on the sole of her boot, and inhaled, relishing the feel of smoke rolling down her throat and into her lungs. She exhaled with a contented sigh.

"He'll be annoyed you're smoking in his house."

Lou smiled to herself, and looked up to see a woman sitting on the horsehair sofa, staring intently at the buzzing mechanical bee. She had been a thin, frail creature in life; worry lines creased her translucent forehead, and she looked as though she might startle like a nervous horse at any moment. When Lou spoke, she spoke gently.

"Mrs. Siegert?"

"Yes?"

"Howdy. My name's Lou Merriwether. I thought we might could have ourselves a little chat."

"A chat?" Only with difficulty did the woman tear her eyes from the humming metal insect. "About what?"

Lou took another slow drag on her cigarette. She was guessing Mrs. Siegert knew she was dead, but lest the lieutenant's reports proved unreliable Lou preferred to feel out the situation on her own. Surprising the deceased with the knowledge of their situation was almost always a terrible idea.

"You're a psychopomp, you said."

"Yes ma'am."

"Cyrus hired you." She looked back at the bee. "Because of me."

"Yes he did," agreed Lou. "Any idea why?"

"I like that sound," said the ghost. "The bee. It's soothing."

Lou was used to the circumlocutions of the dead, and decided to follow where Mrs. Siegert wanted to lead her. "I thought you might think so."

"Oh?"

"Bees are funny creatures," said Lou. "Not wholly of this world nor the other."

"Really."

"Yep." Lou dropped the butt of her cigarette into her empty whiskey glass; reached for her pouch and papers to roll another. "Their power over the dead was harnessed by the earliest psychopomps. Did you know—"

"I know why Cyrus called you. But you don't understand, Lou Merriwether."

"What don't I understand?"

Bitterness crept into Mrs. Siegert's voice. "Have you ever been in the army?"

"Me?" Lou sensed they might be getting somewhere. "No, ma'am, but I'd like to hear anything you care to tell me about it."

"It's common enough, *I hear*, for discharged soldiers to pay the occasional visit to their former commanders."

"Seems natural. My father was a professor. Students came by our house all the time."

"Not once in five years of marriage, did anyone come to visit us." Mrs. Siegert smiled. "Cyrus is a… particular fellow. He likes everything *just so*. Tidy, neat, on time, no mistakes."

"Sounds like a real pain in the ass," said Lou. A flash of alarm passed over Mrs. Siegert's shadowed face, and then she chuckled, a sound like dry autumn leaves crunching under shoes.

"It was a hard pregnancy. The doctor put me on bed rest. But houses get dirty, and meals have to be cooked. Cyrus wouldn't hire anybody. He said he liked things the way I did them—and that it was my job, as his wife, to do them." Mrs. Siegert sighed. "He harassed me until I got back on my feet… and now, here I am."

"That's terrible. I'm real sorry."

"How I always wanted to give him a dose of his own medicine! I'd love to knock things off shelves, misplace his socks… I've tried, but I can't seem to touch anything. So I've hassled him in other ways."

"He said something about roses?"

"At first, it was how they were arranged." She giggled dustily. "Then I told him I hated roses entirely. It's petty, I know, but it feels so *good* to see him get so annoyed."

"I can see that. I'll tell him to dig them up and put something else in their place."

"I want tulips," she said. "And daffodils. It'll be expensive. He'll hate that."

"Okay," said Lou. "I'll tell him that's the only way to seal the nekuia."

"Seal the what now?"

"Nekuia," said Lou. She stood, stretched, sidled over to the circle containing her various instruments. "From the ancient Greek. Getting you to chat with me so you can feel good about giving all this up."

"Giving it up?" asked the ghost. Lou watched her closely out of the corner of her eye—the spirit had gotten to her feet as well, and was edging away from her. "I'll leave Cyrus alone, afterwards I mean. I promise. I'll—"

"It's no good, sorry. As I was telling Lieutenant Siegert, souls rot, same as everything else. You tell me you'll leave him be, but sooner or later your feelings about that'll change. Maybe you'll get bored of never going anywhere, and start thinking about hopping inside his skin so you can go for a walk on a fine day. Maybe you'll start thinking about doing other stuff, too, like—"

"I won't," said the ghost, sounding panicked. "Please—I won't, I promise! I just want to live a little longer, I mean... be here a little longer."

"Mrs. Siegert," said Lou. "It's too late. I'm sorry. I am, really. I've heard stories like yours before, worse even sometimes. The thing is... I work for the living. Even if they're assholes."

"But I'm *dead* because of him," cried the ghost of Mrs. Siegert.

Lou crouched down and reached inside one of the chalk circles she'd drawn, closing her fingers over the pitch pipe. Mrs. Siegert had retreated to the edge of the parlor, but her eyes kept returning to the buzzing bee. That was, of course, its purpose—the sound held her, transfixed her, kept her where Lou could get her. Lou felt the stirrings of regret, seeing the desperate way Mrs. Siegert wriggled and squirmed in her desire to be free, but steeled herself against compassion.

"You can't stay here," said Lou firmly. "The questions I asked you were a courtesy to you, so you could feel okay moving on—but you're moving on whether you want to or not. I won't add insult to injury by lecturing you about balance, making sure the worlds aren't contaminated by one another, that kind of thing. You just gotta accept it."

"You're a monster!" Mrs. Siegert was writhing now, abortively pulling away from what held her in place.

Lou had heard the same allegation out of countless spectral mouths. It stung every time, but she could not allow herself to sympathize with the dead. Reluctant spirits would say or do just about anything to keep from passing into the world of the dead, but it meant bad news for the living the longer they remained.

"It's nothing personal," she promised.

Before Mrs. Siegert could speak again, Lou blew on the pitch pipe. The note hung in the air even after Lou stopped blowing, and Mrs. Siegert screamed and clawed at her ears, rooted to the spot.

"Just go along with it," advised Lou as she snatched one of the yellow papers from the stack and stepped toward the ghost. "It'll be worse—for you, I mean—if you resist."

Unfortunately—but unsurprisingly—Lieutenant Siegert had been lying about how long he'd been allowing his wife's ghost to haunt him. The shade succeeded in freeing herself from the vibrations with a great rending sound, and launched herself straight at Lou, screeching.

Lou tripped over the edge of the coffee table in her haste to get out of Mrs. Siegert's way, and grunted as she fell flat on her ass. Too dizzy to attempt a further retreat, she lifted the pitch pipe to her lips a second time, but it was too late—before she could sound the tone, Mrs. Siegert grabbed Lou's left wrist.

Lou hollered as spirit-fire burned her arm. Footsteps pounded on the floor above as she grabbed her gun, and she heard Lt. Siegert clattering down the stairs before she shot the ghost point-blank between the eyes.

The blast was deafening, and Lou felt rather than saw Mrs. Siegert let go her wrist; the thick cloud of smoke produced by the revolver obscured the spirit momentarily. Lou was on her feet quick as she could manage and sidestepping the miasma saw the ghost clawing at the bullet now lodged in her ethereal head. She was backing away from Lou—but slowly, as if through deep water.

Lou's arm still felt like it was on fire, but she ignored the pain as she leveled her gun again.

"Sorry, ma'am," she said through gritted teeth—and fired on the ghost a second time.

The bullet hit Mrs. Siegert where her guts used to be, freezing her completely this time, mouth open, fingers at her face.

Lou exhaled, relieved, as Lt. Siegert burst into the hazy room. He stared at Lou, one arm curled against her chest, the other still holding the smoking LeMat. He opened and closed his mouth stupidly a few times. Lou would have laughed if her arm hadn't hurt so goddamn much.

"Sorry for the ruckus," she said. "There won't be any bullet-holes, I plugged her with both shots."

"Uh?" said the lieutenant, still gaping.

"Just sit tight. I'm almost done."

After tucking her gun into its holster, Lou took up her tongs. Clasping Mrs. Siegert by the arm, she dragged her toward the door in the floor. When Lou had wrangled her directly over the portal, she lowered the ghost carefully, feet first. She pressed firmly against the slight resistance and watched the spirit sink into the flat flowing blackness like a bison falling into a tar pit.

When Mrs. Siegert's head disappeared beneath the surface at last, Lou grabbed the edge of the door with her tongs and laid it back over the portal into the beyond. Green light seeped through the edges again.

Lou stepped away from the door and withdrew from her waistcoat pocket the object that looked like a silver pocket watch. It was not a timepiece, however; when she flipped it open, the face looked more like a compass—only the needle didn't point to magnetic North. It was her father's antique skiameter, and had there been any sort of undead presence in the house, the needle would indicate where it lurked. Earlier it had pointed straight to the couch, where Mrs. Siegert had been sitting. Now, it spun lazily around and around the face. Satisfied she had completed the nekuia, Lou closed it again. The hard part was over.

"What the hell happened?" asked the lieutenant.

"You really let her bide for a while, huh?" Lou shut her mouth and retched. Now that the excitement had passed, the spirit-burn on her arm ached hot and cold, just as if she'd burned it under far less uncanny circumstances. "Closer to two, three months, I'd warrant."

Lt. Siegert didn't say anything. Lou shook her head but didn't give him any more crap. The ghost might be gone, but her work was not yet done.

Out of her bag she pocketed a spool of psuilver thread and a piece of felt with a shimmering needle stuck in it. With no more ghosts hanging around Lou replaced the pink lens in her goggles with another blue one. Once the edges of the door came into better focus, she painstakingly whip-stitched it shut. She slapped a yellow ward over the area, just to be safe.

"The rug should cover that," said Lou. She rose and almost stumbled—

she was completely exhausted. "You don't have to keep it there forever, just a few months."

Lt. Siegert had apparently had his fill of asking questions. "All right," he said. "So you're done? We can clean up?"

"All taken care of." Obvious relief brightened Lt. Siegert's eyes, but he still looked testy. Lou wondered what was coming next.

"*And?*" he asked.

"Oh." Lou realized what he was after. "Right. Turns out she always hated roses. Go dig 'em up, or she might come back." That part wasn't true, but she *had* promised the ghost, and in spite of everything Lou had still liked her more than her husband. "Go buy some tulips and daffodils."

"Damned nuisance even after she's dead," muttered Lt. Siegert. "Fine, fine. Well, just one other thing. I was curious…"

Lou, busy replacing all of her materials, glanced up at him and knew his question before he asked it. She'd seen the look before, and she'd see it again.

"I think if you'll look at the contract we both signed, you'll see I don't discuss the afterlife," she said. "I send them on their way because I have to. It's not my business what happens to them. Now, I *do* know a few preachers who'd be willing to talk with you, though I can't vouch for the accuracy of their predictions. Only have their word on the matter, of course."

Lt. Siegert nodded once, tersely. He told her to wait a moment, disappeared into another room.

Once he left, Lou collapsed into an armchair. She felt awful, chilled to the bone, weak, and stomach-sick. She'd grab some food on her way back into town; that would help. She was close to the Bear Market, and as her favorite chili-vendor was citified enough not to hibernate she could get herself a cheap bowl of hot stew. This thought cheered her significantly—until she saw Lt. Siegert emerge, not with a wad of bills or a check in his hand, but two shovels.

"Uh," said Lou.

"You'd come along with me to dig them up, I thought. It's in the contract we both signed," said Lt. Siegert, looking pretty pleased with himself. "*All sundry duties related to the successful completion of the nekuia.* I just checked. You said it wouldn't take if we didn't, so…"

Damned if she'd let on how truly inadequate she felt to the task. With a nod Lou got to her feet, consoling herself with a promise that first thing when she got back to the office she'd demand Vilhelm remove that particular clause from the standard contract.

Chapter Two

Lou felt pure, unadulterated joy when she spied Uncle Bjorn through a cloud of rich, spicy steam, still selling bowls of hot stew to the bears, men and women going about their evening shopping. She was beyond weary; hacking roots out of iron-hard gravedirt with a wobble-bladed shovel and only an ornery veteran for company had taken all the remaining starch right out of her.

"You all right, Lou?"

"Huh?" Lou realized she'd been staring at the two pots for a while, and deciding between rabbit stew and venison chili shouldn't take so long. "Sorry, Uncle. Just tired. Gimme a bowl of the chili, unless you think the rabbit…?"

"Go for the venison." He ladled her out a hearty serving, then reached for a small bucket of fat white maggots. "Grubs?"

"No, thanks," said Lou. The sight of the writhing larvae didn't help her lingering nausea. She looked away quickly. "Any news?"

Some would call Lou a cheapskate; she described herself as thrifty, which was why she'd gotten her meat and mushrooms at the Bear Market for years now—long enough that most of the stallkeepers trusted her enough to gossip with her, or at least freely grumble about whatever recent trumped-up charge some local bear had gotten saddled with to spare some human the shame of justice. It was easy enough for her to believe; the same sort of bullshit was spread calf-deep around Chinatown, too.

"Nothing directly involving any of us. Some muttering about some mauling up north. Obviously wolves, but you know how it is. See a claw mark…"

"Yeah," managed Lou, after burning the roof of her mouth on her first bite. "All right. Well, think I'll check out the Wanted board, see if there's anything that catches my eye."

"You're lookin for love in all the wrong places, Lou."

"Don't I know it," she said, and, after acknowledging Bjorn's request that she bring back the bowl, spooned meat and sauce into her mouth as she ambled away, cutting in among stalls and dodging shoppers as she headed toward the sheriff's office.

There wasn't much. All the crimes had apparently been committed by villains of the usual sort. There was a notice for a prospector who had sold his silver claim after getting treated for what he said was coyote-bite, and was now wanted on suspicion of being a werewolf, and a woman had fled town after giving birth to a halfsquatch, possibly headed towards the San Bernardino range to the south. Both were jobs for monster-hunters rather than psychopomps.

Cruising the Wanted posters wasn't something most psychopomps did, but Lou had made some decent cash off of bounty-hunting when contract work was slow. Thankfully, there had been plenty of regular work for her of late.

Realizing she'd been doing more sucking on her spoon than actual eating, Lou headed back towards Uncle Bjorn's stall. She'd only been able to force down a small portion of her meal. Sheepishly, she returned the bowl to Uncle Bjorn, explaining her stomach's unruliness when he raised what passed for his eyebrow to see so much food left over. At least the stew didn't go to waste, he scraped out what remained with his paw and gulped it right down. Lou tipped her hat to him and took her leave.

Food had helped, but Lou knew she was in a bad enough way to need a cab. She hailed the first one she saw, and angling her hat down low as the driver slowed, grunted a Post Street address. She spent the ride trying to stay awake as they rattled into the center of town.

It had been a long day. Six jobs was a lot, even without any as irritating as the Siegert haunting—but she'd done more work for less money. Tonight she'd relax, take a hot bath, eat a good dinner… and as for after,

Lou thought she'd left a little whiskey in the bottle, and she had the bulk of *Buffalo Bill, King of the Border Men* left to read.

"C'mon now!"

"Buh?" said Lou, wondering where the hell she was, as it certainly wasn't in her bed with a bellyful of Old Monk and a dime novel falling from her hand. Someone was shaking her shoulder roughly and shouting at her. She looked up blearily at the cab driver as she pulled away from his grip.

"This ain't no damn hotel. You speakee English? Pay up and get out, or I'll—"

"Oh shit," said Lou, genuinely apologetic when she realized where she was and what had happened. "Sorry—didn't mean to—"

"Lazy goddamn chink," muttered the cabman. "Shoulda got a better look at you 'fore you hopped in. This ain't no garbage cart."

Lou was too exhausted to do more than just pay the man—though she stiffed him on the tip. As he counted the coins she stepped down from the cab and onto the sidewalk without a backwards glance. A volley of cusswords followed her up the stairs to the Merriwether Agency's shiny black door; Lou flashed the driver her brightest smile, waved in a friendly fashion to his obvious irritation, and ducked inside before he could think of anything else to shout after her.

The office was deliciously warm, and the tinkling of the silver door-bell sounded friendly and cheerful, as always. Hanging up her hat and overcoat, Lou noticed the chair behind the great wooden desk was empty of its usual occupant, but she heard Vilhelm messing around in the kitchenette. She called out a greeting so he would know it was just her and not a client.

Curious, Lou sniffed the air. It smelled like lemon oil, the dusty-sweet scent of books—and tea. Glancing at the ornate green and gold mantle-clock that squatted atop one of the bookshelves she saw it was indeed teatime, a ritual still considered sacrosanct by both Lou and her business partner even though its high priest had passed on. Cheered by the prospect of a revivifying cuppa, Lou retrieved the money she'd earned that day and knelt down behind the desk to lock it into the strongbox.

"Hey, you," said Vilhelm, poking his head out as she stood. "Come help me set up the tray. Tea's almost ready."

"Tray?" asked Lou, and entering the kitchenette she saw a paper packet of meat sitting beside her father's antique blue and white tea service. Vilhelm was buttering thin slices of bread with efficient, practiced movements.

"Fancy," she said. "What's the occasion?"

"I ran out for tarts and some cold sliced beef when the rain let up," said Vilhelm over his shoulder. "You had a busy day, and a wet one, so I figured you could use something hardy."

"Thanks." Lou was plenty used to long hours and wet weather, but as Vilhelm layered some cress on top of the buttered bread, she had to admit high tea was a nice treat. Not that she was particularly inclined to eat more at the moment.

"Can you grab that box—the one on the second shelf? They're raspberry jam."

Lou fetched the pink pastry-box from the cabinet and brought it over, but she let Vilhelm arrange the tarts as he saw fit while she washed up in the little sink. The pleasure of hot water on her chapped hands was almost dizzying; the amount of grime that sluiced away down the drain, disgusting. Afterwards, she followed Vilhelm into the front parlor.

"Very nice," he said, stepping back to admire his efforts. "I used some of the gold tips. All taken care of?"

"The tea?"

"No, the jobs," said Vilhelm.

"Oh. Yeah," said Lou, settling into a chair with a groan. "That last one was a doozy." She eyed the repast, but knew the beef sandwiches were beyond her power. The tea on the other hand looked wonderful, and she inhaled the delicate steam gratefully after accepting a cup. A few sips strengthened her enough that she felt able to retrieve her tobacco pouch so she could roll herself a cigarette. She spilled a lot of shag. Her hands were shaking.

"Not hungry?" Vilhelm was as surprised as Bjorn had been.

"Just tired. This last ghost tried to take me with her. Got me real good on the arm. Just look at that." Lou rolled up the cuff of her sky-blue shirt, revealing a mark, neither bruise nor burn, in the shape of a clutching hand.

"Christ, Lou," said Vilhelm, standing quickly. "Put some salve on that!"

"In a minute," said Lou, motioning for her partner to sit back down. "It's nothing to get all excited about."

"Don't be stupid, it'll suppurate if you don't treat it," said Vilhelm, striding to the back of the office.

"Not *instantly*," argued Lou, as Vilhelm retrieved a jar of ointment from a cupboard. His hand-wringing both amused and irritated her. She was no newcomer to psychopompery; she'd begun assisting her father when she was fourteen years old, and had been working full-time at the Agency even before he got sick. Since his death nine months ago, she'd handled every-thing—meaning, she knew what she was doing.

Vilhelm set a fat jar down in front of her. "You can't neglect yourself."

"You told me to come help you in the kitchen," said Lou, ignoring the salve.

"'First thing, take care of yourself,'" quoted Vilhelm piously.

Lou scowled at him, annoyed to hear her father's wisdom flung at her. Vilhelm, immune to her ire, took off his brass-framed pince-nez and peered across the low table at Lou.

"Sorry you had a hard day," he said gently.

"Eh." She'd had worse. As far as professions went, psychopompery wasn't the easiest. The active portions of the job required intense concentration, physical stamina, and quick reflexes. Even preparing the necessary materials for banishing ghosts and shades carried their own risks, mercury poison-ing being one of the worst. Frequently handling vermilion was dangerous enough, to say nothing of inhaling the dust from grinding it at home. But she'd known all that when she got into the business.

What she hadn't known was how soon after taking up the job the whole of it would fall upon her shoulders... but that also wasn't to be complained about. It wasn't her father's fault that in the early years of his business he'd ground his own cinnabar to save money. He'd been thinking of his new family, never suspecting that decades later in spite of all his precautions his skin would turn pink and begin to peel away, his teeth would fall out, his body would weaken, and eventually, his kidneys would fail...

"Lou," said Vilhelm, suddenly very serious, "I think you've taken too much on your shoulders. You need a partner. I know you don't want to hear that, but—"

"Already got a partner," said Lou. "He's a lippy old cuss, and a foreigner, but he makes a decent enough cup of tea. Now his coffee, on the other hand—"

"You know I mean a field partner," said Vilhelm. "Archie had you, didn't he? We're making plenty of money, we can afford it."

"Who, though? Haven't heard of anyone promising who hasn't been snapped up yet."

"What about Erasmus?"

"Dead."

"Of what?"

"Peritonitis."

"Jasper?"

"In jail."

"Really? For what?"

"You don't want to know."

"Damn. Imre?"

"You know very well he's still finishing his degree. I wouldn't want to distract him. Plus there's—"

"His limp isn't some big deal. He can walk. He's strong."

"Maybe so."

Vilhelm sighed but said no more on the matter, instead picking up the day's newspaper; Lou rolled and smoked a second cigarette. It was so quiet they both jumped when a sudden volley of fat raindrops hit the windows.

Lou was just about to announce her intention to head home for the day when she noticed Vilhelm kept peering at her, over the edge of his paper. There was something strange about his expression—he looked smug, like there was something smart he wanted to say to her.

"What?" she asked.

"I beg your pardon?" Vilhelm's expression was too innocent.

"Out with it," said Lou, annoyed.

"Oh, I was just perusing today's *Chronicle*. Read it yet?"

"No, why?"

"There was a break-in at the Academy of Sciences. Agents unknown." Vilhelm raised his bushy eyebrows dramatically.

"Oh." Lou was underwhelmed by this intelligence.

"Yes, they said at first they thought it had to do with the dragon, but—"

"The *what?*"

"Really, Lou." Vilhelm shook his head. "The tianlung they recently found in China? Still flying, months after it died?" He said all this slowly, as if expecting something to register with Lou. "The skeleton's been on display in the city for two weeks!"

"Okay," said Lou. "So someone stole it?"

"No. Nothing seems to have been stolen. That's the mystery."

Lou considered this. "That's news? Good Lord, the state of the press these days."

"It shows an appalling lack of security at the Academy, that's why it's news! San Francisco won't get any good cultural exhibitions if we get a reputation for... you don't care."

Lou shrugged. "Saw a dinosaur once. Just a bunch of bones."

"You're missing the point."

"Am I?" Lou realized she'd been sidetracked. "And reading about some break-in gave you a case of the giggle-snorts?"

"No—that was something else."

"What then?"

"Nothing... I mean, nothing *you'd* be interested in, I should say."

Lou, frustrated, chewed on the edge of her thumbnail as Vilhelm went back to his paper, and then said, "Fine. I'm interested."

Vilhelm gave her a look of stage-surprise over the top of the paper, but then stood and walked over to his desk. She watched him coolly, slouching in her chair as he withdrew a lone piece of paper and brought it to her.

"I know you're tired," he said with an innocent air, "but if you could take a look at this, it's pretty urgent. And you know... since you *like* working alone, by your own admission, there shouldn't be any issues."

Lou skimmed the document, and upon realizing it was a just the usual Merriwether Agency contract, was mildly baffled. "Why're you showing me this? I want the notes, not... wait. Why does this say pro bono? I don't—" Lou scanned the page and straightened up; crumpled the contract into a ball and pegged Vilhelm between the eyes with it.

"Hey!" he cried, resettling his pince-nez. "At least that answers my first question, but—"

"And what was your first question?" snarled Lou.

"If you were still avoiding your mother."

Lou bristled. "What the—"

"I knew you rarely spoke after—after everything that happened," said Vilhelm, "but Ailien never said... I can't believe you're actually *estranged!*"

Lou rolled a third cigarette to avoid meeting Vilhelm's reproachful gaze. "It's none of your business if we are."

"Ailien is my friend," said Vilhelm in a patient tone that made Lou feel murderous. "So are you. I know she misses you. When she came by, she said something like 'please tell Lou she's welcome to drop by if she's ever in Chinatown.' Lou, you're over there three times a week if you're there once! I didn't realize you never—where are you going?"

"First it's my health," she said, stomping over to the peg where her coat was hanging, "then it's my lack of appreciation for science. Now it's—I dunno—*filial piety?* I'd enroll at the college if I wanted to attend lectures!"

"Did you even read the contract?" asked Vilhelm. "She needs you."

Misery welled up inside Lou, making her feel mean and ornery. She didn't need this, not after the day she'd had. "What that woman needs isn't my concern."

"Lou." The pleading in Vilhelm's voice further enraged Lou. "Please, just this once, I—"

"No!" Her voice was high, hysterical, and she took a deep breath to calm herself. "I should've known it wasn't me being out all day in the rain that prompted you to have high tea in my honor. Joke's on me, but you know what they say. Fool me once, shame on you. Fool me twice—"

"Why won't you help her out?"

"Because if she needed a psychopomp—" Lou could say no more. The lump in her throat was too big.

"Elouise Merriwether, you sit your narrow behind down in that chair and listen to me!" Vilhelm was now also on his feet, looking fierce enough that Lou obeyed him. Since she was a child she'd always taken a great deal of pleasure in getting Vilhelm so upset that he started sputtering and went red in the face, but this was something else entirely.

Vilhelm sat down as well, and folded his hands in his lap. He looked pointedly at the jar of salve on the table. Meekly, Lou picked it up and smeared the ointment over her arm.

Though they looked much alike, spirit-burn was far more pernicious than frostbite. It tended to sap the energy of the victim, and if left untreated, made them dizzy, nauseated, and irritable… Lou didn't want to admit it, but Vilhelm had been right. She should have seen to the wound as soon as she got back, and not let her dislike of being told her business interfere with her common sense.

"It's gone on long enough," said Vilhelm as she re-capped the medicine. "Your father wouldn't like it, this silence between the two of you."

"Papa can't like anything anymore," mumbled Lou, picking up a sandwich. She was suddenly ravenous.

"Lou, it wasn't her fault. You can't hold this against her. He's lucky he had a skilled apothecary like Ailien to look after him when he got sick. A doctor would've just given him laudanum, and he would have gone away from us long before he did. And as for the other... he chose his moment. You know that."

Lou actively tried to keep from imagining her father the last time she'd seen him alive, lying in bed with the curtains drawn to protect his eyes from the sunlight, the skin of his face pink and wrinkled around his toothless mouth; the way the sweat-soaked sheets had clung to his withered body as he looked up at her mother...

"Lou?"

"He wasn't rational! He was hurting, desperate. There might've still been a chance—"

"Do you really believe that?" Vilhelm looked shocked. "Even now? It's been the better part of a year! You've got to come to terms with this, Lou. Nothing could have saved him." Vilhelm sat back in his chair. "I know things have always been difficult between you and Ailien, but this isn't the same as her scolding you for wearing men's clothing or whatever else the two of you always fought about. Your father *asked* her to do what she did. Do you think she wanted that responsibility? She loved him, too."

"But—"

"But what?"

Lou shuddered. "How can she ever know, at that last moment, that he..."

"He had nothing to fear. Surely you of all people should understand that." Vilhelm paused at Lou's sudden exhalation of breath. "Lou... I can't see how refusing to make peace with your mother will make you any happier."

He was right. *Again.* The truth was, avoiding Ailien and the apothecary shop off of Stockton Street had made Lou feel even lonelier since her father died.

"All right," she said heavily, grinding out her cigarette. "I'll go."

When Vilhelm didn't say anything to this, Lou looked up and was shocked to see his eyes red and his lower lip trembling.

"Vilhelm!"

"I've been so worried about you!" he snuffled. "You've—you've been so different ever since Archie—and I just, I miss the old Lou."

"What are you talking about?"

"You used to… you used to smile—*sometimes*—and you were happy, at least with work. These days… I know you like it, but you seem so overwhelmed. And I didn't realize you and Ailien weren't speaking."

"Vilhelm," said Lou, leaning across the table and patting him awkwardly on the knee. "You're the best. Shucks, I didn't—"

"I always, I just, your family… I know things weren't perfect, but I always envied Archie so much, having you and Ailien. I shouldn't have let things fall apart."

Lou felt a flash of guilt for never having known all this about Vilhelm; for crowing about things like moving out and living on her own while he, apparently, had wanted nothing more than for her to go home to her mother and have a happy family dinner when she was done with her business at the Agency. Well, *that* wasn't going to happen, but for his sake she could make a brief foray into Chinatown and see what her mother wanted. It wouldn't be so bad. She could always leave.

"You didn't let anything fall apart," she said. "If anyone did, it was me."

"You loved your father. I did too. I don't want you to think I want you to stop caring about him… remembering him. I just want to see you come in out of the fog."

Lou looked at him skeptically. "And you think going to see my *mother* will help with that?"

"Well," said Vilhelm, "you never know, right?"

Lou sighed, and grabbed another sandwich—and a raspberry tart. She bolted them both and washed it all down with a cup of lukewarm tea.

"First thing tomorrow I'll go," she said, reaching for a third sandwich. "Okay? I'm too tired to deal with her right now."

Hoping it would dispel the last of the awkwardness between them, Lou stayed to help clean up the tea service before gathering her things and heading out into the chilly February evening. She was glad to find the rain had let up again. She loved this walk, especially at this time of night, when dusk flooded the city with blue-grey shadows. But walking alone did have its perils. A pack of men lurched out of a saloon, clinging to each other like a cluster of grapes in the jewel-bright puddle of light spilling out of the doorway, loudly serenading passers-by with ribald songs. A woman with a basket of onions and meat hissed her disapproval as one of the drunks vomited all over himself. His companions jeered at her while pounding the gagging man on the back.

Lou gave them a wide berth, but in her attempt to avoid eye contact she inadvertently glanced down an alleyway and caught sight of two men fucking in the shadows behind some piled crates. One grunted into the other just as Lou averted her eyes, a flush rising to her cheeks.

Then the group of men saw what Lou had spied. As they shouted epithets into the gloom, the couple broke apart and ran for it. Likely they knew what lay in store for them if they lingered.

"Like the sight of that?" called one of the men after Lou. She had not stopped walking during any part of this exchange, and she did not stop now to answer him. She did, however, lengthen her strides, not so much as to be obvious, and kept her eyes forward. These days, with jobs scarce and fresh food scarcer, it made men grumpy and rowdy—men, who under the best of circumstances, would likely consider it a hoot and a holler to beat up some random Chinaman.

"He was next in line!" guffawed another. "You ruined his night!"

They did not follow Lou, and unmolested she arrived at the building where she rented a small suite of rooms. She had chosen this apartment not because it was particularly nice, which it wasn't, but rather due to its cheapness and its having a private entrance. After letting herself in, the familiar *plink plink* of the pump dripping into the basin greeted her ears while she lit the wick on her kerosene lantern and settled the chimney over the blaze.

It was a shabby space. The advertisement had claimed the apartment was "furnished," and technically, that had been true. The front room was outfitted with a threadbare sofa, a rickety table, and two wooden chairs. As for the bed—Lou had splurged on a mattress and stuffed the provided one in a closet lest she be forever plagued by bedbugs.

Whatever their quality, the rooms were hers, and the look on her mother's face when Lou had announced her intention to live on her own had been worth every night of coming home to damp darkness rather than a warm kitchen steamy with hot pot or roast goose.

The thought of goose reminded Lou of the bare state of her pantry. Stew and sandwiches had set her up just fine for tonight, but as for breakfast… she headed to see what she had in the pantry and discovered a sprouting onion and one half-slice of salt pork in the barrel. At least she could eke it out with a handful of cornmeal. Good thing she'd be in Chinatown tomorrow, and could do some shopping after visiting her mother.

She was both too antsy and too tired to heat water for a bath. Instead, she built up a fine blaze in the potbelly stove and retrieved the whiskey bottle from where it lay, for some reason, under the sofa. There was a slosh, and that brought a smile to Lou's lips as she pulled the cork out with her teeth and took a swig.

"Everything'll be just fine tomorrow," she said aloud to the dim room. The hollow sound of her voice did not lend her any confidence, so she took another swallow, and said no more.

Chapter Three

The next day, Lou was on her way just as the sky began to brighten, whitish yellow shining out from between bands of slate-grey clouds. She did not care much for the beauty of the dawn. Even with the whiskey she hadn't slept well, tossing and turning as she dreamed of running through a dark wood, in danger from some terrifying, unknown thing. She'd awoken shivering, and with her jaw aching something fierce.

Lou had never been one to pay much heed to dreams; she anticipated her day would be annoying enough without letting her nightmares put the spook on her. Ignoring any residual uneasiness, she dipped and dodged between packs of bleary-eyed people, some heading to work, more looking for it. The recession gripping the nation was never so obvious as in the morning. Only two types of entrepreneurs were turning big profits these days: psychopomps like her, and saloon-owners.

She inhaled deeply through her nose as she walked towards Chinatown, reveling in the scents of the city. San Francisco stank, but the different times of day all had their unique chords of odor. She knew them all. Afternoons reeked of bad stew, sweat, horse shit, and boot-leather; early mornings of vomit, freshly baked bread, and the fishy-salty aroma of the bay. As Lou made her way toward Stockton Street, the scents changed subtly—Chinatown was equally noisome, but in its own way. More pig shit and smoke-smell, less human filth.

Lou was one of the only psychopomps in San Francisco who worked inside and outside of Chinatown, at first courtesy of her parents' sterling relationship within both communities, now due to her own. Inside of what some called the "city in miniature" she often had clients ask her questions about working beyond the intersection of Dupont Gai and Bush Street—if lawmen hassled the business-owners as much, what was cheap at the other markets, and if white people dealt with the same kinds of undead as Chinese folks.

It was far more common for Lou's white clients not to ask questions, but instead to wax prosy about their experiences visiting Chinatown. They'd speak of hearing street musicians plucking gu kahms or playing bamboo flutes, of seeing the grocers' shop windows filled with whole ducks and rabbits, watching the people going about their business twittering like birds; how they always feared becoming the victims of pickpockets or white slavers. Invariably, they remarked that it was like visiting another country.

Not to Lou. To her, Chinatown was just another part of San Francisco, nothing more or less than that. She'd grown up on these streets, purchasing bok choi, silk, rice, and incense at these stores and stalls. Even so, she'd never felt like she really belonged.

She'd hated feeling different more when she was young, when people stared at her all the time, either for being Chinese—or not being Chinese enough. It was bad when her mother took her on visits to her Chinese patients, who would invariably make Lou's appearance a major topic of conversation, but the worst was being taken on errands with her father. His unremarkable shabby-genteel tweeds made her even more conspicuous in her bright, frogged tunics, so eventually she began to refuse to wear the clothes her mother sewed her. While American-style dresses, stockings, and tight shoes were far less comfortable, Lou had hated the names the white kids called her; the looks on her father's clients' faces when they saw his daughter looked like she'd just been carried off the boat from Toisan.

No, it wasn't just the tension between her and her mother that had driven Lou out of Chinatown. She resented the idea that she should live in some specific place just because she'd been born half-Chinese. After all, if there was one thing the two communities agreed on it was that Lou Merriwether was an outsider—so, Lou had concluded, fuck 'em both. She'd do what she wanted, and everybody else could lump it.

Lou's mother Ailien still lived above her apothecary's shop, in the rooms that had once been the Merriwether family's home. Before moving out it had been the only place Lou had ever lived; just seeing the sign brought to mind such a flood of memories that she walked past the door and back again five times before she was able to make herself approach the shop. Even then she sat on the stoop and smoked a cigarette—and a second—before mustering sufficient courage to duck inside.

Upon entering the shop, all dark wood and stone countertops and shelves full of blue and white porcelain jars, Lou was surprised to find the familiar bitter-sour-dusty-sweet scent of herbs and roots and stranger medicines brought a smile to her face; it smelled like coming home. But then she caught a snatch of women's conversation emanating from the kitchen where dinner and deer horn tonic were prepared side-by-side. All pleasant feelings faded and something close to panic gripped her. She was halfway back out the door when her mother's voice brought her up short.

"Coming!" called Ailien, in Toisanese.

Lou steeled herself, remembering her promise to Vilhelm. "It's me, Ma," she said, in English.

"Lou?"

"You got another daughter?"

"Lou!"

Lou winced as she identified the second voice. It was Mui Wong, her mother's oldest friend. She'd been so eager to get the visit out of the way she'd forgotten that to come this early might mean encountering familiar faces rather than anonymous patients.

"No need to get excited," said Lou, sidling between a carved wooden screen and a large vase filled with dried lizards spitted on bamboo skewers. Approaching the kitchen, her stomach grumbled as she smelled juk cooking. She'd been too antsy to eat her old onion and salt pork before leaving her apartment, but the brisk walk and morning air had given her an appetite.

"Well, well, just look at you!" Mui emerged first, wiping her hands on her apron. "But what are you wearing? Ailien! Come here and see your daughter!" Mui embraced Lou. "A real American cowboy!" she said in her heavily accented English. The older woman rose up on her tiptoes, pulling off Lou's Stetson and placing it on her own head. "One shot, one kill!" she proclaimed proudly, pantomiming aiming a revolver at Lou.

Lou laughed. "I can't believe you remember that."

"Of course I do!" Mui exclaimed. "I still have Bo's old Natty Bumppo books if you want them."

Lou's smile fell from her face like a fish sliding off the back of a cart. "He'll want them when he comes back," she muttered.

Ailien emerged, and for a brief moment Lou was actually relieved to see her mother, as the topic of Bo and his homecoming were nothing she wished to discuss... but any joy she felt quickly soured when her mother gasped and pointed at her.

"Lou Merriwether! What have you done to your hair?"

"It's been like this." It really must have been a while since she'd visited.

"It's so *short!*"

"I like it short," said Lou, ducking out of reach of her mother, who clearly had designs on running her hands through the black mop. "It's easier."

"She looks like a boy," observed Mui from under the brim of Lou's too-big hat, not helping the situation one bit.

"And you're proud of that!" cried Ailien, looking keenly at her daughter. "Are you trying to pass as a man?"

"Not trying," said Lou wickedly. "Succeeding."

Mui chuckled at this. Ailien did not. Seeing her usually unflappable mother so upset by her confession, Lou regretted saying anything at all about the matter—most especially the truth.

Perhaps sensing the awkwardness, Mui embraced Ailien and glanced toward the door.

"I've chatted too long," she said. "It was nice to see you, Lou. Come by and visit me? And in case you were wondering, no—I haven't had a letter in a long time."

Lou paled, then flushed. "I, uh…"

"I knew you wouldn't ask," said Mui, and before Lou could protest, Mui plunked the Stetson back on Lou's head, gave her cheek a quick pinch, opened the door, and was gone.

"Well," said Ailien, crossing her arms over her chest.

Lou looked at her mother. "What?"

Ailien sighed. "Hello, Lou."

"Vilhelm said—"

"Have you eaten?"

"Not yet..."

"Come with me."

Already wondering if agreeing to this visit had been a bad idea, Lou followed her mother to the back of the store.

Though full of her mother's organized clutter, the kitchen felt empty to Lou without her father reading at the table, or frying up some bubble and squeak—or mediating arguments between his wife and his daughter. Too antsy to sit, Lou rolled up her sleeves, picked up a rag, and began to wipe down the countertops, collecting bits of green onion and radish in her palm to throw into the compost bin.

"There's an apron if you want one," said Ailien, as she stirred the pot. "Or is that too feminine for you?"

"Sure smells good in here, Ma," said Lou, refusing to rise to Ailien's bait. "I'm starving."

"It's ready enough if you want to eat."

"Want some?" Lou asked, hesitating before retrieving only one bowl from the cabinet.

"I'll be fine."

Oh, how Lou hated it when her mother got like this. "I didn't ask if you were fine," she said through clenched teeth, "I asked if you wanted any breakfast."

"I'll let the man eat first."

"Huh?" Lou stared at her mother, then turned back to the pot full of simmering rice porridge. "Oh, I get it. That's really funny, Ma. *Hilarious.*"

She dished out some juk and doctored it with pickled vegetables and tofu. Her mother sat across from her, apparently perfectly at ease. Lou would have bet a whole dollar that wasn't the case, but she knew from experience it was best to let Ailien speak in her own time. So she blew on her juk and picked up a morsel of pickled tofu with her chopsticks.

"This is really good," she said, after chewing and swallowing. "I can never get the texture just right."

"All it takes is practice."

Lou kept her eyes on her porridge, watching the tofu and vegetables as they sank into the soft rice. She didn't know what to say—didn't know why her mother had wanted her to come over. It felt like they had nothing to talk about now that the one thing they'd ever had in common was gone forever—though to be fair, well before her father's death this sort of frustrated silence had been typical of their interactions. Lou took another bite of food, then sucked on her chopsticks just to be rude. She tried not to smile when she saw how much it irritated her mother.

"Would you like a spoon?"

"Nah," said Lou. "Thanks, though. Anyways, what's the rumpus, Ma? Did you need me to do a job for you, or…?"

"Would it be a problem if I just wanted to visit with my daughter?"

"Nope," said Lou cheerfully. "But were that the case, you could always just drop by."

"Could I?"

"Why not?"

Ailien looked like she wanted to say something, but then shook her head. "Lou—I worry about you…"

"Oh? Why's that?" Lou sensed danger, a thickening in the air like imminent lightning.

"I just hate to see you so unhappy."

Her mother's words surprised her. Lou didn't think of herself as being unhappy, but before she could protest the assertion, Ailien cut her off.

"I know things haven't been easy for you… being different. Your father and I knew when we—"

"Don't talk to me about Papa."

Ailien looked genuinely surprised to hear the venom in Lou's tone, but Lou didn't care. It was a wound that was still too raw to touch. She hid her hands under the table. They were trembling.

"So that's it," said Ailien quietly. "I'd wondered."

"I said I didn't want to talk about it," said Lou, just as quietly.

"Lou… you know, if he hadn't asked me—*pleaded* with me…"

Lou frowned to hear Vilhelm's words in her mother's mouth, but she said nothing. If her mother wanted absolution, she would have to seek it elsewhere.

After a long heavy silence, Ailien sighed. "You look tired, Lou. Are you tired?"

Lou shrugged. "Maybe. Yeah."

"If I made you some medicine, would you take it?"

Lou frowned, knowing whatever Ailien made her would be some kind of hideous concoction that would look bad, smell terrible, and taste worse. On the other hand, Lou figured if she agreed, the sooner she'd be on her way, and her mother would never know if she drank it or not.

"Thanks, that sounds great," she said. "And thanks for breakfast, too," she added, a moment later. "Your cooking's the best, Ma. Always has been. And you look great, and the place…"

Ailien pushed her chair away from the table and stood. For a brief moment, Lou hoped that maybe her mother really had just wanted to visit; that she was getting up to sift about a million weird bugs and roots and fungus and whatever into folded paper packets.

But Ailien did not head back into the shop. She made tea—the regular kind.

Neither mother nor daughter spoke as the older woman heated the water until it looked like bubbling fish eyes, nor as Ailien poured it over the oolong she'd carefully measured into the Yixing teapot that had come with her all the way from her home in Toising. The muffled thumps and cries of morning activity on the streets beyond the kitchen walls were the only sounds in the room as Ailien let the leaves steep; the splash of the tea into two tiny clay cups felt so shockingly loud it made Lou twitch. Then Ailien sat again, handing one cup to Lou.

After taking a small sip, she said, "Before I make your medicine… I confess, I did ask you to come visit because I need your help."

Lou relaxed ever so slightly. Talking about a job was better than talking about anything else. "Sure, Ma. Whatever you need."

"Good. Because… I require the services of a detective."

Lou almost laughed. "What?"

"A detective. Surely you remember when Papa would read you tales of Justice Bao and Judge Dee and Auguste Dupin? Men who solve mysteries, and—"

"I know what a detective is," interrupted Lou, setting down her teacup. "It's just kind of an odd request. I can ask around, but—"

"You misunderstand me," said Ailien. "I mean that I need *you* to become a detective."

"Why? Do you need a ghost… detected?"

Ailien smiled. "No, thank you, but not at this time. Lou, several families in Chinatown have come to me over the last months. There have been a lot of… for the sake of argument, or perhaps for the sake of optimism, let us call them *disappearances*. Many sons and brothers and fathers who left to work on the railroad have not returned."

Lou wondered what her mother was getting at. It had been common enough for sons and brothers and fathers who had worked on the Transcontinental to "go missing"; the mortality rate for Chinese working on the railroad was outrageously high, especially if they worked with dynamite, as so many Chinese had.

"The more curious thing is," continued Ailien, "even more men have disappeared since the *completion* of the Transcontinental. And they all seem to have left the city chasing after promises of steady work in the railroad line—and you know how *that* sounds."

Lou nodded. The Gettysburg Concession had been the condition of the bear tribes whose troops had secured the victory for the Union during the war; the terms had been no more or less than a moratorium on all railroad construction west of the Mississippi after the completion of the Transcontinental. The resulting recession meant that out west at least most rumors of steady jobs in the railroad line were cock-and-bull stories. To hear of such being offered by anyone, even railroad representatives, would—or at least *should*—ring a warning bell in any reasonable person's mind.

"So some local suckers got taken in by some offer that was always going to be too good to be true. Sounds normal enough to me." Seeing the look on her mother's face, she shrugged. "I don't mean to sound heartless, but everyone knows there's no jobs, especially not for coolies."

"There aren't *supposed* to be, no." Ailien poured them more tea. "And yet, I cannot help but think… well, given this nation's respect for the treaties they've made with the Indians, there might be companies who are operating in spite of the law."

Lou had to admit it was a plausible theory. "Fair enough…"

"And even if the jobs never materialized, that doesn't explain the total lack of word from everyone who has gone off to take them. Too many of them are, according to their families, men who would not fail to come home, or at least write were they delayed. In many cases, while helping build the Transcontinental they sent letters home as often as they could."

Lou was beginning to see what her mother was getting at. "Okay. What else?"

Ailien hesitated. Lou, surprised, sat forward in her chair a little. Her mother's reluctance to speak intrigued her more than anything she'd said—Ailien would beat around the bush, but she wouldn't fail to speak her mind when it came down to it. Seeing her so uncomfortable meant something big must be going on.

"I've heard talk—rumors, really—of a ghostly railroad, a line being built to another world. Those who travel on it… well."

Lou was flabbergasted. "You think someone opened a door to the land of the dead and is—"

"I do not think anything. I am repeating theories that may or may not be true. I am inclined to believe something more earthly is stealing away the sons of the Middle Kingdom, but I do not know what it might be." She looked Lou in the eye. "I want you to look into it."

As she contemplated what she could possibly do Lou took a long sip of tea and swished it around in her mouth. Investigating this kind of scandal seemed well beyond her purview as a psychopomp.

"I dunno, Ma. If we knew they were already dead I might be able to help. As for the living, the sheriff might be a better—"

"No white lawman would spend even a moment of his time looking for a single missing chink, let alone many," said Ailien, and Lou's mouth fell open upon hearing such a word spoken by her mother. "Oh, *please,*" said Ailien, seeing Lou's reaction. "You know as well as I do that most people will consider it a blessing that someone or something is taking the Chinese away from San Francisco—every missing Chinaman is one less Chinaman looking for a job that some white boy should have."

Ailien was right. Though Lou might feel little personal connection to the Chinese community, she was of course aware of the recent increased violence against individuals and attacks on businesses. It was a scary time to be Chinese in San Francisco; lawmen were notoriously disinclined to investigate any claims made by the Chinese, and the newspapers rarely ran stories sympathetic to the community.

And it wasn't as if Lou needed to read the papers to know that public opinion was ruthlessly anti-Chinatown. A few months back, after several would-be clients had stalked out of the Merriwether Agency upon seeing Lou sitting behind the desk, Vilhelm had gently advised her to keep away from the office as much as possible, to let him handle that side of things.

"All right," she said. "I'll see what I can do."

Ailien surprised Lou by reaching across the table and putting her hand over her daughter's. They had never been physically close, and certainly not these days—but Lou did not take her hand away.

"Thank you," said Ailien. "I know it's unfair of me to give you so little to go on and ask for so much, but I suspect your ability to move in between our community and the rest of the city will help our chances of finding out *something*."

"Maybe," said Lou, reclaiming her hand. "You're closer to the families than I am."

"True. I could talk to the people who have lost family members and see if they knew exactly where the missing men were heading… and see if they've heard any more stories, from people I don't know…"

"That sounds good. There might be some kind of pattern." Lou sighed. "I'll try my best, but it might come to nothing."

"I know you cannot promise me success," said Ailien. "But I know you, and therefore I know that you will do your best."

They sat quietly for a little while, finishing their tea. When Lou realized she was enjoying herself she stood up. The longer she stayed, the bigger the chance something would screw up the moment.

"I guess I should go… clients to see, and all that. I'll come by soon and let you know if I've found anything."

"I'll get your medicine," said Ailien, also rising. "Do you need more wards? I have time to write them out for you now…"

"I still have a big stack," said Lou. "Thanks, though."

Ailien trotted into the shop proper as Lou collected her coat and hat. When she rejoined her mother, Lou found her weighing out some sort of resin with a set of ornate brass scales. Six white squares of paper already held an assortment of dried berries, herbs, and bark.

"How's business, by the bye?" asked Lou.

"Who can say in these uncertain times?" said Ailien, crumbling the resin into the mix. "But, muddy water will become clear if left to stand."

"Heaven and earth, Ma," said Lou.

"I'm not entirely certain what you mean by that, but all right," said Ailien patiently. Folding up the papers into little parcels, she packed them into a paper bag and handed over the earthy-smelling bundle, along with a five-dollar bill. "Take a cab home. It's not safe, walking everywhere like you do."

"Thanks, I will," said Lou, though she had no intention of wasting the gift in such a frivolous manner. Five dollars was a lot of money, too much to blow on a few minutes' comfort.

"Boil the medicine in two cups of water, until it becomes one, then strain it and drink it while it's hot."

"Gotcha," said Lou, opening the door.

"And Lou?"

"Hmm?"

"Your hair was so beautiful… at least consider growing it out again?"

Lou shut the door behind her with the utmost care.

Chapter Four

It was only with difficulty that Lou bit back the *fuck you* she'd been longing to say for the better part of half an hour; instead, she took a deep breath and tried again.

"What about the Shaw brothers?" she asked, mostly succeeding at keeping her voice neutral. "All four boys were American-born, so maybe you'd have a record of them? Runje and Runme and Runde bought their tickets last August from this station and headed to Cheyenne. Their father told me that their youngest brother Run Run, who'd worked for the U.P. for a while—and got his job here, at your recruitment office—had written that there was work for those who wanted it, so they should come on out."

There was a long moment of tense silence, punctuated only by the calls of the seagulls as they soared on the damp wind, and the barking speech of the sea lion ferrymasters bringing folks back and forth across the bay. Lou tried to look like she didn't much care if she got an answer. So far she hadn't learned a single helpful thing from the recruitment officer who slouched behind the window at the Oakland office of the Central Pacific Railroad, but she held out hope that if she played it cool for long enough she'd find out something.

Eventually the man blew out a sigh through the straggly ends of his tobacco-stained mustache. "Look, boy," he said. "You can me ask about every chink in Chinatown, but no matter *where* they were born, I'm gonna keep tellin you the same thing: there ain't been work for coolies for damn close to a year now, so anyone who's decided to head east has done so for his own inscrutable reasons. As is, I suppose, fitting for a Celestial."

Lou could taste the salt from the bay on her lips when she spoke. "Just seems strange, is all."

"World's a strange place."

"Sure is." Lou produced a letter from the inside breast pocket of her over-coat. The paper fluttered in the breeze as she showed him the front of the envelope. "But here's the thing, this letter? It's postmarked from Cheyenne, Wyoming."

"So?"

Lou took the letter out, and placed it on the counter, holding it down with her fingertips. "It's from one of the men you said you couldn't trace because of—what was it? Mildew destroyed the records?"

"*So?*"

"This is from last May." Lou paused, trying not to stare at her adversary, who was now picking his teeth with a grubby thumbnail. "It says our man here had hopes of finding some work in the railroad line."

The recruitment officer leaned forward to eye the calligraphy suspiciously, and then spat out something he'd dislodged with his makeshift toothpick. "That could say anything."

"Ah, but it doesn't," said Lou, raising an eyebrow. "It says, and I quote, *Dear Father, I regret I shall miss the celebration of your sixtieth birthday, but after traveling to Cheyenne to see about another job with the railroad, I have been told there is work for men with blasting experience south of here, in the Colorado Territory. I have signed a contract but know little more other than that the pay is good. I think for the sake of our family's finances I have made the right decision. Expect a letter when I arrive, your loving son, Chan.*"

With his drooping whiskers and narrowed eyes, the man resembled a grouchy housecat when Lou looked up at him after finishing.

"By all accounts," said Lou, when it became obvious the man had nothing to say to this, "there shouldn't be any railroad work anywhere, and certainly not in Colorado, right? Papers all say things are pretty desperate in Denver, with no rail line feeding them, and stagecoaches running up to the depot in Cheyenne. But Chan here isn't talking about working as muscle on a stage, is he?"

"No."

"So you can see why I'd have reason to believe I might be able to trace these missing men through your company's records?"

"I can see why you'd think that. Too bad it's not possible."

"Because of the mildew?"

"It's a curse and a blessing, the bay. Lots of fresh fish, but paper just crumbles away."

Lou sighed. "This is the last letter his family received from him."

"Maybe he died."

"Maybe," she allowed. "But I've heard fifty stories like this if I've heard one. That's a mighty high death toll for a job that doesn't exist."

The man sighed and sat back in his chair. "Maybe you should wire Cheyenne, see what they—"

"Being both intelligent and thorough, I did that before I came callin'," said Lou. "They said there was no work anywhere. Not in the Dakota Territory, not in the Colorado Territory. Nowhere."

"Well, there you go."

"So what about all these missing people who were told there were jobs for them?"

"People get hoodwinked all the time. If they traveled by train, we transported them safely wherever they wanted to go, but we can't do nothin once they get off the car."

"But—"

The man held up his hand. "I'm sorry, but we're going to be shutting down for the day soon, so…"

"It's two in the afternoon!"

"Winter hours," said the man blithely. "Sorry."

Lou didn't want to leave without learning something, *anything*, about where all the men might have gone. "But—"

"Scat, kid," said the man, and closed the shutter in Lou's face.

Lou stood there, staring at the now-opaque window, deeply unhappy. She'd hoped a personal visit to the Oakland office would yield better results than her telegram to Cheyenne, but it seemed no one wanted to talk. That had convinced her something was not on the up-and-up, even more than the sheer volume of missing people—and the similarities among the stories told by their family and friends. The hard part was finding out *what*.

Defeated, at least for the present moment, Lou headed back toward the Long Wharf. The ferrymasters were sunning themselves in a pile. Feeling it would be rude to holler at them, Lou walked down the clattering steps onto the beach proper, where the heels of her boots squeaked on the hard-packed sand. It smelled like dead fish and salt spray. A sea lion smell. Lou ambled along the beached private sedans and paused beside the big heap of snoring, bulky bodies. A big bull noticed her and extricated himself from his companions. He rippled over to where she stood, his flanks glistening in the pale sunlight.

"Back across, please," she said.

"Too choppy," he horked at her. "Next ferry's due in soon."

"Too choppy?" Lou glanced over at the glass-smooth bay.

"Storm this evening. It'll get rough." He pulled his head down towards his shoulders in the sea lion equivalent of a shrug.

"But…" began Lou, but the creature was already shuffling back towards his fellows, leaving Lou to walk back to the dock, find a bench, and shiver while scanning the lapping water for any sign of the ferry.

"Not long" meant something different to the sea lions, apparently. Jealous, Lou looked over at them as they snoozed in comfort, warm under their thick layers of blubber. Well, between pulling a sedan through the frigid waters of the bay and taking a nice nap, she wouldn't necessarily choose the former, either.

Then something occurred to Lou that made her sit up and forget the chill breeze that gusted down the collar of her duster and right through her clothes to her very bones. An image of herself attached to a sedan chair and bearing it along the streets of San Francisco had flitted idly across her mind.

It wasn't that the man wouldn't talk to her because she was Chinese. He wouldn't talk to her because she wasn't Chinese *enough*. She should have realized that sooner, given that it was always one or the other with her.

A plan came together in her mind just as the ferry appeared on the horizon.

***

It took Lou only a day to collect what she needed to put her idea into action, but she delayed the execution in order to put in some long hours at the Agency. But when March arrived, just like a lion as the adage went, she felt she could delay no longer. The first Friday of the month was decided as the day she and Vilhelm would close the Agency early and implement her scheme.

"You're sure you want to go through with this?" asked Vilhelm, as he walked out of the Merriwether Agency's back room, dressed in a threadbare, grey-checkered three-piece accented with a jade-green cravat. The clothes were so seedy that at first he'd objected to wearing them at all… but when Lou showed him *her* costume he'd quieted down quick enough.

"Far as I can see it, it's the only way." Lou fastened the last few frogs of her father's old silk tunic and shimmied her shoulders to get the garment to hang correctly. It was too large for her, but she figured no one would notice. "Just don't mess up, okay? We only have one chance to get this right."

"Should I hail a cab?"

"We'll walk." Lou rolled her eyes when Vilhelm pouted. "I'm going to freeze to death in this getup if I don't keep my blood moving."

"Just mind you don't lose that moustache somewhere along the way."

Lou tugged the brim of her conical straw hat down low over her face. It wasn't appropriate to what she was wearing, but it hid her face, and again, she figured no one would notice. "Come on, let's go."

In spite of her bravado Lou knew she looked ridiculous, and felt the indignity keenly. Not only were all the clothes too big for her but they were decades out of fashion, relics from her father's trip to Canton that had yielded many valuable insights into the art of psychopompery—and, unexpectedly, a wife. But Lou was betting on the nuances of Chinese dress being lost on most white folks; indeed, it seemed, as she and Vilhelm hurried along, that she received far fewer looks than usual.

She forgot her self-consciousness when they reached Fisherman's Wharf. The open market was one of her favorite spots in the city, with all the cart stands selling fried squid and chowder, the boardwalk, and the strong smell of salt coming in off the coracle-speckled bay. It was always and never the same, busy and noisy and stinky and beautifully anonymous.

Unlike the Bear Market, here human fishermen sold their catches beside sea lions barking about the superior virtues of their heaped piles of sturgeon, perch, and salmon. Lou paid a few pennies for a skewer of fish balls to nibble on while they waited for the ferry. Vilhelm eyed them with suspicion, but eventually grabbed one for himself after Lou said they tasted fresh and weren't too spicy.

Licking salt and grease from her fingers, Lou idly watched the human children who were often employed by sea lions to collect money, make change, and run hither and yon on errands, their screeches not too different from the pups who stumbled and frolicked alongside their parents. Not having hands like their ursine cousins, many of the pinniped shop-owners used humans for tasks requiring manual dexterity—but some, of course, did not care to do so. Instead, they sported leather bags around their neck with "exact change only" scrawled in Chinese, Spanish, and English—and woe betide the person who sought to cheat the system. There were always reports of folks who thought themselves crafty needing stitches after receiving horrible bites, or losing entire fingers for the sake of a coin.

The dock had grown increasingly crowded as they ate, so, after they finished their snack, they meandered over to the booth that sold ferry-tokens.

"Two round-trip tickets, please," said Lou, handing over a few coins.

"Shouldn't be long." A young cow wearing a blue scarf around her neck nosed two wooden tokens across the counter. "Thanks."

"Thank *you,* m'dear," said Vilhelm, who bestowed his avuncular courtesy upon ladies of all species. "We appreciate it."

The ferry crawled into view, a large catamaran powered by enormous bulls who, harnessed in the empty space below the two hulls, tugged the vessel to and fro across the bay all day. Vilhelm looked nervous as they waited to board. He was prone to seasickness, but there wasn't an alternative, and anyways, it wasn't a long trip.

The breeze was colder once they were out on the water. Lou was covered in goose-pimples long before she stepped off onto the dock that led to the Terminus of the Central Pacific, and Vilhelm was looking green about the gills. Maybe the fish balls hadn't been such a good idea.

Most of those who had crossed with them hurried to buy tickets for the train, so Lou told Vilhelm to take a few moments to recover his composure. Once the crowd thinned a bit, they headed over to the window that said Recruitment.

The same horseshoe-mustached man sat there, scribbling. Lou shoved her hands into her sleeves, trying to look as obsequiously Chinese as possible. Vilhelm, for his part, adopted a casual sneer as he waited patiently for the man to look up.

"Can I help you fellas?" he asked. Lou looked at Vilhelm as if confused. Vilhelm smiled with all his teeth.

"I heard a rumor about there being work for coolies," he said. "My friend here—see him? He needs a job."

"Sorry," said the man behind the counter, looking back down at his paperwork. "No jobs."

"Help a man out," pleaded Vilhelm, when Lou shot him a look urging him to put a little pressure on the guy for goodness' sake. "He don't speak English, and he's had some hard times of late."

"Too bad," said the man. "All jobs are east of here. East," he repeated, pointing east.

Vilhelm didn't speak much Toisanese, but he had enough to make a convincing show of turning to Lou and explaining what the man had just said. Lou pretended to be listening intently, then began nodding vigorously. Turning to the man behind the counter, she said "East," in accented English.

"Your boy sure?" asked the man, turning back to Vilhelm.

"He's not my boy, he's my friend… sort of. He's fallen on hard times, like I said," said Vilhelm, launching into his prepared spiel. "Five brothers, no work." Then he grinned. "Plus he gave a girl *happiness,* as he'd tell you—if he could speak English."

"Happiness?" The man looked confused.

Vilhelm winked at the man and made a motion like he was caressing a large, pregnant belly. Lou tried not to react to this improvisation on Vilhelm's part.

"Hmm," said the man, looking Lou up and down. "It's dangerous work, if he's a family man. Might not come back, and it sounds like he's got some folks who'd want him to stick around…"

Vilhelm was thinking fast. "It's his brother's wife who he… we're both men of the world, aren't we?"

"Speak for yourself," said the man coldly. "That's no good, if he's *that* sort of boy. We need workers—good ones, not the sort who'll be lazy and idle, chasing after women and—"

"Trust me, he's learned his lesson," said Vilhelm smoothly. "Look at me." He gestured up and down his body. "Do you think a gentleman such as myself would associate with a hardened ne'er-do-well?"

54

The man didn't say anything for a long few moments, assessing Vilhelm and Lou both. Lou cast her eyes downward, hoping she looked penitent and hardworking, not nervous.

"Come on," urged Vilhelm. "Please? Just between you and me... I want to be rid of him. We're old fan-tan buddies, he and I, and so I gave him a place to stay when the... *incident* with his brother's wife was discovered. But he's outstayed his welcome, what with not being able to find work. I want him out of my house. It's impossible to bring a girl back or—I need not trouble you with my concerns."

After a long moment, the man asked, "What's his name?"

"Bo Wong," answered Vilhelm. This time Lou *did* choke, but played it off as if she was startled to hear her name during the queer, confusing English conversation.

"Can he sign it?" asked the man. Vilhelm chattered the question at her in Toisanese.

Lou looked up and nodded.

"Hmm," said the man again, producing a contract from the top drawer of his desk. "Show me."

Lou scanned the document. Strangely enough, it didn't seem to mention a railroad anywhere, but she couldn't spend too much time scanning the legalese for fear of—

"Here," said the man loudly, as if increasing his volume would help Lou understand him. He stabbed a finger at the line where she was to write her name, his hand obscuring the rest of the writing. "This is where you sign."

Lou smiled blandly and drew an X on the line. The man seemed pleased by this, and tapped something on the telegraph line with his right hand.

"Well, that's some good timing, friend," he said to Vilhelm, taking the contract and opening a drawer that Lou could see was full of sheets of paper most definitely *not* mildewed into illegibility. "Just told my people in Cheyenne that your friend Mr. Wong'll be on the 5:09 from Oakland. He can go today—tell him to go on in and wait. It's warmer in here."

"No," said Vilhelm, startled.

"Huh?"

"He's not, ah, packed," said Vilhelm, more calmly. "He didn't know if there'd be anything for him, see."

"If he doesn't leave today, then he's gotta wait till Monday."

"He'll be on the earliest train. Promise."

"Because he signed a contract, right? And he knows what that means, right?" The man gave Vilhelm the hard-eye. "Well.... all right. I can wire and say he'll start out Monday instead." The man tapped something further on the telegraph, then he rummaged in a file and extricated a ticket. "What was the name again?" he asked. "Bo Wong?"

"Yessir."

"Easy enough." He wrote something on the ticket, then handed it across to Lou. "Complimentary," he said, with a smile that unsettled Lou with its casual friendliness. "I won't see him Monday—my shift starts later—but the ticket should be enough. If not, tell 'em Ralph said it was okay. Can you remember that? *Ralph.*"

"Ralph," Lou repeated, pretending to stumble over the name as she looked from Ralph to Vilhelm.

"Close enough," said Ralph. "Oh, and be *on time.* Six fifteen sharp."

Lou was quiet as they rode the ferry back to San Francisco, trying to parse the grammar of her feelings. She was happy that she now had evidence that the railroad office was indeed recruiting Chinese laborers for work somewhere in the Wyoming Territory—or maybe Colorado. She'd seen both Cheyenne and some place called "Estes Park" mentioned while scanning the strange document she'd signed. But the contract had seemed, for lack of a better description, *really weird,* and she hadn't had time to look at it long enough to figure out why.

"Penny for your thoughts," said Vilhelm.

"Oh." Lou shook her head. "Just... everything I guess."

"What—you mean like how your contract wasn't on letterhead?"

"Or had any kind of identifying markings? And he wouldn't let either of us take a good look at it?"

"And how the moment it seemed less like I was doing you a favor, and more like I was trying to get rid of you any way I could, he warmed up to me?" Vilhelm nodded. "Queer indeed. But at least you have something to tell Ailien, right?"

"I guess." Lou looked up at the sky, noticing the air had begun to feel heavier and wetter. They were close to docking; she'd have to book it across town unless she wanted to hunt for a cab. "I'm not crazy, am I? There's no more railroads being built... not right now. Right?"

"Right."

"So what do they want coolies for?"

Vilhelm shrugged. "Guess you'd have to go there to find out."

"With my ticket says Bo Wong? Thanks for that, by the way."

"I had to give a boy's name, didn't I?"

"Uh huh."

Vilhelm was having a difficult time not saying more, Lou could tell, so she was grateful when he just asked, "So, are you going to go?"

"Hell no." Lou stood. It was time to disembark and she wanted to get off the ferry and home again as quickly as possible. It was getting colder, and her silk tunic was feeling thinner by the moment. "I can't. Who would run things here? I'm gonna tell Ma what I found out, and she can tell the families she knows their sons went east, and I'll help her spread the word that no one should take any more of these jobs until it's clearer what's going on." Lou shrugged unhappily. Something felt wrong about abandoning her inquiry without seeing it through to the end, but she couldn't just hop onto a train Monday morning and leave her business behind. "I don't really know what else to do."

"If you're worried about work, I'm sure Imre would—"

"Oh no," said Lou, as they walked along the wharf. "He's busy. I wouldn't want to impose."

"Lou... I saw him at the synagogue last Saturday. He asked about you, said he'd be happy to help if you ever needed any."

"He's got enough on his plate with school."

Vilhelm shrugged. "That's his business. Seemed to like the idea of getting his hands dirty again. Maybe the air in the ivory tower's gotten a little musty for his taste."

A peal of thunder jolted Lou's mind away from the notion of temporarily handing over operations to one of her father's former graduate students. "I'll think about it," she promised. "But I should go."

"Want to split a cab?"

"Nah. Walking helps me think."

"Suit yourself." Vilhelm eyed the sky. "Stay dry, Lou—see you Monday?"

"No reason you wouldn't."

As she walked Lou chewed over the idea of traveling across the country to pursue her investigation, but she couldn't think of anything she'd rather do less than go all the way to goddamn Cheyenne to look into whatever shady reason the Central Pacific had for recruiting Chinese workers to build a railroad that shouldn't exist. Surely warning any more young men against taking these jobs would be enough? Likely she couldn't do anything for anyone who'd already gone.

So why did she feel like such a coward?

A sudden chill downpour soaked Lou to the bones and set her teeth chattering. She was almost home, but not close enough that running would do anything to save her clothing. Depressed, wet, and cranky, Lou turned the final corner—and froze.

Through the deluge she could see light shining from the windows of her rented rooms, and she certainly hadn't left a lantern or candle lit when she left. A figure crossed in front of the window, but the curtain was drawn so Lou saw only their outline.

Fucking hell, she thought. And she'd left her gun at home. The shoulder holster hadn't looked right under the silken tunic.

The person walked past the window again, and the notion that some burglar was in her warm house, out of the rain, dry and safe and chuckling as he rummaged through her personal effects jolted Lou out of her momentary stupor. After the day she'd had she'd earned her goddamn respite.

But assuming she could surprise the intruder, perhaps she could get at him before he reached for his weapon. Lou figured she was probably a match for most thugs; fists weren't her weapon of choice but she'd used them often enough to know what she was about. If she could get in a few good strikes she could dash for her gun in her bedroom while he was reeling. Your average burglar wouldn't want to take his chances against a LeMat.

Lou approached her door stealthily, turning the knob as gently as possible and wincing at the click. To keep her advantage, she put her weight into the door, slamming it open as she bounded inside.

A scream answered her entrance; as Lou rushed the intruder she felt a missile collide with her face. She stumbled backwards, spitting out something that blocked her mouth.

It was… cabbage?

"Get out!" cried a female voice, in clear, strong Toisanese. "I have a gun!"

Chapter Five

Lou wiped away a few leafy shreds from her mouth and eyes. Her vision was a little blurry and her nose was running from the impact of the half-cabbage, but she could still see who had hit her. "Ma? What are you doing here?"

"Lou?" Ailien was by her side in an instant. Lou allowed her mother to help her half fall into one of the kitchen chairs. "I didn't recognize… is that a *moustache?*"

Lou felt her nose to make sure it wasn't broken. It wasn't. "I can explain."

Ailien looked her daughter up and down. "I hope so. You've ruined your father's clothes. What a waste!"

"Not entirely. I found out some stuff," she said. "The chucklehead at the Oakland office who sassed me so hard offered me a job when I showed up looking like a coolie. Or whatever." She paused as Ailien walked back to the small stove and stirred something. It occurred to Lou that it smelled good in her house. Really good. "You're cooking?"

"I was making you dinner," said Ailien. "I thought you might be hungry."

For the first time that night Lou didn't regret having given her mother a spare key. "Thanks, Ma. That's real thoughtful of you. About how long do I have until it's ready? Is there time for me to take a bath?"

"Of course. Let me heat up some water. I should have thought of that when it started to rain."

It was warmer in the kitchen, so Lou chopped green onions until the water was hot. After taking the cauldron into her small bathroom, she finally peeled off the wet silk and sponged herself down. It felt heavenly to be warm and dry, and she felt even better after donning fresh twill trousers, a green shirt, and a pearl-grey waistcoat. Her favorite bolo tie completed the ensemble: black braided leather with real silver tips, the clasp was a lucky Chinese coin embossed with her zodiac sign, a tiny prick-eared pig. Though the metal had gone green in places with age, she refused to polish it; indeed, she never had. It might be sentimental, but didn't want to erase the fingermarks of the person who'd given it to her, long ago.

By the time Lou emerged, her apartment was redolent with the rich smells of pork, choi sam, and ginger. Her mother was ladling the hot soup into two bowls.

"I can't say how grateful I am," she said, accepting her portion. I never expected such a treat tonight."

"You're very welcome," said Ailien, looking pleased.

After slurping a few spoonfuls of broth so spicy it warmed her right to her toes, Lou felt able to tell her mother the news. "So…" she began, not looking at Ailien, "it looks like the railroad really is handing out jobs to Chinese who come asking—at least, Chinese what don't speak English and can't write. The man told me I could ship out today if I wanted. But it seems weird, Ma. I couldn't tell if the job was in Wyoming—"

"I have reason to believe at least some of the missing men have gone south of there, to Colorado," interrupted Ailien. "A place called Estes Park."

Lou was faintly annoyed to find her news wasn't… news. "That's the other place I was gonna tell you they might be."

"And?"

"And what?"

"That's all? That's everything you found out?"

"Well, they're being shady, aren't they?" Lou deeply resented this dismissal of her efforts. "I can't help it that you sent me on some wild goose chase to find out information you already knew."

"Calm down before that vein in your forehead bursts. I just came into the information today."

"Anyways, it seems like a dead end," grumbled Lou. "I'd have to go there myself to find out more. I was, uh…" Lou trailed off, seeing her mother's displeased expression, but then she rallied. "I can't leave the Agency for that long, but if you know anyone else, anyone without a business to mind, he can use my ticket."

Ailien did not reply. Lou watched her out of the corner of her eye as they both ate. After her mother finished, she set down her bowl and sighed.

"I'd like you to come with me to a friend's house tonight."

Lou grimaced into the dregs of her soup. She should have known Ailien wanted something. Coming here to make her dinner… being so pleasant about everything… it was all starting to make sense. Apparently everyone in her life thought they could bribe her with food. Well, they weren't wrong…

"A friend's house where?" she asked.

"Chinatown. A client of mine received an unusual package this morning. It was sent from Estes Park. Will you come?"

"What was the package?"

"It's easier to show you than explain."

"Come on, Ma, it's cold, and it's raining, and I've had a long day—"

"How's your Chinese these days? I know you rarely practice."

Lou conducted most of her business in Chinatown in Toisanese, but it wasn't worth arguing about. "I get by."

"I can translate if you need me to. Will you come?"

Lou figured if she was abandoning her investigation, she could at least do this one last thing. "All right."

Ailien stood. "I'll get the dishes."

"I'll get 'em," said Lou. "You cooked."

"I'll do them while you change your clothes."

"Change into what?"

"Something a little more feminine?"

Lou laughed. "Keep hoping, Ma. In the meantime, I'll be more comfortable like this."

Ailien seemed amused rather than annoyed, which made Lou more curious to find out what was really going on. "Suit yourself. These won't take but a moment, so get your coat—and that hideous bag you cart your things around in."

"What? Why?"

"It's where you keep your gun, isn't it?"

"No, I got a holster for it."

"Well, bring it. You never know. Do you have an extra umbrella? We'll hail a cab, but until then—"

"Ma! Why do I need my bag?"

"It always helps to be prepared, doesn't it?" Ailien was clearly having a good time stringing her daughter along. "Get yourself together, and we'll go."

Lou sensed asking more questions would only further delight her mother. *Fine.* If Ailien didn't want to give any answers, she could deal with no conversation at all. Handing her mother her an umbrella without a word, Lou locked up, and they dashed into the rainy night.

The silence continued as they hailed a cab, and deepened as they traveled deep into Chinatown. Lou was cranky. The sound of rain pattering against the cab windows and roof was tiresome, she was cold and wet again, and still without a clue where specifically she was going, as her mother had called the direction after Lou had climbed inside, probably on purpose. Wherever she was going, she didn't want to be going there, didn't care about this stupid package from Colorado. An existential gloom replaced Lou's grumpiness as she stared out the window, her mother's fixed, serene expression only adding to her melancholy.

Even with the rain the roads were thick with cabs and pedestrians. It was Friday night, and Chinatown offered many entertainments for all the people of San Francisco—at least, those with money in their pockets. Lou couldn't make out the street signs through the downpour and the fog of her breath on the window, but when they stopped just before reaching a narrow alley ablaze with light, crowded with hustling from awning to awning, pushing each other through open doorways, Lou realized where she was. Known as Lu Song Hang to residents and Ross Alley to outsiders, the place was notorious in any language for being one of the best places in San Francisco to pull a cork, gamble away some hard-earned money—and find a girl whose time was for sale.

"Fan-tan or whores?" asked Lou, at last breaking the silence.

"Whores," replied Ailien mildly, as she opened the cab-door.

Unfurling Lou's umbrella with a *shoof,* Ailien handed her payment up to the cabman and beckoned to her daughter before disappearing into the throng. Lou slid out after her, only to come down hard with both feet in a frigid puddle. Feeling justified for having worn her usual clothing, Lou pulled up the collar of her coat and darted quickly in among the multitudes. The primarily male crowd had parted slightly to allow a lady like Ailien through, but Lou was just another face in a sea of faces; she bumped many a shoulder and received many a cuss in her attempt to keep up.

Ailien disappeared inside Madame Cheung's Flower Garden before Lou even made it to the step. It looked like a rich, popular house. Beautifully carved stone lions guarded the entryway, mouths open and teeth bared. Beyond them, patrons were shedding their coats in the brightly lit parlor.

Once inside, it was even more lavishly decorated than Lou had expected. The only thing more dazzling than the walls hung with brocaded satins and deep velvets of scarlet, jade-green, and jet were the girls. Squeezing in between the well-dressed men chatting up pretty women of all ages, she ignored some miffed looks as her sodden duster brushed against wool and silk.

She looked everywhere for her mother in the big main room but Ailien was nowhere to be seen. Lou sighed. There was a long hallway at the back of the parlor, with many closed doors on either side, as well as a grand, red-carpeted staircase that curved upwards gracefully to the second floor. Where might she have gone?

"Ah, very well-come," breathed someone in Lou's ear, in a voice as sultry as its source's sandalwood perfume. Lou stiffened as she felt an arm snake under her coat and encircle her waist. "What-ever you look-ee, we have-ee. Mahjong, pretty girl, any-thing. *Promise.*"

"Actually, I'm trying to find my mother," replied Lou, turning to see a lovely Chinese girl of about her own age, who looked understandably surprised. Lou grinned at her. "She came in just ahead of me, but I lost her in the crowd. Ailien Merriwether?"

"I don't know her, sorry," the girl said in perfect English. "Is she a friend of Madame Cheung's?"

"Probably. She brought me here because somebody got a strange package today?"

"Oh," said the girl, now much more serious. "Yes, of course. Heung-kam's down in the cellar. I'll show you."

"Do you know what's going on?" asked Lou. "My mother wouldn't tell me."

"No," said the girl. "I just know after the box came Heung-kam got the night off."

"Thanks," said Lou, dodging a drunken man who was guiding a plump, giggling woman in a cherry-red cheongsam toward the staircase. "What's your name?"

"Ting-Ting," she replied, and then, with a sly glance over her shoulder, she asked, "Will you be staying long?"

"Not sure," said Lou. "Why?"

"Here's the cellar," said Ting-Ting. "If they're not there, come and find me. I'll take care of you."

"Thanks."

"And even if you *do* find them down there… come and find me? After, I mean. If you like."

Lou blushed as pink as Ting-Ting's dress, and leaned over to whisper rapidly in the other girl's ear. Ting-Ting winked at her.

"Even better," she said, and melted into the crowd. Lou watched her go with mixed feelings.

She heard murmured Chinese as she descended into the gloom. Recognizing her mother's voice she quickened her pace, and discovered two women gazing up at her in the dim lantern-light.

It was a decent-sized cellar, cluttered with stacked boxes and scuffed furniture. She shivered—it was cold down here, and damp. Lou nodded a greeting to the stranger, an older woman with pink, puffy eyes. Lou put her at about her mother's age, but she looked more careworn than Ailien. There was a large packing crate between them, its lid slightly ajar. A pallet of glass bottles sat off to the side, on the floor.

"Lou, this is Heung-kam," said Ailien. Lou nodded a greeting. "Her son's come home from Colorado."

"Okay," said Lou, slightly confused. "From… Estes Park?"

"Yes."

Puffy eyes… a night off work after receiving a package… Ailien insisting she bring her work bag… it all added up to one thing. "He's in the crate, isn't he?"

"Yes," said Ailien.

"And you want me to…"

Ailien nodded. "You'll understand when you see him why I thought you should be prepared."

Lou didn't need to see him to know if her services would be needed, but she elected not to mention this. Throwing her coat and bag onto a threadbare divan, she sent a puff of dust into the air that made her sneeze as she rooted through her bag for her skiameter. The needle quivered with tension, pointing straight at the crate.

The pull of undeath was surprisingly strong. More was going on here than just a dead boy in a box.

"He came this morning?" Lou asked.

"Yes, why?"

"What did the delivery man look like?" Lou asked Heung-kam, in Toisanese. She was gratified to see her mother's eyebrows shoot upward in surprise.

Lou's smugness faded when Heung-kam began to speak. She understood only about two thirds of what the woman said; she had a thick country accent and spoke very rapidly. Still, Lou thought she'd caught the gist of it. Heung-kam hadn't seen the postman. Someone else had accepted the delivery.

Lou nodded. "Did he ever write?"

"Yes," answered Ailien, when Heung-kam burst into tears. "She always brought his letters to the shop so I could read them for her. The last of them said he was heading to Cheyenne with his brother and a group of friends."

"Interesting. And yeah, this is postmarked from Estes Park... he must have heard the same story I was told, or similar." Lou set down her bag and rubbed her hands together in anticipation. She loved her work, and an impromptu nekuia was the best possible justification for having gotten wet and cold twice in one day. "Well, it's high time to figure out why he's only dead—and not dead-dead."

"Lou!"

"Sorry." Heung-kam might not be able to understand what she was saying, but body language spoke volumes. "It's just exciting—we might learn something new once we figure out what's going on with him, right?"

"You tell me."

Lou lifted the lid and saw why her mother found her behavior unseemly. Though Lou was as inured to the sight of death as any psychopomp had to be, a wave of nausea hit her as she saw what had been done to the boy who lay in the crate.

"He was under that," said Ailien. Lou, all too happy to have a reason to look away, saw her mother indicating a pallet of little bottles lying on the floor.

Lou took a steadying breath and turned back to the boy. Someone had dressed him in a clean workman's uniform, but where his skin was exposed Lou could see great violence had been inflicted upon his person before he died—his body was marked by several large contusions and lacerations, and in a few places his skin had been torn off entirely.

But what was most concerning, to her at least, was that the body had not decomposed at all during its journey. The boy could have just passed on that morning. The corpse did not smell of decay; no maggots writhed and nibbled where they ought to be flourishing.

"That's not good," muttered Lou. She retrieved her goggles and fitted the pink thumoscopic lenses into place. Peering at the body through the treated glass she saw a weak purple-red glow flowing through the young man's veins... exactly as it shouldn't be. Not anymore.

It was a very faint soul-residue, but just the same Lou would have to extract it, draining and then expelling it into the world of death where it belonged. If she didn't, the body would spiritually decompose, remaining physically unchanged, until it rose again to feed on the souls of the living. It would become a geung si: a mindless, re-animated corpse with a powerful hunger for qi.

As she scanned the corpse, Lou noticed something strange about the body itself, rather than the spirit within. The boy's left cheek was oddly distended. Her enhanced vision showed nothing peculiar, so she pushed her goggles onto her forehead and poked experimentally at the boy's face. Nothing terrible came out of his mouth, like maggots or spiders, but something was definitely in there.

All in a day's work. Parting the young man's cold, stiff lips with her fingertips Lou pried open his jaws with one hand and inserted her other into the cavity of his mouth. His teeth and tongue were there, both normal, so she poked her fingers sidelong into the bulge, and touched what felt like soggy paper. She tugged on whatever it was experimentally, and like a cabaret magician performing a scarf trick she withdrew a wad of paper from between the boy's lips.

"What the..." she muttered to herself, uncrumpling the slightly damp mass.

It was a stamped envelope, and the address was Madame Cheung's. Lou flipped open the flap and withdrew the letter.

Dear Cousin, I write to tell you of a job offer, she read—and then she heard a scream. Looking up, she jumped back in alarm.

The corpse had sat up in its crate. It turned slowly to look at her, eyes blank and filmy, arms straight out, hands dangling. It bared its teeth with a dry hollow groan, lips cracking into a half-smile, half-snarl. Lou looked down at the envelope in consternation—why had the geung si awoken after she removed the letter?

The stamps! Lou noted the distinctive red color of the seven-cent stamp and darted forward between the corpse's clutching hands. The geung si froze after she stuck the envelope onto its forehead with such force it sounded as if she'd slapped it. The guttural moaning stopped instantly.

"Sorry about that," apologized Lou, as she turned to find her mother looking pretty darn pissed off, and Heung-kam holding her hands over her mouth, eyes wide in terror. "It happens sometimes, after death."

She did not add that geung si possession was most often induced by a traumatic or violent death. Ailien knew already, and Heung-kam likely would not appreciate the information.

"That was sloppy," snapped her mother. "You could have been hurt."

Ailien's attitude irritated Lou. She knew her business, and anyways, nothing had gone all that wrong. Performing this much-needed exorcism with her mother looking over her shoulder would not be fun.

"Given the circumstances, I should really deal with," Lou gestured at the corpse, *"this.* So if you and Heung-kam wanted to, I dunno…" Lou trailed off, hoping her mother would take the hint and leave.

Predictably, Ailien did not say anything to Heung-kam, nor did she make any motion toward the stairs. Instead she sat down on the divan where Lou's coat lay, watching her daughter like a cat. Lou decided to ignore her.

After fitting her goggles back over her eyes, Lou unbuttoned the young man's shirt, exposing more of his neck. Then she reached into the crate and tipped him onto his back. When duty forced her to work directly with corpses Lou tried to treat them with all possible respect, but sometimes, with rigor mortis or geung si possession, it was necessary to move them around in ways that did not appear to be wholly polite. This corpse, for instance, had been bent at the waist in a ninety-degree angle when she had frozen him, legs outstretched. Now that he was on his back, his arms and legs were sticking straight up, which meant as Lou worked his feet hovered above her head on one side, hands on the other. The only way to fix the situation was to finish the exorcism.

Once she had him in position she retrieved a black velvet pouch from her satchel. Loosening the neck, she poured out a small handful of sticky rice into her left palm.

"What are you doing?" asked Heung-kam, who had apparently come up behind her. Lou almost jumped out of her skin.

"Oh. Uh… he's becoming a geung si. I'm helping him pass on, so he can rest."

Heung-kam furrowed her plucked brows. "Can I help?"

"Yes, actually," said Lou, pleased. Perhaps if she sent Heung-kam on an errand Ailien would go with her. "If you could get me a kettle of hot water, some black tea, and a tea bowl, that would be a big help. Do you have one he used to drink from?"

Heung-kam nodded eagerly. "Yes, and some of his favorite tea." She paused. "Is all this necessary? Could we not just bury him?"

"It has become necessary," said Lou, and with an apologetic shrug, turned back to the corpse. She heard footfalls on stairs behind her, but only one set. Her teeth clenched when she heard Ailien shift a little on the divan.

"Sticking around?" she said without turning.

"Yes," said Ailien. "Just in case you let that geung si awaken again."

Lou smiled ferociously. "Don't you worry. I'll take care of Mr. Vampire over here."

Lou upended the palmful of rice over the young man's throat where it formed a loose pyramid of white grains. The soul reacted instantly—the purple-red lazily circulating through his veins began to writhe purposefully, and then receded into the carotid artery.

Lou's father had described this phenomenon as the attraction of imbalance to balance. Sticky rice, long understood to be one of those rare, perfect expressions of yin and yang, was the ideal reagent for this particular process. Lou had seen other psychopomps use a host of different catalysts, from dragon bones to chemical powders, but sticky rice was cheaper than anything else, and easily replaceable, too.

Once the soul coagulated into one undulating cloud, Lou opened the tooled leather case and retrieved her extractor, a device that resembled a common medical syringe save for its size and the gleaming psuilver needle, largely invisible to the naked eye. Depressing the plunger, Lou thrust the needle through the rice pile and down into the corpse's throat. The soul recoiled violently from the intrusion, the way a live person might if poked with a syringe of so large a gauge. Lou paid no mind to this, but pulled up on the plunger smoothly. The soul, in spite of its obvious preference to remain inside its host, was drawn up inexorably into the barrel. Lou made sure to get every little bit of purple before she withdrew the needle. She knew when she was done when the boy's arms and legs flopped down at his sides.

Lou pushed up her goggles onto her sweaty forehead. The soul in the syringe disappeared from view, as did the needle. She stood and stretched while studiously avoiding her mother's eyes. Her perspiration-soaked shirt clung to her and she was queasy. She disliked this particular procedure—these days more than ever, after everything with her father—so she worked quickly.

As it wouldn't do to let the soul near the corpse again, Lou set the syringe down on the pallet of bottles. Then she retrieved her lens case and a thin wooden box with a key carved into the lid. Changing out the left lens for a blue, pulescopic one, she peered about. She smiled when she spied the telltale green light emanating from the back of the cellar.

"Lou," said her mother. Heung-kam had returned, bearing a tea tray stacked with a cup, a steaming kettle, and a small bowl of leaves.

"Thank you," said Lou.

She placed the extractor and the key-box alongside the tea service and took it all to the rear of the room. Kneeling beside the rectangle of otherworldly light, she opened the box. Inside lay a psuilver key on a silk cushion. Just like her saw, it was very heavy, and having no insulating handle it vibrated unpleasantly when she held it.

Dialing in the focus on her goggles, Lou found the keyhole, which for this door was located on the very top right of the portal. She inserted the key and turned it counterclockwise until she heard a faint click and the door shifted slightly. Jimmying her key underneath the edge, she flipped the door open without touching it with her hands.

Taking up the extractor, she stuck the tip of the needle into the blackness.

The lightless plane bowed slightly under the pressure until the needle's bevel pierced it. Lou depressed the plunger, and the swirling soul spun out into the uncanny dark.

Once she'd cleared the barrel, Lou withdrew the needle, set the syringe aside, and made tea. She measured leaves into the tea bowl—Lapsang Souchong, from the smell—and then poured hot water on top. Lou allowed the tea to steep for a few minutes, then sucked up the liquid into the syringe. Reinserting the tip, she cleared the extractor's chamber with the tea. After that, all that remained was to shut the door and relock it.

The cellar now smelled faintly of death. That was good. Accustomed as Lou was to feeling pleased after having aided a soul's smooth transition to the afterlife, it rarely occurred to her to be sad for the person who'd lost his or her life… most of the time. But, as she padded back over to where the two women stood by the crate, whispering to one another, something nagged at Lou's conscience.

Perhaps it was the boy's youth. His face was unlined, his brow smooth where it hadn't been torn and ruined. He had been very strong. His clothes were slightly too small for muscles grown large with hard work.

"Is it over?" asked Heung-kam.

Lou nodded. "He's passed on—you can bury him. Everything is all right now."

Heung-kam nodded and thanked Lou as Ailien took the tea service.

"I'll help her tidy up," said Ailien. "Find us in the kitchen when you're all done?"

Lou began to repack her workbag, still feeling unhappy. When she was done she looked at the boy one final time before shutting the lid over his corpse. It was a disgrace, whatever had befallen him.

It was then that the pallet of glass bottles caught her eye. Lou poked through them and discovered they were all identical, rectangular, cork-stoppered glass phials, filled with a clear fluid, and all sealed with yellow wax stamped with the image of a European dragon curled into a circle, biting its own tail. They looked like bottles of patent medicine. She moved closer to the lantern the women had courteously left behind to read the label:

Doctor Panacea's World-Famous
THE ELIXIR OF LIFE!

Made with rarified Colorado mountain herbs
And the purest river-water
In **ALL of AMERICA!**
Dosage:
One Drop As Needed
For **Any** and **Every** Ailment
Bottled in
Estes Park, Colorado Territory

Lou stared at the text for a few moments, then looked from the bottle to the corpse. The boy could not have been seventeen years old when he died. There was no way to know if the condition of his body had been the result of gross negligence or despicable treatment, but due to his resulting geung si possession, she very much doubted he had passed from wholly natural causes.

Heung-kam had said this young man, his brother, and their friends had gone to Cheyenne. The bottles claimed to come from Estes Park. Those two territories, again and again: Colorado, and Wyoming. A shell game that had taken in too many—and taken more than their money.

The body had to be a message, one hidden under bottles instead of inside them, and from someone who had known enough to worry about the body becoming a geung si. She felt a certain friendly respect for whoever had sent the boy home packaged so thoughtfully, whoever he was...

She tucked the bottle into her satchel and sighed. It was a disgusting affair. So many families were missing loved ones. She'd never felt particularly fortunate for knowing how her father had died, and why, and when, and for what reasons, but she now realized it would have been far worse to never know, to wonder for months or years if he was alive or dead...

How many others were wishing and waiting, as Heung-kam had wished and waited? How many more would receive grisly parcels with their loved one's remains? How many more men were so desperate for work that they might ignore any warning—or never hear about it to begin with, and leave their families on the promise of a good job only to die violently, far from home, with no one to care for their flesh or spirit?

Ting-Ting was leaning casually against the wall across from the cellar door when Lou emerged. She straightened up, smiling.

"They're in the kitchen," she said.

"Thanks," said Lou. "Would you mind showing me…"

"Right away?"

Lou swallowed. "Right away," she agreed. When Ting-Ting looked disappointed, she shrugged. "Sorry, but I… it's, uh… not that… you know," she finished lamely.

"Urgent business," said Ting-Ting, tapping the side of her nose. She was really very pretty, and Lou had a momentary vision of how the scene might play out under different circumstances. "Still," said Ting-Ting, "you should come back sometime. Might be nice… for you, and for me."

"Maybe. But don't wait up for me or anything," said Lou. She smiled at the other girl, in that moment finally coming to terms with what she needed—what she *wanted*—to do. "I'm… heading out of town for a while."

Even Ting-Ting's frown was beautiful, a graceful downward dipping of her painted lips, like a swan's wings in flight. "Too bad. Where to?"

"Cheyenne. Wyoming Territory." Lou shrugged. "It's unavoidable."

"Everything important tends to be," said Ting-Ting, with charming regret.

Ting-Ting was right. Though Lou wasn't exactly thrilled about the prospect of leaving Imre in charge of the Agency, and traveling all the way to Cheyenne—possibly beyond—she was the best person for the job. She was fluent in Chinese and in English, she knew the details of the case better than anyone, and she cared about the outcome, whatever it might be.

The younger women walked into the kitchen, where Heung-kam was sobbing her grief into Ailien's shoulder as the two embraced tightly. Ting-Ting took Lou's hand and squeezed it, and Lou squeezed back.

There was no way she was going to abandon this case. Not now.

PART TWO

Chapter One

On the bed lay a corpse, and over the corpse a sheet, soft white folds defining nose, chest, knees, toes. Why did she feel so afraid? It was only a body. She saw them often enough.

Lou couldn't quite recall why she was lingering in this warm, bare room that smelled of illness and felt like grief. She didn't have her bag, it couldn't be for work. It was very quiet; only a faint scratching emanated from somewhere, as if the wind were worrying a loose shingle on the roof. Or a rat tore at the wallboards.

"Lou."

Her neck prickled—but then she noticed the body's chest was rising and falling. The sheet covering the person's mouth caved in and puffed out in steady, shallow intervals. Not a corpse. Just a sick person.

"Lou, I can't breathe," she heard, followed by a gasping, snotty gurgle. "Help me."

She tried to reason with herself—someone thought he'd get cold, so they covered him, and he's too weak to help himself. Step forward. Go. Make your legs move. Help him.

Lou folded back the sheet, revealing her father's face, gaunt and sickly pink. Strings of thick white spittle spanned his slack, toothless mouth. She started backwards and the sheet fluttered down to his waist. His head lolled to the side. He was unconscious.

"Help me," said the voice again, but her father's lips did not move. "I can't breathe."

"What…" murmured Lou.

"Air. I need air." The voice was fainter, more plaintive. *"Please,* Lou."

Her father whimpered and rolled onto his side, taking the sheet with him; the motion caused his flannel pajama-top to shift, revealing a sliver of his abdomen. Lou moved to cover him again but the voice cried out, "Under here—help me," and she paused.

"Hello?" she said.

"Under here," said the voice again. Lou steeled herself and gingerly, with thumb and forefinger, lifted up the edge of her father's nightshirt, and screamed.

A pink-lipped mouth leered at her, embedded in his flesh, closer to his nipple than to his navel.

"Thank you," it hissed, its silver tongue flopping wetly between rows of pointy cinnabar teeth. When it spoke, it drooled liquid mercury that rolled over her father's chest and plopped onto the bed, too thick to sink into the sheets.

Lou screamed, choking on the bile burning the back of her throat—

—and woke with a gasp to find herself in a dingy train-carriage, the deep starry blackness of a prairie night just beyond the cheek-print her greasy face had left on the window. Lou tilted her head left and then right, wincing at the ache in her neck.

That particular nightmare hadn't haunted her for a long time. There'd been a few months where she couldn't sleep without it troubling her, but that time had passed. Likely the corpse in the box and her current journey were to blame for its recurrence.

Lou rolled herself a cigarette, taking comfort in the familiarity of the action. She took a long drag and tried to bring herself fully back to the present; focused on the comforting feeling of thick smoke in her lungs, the taste of shag on her tongue, the sensation of languid energy filling her limbs.

She couldn't see the moon from where she lounged, so she had no concept of how long she'd dozed; how long until they arrived in Cheyenne. She thought she'd felt the train slowing at some point, but couldn't place when. She felt like she'd been asleep for hours, but that might just be exhaustion from days of travel. Real sleep had eluded her since she'd left San Francisco, her only rest a series of jolting, aching cat-naps, and for days longer than she'd anticipated due to a few late winter storms that had caused delays all along the line.

At least the benches in the carriage were wide and deep, decently comfortable for sleeping. She'd been surprised by that bit of luxury, especially after the gruff treatment she'd received from the conductor when she boarded in Oakland. He'd looked at her ticket, looked at her, and, smirking, thumbed her on to the very last carriage, admonishing her to "stay put" and "not make trouble." Lou had expected that kind of bullshit, but not the nice big seats and having the whole car to herself. She found it odd that her isolation had continued the entire ride, but as it had meant she could move about freely, avoiding the sun or sitting in it whenever she pleased, she couldn't complain.

A creak of weight shifting on wood came from somewhere behind her. Lou stiffened and reflexively checked her skiameter. Enough of the dream remained that she'd felt a momentary chill, but that passed when her instrument indicated there was no ghostly presence anywhere close by. She felt even sillier when she turned and saw it was only a large sow-bear knitting on a lace shawl.

Like many of her kind, the bear affected a few articles of human dress, though Lou would have questioned the taste of the hat perched between her ears regardless of her species. Absinthe-green and vaguely conical, it had a flat top supporting what appeared to be a nest filled with little silk birds. Having no hair to hold a hatpin, the sow kept it stationary with a matching ribbon tied in a bow under her chin.

"Hello," said the bear. "I was wondering when you'd wake up."

"Howdy, ma'am." Lou reached to tip her hat, but she wasn't wearing it. "You get on when we stopped?"

She nodded. "You were out cold."

"Do you know what time it is? When we'll be arriving?"

"Late. Conductor said we'd be getting in maybe around ten?" The sow checked her wristwatch, a lavish, gold chatelaine that jingled as she inspected it. "It's half-past nine now. Not too much longer."

"Thank you, ma'am."

The bear made a pleased, chuffing sort of sound, somewhere between a dog's snort and a pig's grunt. "If you get hungry, I have a packet of crackers and a wedge of cheese. I'd be happy to give you some in exchange for a cigarette. It smells delicious."

"Oh, of course," said Lou, standing stiffly. The benches were great for lying down, but not so good for sitting—too long and too deep. It occurred to Lou in that moment, as she moved to sit across from the sow, that perhaps the benches in this carriage had been built for non-human passengers. It would explain the conductor's amusement about installing her here.

"Please, sit," said the sow. "Food's in the basket."

"No need to hand over your vittles." Lou had no wish to come between a sow and her snacks. "You're welcome to a smoke. On the house. May I roll you one?"

"That's right courteous of you," said the bear.

Lou, despite being a regular at the Bear Market, hadn't interacted with all that many bears—not socially. Save for the merchants they tended to keep to themselves in the outskirts, less comfortable with the hustle and bustle than their more sociable cousins the sea lions. She was eager, therefore, to take the opportunity to idly hobnob with one.

After the bear finished her row and set aside her knitting, Lou handed over a cigarette. Though madly curious to see how bears smoked, Lou tried not to seem unduly interested as she lit a match. The sow accepted the light, taking the cigarette and holding it to the very tip of her muzzle, forming a seal with the paper by contorting what lips she possessed. Lou was impressed by her delicacy.

"Ahhhhh," she said, upon exhaling. "That's nice. It's hard to get good tobacco out here. Lots of it's cut with deer tongue—which isn't bad, but you get tired of it."

"Oh?" Lou wondered if she'd brought enough—it hadn't occurred to her that it might be more of a luxury item in the wilds. "I didn't realize."

"Where are you from?" asked the sow. "My name's Victoria, by the way."

"I'm Lou Merriwether," said Lou. "Nice to meet you. I'm from San Francisco, heading to Cheyenne. That's the end of the line for me." Maybe.

"I'll be getting off there, too, but I'm headed northwards. I'm on holiday, actually. I have a piece of land up there, close to the border of the Montana Territory."

"Holiday, huh?" Lou hoped the bear would elaborate further.

"I'm an attaché—I go around the Utah, Colorado, and Wyoming Territories, monitoring mining towns and other industrial areas to ensure they're not in violation of any of the more nuanced clauses of legislation what have been passed since the end of the war." Victoria smiled, the cigarette dangling from her paw, smoke curling upwards in whorls of blue and grey. "Let's be charitable and say sometimes humans *forget* certain regulations during the hibernating season. This year the Council asked for a few volunteers to forgo our sleep to keep an eye on things. Maybe volunteer is the wrong word—the pay was so good it seemed worth it, but it does make one a touch cranky to stay up all winter. I need a rest."

"Cheers to that," said Lou. "Sounds like real interesting work."

"It's a lot of travel," said Victoria. "Do you travel much?"

"No ma'am… I've seen precious little of the world that's not a few miles outside of San Francisco."

"What do you do?"

Lou had heard rumors of shamanism among the bear tribes, though whether these were slander regarding their allegedly heathen ways, or the result of actual arktological study, she didn't know. "I work with the dead," she said, knowing bears valued forthrightness. "I help spirits pass from our world to theirs. If they don't, they can make trouble for the living."

"You don't say. What kind of trouble?"

"Well," said Lou. "The soul—qi—the part of us that makes us, well, *us*—needs to be anchored to a body. Souls become corrupt without a host, and they go stir-crazy from being tethered to the place where their body passed. Maybe it would be better to say they lose perspective… spirits and whatnot—revenants, shades, they start getting strange urges that become unwholesome, and downright dangerous for the living." Lou glanced up to see if she was boring the bear, but Victoria seemed intrigued.

"Ghosts may hang around quietly for a while," she continued, "watching their kids grow up or their wife take casseroles to church suppers, but sooner or later, that wife may meet someone, that kid may do something foolish, and then ghosts get to thinking things like 'I would invest my money so much better than my boy's doing' or 'that widow of mine better not be planning to marry that fellow who keeps hanging 'round the house.' And trying to possess a body… it starts to seem like a good idea, and that's when things get difficult."

"Does it happen often? Forgive my curiosity… I've just never heard that happening, with bears I mean."

"Often enough. I'm not the only psychopomp in San Francisco by a long shot." She felt a jealous pang, thinking of Imre doing her job—she was reasonably certain he wouldn't screw anything up too badly, but still, she wished she was there to oversee him. "It's interesting work… you have to keep on your toes. There's all sorts of ways to deal with the undead, and all sorts of undead, too, like I said. And you have to be willing to learn all your life, too, since no matter how much you know, things are always changing."

"How so?"

Lou couldn't ever remember talking so much about her work. "I don't know quite how to explain it. Just like… how folks from different places have different speech and customs and clothing, there's different undead, too. But when people move, or travel, or trade, more's shared than a favorite recipe for chop suey or chili. Before the Gold Rush, geung si possession—er, geung si are a kind of vampire, sort of—well, it was pretty unusual in the United States. Nowadays I see it all the time in Chinatown of course—but a few times I've dealt with the same sort of possession in different parts of the city, communities where you might never see a Chinese person, really, except for on a Wanted poster or in a nasty cartoon in the paper. And there are more kinds of European-style shades and ghosts in Chinatown than ever before. It's like that in big cities all over. Now, as to *why* that happens, I leave that to the academics. Like my father. He used to teach psychopompic theory at Loxias College in the city. But I always liked field work more."

"I see," said Victoria, tapping out her cigarette on the arm of her bench. "So is… psych—is that what you're doing in Cheyenne?"

"No, actually," said Lou. "I'm…" She didn't quite know how to explain what she was doing, to herself or to anyone else, but the train was slowing, saving her. "I'm here on different business."

"Do you have a place to stay?"

"I'll find somewhere," said Lou. She rolled two more cigarettes, passing one over after lighting both.

"Well, maybe I'll see you around Cheyenne," said Victoria, accepting hers with a nod. "I need to do a few things in town before I head north."

"I dunno how long I'll be there," said Lou, "but if you're ever in San Francisco, look me up. I know a few bear-friendly saloons, and hell, I'd be happy to sleep on my sofa for a spell if you needed a place to stay. It can be hard to find a bed if you don't know anyone. Lots of hotels aren't interested in accommodating bears."

Victoria looked at her keenly. "You would share your cave with me? You are an interesting person, Lou Merriwether. I've rarely received such courteousness from your kind. Thank you."

"Oh," said Lou. She sensed some sort of ritual weightiness to the words, and wondered if the concept of xenia meant more in the ursine than human world these days. She felt a brief but potent pang of grief—the notion of cultural cross-pollination between bears and humankind would have fascinated her father. "Shucks, don't mention it. Just come by the Merriwether Agency. It's on Post. If I'm not in, my partner Vilhelm will make sure you're taken care of."

"The Merriwether Agency," repeated the bear. "I'll remember. And if you're ever heading up north of Cheyenne, well—look me up. Here's my card," she said, and extracted a thin piece of pink cardboard from her knitting bag. "If you're looking for me, mention me by name. Everyone knows me."

Lou accepted the card and thanked Victoria for it, then excused herself to tidy up her possessions. She wanted to set her satchel and traveling bag to rights in anticipation of arriving.

The squeal of the brakes was a welcome sound to her ears. She found herself hoping things in Cheyenne took a few days, just so she wouldn't have to hop right back on a train again. She was ready to spend more than a few hours standing still.

Victoria, having no coat to don nor several days of sprawl to tidy, was already gone when Lou stepped out onto the porch of the train carriage. As soon as she did so, she spied a thick railroad employee and a slender man in a brown suit stopping the sow-bear as she lumbered toward the station. The man gestured at the car where Lou had been riding; Victoria nodded, and Lou suddenly felt afraid—extremely afraid. Her stomach knotted, and cold sweat broke out on her brow.

She ducked back inside the carriage to think. Her plan had been to disembark in Cheyenne, still posing as Bo Wong, and play along with the officials until she found out some information. It suddenly dawned on her that this was actually a terrible plan. Would the railroad employees—or any third parties—be inclined to answer questions posed by someone who'd already signed a contract? Would they let her go when she wanted to go? She hadn't read whatever she'd signed. For all she knew, she could be some kind of indentured servant, destined to sleep on a flea-ridden cot in some hellish labor camp for who knew how long.

Lou poked her head around the door and saw the two men were heading her way. The odds of two against one decided things. No way would she go with them—not if she could help it.

Victoria had disembarked from the porch at the front of the carriage, but there was another porch at the rear. Peeking out the back door, Lou decided her best bet would be to make for a busy, shabby-looking eating-house not too far down the row of buildings that comprised the Cheyenne station. There, she figured she could remain relatively anonymous while planning her next move.

In order to get to the restaurant unnoticed she would have to either run along the back of the train or try to sidle across the open platform as inconspicuously as she could. The rail yard was dark and personnel-free, but distressingly open; the thoroughfare was mobbed with people and their luggage, but brightly lit with blazing torches.

Lou made her choice, took a deep breath, willed her pounding heart to save some vigor for the ensuing run—and felt a firm hand come down on her shoulder.

"Hold up," someone breathed in her ear. "Just where do you think you're going?"

Chapter Two

Lou's fingers were curled around the grip of her LeMat before she even realized she'd reached for her gun, but she thought better of it before drawing. There would be no point. She couldn't possibly commit an act of violence against a railroad employee or layperson in a train carriage at a busy station and hope to escape. Resigned to whatever was in store for her, she turned—and bit back a yelp.

For a brief, disorienting moment, Lou thought she had imagined the voice, the touch; that she had turned only to catch sight of herself in a mirror. The person standing behind her was her same height and build, but she quickly realized the eyes into which she gazed were coffee-brown, not green, and they belonged to a young man dressed in a worn but elegant traveling suit. His sweet, comely face was framed by dark hair that curled over his shoulders, and he had a derby hat pinned under his left arm. He looked as bemused as she felt.

"I—there was a mistake," she stammered, slightly distracted by his intense, almost uncanny beauty.

"Mistake?" His eyes dropped to where she still gripped her LeMat.

"Thought you might be a lawman," said Lou, slowly removing her hand from her gun. Her heart was still feeling like to burst at any moment, it was pounding so hard. She needed to get the hell away from this dude, and *fast*, if she wanted to make a break for it. "Sorry. You know how it is… anyways,"

Lou looked behind her at the carriage door. "I gotta…"

His lips quirked into a half-smile, "Are you Bo Wong?" he asked pleasantly. "No need to go anywhere if you are; I'm here to collect you."

"Uh," said Lou. "See, about that…"

"You're not Bo Wong?"

"Well, no." Lou began to sweat a little. "My name's Lou. Lou Merriwether."

"Lou Merriwether." Lou's name had never sounded so luxurious as when he said it. "Well, Mr. Merriwether, my name is Shai. I'm sorry for the confusion. I thought I was picking up a gentleman by the name of Wong—the Oakland office was very specific about that in their wire—to escort him to my employer's sanatorium up in the mountains above Estes Park. There is a job waiting for him there. So, please feel free to go wherever you were headed. I apologize for being so rude, but… you match his description, I mean beyond also being of Chinese extraction. I made an unforgivable assumption. You have my apologies."

To her alarm, he bowed after finishing his little speech. She would have laughed if things hadn't been so serious—she had to make a decision, and fast. She could either go with him, making up some story to explain her deception, or try to make a run for it before he started asking questions, or checked her out with the railroad officials.

The first option didn't seem as bad as it had a few minutes ago… this "Shai" seemed okay; at least, she didn't get the sense he was going to clap her in irons and drag her by force to the labor camp she'd been imagining. It might actually be in her best interests to let him "collect" her—at least temporarily. He had just confirmed that the Chinese workers she was searching for were in his employer's care, working at a sanatorium close to Estes Park no less. If she could play it cool, come up with a plausible reason for heading where he was heading, she might be able to get more valuable information out of him. A guide would be nice, given how she knew nothing about anything out here, like how to get anywhere on her own, for example.

Lou took a deep breath, licked her lips, and told herself that just like jumping into freezing water, her best bet was just to plunge right in.

"I match his description because I gave a false name at the depot. I heard that Chinamen could get free tickets to Cheyenne if they promised to do some sorta job somewhere out here. Sounded like a deal." She gave what she hoped was a casual shrug. "Didn't expect a welcoming committee to call my bluff."

Shai laughed, and Lou took it as a promising sign that he seemed amused, not angry. "Mr. Merriwether, I appreciate your honesty."

"And I appreciate your not handing me over to the law. I mean, unless that's your plan?"

"Farthest thing from my mind." Shai hesitated for a moment. "I suppose, then, I should let you be on your way."

Plunge right in, she told herself. "Actually... I'm curious, Shai—is it Mr. Shai, or just Shai?"

"Just Shai."

"Well, *Just Shai,* is your sanatorium the one where they make Elixir of Life?"

He looked very surprised, as if this was the last question he'd expected from her. "Yes, it is..."

"Wow, it's real funny you being here, and being from there. As it so happens, I'd actually planned on making my way to your sanatorium once I'd gotten to Cheyenne." Lou silently thanked her parents for their vigilance when Lou was younger—all the times she'd had to come up with something to tell Ailien about where she'd been and who else had been there had made her pretty good at lying under pressure. "I'm sick—nothing catching, I assure you. But it's as strange as it is tenacious, having baffled doctors from Chinatown to Nob Hill. Last one I saw told gave me some Elixir, and suggested I take some time at the sanatorium if I could swing it. So... I swung it."

"Is that so. Well, I'm very sorry to hear you're not well."

"Probably a spell at your sanatorium will fix me right up." Hell if she didn't feel a little guilty for playing him like a fiddle. He'd sounded so sincere. And now he looked awkward and vaguely pained, like her father used to look when he had some question to ask or suggestion to make that wasn't strictly polite.

"Sorry," he said, "I just... I wonder, how were you planning on getting to the San? I don't mean to seem nosy, but if you don't know the area..."

"I hadn't figured that part out yet," confessed Lou, telling him the complete truth this time.

"Then why not come with me? At least for tonight—though I'd consider a longer association? It appears I'm short one Mr. Wong, which means I unnecessarily reserved a second room at my hotel. Surely you don't want to worry about going from place to place tonight, knocking on doors to find somewhere to stay—do you? And it will be nice for you to have one good night's rest before heading to Fountain of Youth, whatever you decide. It's rough going after Cheyenne; you'll be lucky to find a flat patch of land to kip on."

Lou figured "Fountain of Youth" must be the name of the sanatorium; she didn't want to ask, as she should by rights know where she was headed, so she thanked him for his mighty chivalrous offer and accepted it, feeling pretty fine about her prospects. It was a working plan... for now. And if Shai tried anything funny, she had her LeMat.

Not that she thought he would. Shai seemed like a good sort, he even insisted on taking her portmanteau for her. To her surprise he hoisted it as if it weighed nothing at all and then led her through the depot and out the other side, eventually taking her beyond the torchlight and activity of the train station to a large two-mule wagon. Two porters were loading it up with sacks and barrels and crates.

"They should be done soon," said Shai. He winked at her. "You weren't the only cargo I was picking up tonight."

Shai tipped the porters as Lou settled her luggage snugly among the packages in the back. When she was satisfied nothing would slide or crush her satchel she clambered awkwardly onto the seat; after handing her the mules' reins, Shai leaped up beside her, graceful as a dancer. As he settled himself on the board Lou noticed he smelled like some sort of spice—cardamom, perhaps.

"Ready?" he asked.

"Yep. Mind if I smoke?"

"Not at all," he said, chucking the reins.

She reached behind her to grab her rolling papers and tobacco out of her satchel. "Want one?"

"No, thank you."

As they rattled away from the station, Lou relaxed enough to notice that the night was a lovely one, if cold. Geese were honking somewhere out on the prairie beyond the town, she heard their calls in between gentle gusts of wind. The sky was clear of clouds, the heavens were aglow with more stars than she'd ever seen, and the moon was just visible over the tops of the buildings, of which there were far fewer than Lou had been expecting.

Cheyenne, despite being a major depot for the U.P., had turned out to be a surprisingly small town... and upon noting this, Lou began to feel nervous, like she might have made some hasty decisions back at the train station. Only a few people were out and about, and theirs was the only wagon. The further they drove from the depot the more she began to question her decision to throw in her lot with Shai so quickly, especially since the only thing she actually knew about him was that he worked for the person who might be responsible for spiriting away her countrymen—and doing whatever had put at least one of them in a pine box.

What had she done? And why was she only thinking about this now that they were out of the more commercial district—where, despite Shai's speech about it being difficult to find accommodations at that time of night, she had seen several hotels advertising available rooms? Well, she *had* resolved to dive in headfirst... best to roll with it. Surely Shai wouldn't think it odd if she asked him a little about himself. And where they were going. In fact, maybe he thought it was weird she hadn't asked yet.

"So," she barked in her haste to say something. Then she fell silent, embarrassed.

"What's that?"

Lou tried to cover her awkwardness by flicking away the butt of her cigarette. "What exactly do you do at Fountain of Youth?"

"Oh, I'm just Dr. Panacea's assistant. His work at the San is quite consuming, as you might imagine. He relies on me, for many different kinds of things... such as heading all the way to Cheyenne to pick up new employees, like Mr. Wong."

Lou winced. "Sorry to trouble you so much for nothing."

"Not *nothing.*" Lou looked at Shai sidelong. He was smiling. "I met you, and that was worth any trouble. Ah, perhaps I shouldn't tease you, I just met you. I was waiting for the cargo, too, remember?"

"Right." Something else struck Lou about her playing Shai and his employer false. "Hope your boss won't be too disappointed?"

"By what?"

"He's expecting someone to work for him, not a new patient."

"We always appreciate new patients." Shai cocked an eyebrow at her.

"Patients pay us—but we have to pay our workers."

His wry humor put Lou at ease. "All right then. For now, though, where are we headed?"

"I'm so sorry," Shai apologized quickly. "I should have mentioned that the hotel where I've been staying is a little off the beaten path. We should be there soon, though."

"Is it pricey?"

"Depends on what you get." He sounded amused. "Just a room isn't too much."

Oh. *That* kind of hotel. Figuring she could go a little deeper undercover, Lou nodded. "Nice to know, but after that trip, I think I just need a bed. I'd be pretty useless with a girl."

"Or whatever," said Shai. "They cater to all kinds at The Aristotelian."

Lou didn't really know what to say to that. "Okay."

"I should also say, don't be alarmed by anything you might see—it's a reputable establishment. I guarantee in the morning your luggage will be right where you left it."

Lou, though curious what he meant by *don't be alarmed by anything you might see,* elected not to ask further questions, lest she come across as wet behind the ears. "Sounds like my kind of place."

Shai shrugged. "It's not so much 'my kind of place' as a place that serves my needs. I won't be heartbroken to head out tomorrow. Despite traveling so much I'm something of a homebody."

"You and me both."

"You travel often?"

Lou shook her head. "No. I'm such a homebody I rarely travel at all."

"That sounds nice." He sounded a little wistful. "I feel I've spent half my life on the road sometimes."

"So it's a long journey to and from Fountain of Youth?"

"The San's not really close to Cheyenne—or to anything," said Shai. "It's a troublesome trip this time of year, too. The last leg is typically done in a group. We send a guide down to Estes Park every other week or so, to take up newcomers. Fountain of Youth is deep in the Rocky Mountains. It can be a treacherous trek—but well worth it, of course." He nodded at a large hotel with a clean, well-maintained exterior. "This is the place," he said.

For a whorehouse, it looked positively sedate to Lou's eyes. It couldn't yet be midnight, but only a few lamps burned in the windows, and no one was hanging around outside.

They headed around back to the stables. Shai hopped down to holler into the darkened barn. Lou followed him, eager to stretch her legs. A bleary-eyed lad of perhaps fifteen years stumbled out. He yawned tremendously, and took the reins from Shai.

"Evenin'," he mumbled. "I'll take your mules." He turned to Lou and blinked, his expression souring. "You c'mon with me," he said loudly. "You speak Eng—"

"This is my friend," said Shai quickly, looking as mortified as Lou felt. "He's a guest."

"Oh," said the boy. He looked confused. "Sorry."

"Why don't you go inside?" murmured Shai. "I'll take care of this, go get yourself settled. Just head around and in through the front. Tell them you'll be staying in the other room I reserved."

Lou grabbed her portmanteau and satchel and took Shai's advice with the quickness. She was more than a little upset after being so unpleasantly reminded that Shai's friendliness toward her was pretty damn unusual. For an hour or so she'd forgotten she was a half-breed, and therefore worthy of everybody's scorn.

The more she thought on it she realized that Shai's behavior, while pleasant, was actually kind of strange. She'd just assumed whoever was employing the missing Chinese workers would be as horrible as that runt back in the barn… but if Dr. Panacea himself was half as offended as his assistant by shabby treatment of Chinese… well, then she'd be extra curious to hear what accounted for her kinsmen all disappearing so quiet-like. And that dead body in the crate.

Lou knocked on the front door before entering a strange, stark little foyer with a few cushioned benches. It was decorated all in black and silver, the wallpaper a flocked, rose-pattered nightmare that looked like it had been selected by an undertaker's maiden aunt. At least it was warm inside, though the warmth reminded her keenly that she was dog-tired, extremely dirty, and sore all over. She longed to lie down on one of the benches, but just as she moved to take a seat a man came through a door on the opposite wall.

He greeted her cordially and introduced himself as Mr. Barville. He was plump, rosy-cheeked, and immaculately dressed in a grey suit that was so dark it was almost black. Though he looked pleasant enough, something about him—and the hotel itself—made Lou uneasy. She couldn't figure out why, exactly. Maybe it was the combination of severity and luxury, maybe it was the wolfish grin Mr. Barville flashed when, after asking what made Lou choose The Aristotelian that evening, she mentioned Shai's name, and the extra room he'd reserved.

"What?" asked Lou, taken aback by his leer.

"You are *very* welcome, Mr. Merriwether," Mr. Barville replied, and with a flourish, bowed her through to the main parlor.

Lou wasn't sure what she'd been expecting, but she knew she hadn't expected whatever one might call... *this.* The parlor was deserted save for a lone girl who knelt in the center of the room. She was completely nude but for bridle and blinders, and tethered by a leather lead to one of several human-sized hitching posts. A thick horsetail, brownish red like her hair, sprouted from between the cheeks of her round bottom. Lou wondered for a brief moment how she kept it in place—and then blushed furiously when she figured it out.

Mr. Barville either didn't notice her reaction or pretended not to; he did, however, wink at Lou as they passed the tethered girl and he administered an open-palmed slap on the rump that made her squeal. Lou almost said something, but then chose to hold her tongue as he led her to the check-in desk. There, he retrieved a key from a peg as Lou wrote her real name and a false address in the register.

"Salt Lake City! You've come a long way, Mr. Merriwether."

"Business," Lou replied, as she followed him back towards the young woman when he motioned for Lou to follow him.

"And some pleasure, too, I hope?" After unhitching the girl, Mr. Barville handed her the key and clicked his tongue. "Get the gentleman's satchel, Marie. Mr. Merriwether is quite tired!"

"That's really not necess—" began Lou, moving to intercept the nude woman, but Mr. Barville frowned and held up a hand. Lou froze.

"This is how things are done at The Aristotelian," he said. From his tone, she sensed he would brook no argument, so Lou shrugged and forced a smile.

"Ah," said a familiar voice. "I see you've got Lou all set up?"

"Hello, Shai," said Mr. Barville. "Your friend will be well looked after, I assure you. Marie's seeing to his needs."

"The chestnut?"

"She's a reliable little mare," said Mr. Barville amiably. Lou got the distinct feeling she was being messed with. She decided to go along with it.

"Well," said Lou, as Marie grabbed her portmanteau, "I don't want to keep her standing too long without a blanket, so I'll say my goodnights. Thank you, Mr. Barville—and thanks, Shai."

"See you tomorrow. Shall we meet for breakfast? Say… around nine?"

"Sounds fine."

"Good night, then."

"And pleasant dreams, Mr. Merriwether," said Mr. Barville, pressing something into Lou's palm. Unfurling her fingers, she discovered a sugar cube.

Lou didn't know what she found more strange—the fact that he'd handed her such an object as a matter of course, or that it turned out to be the only tip her porter would accept after she unlocked Lou's small but tidy room, set down Lou's bag, lit the lamp, fluffed the pillows, straightened the sheets, lit the candle by the bed, and double checked to make sure there was fresh water in the jug. Lou found herself wondering if all the patrons carried carrot chunks and apple slices in their pockets, but she rapidly jumped off that particular train of thought.

Though she dearly longed for a bath it was very late, and her desire to sleep was overwhelming. She settled for rinsing her mouth, then her hands, and then her face in the jug. The color of the wash-water became increasingly horrifying as she did so—no matter what, tomorrow she vowed she'd soak in a tub.

Feeling even marginally less grimy made her exhaustion keener, so Lou turned down the lamp and performed only the bare minimum of disrobing—boots and waistcoat—before throwing herself onto the bed. After blowing out the candle she stretched out, arching her back to crack it, and shivered with the pleasure of resting horizontally.

Lou had expected to fall asleep instantly, but the quiet darkness of her room sent her mind running through the host of anxieties she'd kept largely at bay since leaving San Francisco. Would her mother keep her promise to keep an eye on Lou's house? Would young Imre really be able to handle the Agency's business as well as he had promised? He was a competent psychopomp, but he was more used to libraries and classrooms than real life...

Eventually her thoughts drifted to Shai. After so many hours contemplating increasingly dark scenarios about where all the missing Chinese workers had gone, Shai's openness and sensitivity felt like a warm ray of sunshine—though she wasn't so naïve as to believe his kindness to her ensured the safety of her kinsmen, not by a long shot. She knew very well it was easy enough to be polite to a Chinese who spoke English without an accent and wore a suit like anyone else—it was another thing entirely to extend that courtesy to someone who dressed funny, spoke weirder, and was pretty much without legal recourse if you abused or cheated him.

It was possible Shai was that kind of rat, or worse... but for now he seemed nice enough, and was proving to be a valuable resource. Though he was a little mercurial, she'd found no real reason to refuse his offer to hitch a ride with him to Estes Park; she'd heard enough tales and read enough books about sasquatch attacks, misunderstandings with local Indians, and whatever else that she wasn't too thrilled with the idea of traveling alone, or with some random, and potentially unreliable group. Additionally, he seemed like he might be more pleasant company than she had any right to expect—and gullible, too. She'd already hoodwinked Shai into thinking she was a patient heading for this Fountain of Youth place; it seemed reasonable she could milk him for more information on the way there.

Feeling comfortable, body and mind, made Lou realize it was slightly chilly in her room. With great reluctance she got out of bed, undressed down to her long johns, and burrowed under the covers. The down comforter warmed deliciously to her body, and she fell quickly asleep. She did not dream.

Chapter Three

A loud knock startled Lou awake.

She sat up, disoriented and feeling like she hadn't slept at all—though judging by the daylight streaming in through the windows, it was late morning already. Picking some crust out of the corner of her eye Lou sat there, confused as to why she was sitting up, until the dull sound of knuckles rapping on wood reminded her.

"Hold on!" Lou grabbed her pants. She didn't worry about her top—she hadn't taken off her breast-binding before going to sleep, and her long johns covered everything from neck to waist nicely.

When at last she got the door open she found Shai standing there, looking perfect as a picture-portrait in a cream-colored shirt and a rather romantic blue and pink silk waistcoat with a high-stand collar. His fawn-colored jacket was slung jauntily over his shoulder. He looked moderately skeptical of her appearance.

"Good morning," he said after taking a brief moment to compose himself. "I thought we were going to meet at nine. I was stopping to see if you'd gone down yet… I didn't mean to disturb you."

"Nuh," faltered Lou. She caught a whiff of his inexplicable cardamom scent, and wondered how badly she reeked. Glancing at the tin mirror in the corner of her room, she wasn't sure if she was amused or revolted by her wild and filthy reflection.

Shai cleared his throat. "If you're not yet ready, I'll just go and have a cup of coffee, unless…"

They seemed to be having a who-could-trail-off-most-awkwardly competition. Lou decided to end it. "Where's the bathhouse?" she asked—and blushed, much to her consternation.

"There's a staircase at the end of this hallway. You cross the back yard to the outbuilding," he said, with one of his half-smiles. "I'll go downstairs and ask someone to take some hot water and towels out for you. We can dine afterwards—that is, if you're still inclined to join me?"

"Thanks, I will."

"See you soon," and after favoring her with another of his odd little bows, Shai ambled off.

Lou shut the door, gathered up some fresh clothing, and quick as she could headed downstairs and outside. There were actually two outbuildings, she was happy to see, so after availing herself of the one with less steam puffing from the chimney she headed to the other.

Upon entering she glimpsed a naked person through the steam. Lou called an apology and ducked out again, resigned to waiting for her bath. A moment later the door creaked open and someone called an affable, "Come on in!"

"That's all right." Bathing in front of others wasn't something Lou felt comfortable doing. "I'll wait."

"I'm just an attendant," said the person, and stepped aside so she could reluctantly enter. That was when she finally caught sight of him, and felt both more and less awkward about the whole thing. He was a handsome, auburn-haired ponyboy with green polo wraps on his forearms and calves, and a matching green harness, but no other garments.

"Usually our clientele expect to be waited on."

"Oh. Right." Lou saw there were three tubs, and realized she was actually pretty lucky to be the only guest interested in a pre-breakfast bath. "I should've thought of that, but, uh… I didn't bring anything out with me—cash, or sugar cubes, so…"

"It's all been taken care of. Please, relax!"

"Thanks," said Lou, moving to help the man pour one of two large buckets of steaming water into her tub.

"Let me do it," he said, as he waved her away—then he paused to peer at her.

"What?" asked Lou.

"You're Chinese," he blurted.

"So? You're dressed like horse."

She regretted the quip instantly. People found her race worthy of remark in San Francisco, so it made sense she'd be even more exotic here in Cheyenne. Still, she'd assumed that if her heritage had been an issue, Mr. Barville would have refused to rent her a room the previous night.

"Sorry," she said. "I meant… I guess I don't know what I meant."

"No, I should apologize," said the man. "I had no right to be surprised. Any friend of Shai's is a friend of ours. Please, let me finish up, and I won't delay your bath any longer."

Lou could tell he was lingering in order to assist her with her ablutions, but she pointedly did not disrobe, crossing her arms over her chest until he got the message and departed. As soon as the door shut behind him she pushed a bench against it, stripped, and slipped into the tub.

The pleasure of hot water covering her skin was nothing short of rapturous, but Lou couldn't completely relax. The bath attendant's mention of Shai reminded Lou that she needed to get clean and confirm her travel plans. He'd mentioned leaving today, so every moment she delayed was one less she could use later to go and wire Vilhelm of her decision. She didn't want her partner worrying if he didn't hear from her—and more importantly, she wanted someone to know where she'd gone, and in whose company.

Lou soaped up her hair and availed herself of the long-handled scrub brush. After getting out of the tub and rinsing off, though the color of the water was truly disgusting, she dumped in her shirt and pants and dripped dry while scrubbing at them with the rest of the soap. She figured they'd be at least somewhat cleaner that way.

She wrung out as much of the water as possible from her laundry once she'd done her best with it. It would be wrinkled, but that was better than gummy and smelly. Satisfied with herself and her clothes, she donned a fresh union suit, pants, shirt, and waistcoat, and trotted back up to her room to set everything to dry on the windowsill.

The wholesome smells of coffee and bacon guided Lou downstairs. She had at some point become ravenously hungry—but after she found her way to the parlor, she paused, momentarily taken aback by the spectacle that was breakfast at The Aristotelian.

A few men and many women were eating their breakfast out of bowls set on the floor, all naked except for various harnesses; others were waited upon as they lounged on the sofas or sat at wooden tables that hadn't cluttered the room the night before. One woman in a sequined black riding ensemble reclined as she was fed morsels of toast and fruit by a hearty greybeard sporting a hempen bridle and nothing else, while a few feet away a man in military trousers, high boots and no top save for his half-unbuttoned red long johns spooned oatmeal studded with raisins and dried apples into the eager mouths of a matched pair of black-haired girls who looked up at him with adoration in their eyes and leather gauntlets ending in hooves on their forearms.

She also saw Shai, who waved her over. Too hungry to ruminate further upon how bizarre The Aristotelian truly was, Lou picked her way across the room and slid into the chair across from him. He was idling over a cup of coffee, and had a handsome leather-bound edition of Plato's *Republic* on the table.

"Morning," said Lou.

"Good morning. You seem... refreshed," he said tactfully.

"You're telling me." Lou grinned at him. "Great bathhouse they have here, and interesting décor, too. You always stay here?"

"Oh, yes. The madam and I are old friends, and the food is excellent."

"Good to hear," said Lou, as the first hot meal she'd seen in days was placed in front of her.

She thanked the waiter and set to without another word, not even attempting to hide her pleasure as she devoured the eggs, bacon, toast, sausage, flapjacks, home fries, beans, and grilled onions.

Wiping up the last few oily smears of syrup with a large biscuit, Lou wiped her mouth, gulped down another cup of coffee, and sighed happily—only to glance up and find Shai staring at her with alarm and admiration. He had not come close to finishing his portion. Lou wondered if he'd find it impolite if she asked if she could have his leftovers.

"Ma always said I had a coming appetite," said Lou, rolling a cigarette and sitting back in her chair. "You inclined to finish that? If you are, don't let me stop you, but if not..."

Shai's lips twitched. "So your illness doesn't affect your digestion? That's good." He took another sip of coffee as Lou tried to think of something to say. "Please go ahead and eat whatever you like. Enjoy it while you can… you won't be getting anything close to this kind of fare on the road. Or at Fountain of Youth."

"No?"

"Well, the San is a place to recover one's health," said Shai, sliding his unfinished breakfast beside Lou's empty-yet-glistening plate. "The doctor is an advocate of a clean diet to promote bodily well-being. We have several hothouses so we can have fresh fruits and vegetables even in the winter, and it's rare for us to have much meat on the table."

"That's just fine by me," said Lou, through a mouthful of Shai's potatoes. "I like food no matter what kind it is. Oh, and about the sanatorium…"

"Yes?"

She swallowed. "Hope you're still wanting company when you head off to Estes Park," she said, trying to sound casual about it. "I'd love to tag along."

"I'm sorry," said Shai, shaking his head. "I know it's terribly rude, but after I thought about it last night, I believe it's simply too big a risk to take you with me."

"What?" Lou was surprised, and a little hurt. "I mean, all right. It's your call. I understand."

Shai looked at her keenly. "Do you?"

"Huh?"

"My route to Estes takes me through the remotest of back-country roads. If I were to travel with someone, I'd need to be assured that he was of sterling character. I'm sorry to say it, but I'm not wholly convinced you are of sterling character."

Lou felt pretty damn dumb—and here she'd been so proud of winning him over! "It's true I don't have any references on me, seeing as I'm traveling and all," she said, trying not to sound too disappointed.

Shai *tsk*ed at her. "You haven't been honest with me, and you and I both know it."

"Do we?" Lou didn't want to say more before she found out what exactly he was getting at.

"You signed a contract with no intention to make good on the terms. You said as much last night."

"That's true," she said slowly, figuring out her next move. She decided it was better to embellish an old lie than come up with a new one. "You're right that I never intended to work for anyone out here, and that's dishonest. But I wasn't lying last night. I'm ill, and I need treatment." She looked down at her plate, hoping to look embarrassed. "What I was too ashamed to say last night was that all the doctors' bills nearly wiped me out in San Francisco. I don't have much money left. Train tickets are expensive—*travel's* expensive. I wanted to save my pennies for the sanatorium." She looked up, grimacing. "I mean… come on, Shai. You think you're worried about *my* character? How do you think I feel? No offense, but a man would have to be desperate or stupid to run off into the wilderness with someone he barely knows—and I'm not stupid."

Shai seemed to relax as Lou spoke. "Thank you for your candor, I appreciate it. It's nothing personal, you understand." Then he looked to his right and left and leaned in close before saying, "Money troubles don't concern me. I was afraid you might be a spy."

Lou managed a chuckle, though his suspicions were closer to the truth than the big story she'd just told. "Really?"

"You've no idea," said Shai, leaning in even further. "Plenty of folks have tried to steal the formula for Dr. Panacea's patent medicine over the years. The Elixir of Life is a better cathartic than Brandreth's Vegetable Universal. And it's actually good for you, unlike Dr. Morse's Indian Root Pills, which, for all they claim to 'cleanse the blood' don't actually do anything. At least, so says Dr. Panacea, and I believe him. We have a very, *very* valuable product—one that would mean a lot of money for someone who got hold of the formula. You can see why we have to be careful. The Elixir's not snake oil, and Dr. Panacea's no mountebank. I ought to know. He cured me."

"Of what?"

"Consumption." Shai shrugged. "Having a death sentence repealed tends to make a man loyal, I suppose. I've stuck with him ever since."

Lou did not trust herself to speak. Her heart was pounding, and her mind was far from her present situation. To think that she might have inadvertently stumbled upon something that could have saved her father! But dwelling upon such things would only lead her back to the dark place where she'd lingered too long after his death. In that moment it finally struck her how much of a favor Vilhelm had done for her by forcing her away from those bleak thoughts and harbored resentments.

Anyways, she had other fish to fry. She had not yet gotten herself invited to travel along with Shai, which was of paramount importance. Her quest was not for a perfect cure-all—it was to find out why so many Chinese had been disappearing, and why one of them had found his way back home packed in straw and thirsty for qi.

"Lou?"

She started in her chair, realizing she'd been mentally elsewhere. Her cigarette had burned out; she jabbed the end into her plate.

"So what—have I been honest enough with you?" she asked, left eyebrow raised. "Can I come?"

Shai smiled. "Your frankness has convinced me that I've sufficiently gotten the measure of your character. I'll even pay you ten dollars for your time, since you'll be riding shotgun—no, don't object. You said yourself that you were hard up for cash. We'll say no more about it, I insist. The only thing is, I was planning to be on the road before luncheon... does that work for you?"

"Perfect. I gotta do a few things in town before I leave, but I'll be back in good time to help you load up," she said, pushing back from the table and standing.

"Anything I can help with?"

"Nah," said Lou. "I'm just gonna buy a blanket and some more shag before I go. Anything I can pick up for you?"

"No, thanks. I have everything I need. Oh, but Lou?"

"Yeah?"

"Pick up a waterproof blanket if you can get one. It'll get snowy."

Cheyenne really was much smaller than Lou'd expected. Within an hour she'd followed Shai's directions into town on foot and compared prices on supplies at a few general stores. She purchased a used but well-made travel blanket that came with a waterproof cover that doubled as a sack to carry it in, some extra lead for making rounds for her LeMat, and a decent supply of rolling papers and shag, cut with deer tongue as Victoria had warned her. She also paid a visit to the telegraph office where she sent Vilhelm and her mother similar messages about heading into the Colorado Territory to find out more information, but Vilhelm's telegram included Shai's name and description, a request that he send someone to check the sanatorium if she didn't contact him in a few weeks, and a few further notes for Imre about how she would like him to conduct himself while standing in for her at the Agency.

After that, all that was left was to get back to her hotel, pack, pay her surprisingly modest bill, and head to the stables. There, she found her new traveling companion supervising a hardy stripling who was rolling a large keg up a makeshift ramp into the now-covered wagon. He had to pull some fairly acrobatic maneuvers to get it upright, wedged into place, and then get back out again—it was loaded down with supplies.

"Hello!" called Shai, waving her over once he saw her. "You all set? We're nearly done here."

"You sure?" Lou eyed the tightly packed wagon. "Doesn't seem like you've got enough shoved in there yet."

"I only make supply runs two or three times a year."

"I gotcha. Well, as long as you've got enough room for my new bedroll back there. I like it a lot. It's even waterproof, just like you advised."

"I can tell already we'll get along well, Lou."

"Oh?"

"I'm inclined to like people who listen to me. So!" He rubbed his hands together. "The weather is fine, the mules are fresh… I anticipate we'll make decent enough time. If we go until dark tonight, and then get an early start, we should be in Fort Collins tomorrow evening. Would you like to drive?"

"I don't think that would be a great idea… I've never driven a wagon."

Shai swung himself up onto the riding board after tipping the porter. "It's easy enough. I'll show you. Oh, and if you look under your seat, I brought sandwiches. Didn't know if you'd be hungry after that breakfast, but…"

Lou was, and to Shai's apparent delight she proceeded to devour everything he didn't want.

It was a remarkably pleasant day, cold, but a dry, crisp cold that didn't bother Lou as much as much as the bone-chilling dampness of San Francisco this time of year. Swallows sang as they drove along, dipping and diving on the currents and in and out of the scrub-brush adorning the low hillocks. Lou watched them—and everything else, completely enchanted by the landscape. She'd never seen anything like the wild, open prairie in her whole life. It fascinated her, the way it seemed flat, but wasn't; seemed empty, but was full of life. Every single thing excited her, which entertained Shai tremendously. Usually Lou hated to be laughed at, but she found she didn't mind Shai's teasing. She was a greenhorn, and he seemed to be every bit as pleased as he was amused by how much she was enjoying herself. In fact, Lou couldn't recall the last time she'd had so much fun... but just the same, she tried to keep her mind on what she was supposed to be doing. She ought to be watching for bandits or monsters, not socializing.

After they were several hours out of sight of Cheyenne, they took a short rest to stretch their legs and answer nature's various calls. Shai immediately turned his back to Lou and commenced watering a convenient tree, but Lou claimed a different sort of errand and carried the shotgun with her to squat in the lee of a hummock. When she returned, Shai had that too-polite-to-say-anything look again.

"What?" Lou was instantly worried he'd figured out her secret. Had he seen something? It was tough to figure out the lay of the land out here.

"Well..." he hesitated, as if not sure how to say what he wanted to, "it's just... I've rarely had cause to be concerned about desperados or anything fiercer on this run. At least, not during the day. I know Colorado has a wild reputation—and I'm not saying I don't appreciate your vigilance, taking the shotgun with you everywhere—but really, Lou, you can probably loosen up a little."

Though embarrassed, Lou was put at ease by his obvious desire not to cause offense. "I take your point," she said. "I reckon it's all this open space what's got me nervous. You can't tell what you can see, and what you can't."

"You get used to it." Shai leaned against the wagon, apparently in no hurry to get moving again. "So, speaking of getting used to things... want to drive for a while?"

Lou eyed the mules. They didn't strike her as too dangerous. "All right. But if they run away and you lose all your cargo..."

"I wouldn't think of blaming you."

After Lou learned that not every bump or birdcall would make the mules take off without an experienced driver keeping them in check, she actually found it pretty enjoyable to drive. She refused to accept any compliments offered by Shai, however, insisting her quick learning process was entirely due to the pair being docile, hardworking creatures.

"It's not bad. Driving a wagon, I mean," said Lou. "All the same, it seems slow, maybe after all that train travel. It's too bad there's no rail spur down to just Fort Collins or something—or to Denver, even."

"Lincoln's concessions to the bear tribes dissolved the Denver Pacific R&T before they got their feeder line going, and the red tape was too much for most of the smaller railroads to try to move in on the territory. Too much impact on the local environment, according to some committee. We'll see part of an abandoned spur along the way, actually. It's sad—Denver folks don't want to admit that the city's 'too dead to bury' as the quote goes, but I don't know what could help them now, short of divine intervention."

Lou nodded. "I imagine that's been tough on your sanatorium. With product to ship, and people to get to your doorstep, that seems like a lot to overcome."

"Product to ship," said Shai thoughtfully. "The Elixir, you mean. Yes, that has been difficult. As for getting people to us… well, Dr. Panacea had once hoped the San would be a much larger operation. He bought the land when the Union Pacific was planning to route through Denver via the Rockies, before they settled on the Sherman Pass up by Cheyenne. But we've adapted. And we're glad to offer some jobs to local youths—and the Chinese."

Lou had to remind herself not to be too charmed by Shai—she was supposed to be covertly investigating him. "That's the first time I've ever heard anyone say they were glad to give a job to a Chinaman."

"Really?"

"In San Francisco it's nigh impossible for Chinese folks to get work outside of Chinatown. And if they do, well, it's funny, but shops and businesses that employ Chinese seem to get vandalized more often than white-only establishments. Kind of a deterrent for decent people who'd otherwise hire us."

"That's a shame, and I'm sorry to hear it. It's none too safe out here, either… there are active anti-Chinese leagues in Cheyenne, and in Denver and Boulder, too. I'm sorry… I hope I haven't been insensitive. We can talk about something else if you'd like."

"No offense taken," said Lou, but truth be told, she was happy to drop the subject. She didn't want to take the first opportunity to segue into a discussion of how Chinese workers were treated at the San, lest she seem too interested. Shai's comments about spying were still fresh in her mind.

"Here—do you want me to drive for a while?"

Lou handed over the reins. "Shouldn't we stop soon?" she asked, eyeing the sinking sun.

"There's a spot I usually camp up ahead." Shai cast a sly look in her direction. "I just want to take the last turn."

"Why?"

"So I don't have to cook dinner."

"You might end up regretting that."

"I doubt it," said Shai.

"Why's that?"

Shai laughed. "I've tasted my cooking."

Not long afterwards, Shai turned the wagon toward a wide but shallow stream that had been flowing beside the trail for several miles. Lou was more than ready to stop. Her ass was aching from all the jolting, and the sound of water had her longing to splash some of the road-dust off her face. Hopping down, she grimaced as the feeling came back into her legs. Tomorrow she would walk more and ride less.

They made camp under the purple dusk of a budding cherry tree, and after they'd picketed the mules, Shai began to gather brush to get a fire going. Lou helped, and soon they had a dry, merry blaze that would easily yield enough coals to cook on.

"Go get whatever you want to make dinner," he said, once the fire died down a bit. "Plenty back there for you to choose from."

After lighting the lantern Lou climbed into the back of the wagon. A brief peek showed her that Shai's cargo was mostly food supplies. There were beans, but they were dry; there was salt pork and cornmeal and flour—but then Lou discovered many of the sacks held provisions she knew how to make an even quicker meal out of. There was more dried abalone than she'd ever seen outside of a shop, sacks upon sacks of rice, jars of preserved ginger, packages of chilies, noodles, tofu skin, and dehydrated mushrooms. There were even several bricks of tea. Lou gathered enough supplies for a hardy hot pot-style soup for two and emerged to find Shai coming back from the stream, carrying a sloshing bucket.

"I got you some water," said Shai. "What's for dinner?"

"Soup," said Lou.

"Soup?"

"My ma's recipe," said Lou. "We'll see if I can do it justice."

"I have never yet sampled the exotic delicacies of the Far East," said Shai. "This is an unexpected pleasure."

"Don't get your hopes up," said Lou, over the hissing sound of salt pork cooking in its own fat. She stirred it vigorously, praying it wouldn't burn.

Shai eyed her supplies. "What *is* this stuff?"

Lou glanced up and saw he held what looked like a jellyfish made of old leather. Given how hard he'd been riding her all day, she smirked at him. "Don't you know? You bought it, didn't you?"

For the first time, Shai looked uncomfortable. "We actually place our orders through a contact at the Union Pacific—they know the right shops, and advise us on what to buy for our workers, and in the correct quantities."

Lou tried not to look like she found this both peculiar and interesting as she flaked some tofu skin into the pot. "Why not just ask your cook?"

She looked up again when Shai didn't answer, and saw clear as day there was nothing he wanted to do more than change the topic of conversation. "Anyways," she said, "it's a dried cuttlefish. Hand it over."

Eager to dispel any awkwardness, Lou talked about Toisanese cuisine as she added the rest of her ingredients to the stew. Shai quickly became interested and even asked a few questions, so soon enough they were back on easy, friendly terms. The only problem was, talking about various Chinese delicacies and cooking methods meant that by the time the soup was ready they were both so ravenous they were hard pressed not to gobble their food; for once, Lou wanted to savor her meal, listening to distant owl-hooting and the wind rustling through last year's dead, dry grass.

"That was a rare treat, Lou," Shai said, as he sat back and began to pack a queer, thin pipe from his own tobacco pouch. "When I'm on the road, I just make myself cornmeal mush with salt pork."

"That's good food, too. Honestly, I eat mush more than I eat hot pot. I can't remember the last time my pantry was as stocked as your wagon."

Having a full belly and smoking with Shai on the open prairie was pretty fine. Shai's tobacco was fragrant, as if sweetened with some exotic flavoring, and the campfire was pleasantly warm, especially after the sun sank and the wind kicked up. Somewhere a coyote yipped, and another answered, and a regular conversation got started. She sighed, wondering what had taken her so long to explore the world outside of San Francisco.

"I wish I'd learned to cook somewhere along the line." Shai took a long drag on his pipe and held it in his lungs for a spell before blowing the smoke upwards to spiral into the night, which Lou thought pretty peculiar.

Perhaps that was how folk stretched their tobacco when supplies were lean. "Turned my nose up at lessons many a time. Silly, I know… but I always thought it was woman's work."

Lou's sense of tranquility fled like a startled deer. Was he teasing her—or was he letting her know he'd guessed her secret? Lou's tongue went to an empty socket in her jaw, courtesy of a former friend's outrage when he'd discovered she wasn't actually a man. She'd given him better than she got… but mostly because she'd been on her guard at the first sign of danger. It hadn't been the first incident where she'd been struck for the crime of trying to pass. Nor had it been the last.

As happy as she'd been, she was now flustered, a little frightened, and deeply pissed off at herself. If she'd let her guard down so much that Shai had figured out her secret… if it bothered him she was a fake… she smoked another cigarette to try to calm down. It didn't work.

"I think I'll turn in," she said, standing and stretching theatrically.

"Would you like to take first or second watch?"

"Oh. Doesn't matter to me."

"I'll take the first, if you're tired," said Shai. He was still smoking in that strange way, taking infrequent but deep pulls, and letting his tobacco go out between each puff.

Lou shrugged and went to fetch her blanket—and the worn copy of *The Cases of Judge Dee* she'd brought along to read. The adventures of the famous Chinese magistrate had seemed thematically appropriate for her journey. She wasn't tired enough to sleep yet, and thought reading about a brave, insightful, and most of all successful detective might be inspirational… as well as a good way to avoid further conversation.

It turned out she was wrong.

"You read Chinese?" Shai asked, noticing her book.

"Yup."

"Do you write it, too?"

"A little."

"Speak it?"

"Of course," said Lou, and went back to her reading.

A few moments later, Shai said, "They'll be pleased."

"*Who?*" asked Lou, exasperated.

"Our employees," he said. "We can't let them send any letters home. We have a rule about reading all outgoing post, and no one reads Chinese. We've told them we'd write out anything they want in English, but few have accepted our offer."

"Amazing they're not thrilled by your generosity," grumbled Lou, still too sore from Shai's crack about woman's work to be polite—or grateful that he was basically telling her everything she wanted to know.

"Like I said, we have to be careful of spies." He took another long drag on his pipe, and left her to read in peace.

Pieces of the puzzling investigation might be falling into place, but Lou was feeling too wary of Shai to engage further with him. After a time she shut her book and lay down.

Lou was shocked by how uncomfortable sleeping on the ground was. Even wrapped in her clothes, coat, and thick blanket she could feel every rock and twig, maybe even the earthworms wriggling beneath the soil. She was certain she wouldn't sleep a wink while they were on the road, and began to wonder how long she would have to endure such conditions—only to be awakened out of a deep sleep by a nudge in the small of the back.

"Get up," hissed Shai.

"Mmph?" Lou slumped up on one arm.

"We were followed," said Shai, in a tone that chilled Lou more than the coldness of the night air. "I don't know if they want to rob us and leave us stranded, or rob us and murder us—but I *do* know I want you awake, and *now.*"

Chapter Four

"**A**re you fucking with me?" mumbled Lou.

"*Shh*. No."

She squinted up at him. He was squatting on his heels beside her, scanning the darkness in all directions, shotgun resting on his narrow shoulder. When he finally looked back down at Lou, his eyes flashed with reflected starlight.

"Are you ready? We need to move fast."

"Who followed us?"

"Scum. Road agents, probably," said Shai. "They're not your average run-of-the-mill dry-gulchers, though. By the time I captured their scout he'd already gotten into the wagon."

"You got one?"

"Oh yes." He chuckled, a low, uncanny sound. Gone was the affable, winsome young man who'd cracked jokes beside her in the wagon; now she felt like she was next to some sort of wild and dangerous predator. "Come on. We need to move quickly, before he's missed."

Lou sat up. "You didn't kill him?"

"Of course not," said Shai patiently. "I kept him alive to see if we could get it out of him where his friends are holed up. Can't be across the river—his feet were dry. Narrows it down, but not enough."

"Why would he tell us anything?"

Shai looked at her, his expression neutral. "If we can get him to talk, we'll have a serious advantage."

Lou wasn't scared, not exactly, but she felt fear rising tight in her throat. She didn't like this situation one bit. It was dark—really dark. The moon was down, and the heavens were thick with an unsettling number of stars. The fire had burned low, casting shadows everywhere. That there were people out on the prairie of a mind to steal from and perhaps murder her and her companion felt substantially less thrilling than reading about such things in dime novels, snugged up safe in her apartment in San Francisco.

"Are you ready?" asked Shai. Lou sensed it wasn't really a question, so despite her desire to stay right where she was, she nodded. Shai nodded back. "Don't stand," he said. "I don't want them to see us if they're nearby. And we need to keep our boy quiet. You have your gun with you, don't you?"

"Yeah…"

"May I see it?"

Lou hesitated; she hardly ever let anyone else handle her LeMat. They were rare weapons, and it had cost her father a small fortune to have this one customized to his specifications. Not only was the grip inlaid with antique Chinese coins, it had been hand-carved from a peach-wood sword of the type used by more traditional Taoist exorcists, and the barrels had been inscribed with a Taoist lesson, *The body may die, but the Tao still exists,* in English on the longer and hon jih on the shorter.

When she withdrew the firearm from under the wadded-up pair of pants she'd used as a pillow and showed it to Shai, he looked impressed. As well he might, it was a large handgun. Over a foot long, it weighed around three pounds, unloaded.

"Hoo," he whistled. "That's a monster. Good, it'll scare him. The shotgun would scare him more, but I'd rather not use that if it comes down to it. You could wing him with that and not have him bleed out." He looked at her sternly. "You're not to kill him unless he shouts, do you understand me?"

"Sure," Lou agreed quickly, having never once used a gun to shoot a living creature, animal or human.

They crab-scuttled across the campsite to the side of the wagon that faced the river. Lou's guts twisted when she saw a figure slumped against one of the cartwheels. He was wheezing and grunting through a gag, and his body looked odd with his arms bound behind his back and his legs akimbo.

When he turned at the sound of their feet shooshing through the grass, she saw he was blinking away tears, they were running down his cheeks and disappearing into his sparse beard. He was just a kid, she realized. She also noted his nose had been crushed. It was leaking a darker fluid than his eyes.

Shai set the shotgun down beside Lou and slunk to the other side of the stranger. The kid moaned when Shai pulled him off the wheel to half-cradle him in his lap, his scrawny legs flopping oddly. It was his ankles that were all kinds of strange—they were wrapped up tight with cloth, but it looked like he was otherwise unhobbled. Lou didn't have time to wonder why he didn't just run away, distracted as she was by Shai's slender hand snaking around to grasp the boy by the hair. In his other hand he was holding a queer knife, a six-inch, curved, single-edged blade. The kid whined through his gag when he saw it.

"All right," hissed Shai. "Listen up—you see that gun? Well, my friend here will shoot you dead with it if you shout when I cut this gag away from your mouth, do you understand me?" Shai paused, but the man said nothing. Shai sighed and moved his knife to press flat against the man's throat. "I said, *do you understand me?* Maybe you think I'm fucking around, but I promise I will slit your throat and let you bleed out like a spring lamb if you don't do every single thing I tell you."

The man made an acquiescent noise, and Shai's blade moved to a safer distance. Lou fancied for a moment she could smell the boy's fear, but realized it was just piss staining the front of his trousers.

"You've already paid a high enough price for a few sacks of beans, don't you think?" asked Shai, and the man nodded, no longer concerned for his jugular. "Well, here's my offer—tell me where the rest of your friends are, and I'll drop you off at the jail in Fort Collins. I'll even tell the sheriff you helped us out, put in a good word for you. Then maybe you won't hang. That's a decent deal, since I can guarantee you'll die if you don't tell me what I want to know."

The man nodded again. Shai's knife flashed as he cut the gag from his mouth.

"North," he said quickly, after spitting the cloth free. "A mile or so from here. We camped 'longside the crick, too, in a hollow."

Lou watched in horror as Shai lifted the man's earlobe away from the side of his face ever so delicately with the point of his knife. "Now tell me if I know you and yours."

"No," mewled the man. He was terrified. "Weren't nothin personal, we just saw you leavin town, and you seemed, you know… *easy*. They sent me to scout what you had to offer a group of humble opportunists such as ourselves. I swear though," he panted, his voice rising a little, "we wasn't gonna kill you!"

"Just leave us here, miles from anywhere, with no food and no transportation? After taking our weapons, and anything else of value we might have?" Shai sounded amused, almost friendly, and Lou relaxed a little bit. She'd been concerned things might get ugly, but the interrogation seemed to be going okay. "Well, that's all right. How many others?"

"Two. Emmett and Pete," he said.

"So if I went north for a mile, leaving my friend here to watch you, I'd come back not feeling unhappy? Because I'm planning to verify your tale before I put in that good word for you with the sheriff." Shai sighed. "One can't be too careful these days."

"I'm tellin you the God's honest," said the man eagerly. "If you had a stack of Bibles I'd swear on 'em, really, I—"

Shai slit the man's throat, and Lou vomited all over herself at the sight of the black blood gushing down his chest. A bubble formed over his mouth as he tried to say one last thing—then he died.

"You're all right," said Shai, throwing the man's spit-moistened gag at Lou so she could clean her face. It hit her in the chest, and fell to the ground.

"Why didn't he run away," mumbled Lou, her tongue gritty and her lips acidic. "He should've run away."

"I cut the tendons of his ankles when I caught him," said Shai.

Lou re-awoke to find Shai sponging off her face with the gag. The side of her head hurt.

"You passed out there for a minute, tenderfoot," said Shai, and he winked impishly at her. Lou shuddered; seeing the playful Shai from that morning looking out of the eyes of this crazy killer upset her more than anything else. "Things get rough out here in the wilds, don't they?"

"You killed him," said Lou. She was trembling. For all she was used to the dead, she'd never before seen a man straight-up *murdered* before. She'd heard about folk dying after getting roughed up in bar fights she'd witnessed—but to see a man bleed out was a new experience for her, and not a welcome one.

"Of course I did," said Shai, standing up and dusting off his trousers. He offered her his hand. "What did you expect? Come on, get up. We've got more work yet to do."

"No," said Lou, seeing his angle. "No—let's just pack up and go, they won't—"

"They'll be expecting him to return sooner rather than later," said Shai, shaking his head, his long, unbound hair falling softly over his shoulders in dark waves. "They've got horses, and we're slow with the wagon loaded so heavy. When their brother doesn't come back... no. We must do this. Now."

"But—"

"Your piece is all right as a second, but go get your holster so you can carry the shotgun in your hands—you said you knew how to use it?" Shai, impatient, grabbed Lou's arm and hauled her to her feet.

"But—"

"Lou," said Shai, in a tone that brought Lou's eyes to his. "You are going to walk over to where you were sleeping by the fire and get the holster for your pistol. Okay? I need you. They'll come after us and kill us if we don't act quickly. I know what I'm talking about. Do you trust me?"

The answer to that question was actually *no, absolutely not,* but Lou nodded just the same, numbly wandering back to the fireside as Shai ducked inside the back of the wagon. As she adjusted her shoulder holster, she took momentary comfort in the pleasant sensation of leather binding her around the shoulders and across her chest, but any relief melted away when she wondered if she'd see more men die before the sun rose.

Lou sensed she wasn't actually wondering so much as dreading the inevitable, but she couldn't refuse to go with Shai. To be perfectly honest, she was afraid of what he might do if she did. The memory of the young road agent, dead and ruined, was too fresh in her mind. She really didn't want to die out here, and *definitely* not like that.

To think only a few hours before they'd been sitting together, smoking, as he complimented her cooking! That would teach her to make snap judgments. She'd been right to resolve to keep him at arm's length, a vow she had conveniently forgotten when he'd proved so nice. Now she wondered if keeping him at arm's length was far enough—perhaps she shouldn't have been so quick to ride with him in the first place. She was just fine-tuning the details of a plan to extricate herself from Shai's company when she felt stinging pain across her cheek.

"I've been calling you," said Shai, shaking out the hand he'd popped her with. "Keep it together, Lou? We've got a mile trek over dark prairie and I need you with me every step of the way—and by *with me,* I mean more than just on your feet."

Shai now had a sword buckled around his waist. Lou laughed when she saw it. He slapped her again.

"What the hell," she said, raising a hand to her face. *"Swords?"*

"Yes, it's a sword," said Shai, and there was an edge as keen as any blade to his words. "Are you with me? Or do you want to die out here?"

Lou couldn't quite tell if he was threatening her, or referring to his earlier claim that the man's friends would come and get them if they didn't go and find them first. Regardless, the answer was *hell no.*

"Come on, then," said Shai, beginning to head north. Lou trotted after him. "Make as little noise as possible. Hopefully they'll have a low fire or something, but keep in mind that they'll be expecting someone and therefore alert."

Lou swallowed. "So... do you want me to shoot them when I see them?"

"No," said Shai. "Don't fire until I tell you."

They walked in silence, starlight silvering the gentle hills to their west. Puffs of wind bent the slender grasses; mist-whorls curled between the trees and scrub-brush patches as if stirred by the passing of a ghostly wagon. Lou spied what she assumed was a fox—pointy ears, brush tail—dart away from them and down a hole. It was dead quiet except for the occasional gust and nightbird's cry. Lou almost jumped out of her skin when Shai cleared his throat.

"For what it's worth... I had to do that back there. To that boy." Lou couldn't tell if he was defending himself or asking her forgiveness. "They'd have hanged him in Fort Collins if I'd turned him in, even if I'd put in a word for him. At least he died quickly this way."

"You could've let him go."

"No, Lou," said Shai. He was definitely pleading with her now. "This is the way things are out here. I've killed before, and I will again. It's not just my cargo I'm defending. It's my life."

"So you say."

"Dr. Panacea trusts me, no, more than that, he *relies* on me, to bring in supplies for the San. And yes, to be a ruthless son of a bitch when it's needed." Shai sighed. "I know you probably hate me now because you feel bad for that boy, but I promise you, Lou, no matter what he claimed while pissing himself scared he'd have come after us, with two other men besides. It wasn't an ideal solution, but this is hardly an ideal situation. Especially with you not really, well…"

"What?"

"You've never killed anyone before, have you?"

She glanced over at him and saw he was looking at her. She shook her head.

"But you're a good shot? You said you were."

"I spoke true," said Lou.

"Shotguns scare people," Shai said, somewhat unnecessarily, as Lou herself was wary of the giant weapon she held in her hands. "Hang back. If we creep up on them quiet enough I should be able to handle them."

"Both of them?"

Shai did not reply and as Lou had nothing more to say, they trekked northward in silence. She knew she needed to keep her eyes on the horizon, focus on what was at hand, but the slender figure striding beside her occupied her thoughts.

Shai's speech had affected her. San Francisco might be a rough town but it seemed people out here played by a more ruthless set of rules. It was strange—contrary to his assumption, she didn't hate Shai for doing what he'd done… but she wasn't going to tell him that. Not yet, anyways. While she understood well enough how it felt to be in a line of work where for the greater good one was required to do things others would consider despicable, Shai's unapologetic attitude toward murder unsettled her a little. Well, more than a little. But she could put herself in his shoes, easily. *Too* easily; she'd heard similar condemnations pronounced upon her character out of the mouths of myriad ghosts and shades.

But she could think about that later. Spying several dark shapes ahead, Lou pointed. Shai dropped into a crouch.

"Three horses," he murmured. "Good."

"How do you know it's them?"

"It's them," said Shai confidently. "Here's what we're going to do. I'm going to walk on up to their camp—"

"*What?*"

"They're expecting to see a man coming, right? Now, while I'm doing that, you keep down and draw a bead on whichever is farther away from me. I'll call to them, talk smooth pretending to be their friend, and once I get close enough, I'm going to put them down with my sword."

"But—"

"I'll take care of them quickly enough, trust me. But Lou, you make sure to keep good watch in case one of them is faster than I'm anticipating. Cover me, but don't feel the need to step in—unless you see me in danger. Then, of course, I'd appreciate the help."

This sounded like an incredibly bad plan to Lou, but Shai had begun to approach the camp in a cocksure manner. The road agents did, indeed, have a small, smokeless fire going. There were two men kneeling by it. Lou took a deep breath to calm herself and followed Shai, keeping as low as she could while still moving at a decent clip.

"Well, sheeeit," called Shai from the darkness, in a passable imitation of the dead man's voice. "What do I see but two sorry cusses lazin about in the dark while I do all the work around here. I tell you what."

There was a pause. Lou eased herself down onto her stomach and, peering through the grass, aimed at the man on the far side of the fire.

"Jim?" called one.

"Who else?" called Shai, but then there was a hiss as someone doused the fire.

Lou could no longer see the man she'd been aiming at. She swore under her breath and crawled closer—only to hear the sound of sliding metal and then a strangled yell. She had no idea if the cry came from Shai or one of the two strangers, so she crept closer still, trying not to freak out.

"Was that Emmett I killed, or Pete?" Shai's voice whipped over to Lou, carried on the wind. "Whoever it was, he's even uglier now!"

"Shut up shut up shut *up,*" muttered Lou. Then she heard the crack of a gun. Unable to control her impulse to sit up and look around, she did so—and saw Shai's silhouette in the middle of the camp, a body sprawled out at his feet.

"You missed," called Shai. He had his sword arm extended, the saber-blade steady as he pointed it into the darkness, turning slowly round and round on his heels. "Try again—or come out and fight like a man!"

Lou, while astounded by Shai's bravery—or bravado, she didn't know which—was also panicking about no longer being able to see the final brother. She was acutely aware her task was covering Shai, and therefore she was failing him. She didn't know what to do. Shai must be assuming she was ready to take down whoever might peek out and try to shoot him. Why else would he be acting so foolishly?

There came a rustle to the side of her, and Lou finally spied the profile of the final brother. He was low to the ground and aiming a revolver right at Shai, who had just turned his back on the gunman. There was no time for her to set up her shot, no time for anything.

"Get down!" shouted Lou as she swung the shotgun around; the man fired into the dark as Shai dropped to a crouch. Lou fired too, but the moment she pulled the trigger something smacked into her. She toppled over with a cry, dropping her gun as her back hit packed earth. Her right shoulder felt like it was on fire and she clutched at it, only to jerk her hand away when she touched her own warm blood flowing freely out of her.

"You got him!" whooped someone, from what sounded like far away. "You're a crack shot, Lou! Lou?"

"I got him?"

"You killed—my goodness, you've been shot," said Shai. He was standing over her. He quickly untucked his shirt and tore a strip from the bottom. "Can you sit up?"

"I think he shot me," said Lou.

Shai crouched down beside her and helped her sit up. "Can you hold this here?" He put the strip of shirt into her hand, and then pressed her hand firmly over the wound. "It looks like the bullet passed through," he said, after looking at her back. "That's good. You'll be all right, Lou, okay? Let me get your shirt off, and I'll—"

Lou panicked through the fog of pain and horror. She'd killed a man—and worse than that, Shai would find out she was a woman. "No," she said. "No, you can't. *Please!*"

"You're not just bleeding here," said Shai, touching her hand. "I have to get your shirt off so I can staunch the flow from both—"

"No," shrieked Lou. The night was getting darker, and to her supreme embarrassment, she began to cry. She clutched at Shai's hand. It was warm and dry. "Don't!"

"It's okay," he said gently. "It's okay, Lou. You'll be just fine."

"Please don't be mad at me," she said. Then she passed out.

Chapter Five

Lou regained consciousness only once during the trek back to their camp. She opened her eyes to see stars above her, the sky a great dome of blazing pinpricks, and wondered why they were bouncing. Perhaps an earthquake. But no—the sky was holding steady. *She* was bouncing. Or rather, being bounced: Shai was carrying her in his arms as if she weighed no more than a baby. Overwhelmed, Lou slid back into the yawning, rainbow-shimmery darkness that nibbled at the edges of her vision.

Upon waking the next morning, she half-remembered being set gently down and tended to beside the campfire that Shai must have built back up. Her shoulder hurt like a son of a bitch, but she was surprised she wasn't in more pain, considering. The throbbing ache was downright manageable when she sat up to the wondrous spectacle of her first prairie morning.

The sky above her was a vast, cerulean expanse that seemed both very near and very far away. Pale, eyewateringly bright sunlight shone over everything, glimmering on the small ripples of the burbling creek, gilding the yellow patches of last year's dried grass, and glinting off the small spider webs that clung to the blades of the new season's fresh green growth. The cherry tree that shaded their camp was a thing of rare beauty, all purple buds and brownish-silver bark, and everywhere barn swallows and martins sought their breakfast, chirping as they dived.

The splendor of the landscape captivated her for only so long. She was desperately thirsty, but when she tried to stand and head for the creek she found her legs were wobbly as a newborn colt's. Feeling sick to her stomach she sat back down with a thump that jolted her shoulder. When she could open her eyes without feeling like she wanted to throw up, she looked down to see if she'd bled through her bandage.

The bandage. Right.

So much for her secret.

That was for later; for now, she needed a drink more than pride or privacy. Though only a few strides from where she sat the creek seemed leagues away. But there was nothing for it, so she lurched to her feet with a grunt.

"Hey!" Shai poked his head out of the back of the wagon. "What're you doing?"

Lou was too busy staggering towards the sound of water to do anything more than shake her head in response. When she made it, she flopped to her knees on the soft bank, then faceplanted in the water. It was shockingly cold but sweet. She sucked up several mouthfuls before Shai got to her and helped her back up again.

"What in the world is wrong with you?" he asked. "I was right here. Why didn't you call me?"

"I didn't know where you were," replied Lou, wiping her mouth on her sleeve. "What was I supposed to do? I was thirsty."

"Well, at least you've recovered enough to grump at me," said Shai. "You were scaring me a little last night, letting me carry you and then thanking me nicely for everything. What, you don't remember?" he said, eyes twinkling merrily as she looked at him in horror. "Come on. Let's get you back. I put a waterskin next to you, you know."

"I didn't think to look."

"And here I thought you could see well," Shai teased. "But really, Lou—that was a great shot last night. He was dead before his bullet hit you, I think. You blew half his skull clean off."

Lou knew he meant the information as a compliment, but his admiration unsettled her. Shai might seem like himself again, she now knew him for what he was. A cold-blooded murderer.

Then again, so was she. She shivered as she sat back down by the fire. Shai frowned and put his hand on her forehead.

"You're not feverish," he announced. "I think you'll survive. I need to see to that dressing, though."

Feeling even fainter, Lou hid her face in her hands. She longed to be back in San Francisco, starting her day not with bandage-changing and discussion of how effectively she'd killed a man, but with a newspaper and a cup of the gritty, tar-black sludge Vilhelm claimed was coffee. Then she'd leave for a day of sending the dead on their way, go home to eat, sleep, and do the exact same thing the next day, and the next, and—

"Lou," said Shai. His tone was gentle, but she couldn't look up at him. "Hey—Lou? It's all right. Really. I already knew you were a woman."

Lou froze. "What?"

"I knew before I drove you to The Aristotelian. At least… I suspected."

"How?"

"I don't know. I couldn't tell you why exactly. I went back and forth on it, and doubted myself plenty… but then you didn't sock me when I said 'they serve all kinds' at The Aristotelian. That's not always a giveaway, of course, but when total strangers imply a gentleman might be interested in the odd bit of sodomy, even fellows with a taste for cock—that was a more colorful expression than I intended, my apologies—tend to get defensive." Shai shrugged. "Sometimes you get a feeling about people, that they're not entirely what they seem."

Given that Lou felt much the same way about Shai, she couldn't really refute his logic. "Okay," she said. "Well, I'm sorry. Usually I don't lie about it. I just let people believe what they want."

"I'm not angry," said Shai. "Trust me, I've run with odder folk than you pretty much my whole life."

"Yeah?"

"Yeah," he agreed. "So… can I see to your wound?"

Lou was so relieved by Shai's insouciance regarding her secret that she was able to bear his ministrations with, if not a grin, then at least a minimum of growling. No longer feeling like she had to hide felt wonderful, as if a great weight had been taken off her shoulders.

Even better, upon removing the dressing Shai said he was happy with how well she was healing up. Lou was pleased by both his studiously keeping his eyes on her wound, and how hardy she was in a pinch—but after she commented on the latter Shai reached inside the breast pocket of his suit jacket and withdrew a bottle of the Elixir of Life.

"Likely it'd be festering without it," he said, with another of his cheeky winks. "Bullet wounds need more than grit, willpower, and determination to knit."

Lou was impressed. This Elixir was evidently the real deal. As she pondered what on earth it might contain to be so effective, Shai ducked inside the wagon. When he reappeared with salt pork and corn grits, the sight of vittles drove all thoughts other than breakfast from her mind.

Waiting for the food to cook was pure agony, and when Shai passed her the bowl of mush and meat she thanked him profusely. By the time she finished her share and what he left in his bowl, and was smoking her post-meal cigarette, Lou was feeling as chipper as the birds who yet swooped and sang over the prairie.

"So are we too late?" she asked. "I mean, for leaving for Fort Collins today?"

"You need to take *at least* a day to rest," said Shai as he stretched out on his back. "And anyways, after all that excitement last night, I'm too exhausted to even hitch up the mules."

"But—"

"Lou, you need to learn to relax. Good thing it's a nice day for a lesson."

Lou glanced up at the sky and had to agree. Taking her cue from Shai she settled down and tried to get comfortable, but quickly realized he had no intention of cloud-watching and napping to while away the hours. He was, as usual, in a talkative mood.

Shai rambled for a time about the journey ahead—how Fort Collins was a decent little town, busier than it might be because of the military presence which lingered in the area to help settlers negotiate disputes with the remaining Indians and local bears, but a veritable metropolis compared to some of the outposts that had once cherished aspirations to township before the situation with the railroad. As he was speaking, Lou scooched herself onto her side to roll a cigarette, and then gingerly returned to a prone position to smoke it. As he trailed off, Lou set to admiring the wild beauty of the landscape and began to drowse after watching a flock of Canada geese fly over in formation, honking. She felt so relaxed that she figured she'd doze for a spell, but then Shai said,

"So, what's your story, Lou? Why the disguise I mean, the trousers, and everything else?"

Lou shrugged; winced. "It's not a disguise. I don't keep a spare sock rolled up in my drawers or anything. I mean, I grew up wearing pants, you know—Chinese women often wear them, if not this style. They're a sight more comfortable when you walk around all the—"

"No," interrupted Shai. "I understand well enough the many virtues of pants, Chinese or American. I was asking why *you* wore them—American pants. I wouldn't be asking if you were dressed like a traditional Chinese woman."

"Oh," said Lou, feeling more than a little self-conscious. What business was it of his? "It's just how I am, I guess. Who I am. I mean, why are you such a dude even out here in the wilderness? It's just how you are, right?"

"Fair enough," said Shai, settling his derby over his face to shade his eyes from the sun.

Lou glanced over at him as he lay by the coals of the morning fire, smoking his pipe in silence, and wondered why she had to be so goddamn prickly all the time. All he'd been after was some pleasant conversation. Getting to know one another would have been a fine way to pass the time, given that in the light of day she was less inclined to attempt any of the escape plans she'd dreamed up in the darkness. Except for the slap to the face and the threats last night—which, come to think of it, had snapped her out of her stupor better and faster than anything else—he'd been nothing but completely gallant towards her. He was still her best bet for finding out more about Fountain of Youth... and, considering how her first night on the prairie had gone, getting there at all.

She cursed herself for snapping at him. If she'd been willing to talk about herself, maybe she could have learned a little bit about him. As usual, she was smart enough to put on socks when her feet were cold, but not much more than that.

"Look," she said, "it's just—there isn't much to tell. Nothing interesting, at least," she added.

Shai flicked up the brim of his hat to look at her. "What's that?"

"About me. About myself," said Lou, frustrated.

"Nonsense." Shai turned onto his side and, withdrawing a flask from his jacket, took a long pull before passing her the booze. "We're all the hero of our own story, Lou. You read, right? So you know how it's done. Tell me a tale of how Lou came to her love of pants. Or start earlier if you like, the adventures of young Lou Merriwether in San Francisco."

Lou took an experimental sip—whiskey, and not rotgut, either. "It's not that easy. I don't know where to start." She took another swallow, for courage, and returned the flask. "I grew up in Chinatown. Mostly on my own. There weren't many other children to play with."

"Chinese children? Forgive me, I don't mean to be rude."

"It's not rude." Lou bit her lip, organized her thoughts. "There weren't a lot of Chinese kids, no... but there just weren't that many kids in San Francisco at all, even white ones, when I was little. Still aren't. In Chinatown, it's mostly because of all the immigration laws... the government's put restrictions on the number of Chinese women allowed in the country, even wives. I guess the muckety-mucks in the government figure if they let in Chinese women, their men might get the idea to set up housekeeping on this side of the Pacific. All the men who helped build the railroad are supposed to go home now, right? White folks want that, especially nowadays." Lou remembered she was discussing her past, not politics. "So, yeah, there were a few children my age that I knew, but mostly they didn't want much to do with me."

"Because you were a girl?"

"No. Because I'm a half-breed. I think it made them feel weird, since they were used to getting hassled by white folks. And even though people liked my father well enough, he was English... the reputation Englishmen had—have—among Toisanese folks—it's complicated. It was always complicated."

"I see," said Shai. "That makes sense about your father, I thought you looked—"

"Yeah," interrupted Lou, never comfortable talking about how she looked.

"Did your parents meet in San Francisco?"

"No. Papa was the second son of a second son or something, some whole boring English inheritance law situation where there was some money, but he didn't get much of it. I think he would've left even if he'd been born a lord, though. He was a Sinologist... among other things... so he went to China to study. Met my mother there. They came to San Francisco when they wanted to start a family, thinking it would be easier on their kids here. It was a real pain in the ass to get my Ma citizenship to hear them talk about it, even though she was poised to become a model goddamn citizen. But they managed, and eventually had me. Anyways, most of the time I played by myself, or helped Ma at her shop. I had one other friend who was also mixed." Lou found she didn't want to talk about Bo, so she paused to reach for the flask.

"Your mother owned her own business?"

"Oh. Yeah. She's an apothecary. Learned it from her father, he was a celebrated doctor, he actually studied with—with a few famous physicians," amended Lou, noticing Shai was frowning. Not wishing to bore him, she hurried her story along. "I grew up mostly at home, and you wouldn't believe how interesting it was… well, I realize it now. At the time I didn't appreciate it."

Lou paused, wondering at herself. She didn't usually talk this much, and especially not about her past. "Anyways, damn near everyone came to see my mother. Sick people, of course, but also working girls not interested in getting themselves in a family way; sometimes rich white folk who were tired of Western doctors for whatever reason. And folks who wanted to see if she stocked opium. Sometimes she even went out to visit people at their homes, outside of Chinatown I mean, if they needed that sort of discretion. But all I ever wanted was to go to school like a white kid.

"My father agreed I should get some schoolroom schooling, so when I was about nine he looked into it and, I think, greased a few palms, so I was allowed to attend even being half-Celestial. I insisted on wearing white kid clothes and made my Ma sew me new dresses. Can you imagine me in calico ruffles? I thought it would make me stand out less." Lou shook her head. "Boy, did I have a time of it. I got called all kinds of names… when the others would talk to me at all."

"Sounds lonely."

Lou nodded. "I guess it was. Never thought much about it at the time, but yeah, most of the kids lived close enough to the school that they went home for dinner, so I ate by myself every day. The teacher stayed to eat, too, but she never talked to me. I spent most of my time at recess by myself, too. I wanted so much to join the boys' games, though! I'd always wanted to be a boy, sort of—I mean, I wanted to be able to act like them. Maybe it's the same thing, I don't know. Anyways, when I saw those white boys in their trousers and copper-toed boots, making a ruckus and carrying on, having so much fun… I wanted so much to join in. I wanted to be one of them.

"I'd played with plenty of boys in Chinatown, but at school, the first time I tried I got chased off pretty quick. Once I got used to being called chink and trash and whatever else, I ventured back and tried again. But they still wouldn't let me. It made me so mad! I came up with all sorts of plans for a dramatic revenge but then I decided the direct approach would work best. So I screwed up my courage one day and knocked the biggest boy down, and—"

"You what?"

Lou had been staring at the tip of her cigarette, watching it burn. She glanced up at Shai. He was staring at her in admiration.

"I knocked him down," she said, blushing a little. "I knew how to fight pretty good, some of the Chinatown boys had taught me how to throw punches after I'd begged. My friend—the other half-blood kid—he was always pretty scrappy, so I got a few boxing lessons from him and his friends, bare-knuckle and Chinese style, too. I'm out of practice now. Once I took to shooting, I didn't keep up with it. Anyways, that day at recess I'd gone up to the boys and asked to play with them. They laughed, and it made me madder than ever for some reason, you know how it is when you're a kid, and I said I wanted to play and they couldn't stop me. So the biggest boy, this tow-headed mountain of a kid, stepped forward and said that even if I'd been a boy, they wouldn't let me. I asked why, and he said—I'll never forget it—that neither team wanted me because they all knew I couldn't see right out of my 'slanty chink eyes.' So I broke his nose."

"Good for you!"

"You think so?"

"Absolutely! But what happened to you?"

"When he fell, all the boys at his back jumped out of the way and he landed on his ass and started screaming when he saw the blood. Everyone looked up at me... and jumped me. All against one. If my friend had been there... he would have loved it. He was jealous, when I told him about it—he was always on about martial tales, the kind where a lone warrior battles a whole host, and wins... well, I lost, being a snot-nosed kid, not one of the Ten Tigers of Canton, but I gave them hell! Busted a few more noses and blacked a few eyes before our teacher dragged me away. They'd got me pretty good, I had a black eye coming too, and they'd knocked out two of my top teeth.

"But I was the one who got in trouble. I had to stand in the corner the rest of the day, and was sent home that afternoon with a note about fighting. As I walked away I heard a bunch of the boys saying I'd never come back, and sure enough when Papa came in and saw me he was madder than a wet hen, said he'd find me a tutor instead. I begged and pleaded, but in the end it was my Ma who changed his mind. She put her foot down and said I could go back after a day." It occurred to Lou that she'd never appreciated how her mother had used to stand up for her against her father's hand-wringing. Lou resolved to thank her, and try to be less of a sorry cuss when she got home. If she got home.

"Knowing me, my parents locked up my school clothes and shoes, figuring I'd sneak off without their permission if they didn't. So I climbed out a window wearing my everyday clothes—tunic and pants, I mean—and ran like hell to school the next morning. I got there right as the teacher was ringing the bell, but she made me stand in the corner again for coming in 'inappropriate attire.' Still, every time she was busy I'd turn around and stare those boys right in the eye. We reached an understanding, I think." Lou smiled as she flicked the long-dead butt of her cigarette in the fire.

Shai was obviously impressed. Lou tried not to notice—or enjoy it too much.

"And they let you play with them after that?"

"Sometimes," Lou said. "I had a few decent years, but then, I dunno. I lost interest in school, I guess."

Lou was unsure how to continue now that she'd come to the end of what she figured was harmless information about herself. Her mother had talked of a ghostly train spiriting away the missing Chinatown men to the world of the dead, and while Lou didn't much credit the theory she wasn't about to tell Shai about her years as a psychopomp-in-training—just in case.

She decided that it was still best to keep mostly to the truth. "I wanted to work, make some money. I helped my Ma in the shop for a while, but when I got old enough, maybe twelve, thirteen, I used my savings and bought myself a decent secondhand three-piece and a shirt or two. I've always liked the look of Western suits. They're so... they're hard-wearing, whatever you do... and they make you look *good* doing it. Maybe it was all the adventure books I read as a kid, or the natty duds forty-niners would sport, strutting their stuff through Chinatown on Saturday nights. And I can't tell you how… *right* I felt, when I finally put it on, at the tailor's… I liked the way I looked, really liked it, for the first time. Ever. Looked a sight better than I ever had in a dress, probably because I'm uglier than a boy-dog's butt and scrawny, too." Lou shrugged. "So there's the answer you were looking for, I guess. Only took me a million hours to get to it."

There was another side to the story—one she wouldn't tell Shai. It had been most efficacious to begin dressing as a boy when she finally made the decision to start practicing psychopompery on the sly.

She'd become fascinated with the science after her father had allowed her to attend an exorcism of a young girl. He indulged her interest at first, was flattered by it, and happily allowed her to paw through his manuals and learn the tricks of using his gear, after completing her homework in the evenings. But he would go no further than that—though she begged and begged her father to train her as his apprentice, it came to nothing. Her father wanted her to pursue her education and go to college.

But more schooling had been the last thing Lou wanted, so she formed a plan. She figured she wasn't disobeying him if she went to school, but spent her mid-day break studying his books rather than hers, and all evening too. Her grades dropped, but she was too enthralled by what she was learning to care.

Eventually she even began taking some of the easier-sounding jobs she saw in the papers and wanted signs. She made herself up a bag of tools from his old gear, and took half-days off to work; went out in the evenings, claiming academic errands.

She had a lot of success, early on, both professionally and when it came to keeping her parents unaware of her activities… until a case went very, *very* wrong. She'd been trying to singlehandedly break up an underground geung si boxing ring, only to have someone recognize her at a crucial, vulnerable moment. She'd come away the worse for wear, with a broken nose, as many bruises as bad memories, and a sheriff asking her a lot of questions as he took her home. After having to explain everything to her parents, Ailien had been the calm one that night. After Lou's father had cried himself out and scolded her to his heart's content, Ailien suggested that if Lou was going to practice psychopompery, she'd obviously be better off with supervision. That had finally convinced her father to take her on as his formal apprentice, albeit reluctantly.

Obviously Lou had to skip over all of *that*.

"Anyways… the hard labor and late hours got to me, I guess. I got sick with whatever's wrong with me, and it was beyond my Ma's skill. Heard about your Elixir of Life from a doctor, and took a few doses. When that didn't do enough, I headed out here."

Shai didn't say anything when she finished her tale, he just nodded and stirred up the fire with a stick, looking thoughtful. Quiet settled over the camp as the afternoon wore on and the shadows lengthened. Lou began to feel embarrassed, but then Shai rose, stretched, and smiled at her.

"It's always hard when you're different," he said, and Lou heard something in his voice that made her feel like he really understood what she'd been saying. "But sometimes, though the paths we're forced to tread in life may seem rockier than others, they take us to good—maybe sometimes better—places."

"Huh?"

A rosy tinge bloomed on Shai's cheeks for a moment—but it was gone so quickly Lou wondered if she'd imagined it.

"I know…" he said, trailed off, then started again, his expression unreadable. "It's very selfish of me—but I think what I'm trying to say—inelegantly—is that whatever the reason you're here, camping out on the prairie with me… I'm very glad to have met you. I never knew there was anyone like you in the whole world."

Lou didn't know what to say. She felt flattered, but also ashamed for telling Shai so many half-truths about her life—and that was saying nothing of flat-out lying about her entire reason for accompanying him to Fountain of Youth. Of course he was glad to have met her—*he didn't really know her.* His opinion had been formed in ignorance. Had he known she was investigating his employer he would keep her at arm's length; had he known she worked so closely with the dead, he, like most people, would probably think her creepy.

Fighting a sudden, intense longing to tell him the truth, Lou told herself that what she had traveled to Colorado to do was more important than her personal wants and needs. Shai might be friendlier after a few days than most of the people she'd known for years, but he was still someone she needed to be wary of. He was an employee of the mysterious Dr. Panacea, and a comfortable killer.

"I'm glad I met you, too," she said, speaking carefully. Thinking about psychopompery had reminded her of her duty. "I can't imagine being out here alone. I don't think I'd have come away from last night with just another interesting scar. And, speaking of last night... what did you do with the bodies? And the horses? You didn't just leave them, did you?"

"No. The horses—it's a shame, but I sent them on their way back to Cheyenne. They'll find their way home. The men I buried on the other side of the river while you were snoring away last night." Shai glanced at the wagon. "Say, did all that talking make you hungry? Listening rather whetted my appetite..."

"I'm always hungry. Haven't you figured that out yet?"

The campfire was bright, Shai's cooking smelled good, and as the sun sank it tinged the bands of clouds bright coral-pink and rose-gold. Lou watched the heavenly show as her stomach grumbled in anticipation of her meal. Shai apologized for it being the same thing he'd made earlier, but Lou told him truthfully that she didn't care. It was tasty, and there was lots of it—and those were the two most important things when it came to food. Shai acknowledged she had a point.

After they set aside their bowls, Lou asked the question that had been on her mind for the past few hours.

"Where on the other side of the river?"

"Hmm?" asked Shai, glancing up from packing his pipe.

"The men."

"Oh. North of here, under a willow tree. Why?"

Lou smiled sheepishly, hating herself as she did so. It was a calculated expression. "I'd, uh, like to pay my respects. Seeing as I killed one and all."

Shai smiled faintly. "Understandable," he said. He sounded a little sad as he described how to get to the place. "I could take first watch if you want?"

"No, no," said Lou. "You were up all night and all day. I'll take first watch and then nip off after I wake you for yours. I'd... like to be alone."

Shai was fine with this plan, and together they scrubbed the dishes and put them up, chattering and joking with one another the whole time. Then he changed her bandage, and not long afterwards he dozed off; it seemed the recent events had indeed taken a toll on him.

Lou waited until Shai was deeply asleep before making her move. She knew it was a betrayal of his trust to abandon her watch, but couldn't see any other way to do what she needed to do without giving herself away.

The likeliest place to find something spiritually amiss was under her very feet—but were that the case, she wanted to save it for last. Shai might be out cold but it couldn't hurt to give him a little more time, just to make sure. And that way she'd be back sooner rather than later, if her hunch proved right.

Several applications of the Elixir of Life meant her shoulder had ceased to hurt, but it still ached like a motherfucker as she walked north along the riverbank, keeping an eye out for any likely looking spots to ford the creek. She'd spied the willows in the darkness; she just wanted to get to them without getting wet above the thighs.

Eventually she found the remains of a campfire. Blood and hoofprints were visible in the dusty packed earth. Lou took out her skiameter from her workbag. It registered nothing, but even so, she set down her satchel and donned her goggles, fitting them with the thumoscopic lenses. A thorough scan revealed nothing eldritch, so she packed up and walked back the way she'd come until she returned to the shallowest spot she'd seen, not too far back. Fording it, she headed toward the stand of willows.

There, too, she found nothing. The single grave was clean of any spiritual lingering, so Lou headed back to camp.

Her shoulder was protesting in earnest by the time she arrived, but she was not yet finished. Taking out her skiameter, it showed her exactly what she'd suspected: she would be performing a nekuia that night. Pulling her goggles over her eyes a final time, the campfire dimmed through the colored glass—but another light shone faintly.

He was under the wagon. Lou crouched down and saw he was seated, curled into a ball with his arms wrapped around his legs.

"Hey," she said softly. "Why not come out from under there? I won't hurt you."

"*Fuck* you," came the muffled reply.

"I want to help," she said. "Really."

Shai snorted and rolled over. Lou lowered her voice even more.

"Look, I'm sorry about what happened. Let me help you."

"Go away," said the boy, but more quietly. He finally looked over at Lou. "Why're you botherin me when I'm already dead? And how come you can see me now? Neither of you could earlier, I waved my hand in front of your faces and everything."

Lou tapped her goggles. "I help the dead move on," she said. "It's my job. Sometimes getting murdered can make a soul cling to this world. I want to help you go to where you ought to be."

"I weren't saved. I don't wanna go to hell." He looked at her. "Unless there ain't no hell? Or heaven?"

"I dunno." Lou shrugged. "To my mind, anyone who tells you with certainty either way's probably a big fraud or selling something. Still, wouldn't you rather find out?"

"No," said the boy. "Preacher says it's the scourge and the burnin lake of fire and the rain of snares."

Shai mumbled something, but it sounded like sleeptalk. His proximity made Lou nervous. She needed to get this done, and fast.

"Well, your preacher probably also told you not to turn road agent, stealing and murdering and then using the money for sinful purposes," she said. "It's a little late to start heeding what he had to say, isn't it?"

The boy considered this. "Reckon so."

"Well, then," said Lou, as if that decided it. "You chose your life, and now it's over. Maybe you didn't want to go out this way but you must've known it was a risk when you did your very first job." That sounded a little harsh to her ears. She decided to try a different tactic. "Thing is, if you don't move on you'll be tied to this spot forever. You liked to travel, didn't you? Stick around on this side of things and you're stuck for the duration on this boring patch of prairie." Unless he successfully possessed someone, of course—but Lou wasn't about to give him any ideas.

"That don't sound neither good," he said.

Lou backed away from the gap in the wheels so he could crawl out without touching her. He looked even younger than last night, now that his face was illuminated by its own light. "So what're you gonna do to me?"

"Nothing to you." Lou switched out a goggle-lens to find a door. There was one a few yards over, under the grass. She took out her psilver key, bid the boy follow her. His eyes widened when she unlocked it and then opened it with her tongs.

"Jesus," he said.

"Maybe," said Lou, with a shrug.

"Well... thanks. I guess. For this part, at least. I still wish your friend hadn't killed me, but there it is."

As if lowering himself into a bathtub or swimming hole, the boy sat down; in went one leg, then the next. After scooting his rear end off the edge to allow his torso to sink into the soft blackness he looked at her a final time, then disappeared entirely.

Lou stared for a few moments after he'd gone, then locked up the door, repacked her bag, and headed back to camp—but something made her turn back. Without her enhanced vision, however, she saw only a patch of grassland.

"Good luck," she said to no one who existed in her world anymore.

After putting her satchel back in the wagon, Lou looked over to where Shai slumbered, and watched him sleep for a few moments. He was beautiful even with his face slack and his mouth slightly ajar. Such a strange person, Lou thought. Not that she didn't like him. She liked him a lot, actually. More than she should.

Only then did it occur to Lou that Shai had not told her any part of his own life's story in exchange for hers. Beyond that he'd been cured of consumption, she knew nothing about him at all.

"Hey," she said, shaking him gently. "Time to get up."

The illusion of his perfection was shattered slightly as he sat up and she saw drool crusting the edge of his mouth. Good to be reminded that everyone puts their pants on one leg at a time.

"You awake?" she asked.

"Yeah," he said. "Yeah, I am."

"All right. I'm off then."

"Huh?"

"Like I said earlier—I want to pay my respects."

"Oh," he said. "Right. Well, good luck, Lou."

"Thanks," she said, and headed off to retrace her steps, her heart heavy with lies, but lighter with the knowledge that she'd done some good that night.

Chapter Six

Again shaken awake to the sight of Shai crouching over her, Lou's heart leaped, but he stifled her yelp by pressing two fingers to her lips before she could make a sound.

"Shh," he whispered. Lou's heart did not stop pounding—but she calmed down slightly when she saw Shai was smiling in the predawn light. "It's okay," he said softly. "It's just that they'll bolt if you make a ruckus. Sit up slowly and look to your left."

Lou obeyed, and saw two jackalopes munching prairie grass a few yards from their camp. Larger than hares, they were both the soft blue-grey of a cloudy morning sky. Only the buck had antlers, his rack remarkably similar to an antelope's. They sprouted just above his enormous ears.

Lou was delighted. "I always thought they were a taxidermist's joke," she murmured.

"Oh, they're real enough," said Shai, "but most of the stuffed ones you'll see around are fakes. They're terribly reclusive creatures. It's a lucky sighting." He smiled. "Maybe it's because we left the flask out last night. They're said to be attracted to the scent of whiskey."

"That's true?"

Shai shrugged. "Probably not. I've never heard one speak, and they're supposed to do that, aren't they? Likely we just woke up at the right time."

"They look soft," said Lou.

"Maybe so, but they're really quite fierce. They'll kill rattlesnakes that go after their young." Shai stood, and the jackalopes froze where they sat, black eyes wide and watching. "We'd better get moving," he said. "Fort Collins is still a ways off, and we need to eat and change your bandage before we go."

Lou didn't think anything could top such an auspicious start to a day, but the ride down to Fort Collins ended up being more fun than travel had any right to be. As the Rockies grew ever-larger to their right, she and Shai chatted with an easy companionability that Lou had not known for a very long time—years, really. They taught each other songs, told tales, and laughed at everything.

It was after dusk when they arrived in town, but exhaustion and shoulder-pain prevented Lou from exploring what nightlife Fort Collins had to offer. Shai hadn't let her drive because of her wound, but it throbbed anyway from the constant jolting of the wagon. Directly after supper at the hotel Lou fell into her narrow bed and was asleep before Shai even came back from his bath.

They awoke early the next morning. One of the mules had thrown a shoe on the road, so they took him to be reshod at a local blacksmith's. They passed the time by visiting a few stores. Shai bought some more salt pork and beef, and a few packets of seeds, along with some dried cherries and peaches.

Lou replenished her supply of shag, but that was it, until they passed a bootmaker's while returning to the farrier. Shai pointed at the shop window. On display were a pair of pointy-toed, chocolate-brown high boots with a scene of jackalopes fighting rattlesnakes stitched over the shaft. Lou loved them instantly and wanted them more than she'd ever wanted anything, but she knew she didn't need them—and she sensed, given the workmanship, that they wouldn't be cheap. Lest she be tempted, at first she refused to even enter the shop, but Shai's insistence that it couldn't hurt to just *look* at them ended up swaying her.

Lou promised herself she was just making Shai happy and that she'd keep her dollars in her pocket, but as soon as she touched the buttery hide and ran her fingers over the cord on the side welt she thanked her lucky stars they were too big for her. The price was indeed high.

Then the wizened, white-haired proprietor mentioned he'd made a similar pair a few years ago, for his son's fifteenth birthday. They'd been long since outgrown, so if Lou didn't mind buying a used pair, he'd bring them out to see if they fit her. Lou hesitated, but when the owner mentioned the price he'd charge for them, she consented.

They fit beautifully.

"I still don't know," said Lou, as she walked around the shop. The heels rang like bells on the wooden floor, and she couldn't help glancing in the mirror again and again, seeing how nicely they fit her calves; how the toes glinted in the light.

"What don't you know?" asked Shai, smoking his pipe lazily while lounging in a chair. "Just look at them! Come on, Lou. Your boots are awful. They don't even keep your feet dry."

"True. But these, they're just so… *fancy.*"

"Well, we get some fancy folk up at Fountain of Youth, so you'll fit right in. And when you get back to San Francisco you'll be the talk of the town."

Before Lou could remark that she'd never once wanted to be "the talk of the town," the proprietor said, "Fountain of Youth? You boys headed up to the San?"

"I work there," said Shai, and then added, "so does my friend—or, almost. Been offered a job."

"Well then," said the man, and lowered the price even further. Lou stared at him. "Dr. Panacea's Elixir helps my rheumatics," he said. "I can keep working because of it. And he gave my boy Zeb a job when no one else would hire him. It was the consumption."

"Zeb's your son?" Shai looked quite interested in this intelligence. "Didn't realize he was a local."

"Yep," said the man. "Say, any chance you talked to him lately?"

"I've been away, but when I left he was fine, just fine."

"Well, that's all right. Tell him his Pa hopes he's keeping out of trouble. Anyways, gentlemen, that's my price, and it's a good one. What do you think?"

Lou's dollars went on the counter, and she couldn't help but grin at the bootmaker as he took them. He returned the expression when she refused a box, saying she'd wear the new pair out.

"Well, well. Don't you look fancy," said Shai, as they stepped out into the main thoroughfare.

Lou looked slyly at her companion as she swung her old boots by the pull-tabs. "Oh, right. I'm sure standing next to you, everyone thinks *I'm* the fop."

"You wound me!" cried Shai, clutching at his chest like he'd just been shot. "I prefer to think of myself as a dandy. It's more respectable."

"Whatever you say, dude."

When they returned to find the mule not yet shod, Shai suggested they sample some of the local libations while they waited. They knocked back a few boilermakers at a local saloon while they waited, and thus it was in rather high spirits that they departed from Fort Collins. As they drove, Lou scarcely noticed when she sobered up—she was drunk on scenery.

Their road ran along the rolling, scrub-studded foothills that Shai called "the Front Range." Beside them, mountains grew ever-larger and impressive. Lou couldn't take her eyes off them. The buckskin-colored, rock-speckled hills were getting bigger, the high green peaks beyond them were enormous, and the white-capped giants behind *them* were downright astounding. She'd heard the Rockies were huge, but the scale of them up close and in person was overwhelming. She felt small and insignificant in their shadow.

"I've never gotten used to it," confessed Shai, when she mentioned the sensation. "Up at the San, sometimes I walk outside in the mornings, alone… you wouldn't believe the freshness of the air, how crisp it feels in your lungs; the brightness of the early sun on the hot springs, or reflecting off the snow. I've always loved the sunlight…"

He looked sad, almost grief-stricken, an expression Lou had not yet seen on his delicate face. Still—even if Shai managed to make sorrow look comely, she wanted to cheer him up, divert him from whatever dark thoughts were troubling him. Reminded of a poem her mother loved, she quoted it.

"Why do I live in the green mountains?

I laugh and answer not. My soul is serene.

It dwells in another heaven and earth belonging to no man—

The peach trees are in flower, and the water flows on."

After she finished, the only sounds were the creak of the wagon-wheels and the jangling of the mules' harnesses. After some long moments, Shai cleared his throat.

"Did you write that?" he asked softly.

Lou snorted, ruining the moment. "Hell no. It's Chinese poetry." Sensing she had been indelicate, she added, "But I never understood it until today, I don't think."

"Oh," said Shai. "It's just… but how could you know…"

Lou got the impression he had spoken mostly to himself. She felt guilty; clearly her attempt to cheer him had failed. Wondering if discussing matters more mundane might distract him better, she asked if they were getting close to the next town. Shai seemed to perk up a little.

"I suppose that depends."

"On what?"

"You." Shai seemed queerly nervous, his smile flickering like a candle in a drafty room. All of a sudden Lou wondered if he might like her. *Like*-like her. But that was impossible. She was pretty sure they hadn't known one another long enough for that, and anyways, she couldn't see any way in the world she'd be his type. He was too pretty to like someone like her, for one thing, and she was fairly certain he was too cool to have any warm feelings like *that,* for another. Maybe he was still drunk.

"How does it depend on me, exactly?"

"There's a few ways we can go from here. We'll come to a fork in a while, and we can either keep running along the base of the mountains to Lickskillet—"

"Lickskillet?" hooted Lou. "Is that a town?"

"After a fashion. Don't expect much civilization from here on out," Shai cautioned her. "Even Estes Park isn't much more than a fishing camp."

"Duly noted. So what's the other way?"

Shai turned fully on the riding board to look at her, his eyebrows raised. "The Devil's Gulch road," he said, lowering his voice and trying to sound spooky. "It'll be a few days longer… if the weather stays good. More if we get snow. But it's a much prettier drive, you'll see the deep woods and the high country and scenic vistas you won't believe. So what do you think, Lou? Are you scared of *the devil?"*

The prospect of some extra days on the road with Shai wasn't exactly anathema to Lou. Sore shoulder notwithstanding she was having a good time, and was—selfishly—disinclined to put an end to her fun. She didn't harbor any illusions of what would happen between them when he found out she was there to investigate his employer.

"Nah. What about you? Can you get back late?"

"Late makes it sound like I'm supposed to be back on a certain day. I could take an extra week and no one would notice."

Once again Lou detected that melancholic note in Shai's voice. Even if it didn't sound like fun, she'd have agreed just to cheer him up.

Scenic the route surely turned out to be, once they reached the turnoff. The rolling hills studded with iron-grey scrub brush and patches of low spiny cactus yielded to true mountain terrain—at least so it seemed to Lou. The canyon walls seemed impossibly high; the cold smell of winter pine trees dizzying, but Shai said they were still barely into the Rockies. There were, he promised, more impressive sights yet to come.

They made camp early beside the river that ran along the road, in a cave that was little more than recess in the rock with a small overhang. They were grateful for even that scant protection. Night was falling much more quickly than Lou had expected and the gusts of wind that rushed down through the canyon were arctic and wet, but by the time they had a fire going and the mules tethered it was a cozy enough spot.

"Could be cozier, though." Shai leaned in conspiratorially, getting closer than Lou was necessarily comfortable with now that she was wondering if he harbored some kind of romantic feelings toward her. "Want to be bad with me?"

She shifted away ever so slightly. "That depends…"

"I happen to know the doctor had me pick up some coffee as well as the other supplies. If I pinched from his private supply, you wouldn't mention it to him?"

Lou relaxed. "I promise," she said. "I've never been so happy to hear the word coffee in my life."

As Shai funneled the beans into a small hand grinder and boiled some water, Lou wiped down the mule team as he had taught her, and, after asking his permission, gave them a few extra handfuls of oats along with their pack. The canyon road wasn't an easy one, and she felt they'd earned a good dinner. After ensuring they were well-covered by their blankets, Lou hunkered down beside the blaze to warm her hands. Shai took the pot off the fire and puffed on his pipe as they waited for the grounds to steep, his fruity smoke mixing with the wood-smell of the fire and the rich smell of the coffee. It was so peaceful that Lou hated having to ask if he'd tend to her bullet-wound, but it was aching again.

"Looks like we can leave off binding it tomorrow," he said, as he sprinkled fresh Elixir on the bandage. "It'll still be sore for a while, but the puncture's knitted."

"Amazing." Lou quickly buttoned up her shirt against the wind and Shai's gaze, trying not to blush. She couldn't tell if she was imagining things, or if his eyes really were lingering on her bare flesh. "That stuff, it's downright miraculous," she said, playing it cool.

"Yes, it is," said Shai, again with that strange, wistful tone in his voice.

The next morning it wasn't just her uneasiness over Shai's sentiments that made Lou glad they could leave off with washing and binding her wound—it was cold as a goddamn grave in the canyon. When Shai shook her awake, her nostrils were rimed with ice.

The next several days were a blur of beauty and happiness and wonder. Winding up Devil's Gulch they entered the forest proper. Lou found she liked the feeling of being beneath the tall pines and ghostly bare aspens. It was almost like being in a city again, though a city where one frequently caught glimpses of shy, majestic elk and smaller, long-eared mule deer, eagle-sized ravens and jabbering black-and-white mockingbirds. Lou had never seen so much wildlife, and she almost squealed with delight when two young longhorn sheep joyfully bounded across their path and then disappeared into the shadows of the pinewood, the only sign they'd been there hoofprints in the snow.

Shai claimed they needed to rest the mules often, and so they stopped to sit and admire the distant peaks and low-lying valleys whenever there was a convenient break in the trees. When she remarked on their leisurely pace, Shai claimed it was all about safety... yet he didn't urge the mules at all when they encountered wider, less steep stretches. He seemed determined to take his time.

Lou was of a mixed mind about this. True, she could be herself around him—at least, more than she usually could, with people. Her only source of anxiety was how queer he made her feel when she caught him watching her. The look in his eyes—it might have been longing, or even hunger. The sexy kind of hunger, like she'd read about in books. She couldn't tell for sure, never having had such a look directed at her, but she was fairly certain her intuition was on point.

The problem was, she liked Shai a lot... just not that way. She had no idea what she'd done to lead him on, but she needed to put a stop to things, quickly. The longer she let it bide, the more likely he was to be hurt when she turned him down—or when he discovered her true purpose for coming to Fountain of Youth. Thus, she began to formulate a plan as they drove through gulches clogged with fresh-smelling juniper bushes and dripping willows crowned with the first golden shoots of spring growth; skirted impossibly blue, half-thawed mountain lakes where rainbow-bright fishes swam beneath the ice. She would show him they were friends, nothing more.

The next time Shai stopped the team to let them rest, Lou sidled into the woods pretending she needed some privacy, but really she was searching for a nice patch of snow. Once she found a proper pile, she spent several minutes packing a host of snowballs, setting all she couldn't carry in her hat. Then she snuck back as quietly as she could manage. Positioning herself to the side of the wagon she armed herself with two missiles.

"Hey Shai, *think fast!*" she cried, and knocked his derby clean off his head.

He squawked—Shai, slick, smooth, calm Shai *squawked,* and it was the funniest goddamn thing Lou had ever seen. She doubled over laughing at him until she saw him barreling at her, his eyes blazing like a demon's.

That was when she lobbed her second snowball and hit him in the neck.

"Dammit, Lou!" he sputtered, cupping his hand to get slush off of his skin. "What is *wrong* with you?"

"Can't take the snow, get out of the woods!" Lou taunted him, gasping. It made no sense, but whatever, he was actively chasing her and she was focusing on keeping her hat clutched in her arms. She managed to get off another volley while running, though it flew by him.

When he caught her by the collar of her coat she threw her hat away and swung around, feigning punching at him. He blocked her assaults surprisingly well, and then started fighting back. They were both out of breath from shouting and cussing and messing with one another, just like she'd planned. Lou was feeling good, fairly certain she'd put things to rights with her horseplay—until he swept her legs out from under her.

She grabbed at him, dragging him down as she fell, and they landed in a jumble of arms and legs in the snow. His sweet face was so close to hers, hanging over her like a moon against the black pine trees. He stared at her, neither of them saying anything, his expression unreadable but definitely dazed.

Being pinned by him, his warm body pressed against hers, was definitely not what Lou had been after. She pushed him off with a grunt.

"Nice one," she said, sitting up and starting to brush the snow off, feeling a mite dazed herself. Her vision was even a little blurry. "Should've seen that coming."

"Lou," he yelped, pointing at the snow. Where her head had been, a smear of blood lingered. She brushed it aside and found a rock hiding beneath the bank. She hadn't even felt it.

"No big deal," she said.

"You can't know that," he said, knee-walking around her to get a look at her injury. "I'm so sorry, Lou, I shouldn't have been horsing around like that. At least it's not a bad cut," he said. "You're lucky."

"Luck has nothing to do with it." She winked at him. "You should be more concerned for the rocks. I'm hard as hell."

Shai looked exasperated for half a second, then he shook his head. "You're something else, Lou, you know that? One of a goddamn kind."

"You better believe it."

He was tender and apologetic while dabbing her skull with Elixir, which sharpened her vision and took away some of the pain. Even better, after they got back on the road, Shai didn't seem to be casting as many significant looks her way. Apparently, she'd made her point.

That evening, just as the shadows were beginning to lengthen, the road took them so high upland that a low-hanging cloud caught on the mountainside enveloped them in soft white blankness. Mist swirled about them, but just as Lou began to shiver the wind came up, the clouds parted, and the last of the day's sunlight cut through the fog. They had reached a swath of high country, and in the distance Lou spied an outpost, not much more than a few cabins, at the base of the highest peaks she had yet seen.

"Is that Estes Park?" she asked.

Shai nodded. "We'll sleep in real beds tomorrow tonight."

"You don't want to press on?" As much as she'd been enjoying herself, the prospect of a mattress and a roof over her head was a welcome one.

"Do *you?*" Shai's surprise mirrored hers.

Lou found herself reconsidering her eagerness. Estes Park was their last stop before they reached Fountain of Youth—and her continuing with the investigation. Her desire to make it to Estes evaporated as it dawned on her that her time alone with Shai was ending. It hit her a little harder than she expected.

"Actually, I'm pretty worn out. Seems like we might as well camp here."

"Sounds good to me." Shai hesitated, then said all in a rush, "You know, Lou… there are plenty of folks who intend to come up to the San but then find themselves happy enough in Estes. It's a beautiful spot, with all the fishing and hiking a man—er, a person—could want."

Lou nodded. "I can see that. Even this far off it's gorgeous."

"Some of our clients, really, they just need a break from their life. Rest… and a few weeks soaking up the beauty of the mountains."

"Better not spread that around."

"What's that?"

Lou nudged him in the ribs. "Didn't you say Dr. Panacea was wanting to attract more patients? Telling people Estes Park is just as salubrious as your San could be bad for business."

"Dr. Panacea's business is healing the sick," said Shai shortly.

Taken aback by Shai's tone, Lou silently helped set up a little camp just behind the treeline. She didn't know what the hell she'd done beyond tease him a little; Shai looked like she'd insulted his mother, or worse. As a peace offering she suggested she might cook the soup he'd liked so much that first night, but that only seemed to depress him further. As he made no move to prepare anything himself she went ahead and cooked up a batch anyway. He might be brooding too hard to notice he was hungry, but she sure wasn't.

"Eat," she urged, after she'd put down two bowls of soup in the time it took him to pick at one. "Gotta keep your strength up. Don't want to end up a patient at the San yourself, do you?"

Shai didn't eat more. "Why are you here, Lou?" he asked, eyes on his cooling bowl.

"Huh? We camped here."

"No, why are you *here?* Here, with me, heading to Fountain of Youth?"

Answers scudded across Lou's mind like the clouds above—men missing and missed; two mothers holding each other, weeping in a whorehouse kitchen; a dead boy sitting up in his coffin, full of rage and hunger; the pressure of knowing any resolution might depend upon her own bravery or cowardice. She longed to give voice to her thoughts, to confide in another soul. But no matter how much she liked Shai, she couldn't tell him—as much as she hoped it wasn't the case, he might even be a part of whatever was going on. So instead of confessing, she looked at him quizzically.

"I told you. I'm sick and I can't seem to get better." She shrugged. "I'm not ready to die yet. Is that so strange?"

Shai laughed a dry, high laugh, and then took a long hit off his pipe. "Ask you no questions, and you'll tell me no lies. Fair enough."

"What do you—"

"It's all right, Lou," he said. "I understand not being ready to die."

Chapter Seven

I *understand not being ready to die.*

Shai's words kept rattling around Lou's skull as she stared at the starlit hills. It had been the last thing he'd said to her before setting aside his half-finished bowl of soup and curling up under his blanket. She'd guessed that meant she was supposed to take first watch.

A deep gloominess settled over Lou. She tried to tell herself that Shai would be his old self in the morning. But, even if he was, it was only a matter of time before things changed forever.

This wasn't how she'd envisioned their time together ending when she'd pegged him with that snowball. Truth be told, she wasn't sure *what* she'd envisioned.

Well, that wasn't strictly true. She'd actually imagined this exact scenario, time and again… only with someone else. Guilt and loneliness gnawed at her as Lou's hand strayed to the bolo tie at her neck, her fingers warming the silver coin as she traced the outline of the plump little pig. Hadn't she dreamed of being out on the prairie—or wherever—under the stars, beside a campfire, taking first watch as a handsome young man snoozed beside her?

But that handsome young man wasn't here. He'd left long ago to go off on his own adventures. Without her.

She got out her satchel and retrieved a greasy envelope. The letter inside was thin where it had been folded and refolded, so she opened it as carefully as she could. It was dated May 1869, postmarked from New York City. She'd read it so often she didn't need to strain her eyes by the firelight to know exactly what it said.

Hey girl,

Gosh but I am sorry to hear about your father. It is hard to imagine Archie unwell! But I am sure he will come through it okay. You and Ailien will take the best care of him in the world, I know it.

So you are handling jobs on your own now! And with your father's permission this time! I always knew you would take over the Agency one day. I am sorry I cannot come home at present to celebrate with you. Do you remember the first night you snuck out and made three whole dollars exorcising a shade? I do. I have never been so proud as when you showed up with that bottle of Old Monk so we could get roostered together on the roof of the Agency. I wish we could do that again, but you'll have to do it by yourself and just imagine me there so hard I can feel it way out here.

I have some news, too! I have started my own business with my friend Thurlow. I will miss working on the stage, but you were right, there is nothing but minstrel work for me, even out here. And even if I was not ready to leave, Thurlow is, and I don't know if I could handle New York City without him.

For our first job he and I underbid everyone else for the exclusive right to take care of the banshee that was haunting the Central Park construction areas. We did a real good job of it if I do say so myself! Used the money to buy a wagon and a mule team, so I figure we are ready to go on the road and do this for a living. (There are too many established monster-hunters in New York for us to really break into the business here.) Oh, and it is not just me and Thurlow any more! The twins decided to take us up on our offer. Jack is a real hand with an axe, and Caitlin, she is something else entirely, let me tell you. I have hopes we will do well on the road, even in the South. Our services are always needed, and if people have a problem with us being the ones offering services, well, we figure a posse of fools is a lot easier to take care of than a banshee.

I miss you, and now I will not be able to even get your letters. But I will keep in touch whenever we find a post office. Be well, Lou. Best of luck to your father but I know everything will be fine.

—Bo Wong

Lou refolded the letter and rolled herself a cigarette, wishing she had the nerve to try to steal Shai's flask out of his jacket pocket. She was yearning for a drink. She'd thought she was over Bo and yet here she was, back to being an idiot about the whole thing, even though she knew perfectly well that things would never go back to the way they were. How could they?

Usually she tried to forget about Bo, but to do so meant forgetting some of her happiest memories. Like the first time he'd performed in a small revue in Chinatown, where performers of all sorts were welcomed. She'd gazed up at him as he delivered a monologue from *Doctor Faustus,* hearing the words, but mostly watching the way the light reflected off his skin, how his cheekbones moved when he spoke with such passion.

Lou couldn't recall a time when she hadn't been half in love with Bo—except for the night she'd realized she was completely in love with him, while they celebrated her first success on the Agency's roof. That the very next day he'd told her he was leaving for New York City didn't sully her memory, but it did make it bittersweet. She'd resisted her impulse to kiss him that night. Now she wondered if she'd ever get the chance to tell him how she felt.

To be fair, she *had* told him how she felt—that he was an idiot, or crazy, or both for heading east to try to be an actor—but not the rest. Not that she longed to know what his lips tasted like, to trade loving whispers instead of friendly punches and insults. She hadn't told him, either, that she'd always hoped that since they'd spent so much time studying her father's psycho-pompery manuals together he would partner up with her at the Agency once Archie retired.

Lou resisted the temptation to throw the letter into the fire; instead, she shoved the envelope back into her satchel only to bark her knuckles on something cold and hard. With a soft cuss she withdrew her hand, which had closed around the bottle of Elixir she'd snatched from the crate in the basement of Madame Cheung's. She stared at the potent reminder of why she was really in Colorado. After replacing the bottle carefully she nudged Shai awake with the toe of her new boot, and went to sleep without a word.

***

The morning came too soon for Lou's liking. It seemed darker than it ought to be when she heard Shai building up the fire. Peeking over the edge of her blanket, the sky was a leaden shade and the wind was blowing wet and cold.

When Lou remarked upon this, Shai said only that clear skies or snowy he was needed back at Fountain of Youth. Taking his hint, she hurried through her morning ablutions by a small stream. After washing as thoroughly as she could bear to in the frigid water, she returned to find Shai had laid out some dried peaches and corndodgers for their breakfast. She eyed the food with distaste. It was the kind of dreary-ass morning where a hot breakfast would really hit the spot, but she could tell there was no chance of that.

Despite the threat of unpleasant weather, the skies cleared after they'd driven for a few hours and sunlight shone down upon them. A little grass had sprouted already, and sheep, even some cattle were grazing. Chipmunks darted out from under rocks and bushes to frisk in the sunshine, heedless of the hawks that circled lazily above. Gazing up at the craggy mountains that enclosed the long dale, Lou wished Shai hadn't fallen into such a sorry mood.

He had not said an unnecessary word to her since waking. Lou let him stew. She'd made a few attempts to coax a smile only to be shut down, and she could take a hint.

Whilst traversing the meadowland Lou swore a hundred times to herself that Estes Park was getting no closer, but then all of a sudden they were there. A fork in the trail was marked with small hand-painted sign that said "Fish Creek Camp" to the side of a half-frozen lake, and Shai turned them toward where a cluster of longhouses and cabins sat a few miles off. Smoke was rising from the chimneys, and Lou felt she'd never seen anything so snug and homey-looking.

Their approach did not go unnoticed. As they pulled alongside the largest of the structures, a hearty old-timer with a long white beard emerged to halloo at them. He was closely followed by four enormous, drooling bulldogs that cavorted about his knees, barking and stepping on one another.

"Tell everyone you're here for a job," said Shai quietly. "It'll be easier that way. Less remarkable, is my meaning."

"Is there something particularly remarkable about a Chinese getting sick?"

Shai shot her a look that told her plainly what he thought of her sass, then hailed the approaching greybeard, calling him "Griff." Griff appeared overwhelmed with delight to see them, as he kept shouting even as they drew close enough to hear him perfectly well at a more moderate volume. He also seemed disinclined to let anyone else speak; Lou found herself wondering if he ever breathed.

"Shai, you're a sight!" he cried over the snuffling and barking of the bulldogs. "Don't look like you've pressed your suit yet today! Haw haw!" Then, unexpectedly, he swung himself up next to Lou on the riding board, shoving her into Shai.

"Budge up there, little brother—say, lookee here, you're a Chinaman!" This revelation clearly amused Griff. He had perhaps a dozen long curly wood shavings caught in among his beard-hairs. "Sure got yourself a big farm up there! Gotta haul myself up to see it 'fore I die! Then again, maybe your doctor friend could push that back a few years? Haw! That's the point, ain't it? Hey, Ching-Chong, can you teach me any of your speakee talkee? Well, probably not! I've heard plenty of your kind jabbering and can't make heads nor tails of it! Would sound like speakin in tongues but for y'all's bein heathens! Oooga-booga-chingy-chongy-chang-ching-chung! Haw!"

Shai needn't have worried about Lou's saying anything inappropriate— she was too shocked to speak. Not that she would have been heard over the ruckus. Griff never shut his fool mouth, and the dogs followed them as they drove, never ceasing their barking and whining. Occasionally they even ran underneath the mules' feet, but the mules, to their credit, ignored them. Lou wished she could do the same with Griff. He did not lower his voice one bit once they got inside the large, warm barn.

"Been a hard road for you boys? Glad you didn't get stuck in this snow, and you're here now! We just finished dinner, but there's leftover trout-fry and bacon and mush and potato pancakes! And I'll have the missus boil up some hot pine needle tea! Oh, and Shai, you'll be happy—buncha of invalids come in since you left. Good for you, but bad for them! Haw! Got some in the longhouse now, waiting for Ned and the Coyote, a husband and wife from out east, and a squarehead who don't talk good English but got himself plenty of coin from a gold strike!"

"Excellent," said Shai, after handing over the mules to a tall, black-haired man in coveralls and muck-boots. "Seen Tom?"

"Tom?" Griff paused to consider this. "Tom Hill? No, haven't seen him since he went on his way out west to Frisco two months ago—or was it three? No matter, ain't seen neither hide nor hair."

Lou winced at the nickname—locals never called San Francisco "Frisco"—but was more intrigued that he'd named her hometown at all. Shai had not once mentioned any associates connected with the city. Sadly, more information was not forthcoming. Shai commenced cussing and called Tom more than a few names before Griff remarked that any number of troubles might have befallen Tom given the way of the world, and then immediately launched into another series of loud, mostly rhetorical questions.

Once they left the barn and commenced moseying to the central longhouse Griff asked, "Will you be waiting for Ned and the Coyote?"

"No—well, maybe," amended Shai. "I'll see how the weather looks in the morning, and the mules, too. They've been working hard, and it couldn't hurt to let them rest. For now, though, that food sounded pretty good…"

Griff gave Lou the hard-eye when she moved to follow Shai into the house, but when Shai said something too low for her to catch, Griff grudgingly let her inside. Lou was unimpressed, but held her tongue.

Inside, it was nice enough. The logs had been chinked against the cold, and the floors had been swept recently. The ceilings were high enough to feel comfortable without being so high as to waste heat. Two windows on each long wall let in some sunlight, as well as the spectacular views of the water and the mountains. Though it smelled of fish, it smelled of fresh fish.

A large pot-stove warmed the space adequately, but Lou's reception by those sitting around it was downright chilly. There were a few rough-looking sorts that Griff said were would-be homesteaders. Lou forgot their names as soon as they came out of Griff's hairy mouth. Sitting together in a cluster, they spoke in whispers while occasionally spitting tobacco into a spittoon.

After being introduced, they grunted a greeting at Shai, then went back to their conversation.

On the other side of the stove were those bound for Fountain of Youth. A well-dressed couple by the name of Willoughby nodded politely at Shai's greeting but looked at Lou as if she'd strutted up and farted right in their mouths. There was also a ghoulishly thin blond man in a fine suit who introduced himself as Mr. Magnusson. He seemed more amenable to Lou's presence, in that he smiled at her, but he said nothing more than his name.

"Take a load off, Shai," said Griff. "I'll fetch your vittles. And as for *you,* Ching-Chong," said Griff, raising his voice as he spoke to Lou, "you go eat in the kitchen. Afterwards, go find Big Joe, that Injun who took your mules. He'll show you to a pallet in the fish house where you can sleep."

Chapter Eight

Shai, to Lou's extreme bewilderment, did not protest Griff's sending her to the kitchen to eat, nor to sleep in the "fish house," whatever and wherever that might be. In fact, he ignored Lou entirely as he pulled up a chair to the stove and began to chat with Fountain of Youth's future patients, leaving her to gape at him. When it became obvious he would not acknowledge her, she blushed, but turned away obediently.

And if *that* wasn't enough to rob Lou of her appetite, Griff's admonition to her back to "Mind you behave," and his wife's baleful gaze did the rest. Confused, wounded, and extremely pissed off, Lou only managed to bolt down two cold trout, six rashers of bacon, a mound of corn mush, two potato pancakes, and a boiled egg before needing to escape from Mrs. Evans' hard-eye—and also the vacant stares of the dozens of carven bulldogs that squatted on every flat surface. Apparently Griff was a whittler.

Not wanting to spend a moment longer in the kitchen than she had to, Lou made her way to the stables, stomping her anger the whole way. Once there, she found "Big Joe" snoozing in the afternoon sunshine on a three-legged stool. Lou mucked about for a few minutes, looking to see if the mules seemed happy. They did, but afterwards, since Joe looked so peaceful she peeked out the back of the barn to scout around for something that looked like it could be called a "fish house." There was a small cabin in the distance, set back a little from the river. She decided to see what it held.

Wandering along the stream, Lou hearkened to the chirps of birdsong and the low babble of the sluggish river. Unfortunately, though impressively bucolic, Estes seemed a lot less charming now.

God*damn* Shai, that two-faced son of a bitch! He had never struck her as the kind of fucker who would champion her in front of a dirt-faced stable boy only to abandon her in front of rich, classy white folks; the sort of man who might come to Chinatown for the "exotic beauties" and then vote to keep Chinese from yellowing up San Francisco. But, apparently he was.

The tight, angry feeling Lou got in her chest when people shoveled that kind of shit onto her wouldn't unwind, even when she told herself she was happier keeping her own company out in the wind and sunshine than cooped in the longhouse making small talk with assholes. Maybe it was unwillingness to lump Shai in with said assholes. Even if he deserved it. Which he did.

The little house by the river was old and weathered, but solidly built of notched logs. When she came within several paces Lou found cause to suspect this was indeed the "fish house." It reeked appropriately, and wasps buzzed and bounced off the windows and around where the roof met the walls. Brushing a few away, she tried the door. It was unlatched.

The heels of her new boots clanged on the puncheon floor as she inspected the dwelling. It was clean, if bare. The only furniture was a square table with three stumps set around for chairs, and the only color in the room came from an old crazy-quilt thrown over a clothesline, partitioning off another space. The fish smell was overwhelming.

Lou pushed aside the quilt and discovered a little living space. A simple shelf held a jackknife, an old tin can stuffed with rags, a lantern, a ball of heavy twine, another wooden bulldog, and a few other odds and ends. Three pegs had been hammered into the wall: One held a heavy coat, another, an iron skillet. The third was empty. There was also a cot with another old quilt thrown over it, and a small stove with one burner. This must be where she was supposed to bunk, but it looked like someone else was already staying here.

When Lou got back to the barn she found Joe awake and chatting with Griff, who had made himself comfortable on Joe's stool. Two large bulldogs panted across his feet as he whittled on another wooden image in their likeness.

"Well, here's Ching-Chong!" cried the white-bearded man. "Wonderin where you got yourself to! Out building a railroad in my back yard? Haw!"

"I was looking at the fish house," said Lou. "It seems real nice."

"Should be!" said Griff. "That's Joel Estes' old cabin—the first human dwelling ever built here, you know. Well, *proper* human dwelling! Big Joe here won't mind me saying so, right Joe? I'm sure he's plenty grateful to have a real roof over his head instead of a buckskin teepee."

"You know I am, Mr. Evans," said Joe, and Lou tried not to smile when Joe surreptitiously rolled his eyes at her. Griff didn't notice, as he had paused in his carving to retrieve a jug from beside him. Hooking it over his arm, he took a long pull before recorking it.

"Wife won't let me drink in the house," he said, as he stowed the jug without offering to share. "Says it makes me mean. Her withered old face that makes me meaner, but she didn't like that when I told her so! Haw! You've seen her, Ching-Chong—so you know as well as I that if she scowled at a new pair of boots it'd curl the leather off the sole! Tell me I'm wrong!"

Lou did not know what to say to this, as neither agreeing nor disagreeing seemed safe, but Griff had already moved on.

"I tell her she should die and let me take a young wife! But she won't have it. Stays alive to spite me. Haw! Just my luck to be born Christian and unable to take some lithe young sister as a second wife while I keep the old bird around to cook my pancakes, like the Mormons do. Hey now, don't both your savage customs allow for that? That don't sound half-bad to me, though of course without the Christ we'd go to hell for it. You boys keep that in mind before you marry twice, now. Though I heard once that Mussulmen's heaven is naught but a lot of virgins waitin around to get poked by the righteous, which sounds like more my sort of reward than eternal rest and gospel-singing! Haw! But don't tell my wife I said so. She gets mad enough when I squaw around in *this* life—I can't imagine what she'd say if she knew I was planning on it after I've got both feet in the grave 'stead of just the one!"

"I think I'll help our friend here make up his bed before I see to the stock," said Joe. "Sound all right with you, Mr. Evans?"

Griff scowled. "Joe's unnatural for his race, Ching-Chong. Never met another Injun like him in all my days. Most of the time you gotta beat a redskin into giving you an honest day's labor, but not Joe! Fine, fine. Run along. Mrs. Evans'll ring the supper bell so you won't miss no meal."

Lou gathered up her things as quickly as she could. As they trotted out of earshot, Joe clapped her on the back.

"Well, that's Griff for you," he said. "Welcome to Estes Park! What's your real name? Met a few Chinese, but never one called Ching-Chong."

"It's Lou."

"Nice to meet you, Lou," said Joe. "I'm Joe. Happy to have you stay with me. Your bed won't be much, I'm afraid. A quilt on the ground will have to do, but we'll put some hay under it."

"I'm not putting you out, am I? Mr. Evans told me I'd be staying in the fish house, but he didn't mention you were already living there."

"Don't bother me none," said Joe. "I snore louder'n anyone; likely I'll disturb you before the reverse."

"I'm a sound sleeper. But it's your house…"

"What's mine is yours, like I said, it don't bother me to have company. Trust me, you'll enjoy yourself more out here with me than in there with them. Most everyone what gets stuck out in the fish house with me agrees. Best part is, Griff swells up if a wasp so much as looks at him, so you never have to worry about running into him out here."

"I was wondering about the nests."

"Yeah. Hope you don't mind I spirited you away like I did. You were looking pretty wide-eyed back there if you don't mind me saying. I understand. Took me a while to learn to only listen to every fifth word he says. Trick is to heed the pauses for when I need to *uh-huh* or *no, sir.*" Lou laughed at this, and gratefully accepted Joe's offer when he added, "Come on and have a drink with me."

Joe stirred up the coals in the stove and prized up a floorboard, revealing three jugs identical to Griff's. Joe encouraged her to have as much as she liked, but Lou took it easy on the booze. She hoped to ask Joe a few questions about the other Chinese that had come through Estes Park, and she figured it would be best to keep her enquiries discreet. Thus she kept to Shai's story, that she was looking for work up at the San. Joe nodded.

"Hope for your sake Shai don't wait around for Ned and the Coyote," he said, tipping more rotgut down his throat. "Being around them hoity-toits gets to be too much for me and I ain't even traveling with 'em. But once you get on up there you'll be okay. Plenty of your kind to keep you company."

"Yeah?"

"Yeah. Talked to a few Celestials what could speak English, all looking for work like you." Joe took another sip. "Must like it up there. None of them leave."

"Huh," said Lou, thinking she knew of at least one Chinese who had come back down from the mountain. "What did they seem to think they'd be doing?"

"Oh, all kinds of work. Some said farming, tending stock. Others seem to think there's a railroad being built up there, but there's obviously some kind of translation issue goin on there. I felt bad pressing the issue so I didn't let them know, but there's no-way no-how about that."

"No?"

"All shipments come through here. I've seen some machinery and some parts come through, but never enough to build a railroad. Plus, it's illegal, and Dr. P seems the sort to keep things on the up-and-up."

"Yeah?"

"So everyone says. I've never met the man, he was settled up there when I arrived, and hasn't ventured down since. But Shai likes him—for what that's worth," amended Joe, as Lou's expression curdled. "And the cured always have good things to say about his bedside manner. Women always talk about how handsome he is, too."

Lou liked Joe, and was grateful for all he told her, but she felt grumpy just the same. The whiskey had soured her mood rather than the reverse, and when the faint sound of a clanging bell interrupted her next sip she felt unaccountably grumpier.

"Time to go beg our supper from the kindly, Christian hand of Mrs. Evans," said Joe, as he replaced the hooch and the floorboard. "After, we'll get your bed made up."

Lou's ruminations went unnoticed or unremarked upon by Joe as they banked the coals; after mentioning Mrs. Evans he launched into a series of ribald tales about his encounters with her since arriving in Estes Park. Apparently Joe's duties involved not just tending horses, but also the missus—which was just fine by him. He'd traveled around quite a bit during his youth, and during that time acquired a taste for widow-women. Given Mrs. Evans' enthusiasm for his attentions, he claimed it was easy enough to pretend Griff had passed out of her life.

The sun had set while they talked, so moonglow was their only light as they made their way back to the longhouse. When they'd gone about halfway, Lou spied a figure coming through the gloaming towards them. It was Shai. As he drew nearer Lou saw he was carrying a plate of food in one hand and a lantern in the other. He waved when he recognized her. Lou didn't wave back. She was still plenty sore about his shabby treatment of her, and disinclined to welcome him.

"Sorry, Joe," said Shai, as the swinging lantern cast light on their faces, and then his own. "Would've brought your supper too if I'd realized you were together. Here you go, Lou." When he offered her the plate, she took it reluctantly.

"It's all right. Mrs. Evans will be expecting me," said Joe, with a wink at Lou. Lou tried not to notice the increased pep in his stride as he wandered off.

"How was your afternoon?" asked Shai, as they stood there awkwardly.

Shai's casual air infuriated Lou. He wasn't the least bit contrite over snubbing her; didn't seem aware that things weren't the same between them—would never be the same again. He was acting as though everything was the same as it had been that morning.

"Fine," she said. "Just fine."

"You're not cross with me, I hope? I know I should have warned you that Griff's a man set in his—"

"Maybe you could've warned me that the moment you had upstanding citizens to socialize with you'd start to treat me like the dirty chink I am?" Shai looked shocked by her words, eyebrows up nearly at his hairline, but he could go to hell. *Cross with him* indeed. "You should've made me sleep in barns the whole way here; not acted all friendly, like I was a human being you'd care to associate with. At least then I wouldn't have expected anything different from you." She shrugged. "Fool me once, Shai."

"Lou, those people are going to be guests of the San in a few days. Part of my job is to make them feel welcome."

His *be reasonable* tone only infuriated her more. "And what about me? I'm not gonna be a *guest?*"

He looked flustered, as well he might. "I told you it would be easier if you pretended to need a job. Just for the time being. Around Griff, it's just... here, and other places, you must understand that I'm expected to... to play a certain role. But that doesn't mean that I was 'acting friendly' on our trip. You can't really believe that I would…"

"I don't know what to believe, so why don't you tell me if there's anything else I should know about this place. Like—how does your boss compare to Griff? Is he as progressive-minded?"

"I'm sorry about Griff's attitude towards your people, but—"

"My people. You mean the English?"

"Probably so," said Shai mildly. "He hates most everyone with an accent."

Shai was only making her angrier. "Well, I better eat this so I can return my plate. Don't want anyone to think I've stolen it. And I'm sure you'll want to get back to being the welcome-wagon to all those rich nice white folks in there."

"Lou…"

"What?"

Shai looked down at his boots. "Have you… yesterday evening, when I said folks sometimes stayed here in Estes… have you thought about that? For yourself? Even if it was in the fish house, it might do you well, for your illness I mean, and if you gave me your address in San Francisco I could send you some of our double-strength Elixir…"

"You don't want me to come with you?" Lou was tired of feeling hurt and baffled and confused and also tired of holding her stupid dinner plate in front of her. "For goodness' sake, Shai. You could've told me in Cheyenne if Dr. Panacea wouldn't want me at the San. As a patient, I mean. Guess you'd be welcoming me with open arms if I'd come here for coolie work."

"It's not that, not at all." Shai ran his hand through his hair, stripping the leather thong from where it bound the dark wavy locks. He shook out his mane before retying it. "Look—can we talk? Maybe somewhere warmer?"

There was pleading in his eyes. Lou sighed. She pointed at the fish house with her plate of food. "Come on, Joe's like to be gone for a while. We can talk at the cabin."

"Fine," said Shai. "That's fine."

Once inside, Lou grabbed her tobacco pouch, nipped the jug of rotgut from where Joe had stashed it, and settled on one of the stumps. Inspecting her plate, she found it had bread and cheese, some applesauce, and beet pickles. She picked up the bread and cheese and began to munch on it.

Shai did not sit. He paced. It made Lou nervous, so finally she took a swig and resigned herself to making her way through the applesauce and pickles after Shai had said his piece.

"All right all right. What's the rumpus?" she asked, rolling a cigarette. "Don't burst something holding in whatever you want to say."

Shai whirled around and stared at her.

"I know the real reason you're headed to Fountain of Youth."

For the first time in years, Lou choked on her smoke. "Wha-*hu*-what?" she gasped, coughing.

"You're not sick. I've been around the sick enough to know them when I see them."

Lou found she couldn't move, couldn't speak. What had she done to clue Shai in to her real purpose?

A coyote howled outside somewhere and she startled, the spell broken.

"Uh," she said.

"I'm not angry. We've gotten too big. Too famous. Of course people would be curious. But... I like you, Lou. A lot. More than I've liked anyone, in a long, long time. At first, I thought that it would be easy to just... but after getting to know you I *can't*. I don't care," he said, maybe talking to himself, and then, more fiercely, "I don't care! Believe me when I tell you, Lou, that if you go on to Fountain of Youth, you will be putting yourself into nothing less than mortal peril—and for no reason."

Lou wanted to ask more directly about this "mortal peril," but she was too curious to know what Shai thought she was up to. "What do you mean, no reason?"

"There's no formula."

Lou paused to consider this, and still couldn't puzzle out Shai's angle. "Huh?"

Shai sighed. "I know it's hard to believe, but our Elixir of Life has only one ingredient. Well, two if you count water. But what makes it work—the substance that makes it so potent—there's only a little in the world, and I have all of it."

This was not anything Lou had expected when he claimed to have figured her out. Easy enough to play along with, though. "How'd you know?"

"You gave yourself away when you mentioned your mother was an apothecary." The dike of Lou's confusion broke, flooding her mind with understanding. Her secret was safe—she'd sent him fishing after a red herring without even realizing it. Well, glory fucking be, she'd gone and done *something* right. Though it pained her somewhere deep down inside to be even more false to Shai, the time for snowball fights and drinking under the stars was over.

And anyways, he'd been the one to end it before it had to end.

"That's disappointing, but I do appreciate you telling me," said Lou, all the while trying to come up with a plausible reason for still wanting to continue on up to the San. "Maybe I could convince you to gimme some of the real deal for my trouble, though? I know I said I was low on cash, but—"

"No."

"All right. Too bad for me. But, at least I have a nice vacation ahead of me to look forward to. I'm not gonna turn around and go home after coming all this way."

"Lou, listen! You have no idea how dangerous the San will be for you."

"I think I can handle a few weeks of healthy living." Lou forced a chuckle. "I'll allow enemas frighten me a bit, but you make it sound—"

"If you know you will fail at your task, why do you still want to go?

Lou was surprised how hard Shai was taking her stubbornness. "If I'm not poking around looking for a formula that doesn't exist, what could be the harm?"

Shai swore and kicked open the door, storming off into the night before she could say a word. Lou sat for a moment, shocked, then grabbed her duster. Tucking her LeMat into the deepest pocket she ran out after him. There was a mystery at the heart of Shai's loss of control and she aimed to find out what it was.

She spied a shadow heading upstream, flitting along the creekbank. Following him at a distance, she kept apace as he hiked at a stern clip for maybe half an hour. The big bright moon above them cast strange colorless shadows everywhere. Birds called from the bushes. Lou wished she'd brought the lantern with her, the forest rimming the edges of the valley was impenetrably dark, and several times Lou thought she saw eyes glinting at her from behind trees.

The third time she glanced away, when she looked back, Shai had disappeared from her sight. Lou swore under her breath, annoyed to have lost her quarry so easily. She paused, looking around, but a brief flare of a match, far higher than a man's height, showed her where he'd gone. She crept closer, and saw he was perched on a large rock that jutted out over the river.

"I see you," he called. "You're not very stealthy. I could shoot you from where I'm sitting, you know."

"With what?" she said, trying to sound brave. "I know you favor a blade, and I don't think even you're good enough to slit my throat from up there."

The hairs on Lou's neck stood up when he didn't respond. Then she heard him sigh.

"I wouldn't anyways."

Lou believed him. The look in his eyes when she'd caught him staring at her on the wagon-ride still haunted her—and as annoyed as she still was over what had happened back in the lodge with Griff, she understood why he'd done it. After all, she'd been doing something close to the same thing, treating him like a friend while keeping her responsibilities first and foremost in mind.

The truth was, sometimes you had to do your job, even if it sucked.

She clambered up beside him, deciding to trust him. It seemed like it would be a dangerous scrabble even during daylight, the crazy bastard, but she got up safely, only barking one shin during the climb. Once she was up she settled in beside him. They sat in silence for a long time, listening to the river, and the wind. Just as Lou was about to ask what the hell they were doing, freezing their asses off on this big stupid rock, Shai opened up his tobacco pouch.

"Want some?"

It was the first time he'd offered. Lou shook her head.

"Got my own shag," she said, patting her pocket. "Never cared for pipes."

"This isn't tobacco." Shai chuckled. "You thought... have you never smoked hasheesh?"

"That's hasheesh?"

"Didn't you notice the smell?"

"Thought it was some kind of funny fop's—I mean *dandy's* tobacco."

Shai crumbled a lump of resin with his fingers into the bowl of his pipe, lit it, and took a long drag. Scooting around to face her, he asked, "So did you want to try it?" without exhaling.

As kids, she and Bo had once nipped a hit off of an opium pipe. Neither had cared for the vomiting, constipation, or hours of floaty, discombobulated languidness that followed. But Shai had never seemed so out of his skull as the opium-smokers she'd known; indeed, she'd never suspected he was high…

"Sure," she said, turning towards him. "Why not?"

Shai ducked forward and pressed his open lips to hers. Lou quickly figured out what he was doing and tried not to flinch away. Inhaling slowly, she accepted the smoke from his body into hers.

"Hold it in your lungs," he advised, and then took another hit.

Lou exhaled, wondering if that exchange counted as her first kiss. She decided no, it most assuredly did not.

"Like it?"

"Dunno," she said. She felt funny all over, sad and light-headed and crazy and hot and tingly, but that might have been the cardamom and smoke taste of Shai's mouth that still lingered on her lips.

"Maybe you need more?"

"Let me try it the way you do it," she said.

"Inhale slowly," he cautioned her. "I gave it to you like I did so it wouldn't be as fierce on your lungs."

Lou tried to execute the maneuver without coughing, but failed. It was thick smoke, thicker than she'd expected even when she'd seen in the matchlight that the black substance bubbled rather than burned.

Shai patted her gently on the back. "Good try!"

"And this makes you high, like opium?" she asked, wiping her watering eyes.

"No… more like being drunk, but nicer. I think so, anyways."

Lou began to feel the hash a bit, a pleasant pressure-fog in her mind, just as Shai was finishing up a third hit. Lou accepted the pipe when he passed it to her.

"I didn't mean to make you so mad," she said, before trying to smoke again.

"I know," he said, as she lit the pipe again. "I just really don't want you to come to Fountain of Youth."

Lou coughed for a while before gasping, "Why?"

"I'm trying to protect you."

"I can handle myself."

"No," said Shai. "You can't."

Something in his tone gave Lou pause. "What exactly do you think you're protecting me from?"

Shai took another long hit off his pipe. "More go up than come down from the mountain."

"Well, it's a sanatorium," said Lou slowly. "Sick people have been known to die on occasion, right? I'm not ill, as you already deduced, so what could possibly be so dangerous? Maybe it's your hasheesh, but right now I'm not exactly quaking in my boots at the thought of a handful of lungers and their doctor."

Shai didn't speak for such a long time that Lou wondered if he'd fallen asleep. She certainly felt drowsy enough, and he'd been hitting the pipe a lot harder than her.

Then he sighed. "You said you were good at keeping secrets. What about secrets more serious than pinching some coffee on a cold afternoon?"

Probably it would turn out that Dr. Panacea was exploiting the Chinese laborers he was luring to the San. Big surprise there. Still, best to play along…

"I promise."

Shai took a deep breath. "Lou, how old do you think I am?"

Lou shrugged. "Nineteen? Twenty?"

"I am three hundred and seventy-three years old."

Something about Shai's tone made her believe this outlandish claim, absolutely, immediately. She shivered. A gust of wind made the moonlit meadow-grass across the river ripple and gleam like the choppy waters of the San Francisco Bay. Suddenly she felt very, very far from home.

"How?" she asked.

He took a deep breath. "Let me tell you," he said, and then he did.

Chapter Nine

You must forgive me, Lou, if this story, *my* story, sounds rough and unpolished. I've never told it before. For obvious reasons I've had to keep the details of my life a secret. But I need you to understand why you must not go on to Fountain of Youth, and if to convince you of that I must betray myself, and others, then so be it.

Close to four hundred years ago I was born in Marrakech, in the Jewish ghetto in Tangier. Recent immigrants—my family left Spain when my mother was still pregnant with me—they were very poor. Given that more of us were arriving all the time, driven out by King Ferdinand and his queen, the resources of that community were already stretched thin. Some left for the country, to scratch a living from the flinty earth, but my parents had no knowledge of farming. They had both been city-dwellers all their lives, and so they decided to stay.

They hated it, being poor I mean. They never became accustomed to it, having both grown up knowing an affluence I could scarce imagine when I was still a child. Meat at most meals, fine clothing, servants… but of course, they'd lost their fortune after Granada was seized and made as dark and dangerous as the rest of Inquisitional Spain.

As for me, I didn't much care, having never known any other way of living. Thus I spent my youth relatively happy, much as any other urchin might, begging for coin and stealing food from street vendors when I wasn't helping with chores. But my world was larger than it might have been. My parents were well-educated, and passed what they could on to me and my siblings when they had the time. By the time I was nine I could read Hebrew fluently, and Greek and Latin competently; I could speak Spanish as well as any Spaniard, and Arabic as naturally as a Moor. I never expected those hours spent learning languages would serve me so well in life, but they have.

Everything changed when I was around... ten or eleven, I think, I cannot recall my exact age. My parents... you will think ill of them, perhaps, but they did what they felt they had to. Their fortune had not much increased over the years but their number of children had. They told me I would be a servant, that I was going to work for someone else for a little while, and they promised me that if I didn't cry and did everything he asked of me I would be able to come home again soon.

I realized quickly enough that they'd lied, and the truth was they had sold me, and I was now a slave. I wasn't a stupid child, given that I was never paid a wage nor allowed to visit my parents even when I was desperately homesick, I figured it out quickly enough.

Not that I was homesick for very long. That sort of sensation fades quickly in the young, I suppose, especially after one's life improves so dramatically over a short time—and when it becomes evident that one is not missed in return.

My new master was an older man, closer to fifty than forty, but healthy and strong and *rich*. I didn't know him, and I have no notion of how my parents knew him, or came to sell me to him, or how much he paid for me. He never told me, but I got the impression the money substantially eased my family's situation. Though it sounds funny, I am actually glad of that. I'm not one to hold a grudge. I never have been.

He was an interesting fellow, my master. The day he came for me, as we drove in his coach to his bungalow on the outskirts of the city, he told me that he was a natural philosopher by trade. He'd lived all over the world, but had settled for the last few years in Tangier. It's funny how perfectly I remember that ride... I had been afraid he would be harsh with me, but instead he offered me clusters of green grapes, chunks of pomegranate, cups of sweet wine, little pipes full of kief. I tried it all, being that I was unfamiliar with luxury but curious by nature. Some children would have wept and carried on, refused any comforts out of spite, but not me. Self-denial has never been my way.

Nor was it my master's, I soon saw. His house was grand, full of fine furniture, ornamented with crystal and gold and wide, leaded glass windows. There was a fountain in the courtyard, and songbirds in silver cages brought life to the otherwise-quiet rooms. There was a library full of interesting books, and a kitchen full of delicious things to eat.

And me. I was there. When I first saw the place—me in my filthy rags, lice in my hair—I assumed I had been brought there to do the most onerous tasks, cleaning the dirtiest things, running errands in the street. Yet when I said this aloud, my master told me my burdens would be light—and he, unlike my parents, was not lying. I was actually *pampered,* if you can believe it, and given everything I wanted. Everything except my freedom.

That part was hard on me at first. I was used to doing whatever I liked, wherever and whenever I liked, but now I was kept indoors unless someone went out with me, and then always under the strictest supervision. You frown, I know it sounds terrible, but my confinement was not long onerous to me. If at any point I became restless I was given hasheesh to smoke, which calmed me and granted me perspective. But actually, I was rarely restless. I had plenty to keep me busy. Given that I could read, I assisted my master with his researches, fetching books and other things, and since I had a decent enough hand I even wrote some of his less personal correspondence for him.

That was it, that was all I had to do. I actually asked for more responsibilities as the years wore on, but was denied. As I said, my master was a natural philosopher—a scientist—but I came to find out that was not *all* he was. His consuming passion was alchemy, as it turned out. He had amassed all kinds of fabulous knowledge during his life, and as years—centuries, actually—had passed since he had managed to create the fabled elixir of life, he had used his immortality to seek answers to yet more esoteric questions.

But he wouldn't tell *me* any of those answers. Or even the questions, really. I was not his apprentice, and while I was quick enough to steal food from the kitchens or extra hasheesh from his supplies, I did not dare touch his notes or more outré possessions, even when he was absent from home for long periods of time.

Why? Oh, of course. I told you this story would be ill told, and here I've failed to mention the other two individuals who also dwelt in that bunga-low. Which is funny, as they're the reason we lived at the edge of the city, and were so secretive when venturing forth into Tangier proper. Then as now what the world claims to be *monstrous* is forced to live on the outskirts of civilization, secretly, and in perpetual fear of detection.

Four of us made up that household, counting myself—me, my master, his lover, and his manservant, and it was the two latter who had cause to worry over the repercussions of simply existing… though to be fair, if their presence had ever been discovered, likely my master and I would have been hanged for the crime of harboring them. My master's lover was a Jinn, an ifreet actually. She mostly dwelt in the ether in her natural fiery form, but would manifest on our plane to tryst with him. They had been involved for over a hundred years, as I understood it. He loved her; I was terrified of her. She and I rarely spoke, but whenever I was contrary she would transmute into flame and threaten to burn me. I never crossed her—well, except the once. I shall come to that.

As for my master's manservant, he had even more to lose, for unlike the ifreet he couldn't disappear at will if anyone took an interest in him. He was a kind of vampire—ah, I see you know the word, and so you will understand why I kept my distance for a long time. Like many of them, he was highly allergic to sunlight, and was very strong and fast. He also fed on human blood… but in spite of that, I came to trust him.

I think it was his smile…. Lazarus—that was his name—had a way of smiling at me from under his thick curly mustache that convinced me he meant me no harm. Really, I mean it! It didn't hurt that he was so hand-some. His soft skin was such a lovely olive shade, he had a long, straight nose, and such *eyes!* Enormous—vast hazel pools, calmly intelligent, but with a calculating look that suggested humor… and, yes, a certain devious-ness.

I spent perhaps a year too afraid to speak to him much, but when I finally trusted that he would obey our master and not feed upon me I came to know him better—and like him. Lazarus was the most interesting person I'd ever met, save for my master, and also the best traveled. He told me had been born in a city called Bucharest, north of the Ottoman empire. He'd been a king, a great leader and freedom fighter, but he'd died in a conflict and was now a mere slave to the man who had returned him to life. This tale, when I heard it, enthralled me—I have always possessed a romantic turn of mind—and helped me get over the rest of my fear of him.

It was nice having another person to talk to, after keeping to myself for so long, and once we became friendly we discovered that we shared many things... a love of languages ancient and modern, for example, philosophy... the natural sciences. He also secretly encouraged my interest in the martial arts, which had always fascinated me though I had never been allowed to learn them. My master said it was nothing I need trouble myself about, but Lazarus had been longing for someone to fence with for decades so he taught me swordplay in secret.

You can imagine what happened next. Children do grow older. I was, I think, fourteen, when I realized I was in love. I kept it from him, and from our master of course, but it was impossible to hide my feelings completely. He brightened my life. And sometimes, when we were alone, I sensed he had feelings for me that went beyond friendship. That perplexed me, for while I began dropping hints with all the subtlety of a fourteen-year-old he never laid a hand on me, or gave me the slightest sign he recognized my adoration for what it was. It was so frustrating I cried myself to sleep many nights, but he was a glacier, a mountain—cold, remote, and utterly beyond my ability to move. Sometimes I wondered if he was able to make love, being undead—but the one time I worked up enough courage to ask him, he refused to answer my question and hurried from the room.

This stalemate lasted for... it's funny, it must have been less than two years, and yet at the time it felt like a lifetime. Ah, youth.

Anyways, things changed suddenly, as they tend to do. Well, I suppose there was *some* warning. I'd noticed the nature of my master's research had shifted, for I was still fetching his daily stacks of books. While I was wet behind the ears in many ways, I wasn't *stupid*. I perceived he was getting ready for something, and often when I came upon him with his ifreet lover they would fall silent, and that silence, along with the way they looked at me while acting too innocent, told me they had been speaking of something concerning my person.

So I began spying. I had the queer feeling it was worth the risk. Being naturally a quiet, nimble child, I had many times gone unnoticed by my master when he was bustling, preoccupied, around his dwelling, and his laboratory. At first I heard nothing other than muttered conversations

about "chrysopoeia of the body," "going beyond the spheres of known elements," and other things I could not understand—but my patience was
eventually rewarded.

I had been listening in on their lovemaking one night, which I had used
to do anyways out of natural curiosity, but more recently because they often
spoke of their plans during the act of love. Lazarus discovered me just as
they were finishing. He looked very angry to find me doing such a thing,
but before he could scold me I motioned for him to be silent. Something
about my manner must have convinced him, so we both leaned in to hear
my master remark that he was excited about the prospect of intercourse
with his lover while she was in her fire form.

But will you really be able to go through with it? she asked him. *You have
grown fond of your slave, don't deny it.*

I am fonder of you, he replied. *I have never allowed myself to grow too attached, knowing what must be. Without a virgin sacrifice, I cannot transmute
myself into an unburnable state.*

I looked at Lazarus, horrified, and when he turned to me I saw my expression mirrored in his own. He took my hand into his and squeezed it.

I don't want to die, I whispered.

You won't, he whispered back. *I won't let him kill you.*

In spite of his reassurances I despaired. To my mind, there was nothing
that could be done to prevent this calamity. Years of isolation had made me
fearful of the outside world; I could not imagine running away. If I did,
where would I go? Surely my family had moved, and it seemed all too likely
that anyone who'd known me as a child would fail to recognize me now. I
knew nothing of the city, nothing of the world beyond.

This is my home, I said. *I have nowhere else to go.*

We'll run away together, he declared, and he drew me into his arms to kiss
me for the first time.

Even in that bleak moment my heart soared. I had ceased to dream of
the possibility that Lazarus would ever return my affections, yet my feelings
for him had never faltered. Thus I told him what I had wanted to say for
some time, that I loved him, and would put my trust in him, following him
wherever he wanted to go. I promised him in the solemnest language that if
he helped me escape, for as long as he wanted me, I would be his.

Not knowing how long we had before the planned sacrifice, we acted quickly. The moment the ifreet disappeared into the ether Lazarus burst into our master's bedroom and fell upon him where he lay naked on his bed. He screamed, but there was no one to hear him; writhed, but there was no way he could overpower a vampire. He died with Lazarus' teeth in his throat, his own blood soaking into his fine sheets.

It was the first time I'd watched Lazarus feed, and while the gore and spurting blood horrified me, I refused to look away. It was part of who he was, and to love someone you must love every part of them.

Not that it was really that easy for me. I had come to look upon my master as a kind of surrogate father... but, as I told myself at the time, his death was the result of his own scheming. I was not the one who betrayed him.

We fled that very night, knowing once my master's consort discovered our treachery she would surely seek revenge. We took only what we could carry. I had little I cared to bring, other than money—a few books, clothes, and hasheesh; Lazarus had to leave behind more, a sacrifice he said he was willing to make for me, though it was painful for him. Before we left, however, we took care to steal all of my master's remaining elixir of life. It was his custom to make the potion in large batches, so we had more than a few jars to split between our packs. We took it all, for neither of us knew how to make more. I was (and still am) mortal—and even then I had no wish to die. Why should I, when I could remain young and healthy forever?

Looking back now, it really was almost too easy. After quitting the house we woke a boatman and bribed him to take us across the strait of Gibraltar. I was afraid of Spain, having heard so much about it from my parents when I was young, but we had few other choices. I could translate for Lazarus until he picked up some Spanish, or we escaped into another country. And most importantly, if the Jinn sought us her abilities would be thwarted by water.

I remember how my heart pounded that night, as we urged the boatman to row faster and faster, then making landfall and racing against the dawn to secure lodgings where Lazarus could hide from the sun. But we managed it. We have always managed well together. The next night, at dusk, we bought provisions and began wandering northward, all the while debating the merits of France or England as possible destinations. In the end, however, we ended up staying in Spain for longer than we anticipated.

What happed was this: one evening, while eating supper in a tavern some miles south of Seville we spied a young nobleman sitting apart from his friends, frowning into his garnacha. Lazarus has always been able to gain the confidence of strangers with uncanny ease, so, thinking that for providing a sympathetic ear we might be able to replenish our dwindling funds, he gambled on buying the sad-faced youth a fresh drink in exchange for his story. I translated what he could not understand.

Alonzo Dionisio Gabriel de Buitre was, as we suspected, from a noble family—but one long fallen out of favor. His father, looking to impress the king, had volunteered young Alonzo for a voyage to the New World, to be part of an envoy to Puerto Rico—or was it called San Juan Bautista, then? I can't recall. Anyhow, once there, Alonzo's plan was to avoid further exploration unless it was unavoidable. He was supposed to ingratiate himself with the government and try to buy land, manage a gold mine, anything, and send the money back home. And yet, he seemed unhappy about his chance to gain wealth and glory.

Lazarus then asked, *What would you do if you didn't have to go?*

The youth replied, *I would buy myself a parcel of farmland far from anyone who might know me, and I would marry a wide-hipped lady who would bear me sons and make excellent cheese. And every July twenty-fifth I would buy a fine wax candle and dedicate its light to Saint Christopher, for his mercy.*

You know, I still remember the dreamy look on the young man's face as he spoke.

I wish I could say that Lazarus and I helped that young man in some way... and maybe, if he really was that unhappy, then... I'll stop. You're upset. I cannot blame you. But, Lou, we were so desperate it seemed only prudent to lure Alonzo away from the inn, take everything he had—including his life—and the next morning tell his friends that after a wild night of drinking with us the young man had absconded with all he had in order to pursue his dearest wish.

And in the end, it was more than prudent. It saved us.

We took more than Alonzo Dionisio Gabriel de Buitre's money and clothing and jewels. We took his *idea*. Well, not the wide-hipped lady who made cheese part, nor the candle to Saint Christopher, but certainly living obscurely and frugally to deflect attention from ourselves. Who would ever think a vampire would settle in one of the sunniest areas in Europe?

It's funny, after resisting the idea so much, we were really quite happy in

Spain. We took a fine house in a busy port city in order to always have a high turnover of locals for Lazarus to feed upon, and after we concocted a story about him being an invalid with no tolerance for heat and sunshine we were even accepted into society. Lazarus can eat a little human food when he must, so we hosted and went to dinner parties and dances and fairs and even midnight mass on Christmas.

But eventually people began to notice how neither of us seemed to age, so we moved, and then moved again when the same thing happened. That was hard on us, but at the same time, it was always nice to meet new people and make new friends, human and otherwise. Yes, we met others like us—more or less—over the years, and we learned much from them. Like what? Oh... like, for example, how Lazarus could feed without killing his victim. That was a fortunate piece of information, for after learning the trick of it he could use me to sustain himself during lean times. The elixir of life heals any and all wounds he gives me, so we can live in perfect symbiosis when he cannot obtain more substantial nourishment.

But I digress. Eventually we moved to France, and then England. We enjoyed that country more than any other, and stayed there longer than usual, once even daring to present ourselves as foreign nobility. We certainly had the money for it by then. Being able to invest long-term has its rewards...

But we could never settle. Eventually we thought it prudent to move to the New World, and that actually turned out to be the best decision we ever made. Jamaica in the eighteenth century was fashionable and profitable, and the blind eye turned by the world towards slave mortality protected Lazarus' feeding habits—as it did in Georgia when we moved there. A neighbor's daughter had fallen in love with me, and after I refused her advances she claimed that I had jilted and deflowered her. There was no truth to the rumor, but the scandal was enough to force us to Stateside.

We might still be living on that small farm in Georgia if not for the war. That was a miscalculation on our part. After centuries of seeing the way humans in power treat those different from themselves, such as the Indian, or the Negro, or the monster—and after seeing also, the way humans defend their property, we never even considered the prospect of a Union victory. The newspapers had all predicted a victory for the Secessionists.

Then came the news that Lincoln had forged an alliance with the bears, and that was that. It was a bad time for us, the first time in centuries we'd had to face the prospect of financial ruin. We had, over the years, made loans to our friends, and too many of them could only pay us back in worthless Confederate dollars. No trains were running, we had eaten most of what we'd stored, and as for the future… we could not possibly operate a farm with free workers. Thus, when our lawyer told us that only if we sold our farm could we escape bankruptcy, it was once again time to move on. We sold what we could, machinery, lumber, furniture… we couldn't sell our slaves, of course. Lazarus had to eat them quickly, which was not how he usually fed, but they had started trying to run off what with the whispers of Emancipation.

It was a dire time indeed, but Lazarus once again saved us, for it was he who hit on the plan that allowed us to regain at least a small part of our fortune. A common mountebank had come by our plantation house one morning, hoping to sell us some snake oil. Lazarus ate him; it had been weeks since we buried the last of our slaves and he was desperate at that point… but when we were looking over the props the quack had with him, hoping to find some money or food, it all became clear to him.

We would become snake-oil salesmen! We still had a supply of the elixir of life; I had, over the years, experimented in diluting it to stretch our reserves, which is why I have aged over the centuries, but only a little. Because of that, we already knew that extremely diluted elixir *repairs* the body, but does not *sustain* it. It was perfect. Most of the patent-medicines out there are just booze, or laudanum, or some treacherous combination of the two. But not ours. All it took was creating a few legends surrounding the amazing curative prowess of a certain "Dr. Lazarus Panacea" and his Elixir of Life. Good names for a quacksalver and his product, you must admit.

Though we had traveled much during our lives, transience was new to us. We adjusted, however, and made good money hawking our Elixir. Still, constantly being on the move was too dangerous a lifestyle. We needed a permanent residence, and preferably one where Lazarus' food would come to him. As we'd done good work establishing the identity of "Dr. Panacea" we settled on establishing a sanatorium, a haven for the sickly, where any deaths that might occur would not be seen as unusual. The only question was where to do it. We wanted a location remote enough that we could go unmolested but still do decent business.

Luck found us on the road to Denver, when we encountered a stopped caravan. Imagine our surprise when we realized the stagecoach belonged to, of all people, the most important of the Colorado Territory bears, a big, grey-muzzled fellow called Blackclaw. You'll have seen his name in the papers, but this was before he engineered all those legislative successes for bearkind as a whole, not just his particular tribe.

He'd taken ill on the road; Lazarus cured him with Elixir and we got to chatting. Lazarus mentioned our interest in settling down… and, well.…

Blackclaw knew Lazarus for what he was—or rather, knew he was not human, and therefore he could be trusted. The kinship of predators perhaps, or maybe just a feeling of mutual dissatisfaction at living among humans. Whatever it was, he leased us the land where we founded Fountain of Youth.

With Dr. Panacea's reputation, the natural beauty of the landscape, and the grace of the bears, we seemed in a perfect position to live comfortably… yet the debacle with the Transcontinental was, I confess, a terrible setback in terms of getting enough people up to Fountain of Youth to keep Lazarus healthy. And to the San remaining financially viable, for that matter, what with our lease. We've needed to continue to supplement our income with selling the Elixir, which of course means less for me when all is said and done… but I have hopes that soon enough we shall be able to dispense with both endeavors entirely. We are making plans to enter another line of business entirely—one that does not require what sustains me to sustain itself.

So that is my tale. I assume you understand now why you must not come with me to the San. I like you, Lou. More than I have ever liked a human, I believe. I see myself in you—well, myself long ago. You are so deliciously innocent, so bold and young and fresh. I felt there was something about you I couldn't understand when I first saw you in the train carriage, and after you told me about your childhood it just confirmed that you and I are kindred spirits. Outsiders both, pariahs undeserving of the scorn we have encountered.

Even so, initially I had no qualms about bringing you up to the San. I've done it before, with other nosy troublemakers, and you were frightfully easy to trick. I've rarely had someone play into my hands so willingly. Hoodwinking you into coming with me, alone, away anyone you might ask for help… it was funny, especially because you were so confident you were pulling one over on *me!* I mean, weren't you?

Well, regardless, I find I cannot go through with it—taking you to

Lazarus, I mean. I have come to regard dispatching people for the sake of my lover a necessary evil; I believe he deserves to live as much as any other. But I would spare you if I could. Please, Lou. Don't go any further along the path to death. You will take it to its end one day, as all—well, most—must. But I would delay the inevitable as long as possible.

Chapter Ten

Lou was foggy-headed from the hasheesh and confounded for any number of reasons. She had no idea what to say, but she knew she had to say *something*. It was just too incredible—incredibly stupid more like—that an hour or so ago she'd been wondering if Shai had inadvertently given her her first kiss; that yesterday afternoon she'd gone and knocked his hat off with a goddamn snowball to try to deter what she'd thought had been his romantic inclinations. Well, that would teach her not to go putting on airs—here she'd been fretting over him having a crush on her and all the while he'd been buttering her up so she'd be extra-tasty for his vampire boyfriend.

"Lou?" Shai's voice was still Shai's voice, sweet, soft, and warm. He was staring at her with anxious hope and moonlight reflected in those huge, beautiful eyes of his.

"Uh," she said.

"I know the whole thing must sound so outlandish…"

"I believe you."

"And?" Shai knocked out his pipe and began to repack it for the… Lou had lost count of how many times. She decided not to smoke anymore. The night was turning out to be plenty crazy enough already.

"And…" Lou, grasping at straws, decided to go for the biggest thing that had bothered her ever since Shai had mentioned it in passing. "So he—Dr.

Panacea, I mean—he can eat human food? But just… doesn't?"

Shai paused in his hasheesh-crumbling and looked at her. "It's not quite so simple as that," he said slowly.

"Oh," said Lou. "I thought you said—"

Shai interrupted her with an annoyed harrumph. "I tell you my life's story and *that's* what you have to say?"

"Well, I mean…" Lou shrugged. "It's just kind of a shock, just finding out the place I'm heading is run by some monster inclined to—"

"Monster!"

"Sorry," said Lou, and she bit her lip. She needed to get it together, and the hash-fog in her brain certainly wasn't helping matters. "I just, I mean… right? If you hadn't told me…"

"But I did!"

"And you're going to go tell all those people back at the lodge, too?"

"No," said Shai. "And you're not, either."

Lou shook her head *no* quickly. Before that very moment she'd never actually heard someone use a "threatening" tone of voice, not really; there had been murder in Shai's words, and she remembered how the blood had smelled when it came gushing out of that young road agent's neck that night on the prairie. It seemed an age ago, though it had only been a few days.

"I told you I could keep a secret," she said, trying to sound casual about it, not like he'd genuinely spooked her out, which was closer to the truth. "I only meant that I'm real glad you liked me enough to tell me. I feel bad for those folk back at the lodge. Is that so strange? I mean, they don't know what they're in for. They signed up to get healed, not murdered."

"Murdered!"

Lou was beginning to get annoyed by Shai's incredulity, but that was actually helping clear her mind a little. "Yeah, *murdered*. Let's call things what they are while we're being all honest and sincere with one another."

"So you consider someone who eats what he must to stay alive a murderer. You're not vegetarian; are *you* a murderer?"

Lou frowned. "Neither am I a cannibal."

"I see all meat the same way," said Shai. "So, who's the hypocrite? You or me?"

"You can't be serious!"

"I wonder how a pig would feel about your ethics."

Lou laughed at that. "Probably like I was a giant asshole! And, you know, if a pig talked to me about it, I'd likely concede he had a case—if only to be polite."

"And you think your 'feeling bad' would make a difference to that pig on butchering day?" Shai was trembling. Lou's fingers itched, she wanted to be holding her LeMat, just in case. She knew Shai was one dangerous bastard, but she'd assumed he possessed some sort of moral compass. She wouldn't make that mistake again. "I told you about—about everything—because I thought you would understand," he said. "When you told me about growing up in Chinatown, a pariah—"

"Hey, hold up. You've used that word twice now, but really—"

Shai didn't seem to notice she'd interrupted him. "I admired how you chose to be what you are, instead of letting others define you. But here I open up to you only to find out you're the same as everyone else!"

"What the hell." Shai was really pissing her off now, telling her she was a hypocrite when he didn't have a leg to stand on in that regard. "How dare you? Especially after this afternoon? The way you kicked me off your shoe like a turd in front of Griff and the rest? *Fuck* you, Shai. Your back's up because I don't feel bad for you? Well, from where I sit, it sounds to me like you've got a pretty good thing going. Better than most, at any rate."

Shai had the gall to look hurt, like she'd slapped him across the mouth with her words. "Were we to reveal ourselves, we would have no rights. No safety. No legal ability to hold property. Nothing. We—people like Lazarus, and myself, and all the other people in this world that are called monsters, we are voiceless," he said, in wracked tones. "We live on the fringe of human society, hunted, reviled, feared—"

"You can vote," said Lou. "I can't."

"Well, yes, I can vote, yes, but—"

"And so could Lazarus. If the polls stayed open after dark, I guess. That's more than plenty have. More than any of your slaves did, before they got munched."

"Are you just refusing to see my point? What is a vote, Lou, when no one represents your interests? No one would ever think of putting a farmer in jail for slaughtering an old hog for his winter's hams and bacon, yet if anyone had seen the inside of the smokehouse on our plantation... are you all right?"

Lou attempted to settle her gorge by inhaling a deep, long, slow breath of cold air through her nose and out through her mouth. "I'm not refusing to see your point."

"I thought you of all people would understand what it's like to be marginalized and estranged—to try to live peacefully in a world that regards you as something disgusting."

"Peacefully, huh?"

"As peacefully as we can! He must eat, and we have never found anything else that sustains him perfectly, I assure you," said Shai. "Have you seen someone with pernicious anemia? Rickets? Look here," he said, rolling back his sleeve. His translucent, terracotta skin shone in the moonlight. "Touch my arm—do you feel that?" Lou recoiled at the feel of his scar-pebbled wrist. Shai looked off into the night, his eyes glistening with tears. Then he said quietly, "Do you think I would not, if I could, sate all his appetites myself?"

The question creeped Lou out big-time, but she sensed it was rhetorical so she shrugged noncommittally.

"Well, I would," snapped Shai.

"Okay, okay. Just—look. I'm human, and so are you," she said, wondering why she felt like she was pleading with him. "Longer-lived than most, but still human. Can't you see why I might be a mite perturbed by your casual attitude toward... you know? Eating people? People like me?"

"No. I can't." Shai stood, dusting off his trouser seat. Lou guessed this meant their conversation was coming to an end. When he offered her a hand up, she knew for sure. "But then again, I live in a world where I've been told almost all my life that I am evil; that my lover is an abomination. Being who I am is enough to get me killed. And not just killed—killed with the government's thank-you, especially if the person in question hacks me to pieces and brings my parts in for a bounty. Which, of course, they deserve as they've gone and sacrificed yet another monster on the altar of manifest destiny, or social stability, or whatever reason for persecuting us is currently in fashion. Or did you not know it was possible to make quite a tidy bit of money as an itinerant monster-hunter?"

For the first time in her life Lou felt slightly ashamed of herself for being a psychopomp. Shai's notion that monsters—that the *undead* should be granted equal rights to the living, allowed to co-exist despite their unnaturalness... every part of her rebelled against that idea. Indeed, upon hearing that Fountain of Youth was being run by a vampire, Lou had automatically added that to her list of things she needed to take care of up at the San. Now she wasn't so sure what she should do, a new sensation for her, at least when it came to the improperly deceased. She'd seen so much havoc wrought by ghosts, shades, geung si, and their like that it was difficult for her to feel any empathy for them at all, especially when she felt the faint throb of healed-over patches of spirit-burn all over her body.

Frowning, she rubbed at her wrist where her most recent burn still itched. It nagged at her—what he'd said, the stuff about living in a world where being yourself was enough to get you killed, that whole thing about people getting swept to the side when they made society uncomfortable... didn't she know just a little about that? After all, what the hell was she even doing out here except investigating the disappearance of a bunch of Chinamen whose deaths would likely please more than they'd trouble? And really, it wasn't like she could get up on a high horse about someone hiding as some-thing they weren't so they could have an easier time of it. She knew a little about that, too.

Maybe Shai was right, and they weren't so very different. Maybe she should be able to see where he was coming from. More than see—maybe she should understand, or even agree.

"All right," she said heavily. "I guess you've got your points. It's just... hard for me."

"If he is compelled to look straight at the light, will he not feel a pain in his eyes?" murmured Shai.

"What's that?"

"Nothing. Just a line from something I was reading."

Lou guessed it was the lateness of the hour and feeling more than a little overwhelmed that made the walk back to the fish house seem like it took a hell of a lot longer than it had going out. When at last they arrived, no light burned in the window, and the faint sound of snoring could be heard ema-nating from within. Lou was hoping to soon add her own to the cacophony.

"So long, Lou," Shai's voice was so soft she had to strain to hear him. "I wish... I wish we could have parted on friendlier terms."

"Parted?" It sounded like Shai was saying something more significant than just an average good night. "I'll see you tomorrow, won't I?"

"I've decided to head up tomorrow. Early."

"Not without me, you're not!" Their conversation aside, she still had to find those missing Chinese workers. As to the big thing she couldn't think about right now—doing what a psychopomp did when they came in contact with a vampire—she'd figure that out later.

"You can't still want to go up to the San?"

"Why not?" Lou shrugged in what she hoped was a nonchalant manner. "It's not like I'll be trying to steal your formula; it doesn't exist. So just tell Dr. Panacea I'm in on the secret, and that you know I'll keep my mouth shut. If you vouch for me I can just enjoy the health food and relaxation, which I feel like I've earned after coming all this way. You mentioned there are hot springs. I haven't had a proper bath since Cheyenne."

"Lou, *no*," said Shai. "There's no way I can do that. Lazarus wouldn't approve of me having told you anything, let alone everything."

"I'm sure he trusts you."

"He trusts me because I've proven myself trustworthy." Shai seemed panicked by this turn of the conversation. "Telling him—it's impossible. Trust me, it would be better for all concerned if you just left."

Shai wasn't just alarmed. He was *frightened*. Lou hadn't seen him frightened before, not when they were driving over dangerous mountain passes or facing road agents in the middle of the night. Dr. Panacea must be one scary bastard when he was pissed off.

Something about Shai's dismay made Lou deeply uncomfortable, but she couldn't figure out why. Unable to put her finger on it, she let it go. "Maybe we're both too loopy to make big decisions right now," she said. "Things always seem more serious at night, don't they? Just… don't take off tomorrow, okay? Get me up, we'll eat some breakfast and figure out how to make everybody happy."

Shai hesitated, then nodded and smiled. "All right," he said. "Good night, Lou. See you in the morning."

***

An insistent beam of sunlight, angling through a gap in the cabin wall, forced its way up under Lou's right eyelid. She groaned. She was in a rough way. Her mouth felt sandy, she had a doozy of a headache, and her ass and back were aching.

Remembering the previous night's weirdness, suddenly the day seemed a bit less sunny. The hay beneath her crackled as she rolled over, figuring that a few more minutes of sleep couldn't hurt.

Then Lou realized her cheek was touching something decidedly different in texture than the bedroll she'd been using as a pillow. When she sat up she saw it was, of all things, a ten-dollar bill. Baffled, Lou stared at it for a few moments—but when she grasped its significance she leaped out of bed and flew out the front door of the fish house without even pulling on her boots.

By the time she skidded to a halt inside the stable, Lou was gasping for breath. She hated running, but she hated getting euchred more, so while her volley of cussing was interrupted by her need to pant she still managed to make it long and creative.

The two stalls where the mules had spent the night stood empty and freshly mucked-out, and the cart was gone. Joe's guilty expression when he saw Lou confirmed her worst fears.

"He told me not to wake you," said Joe. "Left just as I was stumbling in here before daybreak. Already hitched the mules and gotten hisself loaded up."

"He wasn't supposed to," said Lou helplessly. She didn't know if she was more angry or afraid that Shai had gone on without her. She was plenty angry, but not knowing what to do or where to go was distressing her more than a little. Even if all she wanted was to turn tail and go home, how the hell would even she do that? She didn't have a cart, or supplies, or really anything but her own two legs and whatever determination she could muster.

Joe shrugged. "He said to tell you, 'This is the only way to keep everybody happy.' Said you'd know what he meant."

Lou knew more cussing wouldn't help matters, but she didn't let that stop her. When she'd finished, Joe told her she'd feel better with some chuck in her belly and handed her a piece of cornbread studded with dried berries. Lou sat down heavily on the stool and stared at the food like it might tell her some better news.

"Least you don't have to worry about transportation," said Joe, after she had taken a bite of breakfast.

"Huh?"

"You won't have to walk home, is what I mean. Shai, he was real worried about inconveniencing you. Said he felt a little responsible how after coming all this way the job turned out not to suit you, so he bought my old appaloosa mule for you, so's you wouldn't have to walk back."

Lou'd noticed the creature picketed out in the pastureland north of the stable, a stubborn-looking, mean-eyed, knock-kneed piece of crowbait if ever she'd seen one. Suddenly the barn felt oppressively warm and stuffy.

Lightheaded, she gasped "Gotta," and without another word made a break for some fresh air.

The beauty of the morning only served to annoy Lou as she found a nice flat rock by the river and sat down, hanging her head between her knees in the hopes of clearing it. It helped with feeling faint, but not so much with feeling lost, confused, and without a plan. Shai's betrayal—*betrayals,* really—were as absolute as they were overwhelming. With ten dollars and a spotted hinny he'd finished what he'd started in front of those folks in the lodge. He'd laid her low, that was for sure.

Lou wished she really had been a spy seeking the formula for the Elixir of Life. It would make things easier right about now.

But she wasn't a spy… at least, not a spy looking for the world's best snake oil. She was looking for something more important: missing people—people who, come to think on it, Shai hadn't mentioned, not once, for all he claimed to be concerned with those living on the margins, in constant danger from those who would exploit them, knowing they lived beneath the notice of the law.

But Shai *had* mentioned the San being a perfect spot to lure the sickly. Wouldn't it also be a perfect spot to lure other people, people that no one would think it strange—or care—if they disappeared?

Here she'd thought Dr. Panacea was recruiting unemployed Chinese people to Colorado to do some sort of dangerous work for cheap. Silly her. More likely he was bringing them in as additional source of nourishment during these "lean times," as Shai had called them. It was perfect. Well, it was perfect if you were an evil fucker. The Chinese he was hiring were people largely invisible to the law, and often less proficient in English than other exploitable populations. And Shai had been the one to accuse her of hypocrisy! That son of a bitch!

For once in her life, rage cleared Lou's mind instead of the reverse.

She'd been tricked, and not just by Shai's slimy ploy to run off and leave her stranded. He'd put one over on her *philosophically*. Shai and his lover weren't oppressed innocents just trying to get by—at least, not entirely. They might be all Shai had said, but they were also criminals, and not of the sort Lou secretly found impressive, like train-robbers or jewel thieves who planned elaborate heists and such. Despite all Shai's excuses about them just doing what they had to do to live in safety and peace, the two of them were knowingly, deliberately—unapologetically—taking advantage of the sick and the vulnerable. Maybe his argument would've worked under some circumstances, but not those.

Lou felt her doubts evaporate. Obviously she'd be in terrible danger if she continued onward, but if she'd been more concerned about her own skin than anything else she never would've come out here at all. She needed to discover fate of the missing Chinese workers, but that wasn't all. It was also her duty to serve the living. She was a psychopomp, and Dr. Panacea was undead. In the sober light of day, Shai's claim about Dr. Panacea being the world's biggest sweetheart whose only problem was the way society judged him for being a vampire... it seemed a little thin. Why else would Shai—his lover for over three hundred years—seem so scared to cross him?

The only thing to do, the *right* thing to do, was to go and see for herself. Once she got up there, if it turned out her suspicions were wrong and Dr. Panacea really was a great guy who was paying a fair wage to Chinese workers while feeding on the weak and sick, like any other honest predator, well, then she'd figure things out then. It seemed unlikely, but she had to be fair. If nothing else, Shai's lecture had convinced her of that.

"You all right?"

Lou about jumped out of her skin, but it was only Joe. He put a hand on her shoulder as he squatted down beside her.

"You didn't come back."

"I was feeling sick," said Lou. "I'm all right now." Shai's gift didn't seem so insulting now that she was thinking straight. Well, it was still insulting—but pride aside, an animal like that could greatly aid her in getting where she wanted to be, especially if she wasn't able to tag along with the guides up to the San. Shai was the type to dot all his i's and cross his t's. He'd have told anyone she might encounter to keep her from coming to Fountain of Youth.

"Anyways," said Joe. "Shai said you'd need to be taught to ride her. You're in luck. Ridin old girls is a special talent of mine," he said, and guffawed in a manner that made Lou uncomfortable. "Let's go on in and I'll teach you how to saddle her up, all right?"

In spite of her apprehensions, only few hours later Lou was enjoying ambling over the gentle hills of Estes Park. The mule, despite looking ill-humored, was friendly and easy to manage. At least, so she thought when Speckled Betty responded to her gentle rein-pull turning her back toward the barn. When she gently tapped the mule's sides with the heels of her boots, Betty took off like a shot, not even cantering but straight-up gallop-ing over the grassy hillocks. Startled birds flew up out of the grasses as the pair pelted across the high country, a family of rabbits scattered every which way, and there was nothing Lou could say or do to slow the mule's pace.

She managed to hang on with her knees as the wind whipped at her face, chapping her cheeks and blowing her hat off and away. Blinded by the bright sunlight, Lou hunkered down and leaned forward in the saddle, pressing her heels down in the stirrups, just like Joe had told her to do. Even with the loss of her Stetson, Lou felt she was doing pretty okay—until she looked up from between Betty's flapping ears and saw they were fast approaching the little bridge they'd earlier traversed. That wasn't alarming in and of itself, but two men in an empty wagon drawn by four mules were currently crossing, and the bridge wasn't big enough for both them and Betty to pass at the same time.

Betty, in her eagerness to return to the barn, was not to be deterred. Find-ing the bridge occupied, the mule veered right to ford the shallows. Lou gave up trying to guide the animal, and let her have her head.

Mule and rider crashed into the water at top speed, but it was colder than either of them anticipated. Lou gasped with the shock of snowmelt soaking her calves and thighs; Betty, also surprised by the chill, did a high-stepping dance for a few moments on the rocks of the creek bed, then leaped across the rest of the way.

Once she was on dry land, the mule finally went still. Lou relaxed… until Betty started bucking. The sensation was jolting where galloping had been smooth, and Lou, afraid she might injure Betty's mouth by clinging to the reins, loosened her hold—and was dumped unceremoniously on the turf, where she rolled ass over teakettle and then flopped to a stop.

Lou lay on her back for a few moments, staring up at the blue sky and the feathery clouds. She was only vaguely aware that Betty was standing calmly beside her, tearing up grass by the mouthful, until she saw mud-caked boots walking to where she lay. Looking to the side, she saw a man take the mule by the bridle; another startled her when he leaned over her, his face obscured by the bright sunlight.

"Quite a tumble," said the man.

"Ungh," said Lou.

"Feisty," he commented, nodding at the mule. "You were doin all right for a time there, but you can't trust a half-breed," he said, and then spat. Lou was unimpressed. "Anyhow, I'm Ned Clifford—this here's Coyote Bill."

So this was the escort from Fountain of Youth. Lou got to her feet and managed to gasp out "Thanks," before she bent over coughing. Once she recovered, she said, "I'm Lou. That's," she coughed once more, "Speckled Betty."

Speckled Betty, for her part, was less calm now that "Coyote Bill" had ahold of her reins. She snorted and stamped and even tried to rear as the man clucked at her. "Whoa there little filly," he said, but Betty would not be soothed. Lou staggered over to reclaim her mount, lest the mule really start to panic. Once Coyote handed over her lead, Betty quieted. Lou hoped this meant the wretched animal would appreciate her new owner a bit more from here on out.

"Whew," she said, and managed to smile at her new acquaintances. Once she got a better look at them, the expression was somewhat more difficult to maintain.

Ned Clifford had prominent teeth below a straggly mustache, and he wore a shabby tweed suit. A few wisps of thin brown hair poked out from under a derby with a feather stuck in the brim. Lou thought he looked like the sort of man who would flatter old ladies into giving him a glass of lemonade while he sold them junk bonds. His companion, on the other hand, would not look out of place on a wanted poster. He looked almost feral. He had a large knife stuck into his boot, an open-crown hat shadowed his face, and a shabby leather duster obscured his shape. Speckled Betty, while easier now that she wasn't actively under his power, didn't seem pleased to still be near him. Lou couldn't blame her.

"You said your name was Lou?" asked Ned, with a significant glance at

Coyote. Well, she had expected Shai would be too smart to believe she'd just turn tail and flee.

"Yeah. Lou Merriwether," said Lou, figuring there was no point in lying. How likely would it be that some other Chinaman in boots with jackalopes on them would show up at Estes Park after she left for home? "Just bought Betty here." Not wanting to confess to her inexperience on horseback, shrugged and smiled again. "Figured I'd get the feel of her."

"Seems the exercise was mutual," said Ned. "Your hat's blowing around over there."

"I'll get it in a minute. So," she said with an innocent look, "where did you two come from?"

"Fountain of Youth, where else?" said Coyote.

"And we'd better get in 'fore dinnertime," said Ned. "Mrs. Evans likes to know how many to cook for. Are you…"

"I'll come along behind you," said Lou. Betty whickered once as she swung herself onto the mule's back, but then she settled down. Maybe there was something to that old chestnut about getting right back in the saddle again. "I'm staying with the Evans clan, too."

"Oh, really?" asked Ned, feigning surprise badly. "You here to… what, hunt? Fish? Or are you headed for Fountain of Youth?"

"I'm here for the San," said Lou. "Heard there were jobs for those what wanted them."

"Hmm," said Ned. "Hadn't heard that, myself."

"Hope you're wrong," said Lou, with a shrug. "I've come a long way."

Coyote opened his mouth, but Ned elbowed him in the ribs. The look he gave his companion said "we'll sort it later" as clearly as if he'd spoken it aloud.

Betty was much better behaved as Lou rode back for her hat and made her way back to the barn. Upon reaching the stable, Lou unsaddled, curried, and fed the creature, all the while concocting a viable argument in her mind as to why Ned and Coyote should take her with them. By the time she heard the dinner bell, she had a plan. By the time she'd eaten her fill, she felt able to execute it.

Just to be sure she'd be thinking with a full belly Lou mopped up the grease from her salt pork, eggs, corncakes, and pickled plums with her bread and popped it into her mouth. Mrs. Evans looked at her in disgust;

Lou smiled at her with a mouthful of food.

"Delicious," she said, after swallowing. "You're a fine cook. Much obliged. Can I wash my plate?"

Mrs. Evans pointed at the sink. Lou figured that meant just put up her dish.

"Thanks again," she said. "Oh, and if anyone comes a-callin, looking for me I mean, I'll be in the stables."

Mrs. Evans gave her a puzzled look, but she must have passed along the information. As Lou was polishing her new saddle under Joe's supervision, Ned and Coyote showed up, looking smug and more than a little tipsy.

"Afternoon," she said. She felt confident she could handle these clowns.

"We need to talk to you," said Coyote. He pointed at Joe. "Clear out, you."

Joe looked understandably annoyed, but Lou sidled between them before more words were exchanged.

"How's about we leave my friend here to his work and discuss our business over a drink?"

This idea pleased the two guides, so Lou took the two men to the fish house after whispering to Joe that she'd repay him for the dent in his supplies. Once inside, she ducked behind the blanket that separated the main room from Joe's dwelling and quickly retrieved her gun from her satchel, tucking it into her belt behind her back. Then she retrieved the lightest of the jugs from under the floorboards.

Stepping back into the main room, she pulled the cork. Hoping to make them as thirsty as possible she hooked it over her shoulder and took a swig before setting it down and wiping her mouth with a contented sigh. When she was sure Ned and Coyote were focused entirely on her she pushed it across to where they stood.

Coyote was the first to sit and take a drink. Ned watched him, licked his lips, then followed suit.

"Thanks," he said, after taking a pull. "Wish we could return the kindness."

"How's that?" asked Lou, also settling in.

"Met Shai on the way down," said Ned. "We're not supposed to let you ride in the wagon with us up to the San."

"That's fine. I can ride my mule," said Lou lightly.

"That's not really the point I'm trying to make," said Ned.

"You ain't too steady on that mule," remarked Coyote. "Accidents will befall an inexperienced rider on hard trails."

"What my friend is saying," said Ned, "is that we were told to do whatever it took to keep you away from Fountain of Youth."

Lou nodded, having already anticipated this. "How much does Dr. Panacea pay you two gentlemen?"

"No business of yours," said Ned.

"Nope," said Lou. She leaned back in her seat. "Just curious, is all."

"They say curiosity killed the chink."

"Shut up, Ned," said Coyote, leaning forward. He was clearly the brighter of the pair. "I think we's bout to be offered a bribe."

"Dr. P won't—"

"Here's the thing," said Lou, over Ned. "Shai... well, let's just say I wasn't completely forthcoming about my business at Fountain of Youth while we were traveling together. He seemed kinda, I dunno... honest, you might say. Upstanding." Ned snorted. Lou raised an eyebrow. "Maybe I misjudged him, but that smooth skin and pretty face of his made me think he was a, uh, *sensitive soul.*" Coyote was the one who snorted at that. "Thusly, I told him a big story about looking for work at the San."

"What're you sayin?" Ned finally seemed interested.

Lou warned herself not to give in to pride, but she felt she was actually fooling these two... not like back in Cheyenne, with Shai. "Why did Shai tell you to keep me from coming with you?"

Ned shrugged. "Not much. Just that it was worth a lot to the doctor and the San to keep you away."

Lou sighed dramatically and shook her head. "I figured. He and I had a, I guess you'd call it a falling out a few days ago." Lou trailed off, saddened momentarily as she remembered Shai's story, the way they'd parted, and just about everything else that related to their brief association. Putting that aside, she cleared her throat, and though it felt like a grotesque betrayal of what had passed between them, raised her eyebrow. "He made me an offer I had to refuse, is what I mean. Need I say more?"

"Naw," said Coyote. "Everybody knows Shai's sweeter than lemonade at a church picnic."

Lou forced a guffaw, privately marveling at how easy it was to hoodwink ignorant fools just by pretending to be one. "Thing is, I believe Dr. Panacea might be very interested in what I have to offer him, and if he is, then that means profits for me. All this to say yes, I will bribe you gentlemen. Or at least try—with this." Lou took the ten-dollar bill out of her pocket and placed it in the center of the table.

"Not good enough," said Ned. "I need more. Like the truth."

Lou, knowing she was taking a big risk, touched her bolo tie for luck. "All right, all right. I heard you folks have a bit of a labor problem at the San… finding quality workers of a certain type, let's say. Did I mention I come from San Francisco?"

Ned nodded, and both he and Coyote leaned forward. Both were looking at Lou a little more keenly. She knew she'd nailed it.

"Well," said Lou, as casually as she could, "the thing is, I have connections to certain communities that also reside in San Francisco. I told Shai I needed a job. The truth of the matter is, I'm looking to be a middleman. I have no qualms acquiring the sort of labor I hear your employer desires, because as far as I see it, I'll get paid twice—once by those looking for work, and once by him on delivery of what he wants. Adds up nicely, in my mind. That straight enough for you?"

"Yep," said Coyote, taking the ten-dollar bill. Ned still looked slightly sour. Lou didn't know if it was due to Coyote snatching the cash or accepting the bribe in a more general sense.

"So when do we leave?" asked Lou brightly.

"Takes four long days at least to get to the San, under the best of conditions," said Ned. "We'll want to get an early start, so be ready to leave at daybreak."

"Hell," said Lou, "I'm ready *now.*"

PART THREE

Chapter One

The early-morning hush of the shadowy pine glade was broken when Mr. Willoughby suddenly yelped like he was being scalped. Lou glanced up from the pot of coffee she was boiling over the campfire to see Ned Clifford back away from the prone man, his hands raised in apology.

"Shucks, Mr. Willoughby," said Ned, "I didn't mean to stumble over you."

"Watch where you're going!" Mr. Willoughby snapped, as he propped himself up on one elbow. "You kicked me!"

Ned looked like butter wouldn't melt in his mouth. "I was just picking up this branch to throw on the fire when my foot slipped on a patch of ice. I'm real sorry. But it's a good thing you're up, whatever the cause! We want to get an early start so we can make the San today. Looks like Lou's just about got the coffee ready. That'll perk you right up!"

Lou returned her attention to the coffee pot to hide her smile. After four nights camping out with the Willoughbys, she couldn't blame anyone for kicking either of them. Such a pair of whiny, self-absorbed stinkers she had never met, and she hoped never to again. They'd certainly done their best to ruin what might have been a beautiful journey with their constant complaining about the weather, the roughness of the roads, the camp fare, and sleeping on the forest floor. Lou found it telling that Ned and Coyote, though used to trekking through the wilds with invalids, agreed with her assessment of their characters.

If either had been the least bit sick Lou would have been more forgiving, but they'd pretty much admitted they were coming to the San for a vacation on the recommendation of some friends of theirs. The only thing wrong with them was a chronic case of rotten attitude, something that Lou figured even a double-dose of the Elixir of Life wouldn't cure.

Mr. Magnusson was a different case entirely. He was so unwell the occasional dose of Elixir from Ned or Coyote sometimes seemed to be the only thing sustaining him. He barely ate, drank only a little water when begged, and coughed so hard the snow around his feet turned pink with blood whenever he bent over to spit.

That morning in particular he was difficult to rouse, and when they finally got him to open his eyes, he looked worse than ever. Sweat beaded his upper lip, and he did not want any breakfast. Ned and Coyote bundled him in blankets and got him on the wagon before packing up camp.

"So you think we'll make it to the San today?" asked Lou, sharing her cigarette with Coyote. She'd just finished saddling Betty when Mrs. Willoughby had taken off through the trees on a private errand.

"Yeah," said Coyote. "We'll be there before suppertime, even with this crew." He looked Lou up and down. "You're all right, you know that? Not just by comparison, I mean."

"How you do go on." Lou took back her cigarette and took a long drag.

"No, really. Most folk who come up to the San... they're not the sort who'll help you build a fire, or feed the mules, or offer to cook dinner for the group."

"Or take a watch," added Ned, sidling over. "Never slept so much on the trail as this time."

Lou shrugged off the praise like it was no big deal, but she was secretly pleased. While she still felt Ned and Coyote were two of the least pleasant fellows she'd ever associated with, they had good in them, too. Both of them respected the bears, which raised them a little in her estimation—in spite of the Willoughbys almost begging for fresh meat Ned had downright refused to violate Dr. Panacea's agreement with the bears that they do no hunting in these woods. And Coyote's nigh-preternatural wood-sense had kept them out of the way of harm more than once, most memorably when he hurried them along a pass just before a dead tree crashed down to block the trail. At the time he'd claimed it was due to his being one-sixteenth Cherokee, but later he'd confessed to Lou it had been pure luck that he'd heard the creak of wood snapping as it swayed.

Even knowing she'd soon be at Fountain of Youth, and therefore able to occasionally get away from her more obnoxious companions, the morning seemed downright interminable to Lou. Mrs. Willoughby, for once, was more vocal than her husband, going on about how the mist was chilling her to the bone, and asking twice if they could stop to build a fire and warm up a little. Every time she was told "no" she sighed like the very angels were weeping for her. This did little to improve the general morale. It wasn't as though Lou didn't understand her dismay over every part of her being chapped and damp and itchy—but talking about discomfort rarely alleviated it.

Around mid-day some of the haze burned off and the path began to wind upwards at a more dramatic angle than they'd yet encountered. Lou took this to be a good sign, and she was right. After they crested a particularly steep switchback, Lou spied a large, vertical rock just where the trail widened into something like an actual road. Seeing some words had been carved into the face, Lou led her mule up alongside so she could read what it said.

FOUNTAIN OF YOUTH SPA AND SANATORIUM
On this day of April the 12th, 1867
Dr. Panacea himself inscribed these words:
No true physician considers his own good in what he prescribes,
but the good of his patient.
A physician is a healer of bodies, not a maker of money.
—Plato

Lou felt plenty warm after reading that, and not just because the sun was finally shining a little. Anger heated her up just as good as squatting by a campfire. While it was true that during the journey she'd gone back and forth with herself over pretty much every word she and Shai had said to one another back on that rock in Estes Park, she was still wholly of the opinion that tricking sick people was beyond the pale when it came to wickedness— especially now, after seeing how long it took to get to the damn sanatorium.

She shook her head. She had let herself think of Shai far too often during her trek—not just their last night together, but the things she'd liked about him before that, like the sound of his laughter, the wonder she'd felt sitting beside him that morning they'd seen the jackalopes; the tenderness she'd felt after reciting that stupid poem what had made him so damn sad.

She'd decided to continue to Fountain of Youth to try to bust wide open whatever was going on up there, but that didn't mean she didn't have other scores to settle. Shai'd taken off before the dust from their talk had settled. She still liked him; hell, she even pitied him, a little. How could she not? He might have made his own bed, and been happy enough sleeping in it for four hundred years, but there were parts of his story that gnawed at her. Like for instance Dr. Panacea being so willing to sacrifice their supply of the Elixir of Life, the one thing in the world that could keep Shai alive—and the way Shai had felt so guilty that he couldn't be his lover's only source of food.

And then there was that whole thing where Shai had said she reminded him of himself when he was young and naïve… well, he reminded her of herself, too, but not in a good way. Shai's argument—which as far as she could tell added up to all things being permissible when the deck of life was stacked against you—it didn't sit well with her. She'd felt plenty bitter toward the world and its ways, but she'd tasted the sweetness of life, too. People like her mother, and Vilhelm, and Bo, they'd helped her find a balance. She wanted to do that for Shai if she could.

If he would let her.

"All right, folks, this last hill is the worst," called Ned, interrupting Lou's thoughts. "Coyote and me will take turns leading the mules, but given the grade we'll need everyone to walk, except you, Mr. Magnusson. To spare the team," he added, when the Willoughbys both opened their mouths wide as baby birds to protest this injustice. "Plenty of luggage already weighing them down."

"Sooner we get started, sooner we're done." Coyote was leaning casually against the inscribed rock as he chewed on a piece of hay. "I've made this trip a hundred times if I've made it once, and it's a doozy, no denying it. But it's a lot easier if you save your breath for the hike, is my advice."

Grudgingly, and without grace, the Willoughbys clambered out of the wagon. Then, to Lou's surprise, Mr. Willoughby approached her, speaking to her directly for the first time since they'd begun their journey.

"Are you…" he trailed off, frowning, and then began anew. "Mister, ah…"

"Merriwether," said Lou. "My name's Lou Merriwether. You can call me Lou."

"Oh," said Mr. Willoughby. "Thank you. Well, Lou… will you be riding or walking up to the San?"

"What's that, now?" Lou figured she knew what he was after, but wanted to make him ask.

"Your mule," he said. "Might I beg the use of her?"

"The *use* of her?" asked Lou. She heard Ned snigger as he began to lead the team up the incline.

"My wife and I aren't quite as hardy as we might be…"

"Oh, you want to ride her up to the ridge? Sorry, but I don't think so. Betty's awful tired, Mr. Willoughby, just like the rest of us. But I'll tell you what—I'll walk with you. We can encourage each other with ideas of what we'll find once we reach the top. Sound like fun?"

Mr. Willoughby looked pained by this proposition, but even when he offered Lou a few dollars from his wallet she refused. Speckled Betty probably could have borne a rider, but it was funnier to make them walk. Petty revenge, but it felt pretty good.

Lou regretted her prank about half an hour into the ascent, when they were only a third of the way up the slope; by the time they reached the top her heart was pounding and her legs were trembling. Then again, as she gasped, her chest burning, she figured even if she hadn't just climbed straight up the side of a goddamn mountain, the view would have taken her breath away.

The final push had put them on the rim of a shallow bowl in the mountains, a grassy, oblong dale perhaps three miles wide at its broadest point, hundreds of feet below where they stood on the ridge that encircled the glacial valley. Opposite their position, marking the far edge of the lowland, the range swooped upwards dramatically into a series of high peaks with one big snowcapped spire towering above the rest. The cloud cover had broken up enough that a few brilliant shafts of sunlight illuminated the land below her. The light bounced off the remaining fog, creating the most beautiful vista Lou had ever beheld.

A few milch cows grazed in the pastureland, their calves quite literally frolicking beside them in the patchy snow, and with them gamboled some other kind of farm creature. Goats, she saw as she shaded her eyes and peered downward. Elsewhere, a handful of men tilled some patches of dark earth, readying the fields for planting. Lou caught hints of birdsong in the air, and a scent of springtime she had not encountered since leaving Estes. Though for miles they'd seen nothing but bare aspens and snow-clogged pines, here wildflowers bloomed around the edges of several steaming lakes.

"Hot springs," answered Coyote, when Lou enquired. "Makes the whole valley here a hell of a lot warmer, even in the dead of winter. There's a small one almost on the San's doorstep, patients can bathe in it whenever they feel like it. A few we use for heat so we can grow vegetables all year round. See them glass houses?" he asked, pointing at two structures with slanted roofs. "They got small springs at the center, we vent the heat out the top. We can grow tomatoes, squash, greens, even when it's snowin."

Shading her eyes, Lou peered at what she assumed was Fountain of Youth, nestled on a low shelf beneath the big peak in the distance. It seemed to consist of a few clapboard buildings and some decks, all connected to one another by wooden walkways; above them, on a different ridge, there was a low-slung longhouse that didn't seem accessible in any way Lou could determine.

"It's…" Lou glanced at Coyote.

"Huh?"

"It's smaller than I thought." Shai had not mentioned sharing her living space with others, but there didn't seem to be a way even their small group could all have separate quarters.

"Just looks that way," Coyote assured her. "You see those doors, there?" Lou squinted and saw a few smears of yellow.

"Yeah?"

"There's a big cave system under the mountain. Most of Fountain of Youth is underground."

Lou took a moment to reflect on what an ingenious motherfucker Dr. Panacea truly was.

"Amazing," she said.

"Yep. Dr. Panacea heard about this place from the bears, is the story. The caves are all a bit close together for their taste. Solitary creatures, you know? So yeah, all the patients bunk in individual little caverns."

"Coyote?"

Lou and the guide looked over. Ned was in the wagon, as were the Willoughbys, and the ever-silent Mr. Magnusson.

"We're about ready to head down," said Ned.

Lou elected to ride Speckled Betty down the steep embankment, the mule having proven herself many times over to be the more surefooted. The trail, while not quite washed-out, was in need of attention. Ned explained that most construction had to wait until after the danger of snowfall, which was most assuredly not past. Lou only half-listened to his talk of building projects they were expecting to begin once they had a little more cash flow—donations from patients always gratefully accepted.

Once at the bottom they made good time through the valley. Lou felt her excitement mounting, and her curiosity, too. None of the laborers they passed appeared to be of Chinese decent, in spite of what Joe and Griff had assumed.

She trotted up beside her guides. "Guess I won't be recruiting farmers for Dr. P, huh?"

The look they exchanged didn't convince her the Chinese were just working different shifts, or days. "You'll have to talk to Dr. P about all that," said Ned.

Lou shrugged it off. "Your average Chinese gets excited about the prospect of just about any kind of work, these days."

"Never a bad thing to keep an open mind," observed the Coyote.

The road up to the stables was gentle compared to the one they'd hiked. Once they arrived, they were introduced to a dark-haired, blue-eyed man named Paul. He assured Lou he'd take good care of Betty and deliver her portmanteau to her room with the utmost care. Just the same, Lou elected to keep her workbag with her. Paul seemed all right, he was gentle with the animals, but there was something unsavory about him. Anyways, it seemed prudent to keep all her secrets close to the chest.

Lou assumed they'd head right away to the big yellow door she'd spied from the summit. To her surprise, after leaving the stables she couldn't see it anywhere, and instead they made their way to small cabin in the lee of a big outcropping just a little ways from the stables. A sign out front said "Welcome" in scrolling letters, and Ned said that's where they'd meet their liaison.

Both guides seemed hell-bent on herding the Willoughbys and Mr. Magnusson inside as quickly as possible, but Ned pulled Lou aside before letting her follow them. She got the impression she was about to receive a talking-to.

She was right.

"All right, now," he said, all his former warmth gone. "We let you come up here with us even though we wasn't supposed to. You mind on that, now."

Lou tried not to look as guilty as she felt. "I know what you did for me—and you know I know. Right, Ned?"

"Maybe I do, and maybe I don't." His tone was slightly softer, but then he shook his finger in her face. "Just… you mind on what we did for you."

"I'm minding, I'm minding." Lou's hands were up. "What do you want me to do right this second? I'm planning on talking to the doc first chance I get. You think I came up here to eat salads and…" She realized she hadn't the foggiest what on earth she would be doing now that she was here. "You know what I mean," she finished lamely.

Ned eyed her up and down, but then nodded and took his leave, heading back to the stables. Lou hoped he and Coyote wouldn't regret helping her… though on this side of the journey she was regretting taking their help. It was finally hitting home what a difficult position she'd put herself in. It didn't seem like the best idea to come right out to Dr. Panacea, pretending to be a middleman interested in locating Chinese workers for the San… but if she didn't run into Shai before long, she'd have to tell the doctor *something*.

Once inside, a strawberry-blond woman with prominent teeth and eyes of no definite color introduced herself to Lou as Miss Vivien Foxglove. She was wearing a plain, long-sleeved white blouse that buttoned up to a band collar, and a white canvas split skirt that gave her an official, nurselike appearance.

"Welcome, welcome," she said in bland but friendly tones as she handed Lou a pencil and a sheet of paper. The Willoughbys and Mr. Magnusson were already seated at a long table, scribbling away. "Please, sit down and fill this out. Afterwards we'll go on a brief tour of the facilities here, and then I'll show you to your rooms. I know you must be ready to put your feet up."

The paperwork was mercifully short; only name, address, next of kin, any allergies, and a brief description of symptoms. Lou just put down "various," eager to get to the tour and whatever else so she could get a bath and some time to herself. It seemed the rest of her companions felt the same way; they all finished around the same time and forked over the modest deposit without a word of complaint.

"Now that's all settled," said Miss Foxglove, as she wrapped a white woolen scarf around her neck, "I'll take you all in the front door, through the cave we call the Great Hall. I know you're very tired, so we'll soldier through the tour—all except you, Mr. Magnusson. You will be shown to your room directly, due to your condition. The doctor will attend you as quickly as he is able. As for the rest of you, after you've gotten your bearings we'll stop and get you fitted for your uniforms, and then you'll have a few hours to yourselves before the welcome dinner tonight."

"Uniforms?" Mrs. Willoughby did not seem too happy about this piece of information.

"It'll look much like what I'm wearing," said Miss Foxglove. "They're very comfortable and warm, I assure you—perfect for taking exercise or relaxing."

Lou wasn't necessarily thrilled by the prospect of a uniform, either, but she kept her trap shut. She'd signed up for this, for better or for worse.

Lou's mood lifted a bit when they trekked back outside and discovered the weather had cleared up even more. Sunlight streamed down on their necks as Miss Foxglove ushered them around the side of an outcropping.

Once they cleared the prominence they had their first real view of the great golden door, set flush into the side of the mountain. It towered over them, more impressive than welcoming. At that scale, the large black dragon painted in the center, curled into a circle and biting its own tail, looked downright sinister. Lou felt certain she'd seen the insignia before and pondered it momentarily before squeezing the handle of her bag a bit more tightly. It was the same insignia featured on the bottle of Elixir of Youth she had stashed in there.

In spite of the door's size Miss Foxglove pushed it open easily. It swung inward, the hinges groaning and echoing eerily.

Once inside, and after her eyes had adjusted, Lou saw the Great Hall was a large cave lit dramatically by torches set in iron sconces. After pointing out a low-hanging stalactite to watch for, Miss Foxglove directed an attendant to take Mr. Magnusson directly to his room. She whispered a few other instructions before they left through the right-hand passage, but Lou couldn't make them out.

Miss Foxglove waved the rest of them to follow her through the tunnel to their left, taking them up several flights of winding stairs carved directly into the living rock. It was surprisingly bright, lit not with torches but queer, pale lumps of bluish-glowing fungus set into little divots in the stone or iron sconces. Lou found the light a little nauseating and was happy when at last they emerged into the sunshine to see the longhouse where breakfast, dinner, and supper were served. Miss Foxglove told them it was also where Dr. Panacea held lectures on nutrition, the importance of regular exercise, and so on.

Then their guide took them back down again to show them the hallway at the end of which they would find Dr. Panacea's office, also dappled with fungal lamps. Lou felt a chill when she saw the door. It had been painted the same golden yellow as the front entrance, but here it glowed a sickly green from the light. She was the only one of the three of them who felt no disappointment when Miss Foxglove didn't knock to introduce them to the San's physician. She figured that was because she was the only one who knew he was a vampire.

"Don't worry," she said, to cheer the Willoughbys, "you'll meet the doctor tonight, at the dinner, and have your intake appointments tomorrow."

Lou swallowed her nerves as Miss Foxglove led the group back outside to see the chapel. Inside, they found six pews and a small altar with a Bible on it. The space was otherwise unadorned. No stove warmed the interior; it seemed, on the whole, disused.

"Currently we have no minister here, but when she is able, on Wednesday afternoons Dr. Panacea's wife leads a prayer group," said Miss Foxglove.

"Dr. Panacea's *married?*" blurted Lou. When all eyes turned to her, she tried to look only casually interested, though nothing could be further from the truth.

"Oh, yes," said Miss Foxglove, to Lou's consternation. "Eliana Panacea is the flower of Fountain of Youth, but one rarely enjoyed. Mrs. Panacea is… not well. Her delicate constitution was one of the reasons Dr. Panacea founded the San—and one of the reasons he first turned to medicine, to hear him speak of it. I *do* hope she will be able to attend the welcome supper tonight, I know you will all like her very much. She is such a kind, gentle thing. Now," Miss Foxglove gestured with both hands toward the door of the chapel, "if you will all file out and follow me, I can show you the trailhead behind the chapel where our guided nature hikes depart, if you are in the mood for something more than a stroll around the facilities, and then we'll head back inside."

Fountain of Youth was a well-marked facility, with little painted wooden signs at every intersection, and helpful arrows pointing the way to the various attractions. Lou noted their existence but not more than that; she wasn't able to pay much attention to what Miss Foxglove was saying. Her thoughts were elsewhere. That Shai had failed to mention his lover's marriage struck Lou as bizarre. She was perfectly aware that sometimes men who preferred men took up with women for the sake of appearances, but Shai's silence seemed rather peculiar, given his forthrightness about matters far less mundane.

So deep in thought was Lou that she barely registered going back inside and coming back out again to see the hot springs, until, walking along the deck of planed polished boards surrounding the pools, Lou heard a giggle. It had come from a pretty young woman who was lounging in a steaming spring. She had quite a lot of curling auburn hair piled on top of her head, and her plump elbows hung over the edge of the pool. Staring openly at Lou, she motioned her over. Lou tipped her hat, but as Miss Foxglove was leading them to the edge of the deck, she did not stop to make her acquaintance.

Beyond the spring was a large open part of the deck where the morning and evening calisthenics classes were held. Much to Lou's displeasure, these were required for all patients. That she was supposed to wear a uniform already seemed like enough infringement on her freedom.

As they paused to enjoy the view beyond the sturdy railing, Miss Foxglove explained a few things, like the times of the calisthenics classes, the cave air facility, and the other health-restoring amenities. Lou felt her mind wandering, but she was called back to the present when Miss Foxglove began to speak about food. She talked with pride about the greenhouses, the dairy cattle and goats, and the farmland where they grew a little wheat and corn. She also mentioned how they hoped to be self-sustaining in future, but for now they were forced to import some of their grain and all of their sugar.

Mr. Willoughby cleared his throat. "Is the fare here vegetarian?"

Miss Foxglove smiled wanly. "We do serve meat occasionally. Pigs and steer aren't particularly sweet-smelling, nor the sight or sound of their slaughter restful, so their small pastureland is on the other side of the ridge, behind the mountain," she replied.

Lou wondered if that was where the Chinese laborers would be found—pig farming seemed like the kind of shit job they'd get stuck with. She resigned herself to slowly investigating Fountain of Youth, which meant taking goddamn calisthenics classes.

As there were no further questions, Miss Foxglove led them all back through the door into the mountainside. Upon descending another short flight of moisture-slick stairs, they arrived at the gender-segregated cave-air facilities. She took Mrs. Willoughby with her to inspect the ladies' side, while Mr. Willoughby and Lou trouped down to see the gentlemen's.

As she had done during the whole tour, Lou was hanging back a little from Mr. Willoughby, thus when she heard his angry exclamation after he went in she could not see what he might be so infuriated by. She did not have long to wonder. It was a narrow passageway, so when Mr. Willoughby emerged, red-faced and flustered, he bumped into Lou, knocking her into the rock wall.

"Watch yourself," snapped Lou, as she rubbed her derrière.

"What!" cried Mr. Willoughby. "How dare—I can't—well! I must say, this establishment is not at all what I expected!"

"Huh?" Lou craned her neck but could only see swirling steam.

"I was under the impression this was a respectable sanatorium," blustered Mr. Willoughby. "Not a..." He seemed unable to supply the right word. Lou waited for him to gather his thoughts; he repaid her patience by poking Lou in the chest.

"You," he said, "are bad enough. But *that,"* he said, pointing his finger at the vapor cave, "is intolerable. I will be lodging a formal complaint."

Lou's curiosity triumphed over her rage, so instead of socking Mr. Willoughby in the eye, she proceeded into the vapor cave. The hot fog momentarily blinded her, and when she finally saw the reason for Mr. Willoughby's distress, she felt as if the temperature rose quickly and substantially. She forced a laugh, hoping the sound would hide the wild thumping of her heart.

"You're a sight for sore eyes." Trying to play it cool, Lou crossed her arms and leaned against the damp wall. "Why don't you ever write your Ma, huh? None of us have had a word from you in what—close to a year?"

The umber-skinned man seated on one of the stone benches looked up and slowly got to his feet. He did not attempt to hide his surprise or pleasure.

"Jesus jumpin' Christ, Lou!" said Bo. He crossed the cave slowly, wheezing from the steam, and embraced her tightly. "Look at you! Look at your hair! It's so short!"

"It's been that way," she said, squirming away from him even though his arms felt so good around her that she felt she might turn to steam herself. She had no words to describe the sensation of seeing her best friend, childhood companion, and—call things what they were—unrequited love sitting around in a towel in a Colorado sanatorium, hanging out like it was no big deal. It was too complex an emotion, equal parts pleasure, anger, love—and relief that she was no longer alone here in this remote, underground, and dangerous place. Bo fought monsters for a living; she exorcised the undead. Together, they'd be taking out the trash in no time.

"It's really you," he said, refusing to release her shoulders as he stared at her. "What are you doing out in the boonies?"

"Same as you," said Lou. "Why else would I come?"

Bo let her go, his expression shifting from excitement to sorrow. "Jesus," he said. "I didn't..."

"Huh?" Lou realized something was wrong. *Really* wrong.

"City life, I guess." Bo ran his hand over his short hair. "Too many people, too little air. But I feel loads better from my stay here, so maybe there's hope for—"

"No," said Lou, shaking her head. She backed away from him as she realized what he was saying, finally recognizing how thin and drawn was his face, how skeletal his body, how reserved his motions had been compared to the Bo she had known. "I—god *damn*—I thought..."

"Huh?" Now Bo looked confused as well as unhappy. "Wait, what?"

Maybe she was wrong. "You're..." Lou swallowed, glanced behind her, and then she lowered her voice as she leaned in to say, "you're here because of all the creepy rumors about this place, right?"

"What rumors?" Bo asked. "Lou, I'm here—I'm here because..." He trailed off, unable to say the words.

Lou couldn't meet Bo's gaze, so she stared at the rock floor until she felt him take her hand in his.

"Lou," he said. She pulled away from him again.

"I told you," she said. "I told you to come home. I told you not to leave! You run off to New York City—and what did it give you but—what?"

Bo chuckled. Lou looked up at him.

"I hope you never change," he said, and then he embraced her again. This time she did not pull away. She didn't want him to see the tears in her eyes.

Chapter Two

Bo released Lou like she'd stung him, half-pushing her away in his haste. She almost asked him what on earth until she saw he was looking pointedly right behind her. There in the doorway was Miss Foxglove, clearly discomfited to have happened upon them during such a private moment.

"Oh," said Lou, willing the flush from her cheeks.

"I'm sorry to have disturbed you," said Miss Foxglove.

"You didn't," said Bo, quickly. "We were just… we ain't seen each other in a while, my cousin and me."

"Yeah," said Lou, trying not to smile. It felt too good to fall into a routine of lying their way out of trouble, as they once used to do. "I don't think Mr. Willoughby knew Bo here was kin to me when he flew off the handle like that. Then again, I got the impression Mr. Willoughby doesn't like *me* much, either." She shrugged. "They say there's no accounting for taste."

Miss Foxglove smiled slightly and nodded. "Come with me, Mr. Merriwether," she said. "I understand your desire to linger here, but everyone else is anxious to press on."

"Of course, said Lou, leaving Bo standing in the center of the steam cave. "See you later?" she called over her shoulder. Bo was grinning at her. She glared back at him, trying to convey through her eyes and the set of her jaw the importance of him to quit clowning around. He seemed to get it, to her relief.

"I'm in room four, cousin," he said, waving. "Stop by first chance you get. Seems we've got a lot of catching up to do."

Lou's skin prickled. All joking aside, four was a bad luck number. Bo didn't hold with numerology, and she didn't either, not usually… but the way Bo was looking, the traditional association between *four* and *death* didn't exactly put her mind at ease.

"You didn't mention during your intake that you had a relation here," said Miss Foxglove, as they climbed back up the stairs to meet the rest of the group. "Was it unexpected? Or did you plan to meet here?"

Lou couldn't see any advantage in lying. "Happy coincidence," she said. "Uh, after a sort, I guess, given our mutual conditions. Anyways, I miss anything?"

"Not unless you enjoy watching grown men throw temper tantrums."

"That can be pretty funny."

"Indeed it can. All the same, Mr. Merriwether, you may wish to…"

"Yeah?"

"Never mind," she said.

They had turned a corner and found the Willoughbys, who were still looking annoyed. As they approached them, Miss Foxglove gave Lou a curious look that Lou couldn't quite read, but she got the feeling it meant their conversation was not over. She pondered this as they went back outside to the laundry facilities to receive their uniforms.

Lou leaned against the wall of the room as her fellow patients were sized. She was longing for a cigarette and a quiet moment to think. Miss Foxglove's attitude, Dr. Panacea's marriage, goddamn *Bo* being here, it was a lot to process for one day—a day when she was already exhausted from hard travel. She was just contemplating trying to nip off for a smoke when she realized Mrs. Willoughby was hissing something at her.

"Huh?" said Lou.

"I said," she murmured, "don't you think it's strange there's no minister here?"

Lou blinked at the narrow-faced woman holding a pile of white garments, longing to say *Nah, it makes sense—this place is run by the undead.* Instead, she nodded slowly. "It's a long way out here," she said, "but you'd think they could find someone."

Mrs. Willoughby seemed pleased by her answer. "So I told Edgar," she said, as if she and Lou were old friends. "He said I was being silly, but *really!* No preacher? So I said I'd ask you—every Chinaman I've known has been a regular churchgoer, no matter what they say."

"Mr. Merriwether? May I have your attention?"

Miss Foxglove was looking at her expectantly. Mr. Willoughby stepped aside, holding his own uniform and accessories, and as she went to pick out her size in shirts, trousers, and undergarments, Lou fought the urge to snicker. Perhaps Dr. Panacea had spirited away her countrymen just to do all the laundry produced by Fountain of Youth.

"Anything else I need?" she asked, wrapping a scarf around her neck.

"That's all, thank you. All right," said Miss Foxglove, checking her wrist-watch and pitching her voice a bit louder. "It's just five now. Supper is at half past six." Lou's stomach ached to hear that news. "That should give you enough time to bathe, if you wish, and change into your uniforms. Don't worry, you'll hear the bell everywhere. Oh, and please feel free to make use of any facilities. So, if you'll just follow me, I'll take you to your rooms— but after that," she said, with a yellowish smile, "you're on your own."

Even though all Lou wanted was to go find Bo, she decided it would behoove her to retrieve a basin of water from the public hot tap down the hall and sponge herself off. She was filthy from her travels, and while she was now more accustomed to the sensation of feeling grimy, she didn't want to smudge her uniform.

After her ablutions, as instructed she set the basin of gritty, tea-brown liquid outside her door for the cleaning staff and wrapped herself in the white robe she'd discovered in her wardrobe. Once she was dry and warm she hung it back up again, but she paused before donning her uniform after catching sight of herself in the mirror atop the dresser.

Lou usually thought of her body as a tool—something useful, not some-thing to stare at, like a picture on the wall. Even so, she knew enough about her general appearance to see that she was leaner and harder than when she'd left San Francisco, and her hair was longer than she liked it. At least the shagginess hid her face better this way.

She raised her hand and touched the pink new scar in her shoulder, pleased by the addition now that the bullet-wound had stopped hurting all the time. If she made it home alive, it would be an even better souvenir than her boots.

Knowing she had little time to waste on vanity and idleness, Lou opened a dresser drawer to retrieve one of the strips of cloth she used to flatten what there was of her bosom. After wrapping herself up tight, she pulled on the regulation shirt, underclothes, and wide-legged canvas trousers, fastened on the suspenders, buttoned up the white band-collar shirt to her neck, and then shrugged on the waistcoat over it all. She looked like a fright, but at least she looked like everyone else. Pulling on her fancy boots, tucking her skiameter into her waistcoat's fob pocket, and fastening the bolo tie Bo had given her around her neck she swallowed her dignity and went to see if she could find Bo.

It took so long for her friend to poke his head out after her knock that she'd begun to wonder where else he might be. When she saw him, her heart fluttered again. She tried to play it off.

"You busy or something?"

"Nah," he said, craning his head toward the interior of his room. It looked pretty much the same as hers. "Just moving slower these days. Come on in."

"Don't mind if I do."

As she stepped inside, Lou wiped her sweaty palms on her pants and tried to smile.

"So," she said.

"Yeah," he said.

A tense silence followed this exchange. Lou desperately wished there was someone else around to help them ease back into their friendship. It had been years since they'd spoken, and this awkwardness felt all the more painful when she remembered how they'd once been so easy with one another. Maybe the dinner bell would ring, or maybe Bo would say something instead of standing there, leaning against the door, wheezing.

"Nice tie," said Bo.

"Just some old piece of junk I found lying around," said Lou, her cheeks warming.

There was another long, uncomfortable pause, and then they both spoke at once.

"So tell me about these rumors," said Bo, just as Lou said, "Is it consumption?"

They both fell silent.

"You first," said Bo.

"Nuh-uh," said Lou. "Maybe later. We should get out of here first, take a walk or something." Lou tapped her ear as she looked all around the room, hoping Bo would understand. She had no idea if it was necessary to be careful of what she said, but Miss Foxglove's assurances that they'd hear the dinner bell in their rooms had made her wonder if there were vents or holes or something where the curious could listen in.

"All right." Bo sounded surprised. "Maybe if I'm feeling well enough after supper I'll take you down to the camp so you can meet my friends. They'd like that."

"They're here?"

"Sort of. They're down in the woods at the base of the mountain. Out of sight, out of mind for the patients, you know? Miss Foxglove said she figured I'd cause a pretty big ruckus even without my cohorts hanging around, so they're camping while I'm stuck here. Given how your friend acted when he saw me in the caves, she was right."

"He's not my friend."

"Well of course he's not," he said, rolling his eyes. "I see you haven't developed a sense of humor, even if you've grown otherwise." He smiled at her scowl, and then Lou had to smile, too. Oh, but he was handsome, even all rawboned and cadaverous. She felt a powerful urge to throw herself at him, panting and blushing like the heroine of a bad novel. As it looked like doing so might break him into pieces, she kept control of herself. "Anyways. I don't think they'd have let me stay at all except I offered to pay them double." He laughed. "And in advance."

"That's a bunch of bullshit right there."

"Always is." Bo shrugged. "But yeah. Consumption. It's gotten real bad, as you can see. As we were in the area, once we heard about this place we decided it was worth a shot."

"Jesus, Bo. You should have told me! Written. Something."

"Oh, sure. *Dear Lou, I've got a probably incurable illness but don't worry none. You can't write to me because I'm on the road, so yeah, best wishes and all my love. Bo.*" He cocked an eyebrow at her.

He had a point. "Still. I could have—"

"Could've *what?*"

Lou sighed, shrugged. "I dunno. All right. Fine." She shook her head.

"Seems dumb how I always worried you'd get yourself et by a monster or, I dunno. Lynched."

"Life has its surprises for us all."

Somewhere a bell rang. It sounded muffled, but that they heard it at all convinced Lou she'd been right to put off discussing what was really going on at Fountain of Youth until they were away from the San.

"Should we get going?" asked Lou, suddenly feeling queasy, yet full of nervous energy. At last, she was going to meet the mysterious Dr. Panacea. Though Shai had told her so much, he hadn't really told her what to expect from the man himself.

"Yeah," said Bo, as he shuffled over to his wardrobe. "It'll take me about ten years to get there."

Lou didn't know what to say to that. "Hope the food's good."

"You'll eat what they serve you, whether you like it or not," said Bo, as he shuffled over to his wardrobe. "And they're big into something they call 'portion control' which means you can't have more'n what's good for you." He shrugged. "My appetite's about as strong as a newborn kitten's, so it hasn't mattered much to me. For you…"

"What's that? You got your sword in there?

Bo glanced down at the cane he'd retrieved. "Shit," he said. "I can't even lift The Gentleman these days. This is just a cane."

Lou was shocked. The Gentleman was Bo's gim, a plain but beautiful double-edged straight sword he had purchased after saving his pocket-money for a year. Unlike Lou, Bo had stuck with Chinese boxing and gotten quite good at both empty-hand and sword techniques. He had always been the faster, nimbler, and more dexterous of the two of them, so seeing him hobbling around like some old codger brought home for Lou how sick her friend really was.

"Oh, but before we go…" said Bo, his hand on the knob, "it's Mr. Merriwether now?"

"Here? Definitely," said Lou, blushing. "I can, uh, explain. Just… later."

"You don't gotta explain nothing to me," said Bo. "Hell, if you prefer Mr. Merriwether all the time…"

"You know I never minded too much what people called me—so long as they don't call me late for dinner."

"That's my girl." He chuckled, then frowned. "Or… whatever."

"Whatever's fine by me," she replied. "Let's go eat."

Their trek to dinner was not a quick one, as Bo had predicted. There were several flights of stairs and he could only manage so many at a time before he began sweating and trembling as he gasped for air. Lou was so concerned she had to bite her tongue to keep from fretting aloud. Her worry must've shown despite her efforts to be discreet about it.

"I'm much better, Lou. Really. Don't fuss. Gimme a few more weeks and I'll be fit as a fiddle, I swear."

"Don't worry. I'm a patient person."

Bo started to cough. "Don't—make me—laugh."

"Guess there's not much to the whole prairie cure, huh?"

"Nah. That's why we came out here to begin with." Bo stood. "Should've known breathing a bunch of fresh air wouldn't work, no matter what kind of land it blows over."

After a few more stairs they reached the final landing. Lou pushed open the door before them, and moist freezing air gusted over them, knocking Bo back a step. Though the afternoon had been fair, it now felt like snow again. Lou shivered, and Bo coughed a few times before they stepped outside to brave the short walk to the A-frame longhouse.

In the light of day the meeting hall had looked functional but inelegant. The wooden tables were heavy and the benches had no cushions; the ceiling was braced by dark timbers and limed with whitewash grubby from smoke. But by firelight—for the only illumination came from more torches set into heavy iron brackets bolted to the walls, and a pit full of coals in the center of the room—the space was striking, almost Medieval in appearance. All it wanted for was a coat of arms, a throne, and maybe some kind of beast turning on a spit.

Two long tables ran along either side of the firepit, and at the head of the hall was a smaller table, perpendicular to the other two. Those who had already arrived were clustered together at the far end of the table to Lou's left. She spied the Willoughbys sitting with another couple, a plump woman Lou put in her late thirties, and Mr. Magnusson, who looked better, though displeased by the whispered conversation that began when his companions noticed Lou. She caught words like "downhill" and "inappropriate" hissed from pinch-mouth to pinch-mouth, and glanced at Bo.

"Always causing a ruckus, aren't you?"

"I think they're talking about you," replied Bo.

Pleased, Lou strutted the rest of the way to the empty table. She sat across from Bo though it put her further from the fire. The cold evening air seeped through the walls, but it was worth it to look at him.

"So about that herd over there," said Bo, leaning in conspiratorially. "The Rutherfords, that's the couple sitting side-by-side—they're horrible. Coriander says they're faking being sick; that they came out here to hide. Some sort of rotten business deal or something, I dunno the details. The single woman is Euphemia Grosvenor, who's here for, whatsit… 'nerves,' I think. I talked to her once, she seems nice enough. If you'd gotten here yesterday, you'd have met Mr. Gillis, but he croaked last night, in his room. Coriander said he'd been declining for a while now."

"Who's Coriander?" asked Lou.

The door swung open, and the young woman Lou had seen in the bathing pool bounded in. Dressed and with her hair done up, Lou thought she could be a model for cocoa mix or fancy soap. She was bouncy of breast and bottom and slender of waist, this was obvious even under the severe blouse and wide split skirt of the women's uniform, and she had a pert nose and rosy cheeks. The Rutherfords waved her over but she ignored them, bustling over to where Lou and Bo sat.

"It's you!" she cried, plunking down on the bench beside Lou.

"Me?" The way she was acting, Lou wondered if perhaps they had met before. Then she saw Bo wink at her.

"Yes, you! I saw you on the tour. I'm very observant; for example, I've already noticed you're Chinese. Oh, but how rude of me! I'm Coriander Gorey and I'm *very* pleased to meet you."

Lou shook the proffered hand. "I'm Lou Merriwether. Nice to meet you, too," she said, returning Coriander's smile. "Bo was just telling me about you."

"Good things, I hope?"

Bo had said neither good nor bad things about Coriander, having merely described her penchant for gossip, but Lou figured she could do worse than be nice. "Of course," she said, but she couldn't resist adding: "But then again, I've never known Bo to say an unkind word about anyone, regardless of his personal opinion."

"He's a dear," agreed Coriander, untroubled by Lou's teasing. "How long have you two known each other?"

"Since small times," said Lou, as the door opened again.

"And here's Mr. Dumpling!" cried Coriander, waving at a greyhound-faced, wispy-haired old soul who looked like he'd been scrubbed clean of all color by an enthusiastic washerwoman. He hobbled over and sat next to Bo.

"Another one. How sad," said Mr. Dumpling, and Lou didn't know what he meant until he settled in and continued, "I'm always sorry to see new-comers, but I suppose disease is a part of life in this world, is it not? Fruit withers on the vine, or rots on the ground, no matter how pristine the blossom."

Lou glanced at Bo. He gave her a significant raise of the eyebrows and then turned to Mr. Dumpling.

"How are you feeling today, Mr. Dumpling? Any independent movement of the bowels yet?"

Lou did not think she could be any more horrified until Mr. Dumpling actually answered.

"I'm afraid not," he replied. "I had another enema this morning. I do wish they'd let me eat less roughage until we get my digestion sorted, but Dr. Panacea won't hear of it."

"Well, perhaps with enough kale, fresh air, and exercise…"

"That's what they've been saying since I arrived," said Mr. Dumpling, "and yet…" He turned to Lou. "And what are you doing here, my friend? I have heard your race is unusually healthy, except for ailments of the teeth. Are you here for complaints of a dental nature?"

Lou had to consciously shut her mouth. "No, I'm, uh, here for some… general ill health."

"What a shame," said Mr. Dumpling. "I would think with all that bowing you would feel so invigorated. What are your symptoms?"

Coriander giggled. Bo turned to Lou expectantly. The son of a bitch was enjoying her discomfort!

"Well," said Lou, but then a sharp gust of wind hit the building, rattling the timbers. At the same time, a trapdoor set into the floor just in front of the entrance of the longhouse flew open with a bang.

Startled, Lou jumped.

The room went quiet.

The first thing that emerged from the hole in the floor was a lustrous mane of salt-and-pepper hair, and then one of the most handsome faces Lou had ever beheld. He had a long, aquiline nose, high prominent cheekbones, and a smile as warm as summer sunshine. There were friendly crinkles around his eyes, and he had the most luscious mouth. His appearance was an odd mixture of the sensual and the avuncular, and impossible to dislike.

"That's Dr. Panacea," whispered Coriander in Lou's ear, as if there could be any mistake about *that*.

The man's motions were so fluid he appeared to rise up from the trapdoor as if he rode atop a dumbwaiter, and even when he gained the final stair and his legs came into view, he still seemed to float. Part of this was the sheer length of his limbs. He was tall but not lanky; there was an elegance to him, enhanced by his close-cut black frock coat and black trousers.

He straightened his black bolo tie and shot the cuffs of his white shirt, then looked over the room with gentle, honest eyes. Lou wondered if perhaps everything she'd heard about him was just a misunderstanding, a mistake, and he really was just a nice doctor helping people at his sanatorium in the mountains...

"Welcome!" he cried. He sounded like an aristocrat from the deep south, one who had never known hunger beyond what a good day of honest exercise induced, nor want beyond the moment of anticipation between seeing a lovely item in a shop window, and then going inside and buying it. "A few new faces even this early in the season, I see! Welcome—welcome one and all! I know it is beginning to snow again, but soon the storm shall pass, and springtime follow. Fear not! As it howls and blows outside, we shall sup together tonight, warm and companionable, and toast the miraculous ability of the body to heal itself! Tonight we shall make new friends and break bread with old!"

Everyone applauded at the end of this little speech, so Lou did, too. Dr. Panacea flashed a smile. His teeth were as bright as the silver buttons on his suit.

"I, as most of you already know, am Dr. Lazarus Panacea, founder, proprietor, and physician at this sanatorium," he continued, bowing so low his lavish tresses fell forward over his shoulders. "It is my only wish to bring vitality and prosperity to those whom the Lord in His wisdom created with weak constitutions, or provide remedy to those who, through misfortune, have fallen prey to illness. Healing is an art—and that, my friends, is why

I have established this sanatorium in the most beautiful place in this great country I've yet seen. Too often do doctors neglect the connection between mind and body that the Greeks understood so well! As medicine works to heal the body, so is the soul rejuvenated by kindness and beauty! To that end, I settled here—and brought splendor to splendor. I would like to introduce all my new patients to my beloved wife: Mrs. Eliana Panacea!"

A head crowned with a braided bun of mahogany hair was the first thing Lou saw; next, a pair of dark, wistful eyes, and finally an entire face, beautiful, with delicately blooming cheeks and features simultaneously earthly and ethereal. But it was a face all too familiar to Lou's eyes. She tried not to stare.

It was Shai.

Chapter Three

It wasn't Shai. Of *course* it wasn't Shai. Lou inhaled and then exhaled through her nose, telling herself sternly to calm down and be reasonable. The fragile creature leaning into Dr. Panacea's embrace was entirely feminine in appearance and bearing, as unlike Shai as day was from night. The waist beneath her periwinkle gown was slender; her bosom a gentle swell, ornamented by a coral-pink cameo necklace that nestled in the valley between her breasts. Whereas Shai had been hardy, this woman was clearly very frail, and there was none of Shai's mocking humor around her mouth or in her eyes.

And yet, her face looked so very like Shai's that Lou couldn't help but be astonished. He hadn't mentioned having a twin—but then again, he hadn't mentioned a lot of things. It was very strange.

"Hello, all." Mrs. Panacea, whoever she was, turned her gaze upward to meet Dr. Panacea's gentle smile with a trembling one of her own. She nodded courteously at the left table, then the right, and said, "I am *so* pleased to welcome you to Fountain of Youth tonight."

"Well well well," murmured Bo, after the couple turned to make their way to the table at the head of the longhouse. "Didn't know you'd developed a taste for the ladies."

"What?" Lou blinked at Bo.

"What?" Coriander's gaze flickered over to Lou. She felt curiosity radiating from the girl. Goddamn Bo!

"She's real pretty," Bo said, nodding at Mrs. Panacea.

"*Very,*" agreed Coriander. "I've been voluntarily attending prayer meetings for the first time in my life just to—"

"*Shh,*" hissed Lou. Dr. and Mrs. Panacea were still speaking, and she wanted to catch every word.

"Tomorrow," Dr. Panacea was saying, "our new arrivals' journeys will begin—journeys that will take them down the paths of better health and the streets of increased longevity. Tonight, however, we feast! And we always begin the feast with a toast. Miss Foxglove?"

Miss Foxglove emerged from what was presumably the kitchen door, bearing a flagon of something in her hands. There were already tankards set about on the table, and she poured a stream of clear liquid into Dr. Panacea's, then his wife's, and went around to each guest in turn.

As she did this, Lou casually flipped open her pocket skiameter to see if she'd been wrong to suspect the doctor, but the device confirmed he was seriously undead. The needle quivered with tension; every time he made the slightest move, it jerked to point directly at him.

Dr. Panacea stood, lifting his cup above his head, and the skiameter made a final bounce before Lou tucked it discreetly away. "It is our tradition during welcome suppers to draw up a bucket of our wonderful well-water and drink a toast to long life. Please, all of you—join me!" He waited until all held aloft their tankards. "To long life!" he cried, and then took a deep draught as all echoed his sentiment. Lou watched to see if he swallowed before taking a sip. She didn't suspect poison, it was more curiosity to see if he would actually drink with them. He did, but not deeply.

After that, several men came out from behind the same door Miss Foxglove had come through, all carrying various platters and tureens heaped with food. They wore clean uniforms and smiled pleasantly enough at the patients, but all of them had that same rough look as the rest of the staff. More importantly to Lou in that moment, the last two fellows who had emerged carried between them a steaming iron cauldron full of something that smelled completely delicious, and they set it over the glowing coals in the center of the room.

"For those of you who have just arrived," said Dr. Panacea, "you should know that only the most health-promoting foods shall be prepared and served to you here at Fountain of Youth. Our cook works hard to create balanced meals that are also tasty. Right now I think he is occupied with dessert, so I shall introduce him to you later.

"As they dish up your first course, let me again emphasize the importance of nutrition. Those of you who have been here for some time may weary of my little lectures, but I shall not apologize for my passion! No, in my long years as a man of science, I've found that to treat the ailments of the body with medicine, only to allow the patient to ruin his health through improper diet—this is mere quackery and money-taking! Though I love all my patients dearly, I wish never to see any of you again once you depart from the San." He winked at the group. "I truly believe if by repetition I can convince you all to be mindful of what you eat, I shall have done you some good. The body re-makes itself every day from what we put into our mouths, and a body that must struggle to create healthy muscle and strong bone from poor-quality food—you have but to imagine a house, if you would understand my point. A dwelling built of rotten wood and crumbling stone, would that structure resist the test of time? Or would it collapse, leaving its inhabitants homeless?"

"My dear?" Mrs. Panacea put her hand on where her husband's rested on the table.

"My wife reminds me that eating food is more nourishing than hearing about it," said the doctor with a charmingly sheepish smile. "Tonight we start with lentil soup and green salad. Asclepius himself could not wish for more wholesome ambrosia. Dig in, y'all—and bon appétit."

Lou was glad when he sat. She'd enjoyed listening to Dr. Panacea's oration just for the beauty of his voice, but now that supper was before her, she had more important things to do.

After tasting the first bite, she had to stop herself from gobbling down the rest. The lentil soup was hearty enough to be a meal in itself, and she scraped her bowl with her spoon when she'd finished her portion. Then she delightedly tucked into the salad of butter lettuce and cucumbers, dressed with some kind of fruit and vegetable purée.

"Hungry?" asked Bo, and Lou glanced up at him. He'd eaten perhaps half of his salad, and was working slowly on his soup.

"It's nice to see someone with an appetite," agreed Coriander. She'd done a bit better than Bo, but didn't seem inspired to wolf it down as Lou had.

"It's not bad—I just get so bored of it I hardly feel like eating."

"I'll take yours if you don't want it," said Lou.

"Be my guest," she said, sliding the bowl across the table.

Lou was still hungry even after Coriander's portion, as she considered soup and salad more an appetizer than a course. Thankfully, soon the servers distributed larger plates containing a mound of wilted chard with a small pat of butter melting into the greens, and a tin pan of dark stew. The greens were delicious, fresh and tasty, but the meat was tough and the sauce tasted almost burned. Lou was surprised, given the quality of everything else, but wolfed it all down anyways without hesitation.

"I see you are enjoying the food," said Mr. Dumpling, as he spooned a chunk of meat into his mouth. He chewed at her expectantly.

"Oh," said Lou. It hadn't occurred to her it might draw attention to her presence if she ate heartily. Well, she'd worry about that tomorrow. "Yeah, it's all right."

"I agree with you."

"You do?" He hadn't eaten much of anything, and everyone but her was just picking at their stew.

"Certainly! I've been to most of the premiere sanatoria in America and in Europe, and the treatment of food is better here than anywhere else, I assure you."

"Ugh," said Coriander. "Surely not."

"Food is fuel for the body, nothing more," said Mr. Dumpling primly.

"Dull fuel," said Coriander. "I miss my chilis."

"My dear! Perhaps you did not attend Dr. Panacea's lecture on how spices infuse the body with their properties? Even pepper can tinge the blood with—"

"Poppycock," said Coriander. "Surely you're not implying my family hurts people with our trade? The Goreys have a long history as spice importers," she said, for Lou's benefit. "For generations, we've traveled all over the world to bring back the finest flavors. I grew up in the West Indies, and let me tell you—"

"I don't think this is appropriate dinner conversation," interrupted Mr. Dumpling, looking put out. "Dr. Panacea wouldn't like it. He is *most* adamant that only plain food can nourish the body without leaving behind a residue. Have you ever drunk the milk of a cow that had dined upon wild garlic? Most unpleasant."

"Well, have you ever eaten asparagus?" Coriander leaned forward, her impressive bosom nearly grazing her plate. "With or without seasoning, it still makes my piss stink."

Lou guffawed, but quickly controlled herself when everyone in the room turned to stare at her. Not attracting attention was turning out to be more difficult than she'd imagined, especially with Mr. Dumpling sputtering and Coriander teasing him. Still, if she could keep her shit together, their argument might allow her to eat and seem social without actively participating. She was more concerned with discreetly watching the doctor and his wife than adding her two bits to the debate.

Dr. Panacea wasn't eating much, taking small bites only occasionally. Mostly, he made a show of feeding bits of meat and slivers of vegetable to Eliana Panacea, who took the morsels off his fork with delicate little bites and modest pink blushes. The effect to the unwary would be charming, but Lou saw it for what it was. Simply by flirting with his bride, Dr. Panacea's plate emptied quickly without him needing to eat much at all.

"Looks like strawberries for dessert," said Bo, as Lou fought the urge to lick her stew-bowl. Gross as it had been, she was still hungry.

A thin man with a face like a hatchet blade and eyebrows like a crow in flight had entered as their plates were whisked away. For some reason, he made Lou slightly uneasy, but as he was bringing out more food she decided to table her judgment. In his gnarled hands he held a metal bowl full of bright quartered berries, the moist white centers making their deep redness even more dazzling.

"May I have your attention?" said Dr. Panacea. The chatter subsided. "It is my pleasure to present Mr. Haggard, our chef. Mr. Haggard—thank you for our supper." Mr. Haggard bobbed his head once and set the tureen before the Panaceas as two other men came out with stacks of smaller bowls for the patients.

Looking over in what she hoped was a nonchalant fashion, Lou saw Dr. Panacea place a large red berry between his wife's full bow lips, which brought another fresh bloom to her rosy cheeks. Lou blushed as well, and looked away… before turning back to stare again. They were charming, and entirely without heed for those who might be watching them, hungry for more than dessert.

Right then and there Lou decided she would not leave Fountain of Youth without telling Bo how she felt about him. Dr. Panacea's tenderness toward his wife inspired her. Though in all likelihood she would have to destroy him, watching him with Eliana was mesmerizing. Like a couple long accustomed to dancing with one another, their motions were practiced and perfected, yet neither seemed the least weary of the routine. Their little touches were innocent, urgent, simmering with a private passion that made Lou uncomfortable. This was not helped a bit when Dr. Panacea's blood-red tongue quickly snaked out from between his teeth to lick his lips as he watched his wife dab at her mouth with a napkin.

"Well, my friends," he said loudly, startling many, "a good meal, and, I think, even better company! But my dearest Eliana needs her rest, so we shall retire. I look forward to meeting with my newest patients tomorrow during your intake appointments, and perhaps seeing some of you around the San. Good evening, and sleep well, all!"

"That was abrupt," remarked Bo. Lou chuckled, but sobered when she saw that the Panaceas were taking the time to bid everyone good night personally. She hoped that being the only new kid at her table, they might skip her, but no such luck.

"And you must be Lou Merriwether."

Lou swung her legs over the bench and stood to shake Dr. Panacea's hand. His palm felt cool and dry. Lou kept her eyes fixed on his; it took every ounce of willpower she possessed not to look at Eliana now that she was so close.

"Hi," she said. "Nice to meet you."

"Likewise, I look forward to working with you. I can see you're nervous," he said kindly, which only made Lou more jumpy. "It's all right—I've reviewed your case, and I have every confidence I'll be able to help you."

"Reviewed my case?" Lou's eyes flickered involuntarily to Eliana. She really was the spitting image of Shai, so much so that Lou kept going back and forth on whether they could possibly be the same person. Shai had been the prettiest man Lou had ever met; Eliana was in the running for handsomest woman. But despite their similar looks, Shai would have been smirking at her with those pouty lips, and neither would he look like he'd just been rescued from a nunnery and was meeting strangers for the first time in his life.

"Yes, of course," said Dr. Panacea crisply. Lou quickly looked back to him. "I review all my patients' cases."

"Oh, yeah, yeah," said Lou, giving him a smile she hoped said *I never suspected otherwise.* "I'm, uh, looking forward to it."

"Good," said Dr. Panacea. "I believe you're scheduled to meet with me after the morning calisthenics class. Please be prompt."

With this, he turned his attention to the other patients at the table, politely enquiring after their health and whether they were happy about the impending snowfall or not.

"Did you by chance travel here in the company of a gentleman called Shai, Mr. Merriwether?"

She could feel Dr. Panacea's gaze hit her like a falcon swooping down upon a vole. All conversation at the table ceased, as did Lou's breathing. Bo was staring at her, too. She swallowed.

"Part of the way," she said, hoping no one could smell her sweating through her uniform. "Why do you ask?"

"Forgive me—it's just, Shai is my brother," said Mrs. Panacea. Her voice, when she was not projecting out over an entire room, was a sweet alto that had none of Shai's devil-may-care brashness. "He is very like me—my twin, in fact. Do you not see the resemblance?"

A twin? An *immortal* twin? It seemed so very unlikely, and yet Lou still couldn't decide if Eliana was lying, even being this close to her. Then Mrs. Panacea caught her eye as she reached up to adjust her necklace. Hadn't she seen Shai pissing standing up a hundred times if she'd seen it once? But there were Eliana's bosoms, unmistakably real, pressing against the blue-grey silk of her gown.

She had no time to ponder. Lou canted her head, peered at Mrs. Panacea, and pretended surprise. "Hey, now that you mention it you and he do look a bit alike. I can't believe I didn't notice before." She decided to fish a little more. "Real nice guy, Shai. Wish we'd been able to travel longer together. He kinda just took off one day, but some folks gotta travel their roads alone, I guess."

Mrs. Panacea's smile was sweeter than a summer peach, and did not falter. "I don't believe Shai had any idea of your intention to come to Fountain of Youth, Mr. Merriwether! When he mentioned you, he seemed to think your business was with the Evans clan, down in Estes. It might have saved you some delay had you been more forthright with him."

Lou honestly didn't know what to say. It was goddamn confusing—not to mention really strange—that it was this difficult for her to decide if Shai had lied to his sister... or was pretending to *be* his own sister. On the one hand, the illusion was so complete Lou doubted anyone could pull off such a perfect, undetectable swap. On the other hand, Shai had had several lifetimes to perfect the art of impersonating someone else, and pretending to be Dr. Panacea's invalid bride seemed like something he'd do—enjoy doing, really. Either way, it seemed that Shai was trying to cover up the details of his association with Lou, most likely to protect himself from Dr. Panacea's wrath. He must have trusted in Ned and Coyote's ability to keep her in Estes and not mentioned much about her to anyone...

"Well, a man doesn't like to admit he's sick," said Lou, deciding that whatever the truth was about Shai being Eliana, or the reverse, she had to play this game the same. She'd worry about it later; now was not the time, not with Dr. Panacea looking daggers at her.

"Being sick is nothing to be ashamed of," Lou heard Eliana saying. "At least, *I* think so—then again, I have been an invalid for quite some time, ever since—"

"My dear," said Dr. Panacea. He strode over and put his arm around Mrs. Panacea's waist, drawing her protectively into his body. "You mustn't aggravate your throat by speaking so much!"

Mrs. Panacea looked up at her husband with limpid, adoring eyes. Lou felt another twinge of uncertainty; she doubted Shai could manage such a mawkish expression without cracking a smile, even with four hundred years of practice. "Please excuse me," she said, turning back to Lou. "I mustn't overtax myself."

"Of course," said Lou. "But hey, if you see your brother, please tell him to come by my room and say howdy? As I mentioned, we parted without saying a proper goodbye."

"I've already sent Shai on an errand to the far side of the mountain," said Dr. Panacea. His eyes were glittering in a way Lou found troubling. "He is looking to our beef and pork. I expect him to be there for some time."

"A pity," said Mrs. Panacea. "But I'll make sure to tell him when he returns. Good night, Mr. Merriwether."

As Lou slid back onto her bench, the doctor and his wife disappeared down their trapdoor, her first, him after. Before disappearing entirely, the doctor looked a final time in Lou's direction. Lou managed to smile and wave farewell, but she felt curiously drained after Dr. Panacea pulled the trapdoor down over him. The muffled sound of a latch scraping could be heard, and then there was nothing but the hush of the longhouse. All eyes were on Lou, including Bo's.

"What?" she asked.

"You're such a troublemaker," said Bo, shaking his head. "I think you struck her fancy, Lou. Better be prepared for a midnight visit!"

Lou felt her face go crimson. "Shut up. Can we—let's go, do you want to go?"

"Where are you going?" asked Coriander. "Can I come?"

Lou glanced at Bo.

"Not tonight," he said firmly. "Lou and me, we've got some catchin up to do."

Coriander looked so disappointed that Lou elbowed her in the ribs.

"It's been a long time since Bo and I seen one another—you'd be bored. But hey, I tell you what." She lowered her voice. "Tomorrow, what do you say we pinch a bottle of cough syrup or whatever they have around here, and we'll have a private party in my room, okay? That suit you?"

"You really mean it?"

"I'd never disappoint a lady."

Lou wondered at herself, that she should care about mollifying this strange girl, but the delight on Coriander's face delighted her in turn.

"All right," said Coriander. "It's just so tedious here after dinner. Everyone goes right to bed!"

Mr. Dumpling patted Coriander's hand across the table. "I have an idea! After we finish up here, we'll go to the library! I'll find us an improving book, and you can read to me."

Coriander's pained expression made Lou regret the necessity of secrecy that night, but there was nothing to be done. She'd just have to do her damnedest to make it up to her tomorrow night.

The weather had turned much colder during the feast. As Lou and Bo made their way back into the mountain it was flurrying but still not really snowing, just a few white flakes whirling about in the chill breeze. The overcast sky made the whole mountain bright but confusing. Lou was not fond of heights—she wasn't *afraid* of them, she just avoided them when she could—but in the darkness the ridge holding the longhouse seemed higher, the drop-off dizzying. She was happy when they were back inside the mountain, out of the wind.

"So what do you think? Up for a stroll?" asked Lou, after they'd gotten down most of the stairs and were heading back toward the Great Hall. She wouldn't have asked, but Bo seemed stronger after his meal.

"If I bundle up, seems fine," he said.

Lou checked her skiameter again once she was in her room, just to make sure there was nothing spooky hiding anywhere close by. The doctor's strong undead presence and stronger dislike of her had her looking for ghosts in every corner. Reassured, she grabbed her scarf and her duster, and her satchel, too. She didn't like the idea of being out in the darkness unprotected, for the same reason.

She wished her first meeting with Dr. Panacea hadn't been so strained. A vampire of his sort would be a formidable threat under the best of circumstances, which her circumstances were most assuredly not. She didn't know her way around, and he would be free to stalk her in daylight, or in darkness. She was on his turf, and apparently encroaching on his territory, both stone and human. Things did not bode well for her if she provoked him into a jealous rage, however inadvertently.

As Lou locked her room behind her, she wondered why nothing was ever easy. It wasn't like she'd come to Fountain of Youth looking for trouble. At least not *that* kind.

Chapter Four

Lou insisted they stop by the stables before heading down to Bo's friends' camp. She said it was so she could check on her mule. She didn't really think Speckled Betty would be mistreated, but Bo was more willing to take short rests when there were reasons to do so other than his health. While her friend recovered his wind, sitting on a bale of hay, Lou had a proper chat with the groom about her animal's temperament and care. She also made sure the front door would remain open all night. Paul assured her it would.

The road down the San was easy enough, but once they cut into the woods things got interesting. There was a trail, but it was dark, and the snow had begun falling much harder. Lou had neglected to bring a lantern, but they did well enough. The trail more or less ran along the mountain, so as long as she kept the rock face to her left upon her return Lou figured she could find her way even if conditions worsened.

"There," said Bo, after they'd been walking for maybe a quarter of an hour. Lou peered along where he pointed. Under a substantial outcropping of rock that curved down to form a windbreak a cheerful orange glow shone through the pines. A campfire!

Lou was suddenly nervous. It had been a long day, and the prospect of meeting more people was in and of itself overwhelming, even without said people being Bo's mysterious, monster-hunting friends. She'd wondered about them for so long, ever since he'd sent her that letter. Wondered about them—and maybe, if she was honest with herself, envied them a little…

"Easy, Lou," said Bo.

"Huh?"

"Nothing to get antsy about. They don't bite."

Lou snorted. If only he knew what *did* bite around here. Still, he was right.

"Say," said Bo, "can you hoot?"

"Can I *what?*"

Bo sighed. "I'm supposed to hoot like an owl to let them know it's me and not a bear or something, but it makes me cough."

"Good signal."

"Shut up and do it."

Having only a limited idea of how to imitate an owl, Lou called, "Hootie hoo!" at a volume that she assumed would reach the campers. She heard distant laughter, and they kept on walking to the clearing.

A large, ebon-skinned man and a formidable Indian woman were passing a flask back and forth as they lounged by the campfire when Lou stepped out from behind the treeline. She said, "Hi," and they jumped to their feet, both staring her down. The woman somehow had a shotgun in her hands and trained on Lou before she could say, "I'm Lou Merriwether."

Then Bo hobbled into the firelight.

"Put it down, Millie," he wheezed. "This is Lou, my friend I told you about."

"Nice to meet you," said Lou wryly. "Thanks for not shooting my ass."

The concern in the woman's face vanished only to be replaced by consternation as she lowered her gun. As for the giant, he headed straight for Bo and began to help him with surprising tenderness toward the crate upon which he'd been sitting. He was older than Bo, white whorls bright in his short black hair. Lou kept glancing his way, but he had eyes only for Bo.

Millie, however, was entirely focused on her.

"Lou?" Millie's voice was hard as nails. "From San Francisco?"

"The very same." Lou tried not to smile. It was strangely thrilling to know Bo had mentioned her to them.

"How'd you know we were here?"

"Bo brought me down," said Lou.

"I mean here at the San."

Lou wished she could make out more of Millie's face. It was difficult to get a read on her with that enormous fluffy scarf wrapped around her neck and her hat pulled down low. All Lou could really see were her bright black eyes and two long black braids that fell over her shoulders.

"Oh," said Lou. "I didn't. Just lucky I guess."

"Hell of a coincidence." Millie sounded skeptical.

"So I keep hearing."

"Relax," said Bo. "There's an explanation."

"Well, what is it?" asked Millie. "I haven't lived this long taking shit like that on faith."

Lou chose not to answer; instead, she withdrew her tobacco pouch from her pocket and rolled up a cigarette. The cold reception was making her cranky. What the heck was their problem? And where were the rest of them? Bo's letter hadn't mentioned a "Millie," though he had written of a pair of twins.

"Anybody else want a smoke?" she asked, but no one took her up on it so she hunkered down and lit her cigarette with a stick from the campfire. She took a long drag and took care to blow the smoke away from Bo.

"Nice gang you got here, Bo," she said. "Real welcoming. Anyone gonna offer me a seat or anything? Or should I just stand here while you all gawk at me like I'm some sort of natural oddity?"

"Take a seat, Lou," said Bo. "I should have mentioned that we've all been a little edgy ever since we had some trouble with a nest of doppelgängers outside of Omaha. Spooky crew. But Millie, really, it's her." He winked at Lou. "Nothing could imitate *that* kind of ugly, even if it wanted to."

Lou often joked about her looks, and her face had always been something of a punch line between her and Bo... but for whatever reason, tonight his teasing smarted. Apparently he'd noticed that she'd never grown into her face like he'd always swore she would.

"Yeah," she croaked. "Good thing for everybody there's only one of me running around. For a lot of reasons."

"Sorry, Lou," said the big man, who must be Thurlow, who Bo was always on about in his letters. "Whatever your reason for being here, we're glad to meet you. Bo's told us loads about you."

Lou settled down and stretched out her legs in the slush around the campfire. She was still a little annoyed, but she didn't want to give these jokers the pleasure of seeing her flustered. "Oh yeah? Like what?"

"Like how you'll fight just about anyone in the world when you're drunk—and you're a crack shot with a pistol—and how every ghost in San Francisco turns blue when they hear Lou Merriwether's coming to send them on."

"Well," said Lou, feeling a little better after hearing this flattering portrait, "to be fair, they're kinda blue to begin with."

Millie stared at her for a moment, then laughed. So did Thurlow.

"You understand how it is when your whole job is dealing with eldritch weirdness, right?" Millie shrugged. "We've got to be cautious."

"More so these days," added Thurlow. "With Jack and Cait off working while Millie and I hang around here, we're not exactly in the best place to defend ourselves if push comes to shove."

"True." Bo coughed, cinched the blanket Thurlow had put over his shoulders tighter about him as the wind gusted. "Even before that, ever since I took poorly."

"You warm enough?" asked Thurlow anxiously.

"Cluck cluck, mother hen," said Bo, smiling his smile that Lou always said could melt the ice caps. It seemed to melt Thurlow, too. The older man's gentleness toward Bo intrigued her, as did their willingness to cuddle up so close on their shared crate. They seemed damn comfortable with one another, more comfortable than just traveling companions... but then again, she and Shai had gotten right friendly after only days on the road. Lou realized she was staring, and looked away.

"So what's the what, Lou?" Bo cleared his throat. "Whatever you wanted to tell me, we're about as away from the San as we're likely to get. Lou seemed to think I'd be here for some other reason than the cough," he explained to his companions.

Lou suddenly wished she'd told Bo about Dr. Panacea during their walk to the camp. She knew he would take her seriously—but the other two? Her story was wild, and she knew it. Feeling shy, she rolled another cigarette.

"Uh," she said. "Well..."

"Would you like a drink?" Millie winked at Lou over the edge of her colorful, shabby scarf. "It's a long walk down here. Maybe you'd like to wet your whistle?"

"I'd love a drink," said Lou, accepting the proffered flask. "I'm, yeah, so I should just say I'm shit at this kind of thing. Explaining, I mean. I usually work alone, so you gotta forgive me if I don't do a good job with this."

"Oh, we don't care." Thurlow smiled at her. "We earn our bread going around to one-horse towns talking to yokels about their monster-troubles, so's we're pretty good at parsing stories."

Lou took several swigs of something that almost passed for whiskey. Afterwards, atmosphere in the camp seemed a little warmer. She checked her skiameter, but it spun without settling anywhere, so she leaned in close. The firelight was warm on her face, and Bo was looking at her encouragingly.

"Well," said Lou, "I'm not quite sure of everything yet, but…"

She told them about the disappearances, the strange rumors about available railroad work, and how she'd managed to get more information on such. Bo laughed until he coughed when Lou described her disguise, which caused Thurlow so much consternation that Lou got all tongue-tied for a while. Another drink helped her move along the tale, but she consciously tried to avoid any humor. Not that there was much funny about her exorcising the body in the box full of bottles of Elixir of Life, or her ride to Cheyenne.

She kept it brief on the subject of Shai. She wasn't eager to talk about him, especially not in front of Bo. His existence, offering her the job to ride shotgun on his wagon, and his confirming her suspicions that the missing workers had come to Fountain of Youth she covered in about three sentences.

"So wait, hold on. This guy works for Dr. Panacea, who you think is behind all the Chinese folks going missing, but he helped you, and told you what you wanted to know?" Millie looked a little lost. "Sorry… just, why do you reckon he was so friendly and forthcoming if what's going on here isn't on the level?"

Lou took a long drag on her cigarette to cover her discomfort. She was still undecided on how much she wanted to tell them. Shai had trusted her with all the secrets of his strange life—well, most of them—and the idea of betraying his confidence, even now, made her uncomfortable. She figured important part was telling Bo and his friends about the vampire in their midst. Shai's personal history wasn't necessary information.

"Well, at first I think he was trying to get the measure of me," said Lou, as she exhaled. The wind gusted at the wrong moment, however, and blew the smoke in Bo's face.

He began to cough again, and Lou hastily threw her cigarette into the fire.

"Sorry," she said, as she noticed Thurlow staring at her accusingly. She took a moment to size him up as Bo got ahold of himself. Thurlow wasn't as handsome as Bo, but he was a fine-looking man in his own right. Except for a slight paunch he was all muscle. Lou put him at about forty-five or fifty.

"Go on," insisted Bo, when he could. "I haven't," he hacked up something gross and spit it into the fire, "met Shai. He's the little missus' brother, right? I've seen him around, but he doesn't talk much with the guests."

"He's kind of Dr. Panacea's right hand man, deep in the doc's council as I understand it." Well, it was close enough to the truth. "Once he thought he knew what I was up to, going to the San, he tried to convince me to go home—in spite of what Eliana said, he knew I was on my way," she amended, when Bo looked like he wanted to say something. "I never let him know what I was really doing. Let him draw his own conclusions."

"And what were those?" asked Millie.

"That I was a spy," said Lou. "He knew I wasn't really sick, but when I told him my ma's an apothecary he figured I was after the formula. I guess there are a lot of people eager to get their hands on it. He said that's why he couldn't let his workforce write home, they had to be certain the letters didn't have any secret information, and neither he nor the doc can read Chinese."

"Lou," said Bo. "I hate to say this, but you know… I ain't seen a single heathen Chinee since I come here."

Lou wouldn't accept it. "They've gotta be here, Bo. Shai's wagon was full of dried cuttlefish and noodles and rice and all kinds of stuff, but it sure doesn't seem like you've been getting small pan rice for dinner."

"No," said Bo. "But still."

"I know it sounds crazy, but I don't think Shai was lying to me." Well, about that part, at any rate.

"So you're out here searching for some missing Chinese," said Thurlow thoughtfully, "but no one's seen any. Why's that, do you think?"

"Well…" Lou took a deep breath. Here goes nothing, she thought. "So," she began, "yeah, Shai and I ended up getting along pretty well." She blushed, much to her annoyance. She didn't want Bo getting the wrong idea. "Because of that, he told me… confessed, really, that…"

"Lou?" Bo was looking at her, brow furrowed. His playful smile didn't help Lou's tongue untangle itself.

Lou checked her skiameter one final time, took a deep breath, and blurted, "He told me I shouldn't come up to the San at all, because the Elixir of Life doesn't have a formula I could steal… and…"

"And?" asked Bo.

"And Dr. Panacea is a vampire." Lou felt a lot better after she got the words out. "I think he might be eating people—I mean, I know he's eating people. I mean, I think he might be luring out-of-work Chinese here specifically, to eat them. Maybe do some work, too, because he's feeding them, but maybe he tries to keep them alive as long as possible, to…" She swallowed. None of them believed her, she could tell. "Seems like an expensive gambit, but Shai said it's been tough times for them, because the railroad went north to Cheyenne instead of through Denver, so the San hasn't had a lot of clients he could, uh, *polish off.* I guess."

A profound silence fell over the camp.

Then Millie laughed. Everyone laughed.

"You really had me going for a while there," said Thurlow.

"Great job, Lou, really," said Bo. "I thought something was actually wrong!"

"And to think Bo always said you were born without a sense of humor!" chuckled Millie.

"I'm not joking!" snapped Lou, not bothering to check her pissed-off tone. The frivolity halted pretty damn quick. "I'm serious!"

"Really?" Bo looked genuinely taken aback.

"Yes, really." It hadn't occurred to her that this group of monster hunters would outright laugh at her story—at *her.* "Seems like a good set-up to me, from what I know of vampires."

"I think you should consider whether your leg got pulled." Bo's gentle tone did not exactly soothe Lou. "You know I think the world of you as a psychopomp, but it's just…"

"He must've been lying," said Millie. "I don't know how many vampires you've dealt with, Lou—this kind of vampire, I mean—but this ain't a good set-up for one, not at all."

"Why not? He can run around all day inside the caves, where there's no sunlight. Seems perfect."

"Vampires are reclusive," insisted Millie. "Their impulse to feed is difficult to manage, and it's a pretty good clue that someone's a bloodsucking fiend if they jump on you and start gnawing on your neck. Most of the ones that associate with humans are the young ones, and they get caught quick 'cause they act like fools. Running a sanatorium would be... it would be *impossible* for a vampire."

"Though, you know, I never seen him outside during the day," said Bo. "I've seen him up and about, but always inside. I wonder..."

"I checked him out." Lou heard her own voice, too high, too tight. She took a deep breath. "My skiameter trained right on him like—"

"Your what?" asked Millie.

"My skiameter." Lou wanted to kick herself. She'd forgotten she had proof! Withdrawing the silver instrument from her waistcoat, she flipped open the cover and showed them. "It's like a compass, but instead of pointing north, it points at undead. My father had it made to look like a pocket watch so it could be used anywhere. Even at a welcome dinner."

Bo had the decency to look abashed as Thurlow and Millie stepped forward to get a look at the curious object. "Sorry, Lou," he said. "I should have known you'd confirm all this before telling us."

"Is this thing ever wrong?" asked Thurlow. "How does it work?"

"When the undead remain in the world of the living, their spirit-matter is... distinctive. The skiameter's needle is drawn to it. I'm sure somebody else could give you a better description, but that's how it was explained to me."

"Oh," said Thurlow. "That's really..."

"Weird," supplied Millie. "No offense, but your kind—psychopomps—kinda put the spook on me, what with y'all hanging around in graveyards, looking at dead people all the time."

"I was raised around the dead, it doesn't bother me much." Lou put her skiameter away. "It's not for the faint of heart, but I'm not as yellow as I look."

"Well, all right," said Thurlow, as Millie giggled. "So you checked it out, and he's a vampire—or at least some kind of undead. So why are you telling us this?"

233

Thurlow's question took Lou by surprise. They were monster-hunters, and she couldn't think of what monster-hunters might do other than hunt monsters. It seemed the entire profession was explained by its title. Something really weird was going on.

"Uh, well, to be perfectly honest, I've never dealt with this kind of vampire before, only geung si. I was hoping you might have some idea as to how…" She swallowed. "I think I'm going to need some help with this one. And I was hoping you would help me."

Many times during her travels Lou had marveled at how quiet the snowy forest became at night, but the silence around the campfire was nothing short of profound. Every crackle from the fire sounded loud as a gunshot. She shifted her butt on the crate, and the creak of the wood was deafening. Then everyone spoke at once.

"Of course," said Bo, as Thurlow said, "Not happening."

Millie was the lone person who seemed amused. "You want to take on a vampire old and crafty enough to pass himself off as human with only *three people?*" she asked, as Lou sat back and said, "Forget I asked; I can handle it on my own."

There was a long pause.

"No, you can't," said Bo, looking at Lou. "Lou, you're a whiz with geung si, but hell… the one time we took on a vampire—*this* kind of vampire, like you're talking about? It was a close shave."

"Asshole could turn into *bats,*" said Millie. "Hardly a fair fight. We didn't know to bring a net."

Thurlow nodded. "If Jack and Cait were here—and if Bo were well—then *maybe*. But as it stands… better to leave sleeping dogs lie."

Lou had felt so confident moving forward with her investigation after learning Bo was at the San with his friends; had felt enthusiastic about the possibility of liberating any Chinese that still might be alive. But to hear them talk, tangling with the doctor at all would be the craziest idea in the world. Yet even seeing them pass sober looks to one another like a bottle of booze, Lou had a hard time believing that things could really be *that* bad.

"I say we go for it," said Bo. "Tomorrow, I'll—"

"Tomorrow you'll take your medicine, rest, exercise how they tell you, and work on getting better." Thurlow's tone said he would brook no argument.

"No." Lou loved the stubborn light in Bo's eye, knowing it well. "Lou came here for a reason. We owe it to her to help her."

"How's that?" countered Millie. "Look, Bo—think about it. We ain't a full team, and there's no profit in this. Who'll pay us for risking our necks if we white-knight on in there? *You,* Lou?" Millie shot Lou a skeptical glance. Lou looked away; it was true she had not considered the issue of payment. "For being such a bad dude I haven't heard any mention of a bounty on Dr. Panacea's head."

Bo alone protested. "Public service or not, we—"

Thurlow leaned into Bo and whispered something. Lou didn't catch what it was, but it silenced Bo. He looked ashamed, but then Thurlow said "please" so gently it almost brought tears to Lou's eyes for some unfathomable reason. Bo hung his head, looking as miserable at the prospect of not taking the job as Lou was for proposing it.

"Thurlow—Millie—they're right," said Bo. "This isn't the best—" and he broke off to cough for a while. "Shit," he gasped, "I'm sorry."

Thurlow put his arm around Bo and held him tightly; put his fingers under Bo's chin and lifted it so they were looking into one another's eyes. Lou looked away, still a little mystified by the what-all going on across the campfire from her.

"This ain't your fault," Thurlow told Bo, "and thinking like that don't help. There's no shame in letting this bide until you're better—or just leaving it alone altogether, for that matter. We never set out to kill *all* the monsters, did we? Much less the ones who are helping you get well. Now drink this," he said, and tipped the flask into Bo's mouth. The liquor seemed to soothe Bo's cough, at least temporarily.

"You understand, don't you?" Millie asked Lou.

Lou did… mostly. She'd kept working the whole time her father was sick, taking on every case she could even if it meant late nights or the occasional day she didn't get to see him. She'd never once questioned that decision—hadn't really thought about it as even being a "decision" in the first place. Work was something one did, rain or shine, hungover or healthy, good mood or foul. Her father had taught her the best habit a psychopomp could cultivate was to relentlessly abjure pride or egotism; to keep in mind that the vocation of putting the dead to rest was always more important than the person doing it. Even when her mother and Vilhelm had begged her to take some time off, days, or weeks even; encouraged her to turn over some of her caseload to Imre, or just refer people to other good psychopomps in the area, she'd taken her father at his word, and she knew he'd respected her for it.

But as Lou watched Bo struggle with his cough, looking brittle and forlorn over his having to turn her down because of his illness, she felt that maybe she should have been there more for her father—been there more *with* her father. She would never see him again, never speak with him again. Never get back the hours she'd spent tramping around San Francisco dealing with death while he contemplated his own in the apartment above Ailien's shop.

Of course, it was always easier to judge things in retrospect.

"Shucks, of course I understand," said Lou casually. "I mean, taking down Dr. Panacea wasn't part of my initial plan. I just wanted to help people—if they need it, I mean." She managed a smile. "I only considered the possibility once I knew you and your crew were around. It'll be way better if I just stick to my original idea." Well, it was true she'd be better off doing things that way; whether or not she *would* was another question.

Not right now, however—for right now, she felt exhausted and overwhelmed. This had been a surprisingly emotional visit. She decided it was time for bed.

"Seeing as it's not getting any warmer, I guess I'll head back." Lou's head swam momentarily as she stood up. Definitely time for some sleep. "I'm sorry, but I'm dog-tired. Will you excuse me?"

"Hold up," said Bo, "I'll head back with you. I'm tired too. Good night, everybody." Bo got unsteadily to his feet with the help of his cane. "Hopefully I can get down tomorrow, but if not…"

"Whatever you can manage," said Thurlow, embracing him and kissing him. "Don't worry about us. Millie and I do just fine by ourselves."

"*I* do fine by *myself,*" said Millie. "Thurlow cries all damn day, he misses you so much."

Lou scarcely heard Millie's sass. She was too busy watching Bo and Thurlow kiss one another. On the mouth.

They weren't just friendly traveling companions. They were in love—more than that, they were lovers. Her guts did a somersault as she looked away, trying not to lose it. But really, holy hell! Lou'd never especially cared when people she met turned out to be that way; Shai, for instance. But seeing the boy she'd loved since she was a kid kiss another fellow… why hadn't he ever told her he liked men? All this time—all these years! If only she'd known…

"Lou?"

"Huh?"

"You ready?"

She blinked. "Oh… yeah. Good night everyone, nice to meet you and all that," she muttered as Millie and Thurlow exchanged looks. Well, *fuck* them. And fuck Bo, too, while there was fucking going on. He could have told her something like *Hey, I'd like you to come down and meet my boyfriend* instead of springing it on her like this. That would have been friendly.

It was slow, hard work getting back up to the San. It had gotten steadily colder as they visited with Millie and Thurlow, and the chill aggravated Bo's cough. He struggled with the ascent, heavily relying on his walking stick. Lou didn't mind the pace or that he had to save his breath for the effort; she didn't feel much like conversation. She had a lot on her mind.

She was happy for Bo. She could say that honestly. The way he and Thurlow had touched with such sweet intimacy, how they seemed to understand one another so well, it was nice to see. But part of her felt shattered by that intimacy, the part that had carried Bo's torch for so long—and the part of her that had always considered him her best friend. Why hadn't he ever told her? Was it something she'd done? Said?

And really, what the hell. Wasn't she close enough to a boy?

When they reached the top, Lou opened the front door and bowed Bo inside. "M'lord," she said, trying to sound cool and casual. Instead, she bleated it like a sick sheep.

"You doing okay?" he wheezed. "Sorry if my friends were a little standoffish. We're pretty tight-knit. Have to be. And it's not just you, trust me. When Millie joined up with us Jack gave her hell for months."

"I wasn't worried," she said, more shortly than she intended.

"Oh, well, that was extremely convincing," he said. "Glad to hear it."

"Look," said Lou. "It's just, I—"

"I was teasing you."

"Save your breath," she snapped. "You need your rest, and so do I."

Bo grinned at her as he pulled a small flask out of his white waistcoat. "That's too bad. I was going to ask you in for a nightcap, after I went to the trouble of stealing this away from Thurlow."

Lou's guts twisted again—they'd been doing that a lot today—but she shrugged as nonchalantly as she could.

"No reason not to, right?"

"Can't think of one off the top of my head," said Bo. "Come on, let's go get drunk. Like old times, right?"

"Yeah," she said, as lightly as she could. "Just like old times."

Chapter Five

Later, when Lou lay awake in her bed long into the night, she could still feel dried tears on her face, Bo's arms around her, the tingling on her skin where he had kissed her; could still smell his rot-sweet breath. She massaged her stomach as she stared up at the stone ceiling in the dim glow of her fungal night-light. Fountain of Youth's health-promoting cuisine was giving her quite the bellyache. She groaned to herself, not just from the pain.

"Better be quiet," Bo had whispered as he slipped his key into the lock on his door. It opened with a low creak. "Folks go to sleep early, like Coriander was saying."

It hadn't been totally dark in his room. One of the ubiquitous wads of phosphorescent lichen allowed them to navigate safely even without a lantern. Even so, Lou got the lamp lit as quickly as possible; the bluish light was unwelcoming and cold. She felt a sense of relief as the yellow flame rose in the glass chimney and the room brightened.

"Whew," sighed Bo, as he settled into his chair. "That's better. That last hill took a lot out of me."

"It would take a lot out of anyone," she said, though the slope had given her no trouble at all. Or so she had thought. It felt overly warm in Bo's room, though that might just be her body quickening as it tended to do around him, even now. Being alone with Bo always made her uncomfortably aware of herself, and tonight she acutely felt the way the cloth of her uniform rubbed against her skin, even the tension of the bolo tie around her neck. She briefly wondered how she'd dealt with feeling so crazy around him before he left... then again, she'd been sixteen and had felt crazy all the time.

"Do you want to sit?"

She looked around. He'd taken the chair, so her only options were his bed and the locked chest...

"Go on, take the bed," he said. "Don't worry. I won't tell."

"Huh?"

"Don't want to get a reputation, do you?"

Lou realized he was teasing her again. She decided to change the subject.

"Seems like you've been having some interesting times since you left," she said, as she sank down onto his mattress.

"You too."

"I always do."

Bo chuckled. "I've missed you, Lou. Every day. You can't know how much."

"I missed you, too. Getting into trouble's not so much fun without a partner in crime."

"Don't I know it," he said. "Wish you'd been able come out to New York when I was there, we could have had some wild times."

"I bet. But you know, the Agency... it keeps me busy." She decided not to point out that he'd never actually invited her.

"Of course. So things are good?"

"Things are good. Plenty of work, as always." Lou steeled herself, sensing what the next question would be.

"How's Arch—"

"Dead."

Bo's mouth fell open. "Jesus Christ," he said, after a moment. "I didn't—I never..."

"Don't worry about it. I didn't know about," she swallowed, "you and Thurlow." Between the two topics, she'd rather talk about Bo's love life, which was saying a lot.

"Oh." Bo looked sheepish. "Yeah. Guess I should've told you."

"Yeah. You should've." Lou felt even hotter and sweatier, but it wasn't lust.

She wasn't *that* mixed up, it was her pain and indignation gathering into a tight knot in her chest. How could he not realize this was a big deal? "You should've—could've—Jesus, what the hell, Bo? I thought we were friends."

"Lou, you're my best friend. It's just…"

"It's just *what?*"

Bo looked at her, but Lou looked away, unable to hold his gaze after seeing what it held. They had been friends for too long for her to not understand what his eyes were telling her: that he had always known how she felt about him, and thus never known how to tell her about his own feelings.

"Sorry," said Lou. "I didn't mean to sound…"

"It wasn't the kind of thing I could put on a postcard."

"Yeah." She took a deep breath. "So you're… happy? Seems like it."

"You've no idea. He's… Lou, I can't explain it. I never thought… I mean, his breath smells bad in the morning just like everyone else's. But I love him." Bo shrugged. "Also, you wouldn't believe how strong and fast he is! You'll give him your stamp of approval, I know it."

"You don't need it."

"No, but I'd like it. But that's not… I didn't mean to… I'm sorry. When did Archie… pass?"

Goddamn it. She'd really rather talk about anything, even what he and Thurlow did when they were alone.

"Lou?"

"Less than a year ago."

"Jesus," he said again.

"Yeah."

"Was it… bad?"

"It got bad." Lou hated herself for choking up, but she could say no more. Through streaming eyes she watched Bo lurch over to her and sit beside her on the bed. He put his hand over hers.

"I wish I'd been there for you."

"It's okay."

"No, it's not," said Bo. "You're my best friend, Lou, and I wasn't there for you when you needed me most. I'm sorry. If I'd known, I would've come home." He took her chin in his fingertips, forced her to look up at him. "For *you*. Not for him."

Bo's words, his touch, unlocked something in Lou. She threw her arms around her oldest friend and cried harder than she'd let herself cry when her father passed away, harder than when she'd first realized he was never going to get better again. She'd hid from herself and from Vilhelm and *especially* from her mother during everything, and even after, figuring everyone had his or her own grief to deal with without her adding to it. But there was no stopping her sorrow now; she buried her face in Bo's armpit and sobbed, clinging to him. He held her tightly, and cried too.

When she was able, Lou told him about how brave her father had been, how much she looked up to the grace and strength he'd displayed, even at the end... but she also told Bo things she'd never once spoken about to another person. What it had been like to see her father enduring such pain; how helpless she had felt watching him suffer. How, as the disease progressed he'd seemed embarrassed for her to see him in such a weakened state, and how she'd kept her distance so he wouldn't have to hide or feel ashamed. How he'd had to relinquish much of his dignity when he'd gotten too weak to care for himself. How she'd avoided both her parents at times, disturbed by how their relationship had changed from husband and wife to child and mother. How towards the end, she'd looked into her father's eyes and seen a different person looking back at her.

Then she realized who she was talking to, and peeled herself off of Bo.

"I shouldn't," she said, wiping her face with her sleeve. "I know, uh, you have your own stuff to deal with."

"Whoa, what the hell," he said. "I'm not there yet, and anyways I'm getting better. Talk about whatever you want. It's hard enough to watch someone pass away, you shouldn't have to do it on your own."

"You don't even know."

"I do," said Bo. "My aunt, when we were kids, remember—"

"You don't know," said Lou harshly. Bo drew away from her, frowning. "You think you know what I'm talking about, but you don't. I remember when your aunt died, but she wasn't, she didn't..."

"What?"

"My Ma, she, I mean, my dad told her to, but she... I haven't told anyone this..." Lou swallowed, her eyes welling up again. Giving voice to the memory was harder than she ever imagined it would be. "Bo, do you remember that book we read, the one my dad had, on the history of psychopompery?"

"That was always your thing, not mine."

"No, come on. We read it together, we were at your ma's house, it was raining, and we read about how for centuries all exorcisms and banishings and whatever else, they were performed by priests, and—"

"Lou, what are you talking about?"

"I'm talking about how we read a bunch of fucked up shit about stealing souls—extracting someone's vital essence while they're still alive!"

"Oh," said Bo. "Okay, yeah, I remember that." His eyes went wide. "Ailien did that?"

Lou nodded. "I wasn't supposed to know, but I found out. I… watched." She shuddered. "For days after she removed his soul he just lay there, eyes open, until his body caught up and died. It was awful, but that way there wouldn't be any suspicion that he, he'd asked her to…"

"How awful." Bo looked grim. "I can't imagine how hard it was for her to do that."

"What?" It was Lou's turn to gape. The memory of spying on her mother and father through the keyhole to their bedroom was so potent that she could almost smell the sour reek of sweat and illness that had emanated from under the door, could almost hear the low whispers of her parents as Ailien made the final preparations. With painful clarity she saw her father take her mother's small hand in his bony, pinkish one. He'd asked her if she was sure she could go through with it, and Lou had been so shocked to see her mother bite her lip, reclaim her hand so she could hide her bloodshot eyes, and shuddering, slouch into her tears. Ailien did not stutter or hesitate. Ailien did not cry. She was always so calm, so sure of herself—almost infuriatingly so, to the point that Lou had, in her darker moments, believed her mother indifferent to her husband's suffering. To see her break down completely had come as a shock… though it was nothing to what she felt when her father's face went slack for the last time once Ailien used the psuilver-needled extractor to withdraw his soul before sending it through the door…

"Lou? Lou!"

Bo was shaking her, and Lou tore herself away as she came back to the present.

"She shouldn't have done it!" cried Lou wildly. "She should have—"

"Lou! If it's obvious to *me*, then *you* of all people have got to know that what she did was the quickest, safest way to put him out of his pain and ensure he'd cross over without any complications."

"Fuck that! Fuck you! People die all the time without, without…"

"Would you rather have exorcised his corpse? Did it ever occur to you maybe they were trying to spare you that?"

No, it hadn't. Bo's words brought Lou up short. The idea that her father had chosen to die in such a way to shield her from discomfort was shocking, mostly because it made sense. He must have known Lou would never have allowed anyone else to do any necessary psychopompic work, and as she contemplated having to argue with her own father's ghost about crossing over into death, she dissolved into tears again.

"You're right," she snuffled. "I never…"

"Hey, it's okay."

"It's not. I wish I was home. I've, towards my mother… I wish I could tell her…"

"You'll tell her. It doesn't have to be tonight. And anyways, I'm sure she understands. She raised you, didn't she? By now nothing you do could shock her."

Lou ran her hands over her short hair with a wry smile. "You'd think that, wouldn't you."

"She's only human."

"I just miss him so much." She found it was easier to admit that now, for some reason. "All the time. I wish I'd had him for longer, for myself, but also, with work… I know how to do it, the job, but not like he did."

"Lou, I'm sure you're great!"

"Maybe."

"Well, what does your partner think?"

"Vilhelm?"

"No, your field partner."

"I don't have a field partner." Lou sighed when she saw Bo looked about ready to strangle her. "Don't *you* start on me now."

"What happened to Imre?"

"He's finishing his degree. I have him covering for me while I'm gone. It'll be good experience for him."

"So what's the problem?"

Lou shrugged. "I didn't want to distract him."

"Wait, so you never—it's not that he said no, it's that you never asked him?" Bo rolled his eyes. "Well, that's just dumb. Some other agency's gonna snap him up one of these days. He was good. What are you waiting for?"

Lou looked up into Bo's eyes, unable to tell him the truth.

"Oh, Lou. I—"

"I know. I know… now."

He seemed to need to explain himself to her. "It's just, the gang and I, we're good at what we do. I mean, you know what this costs, this San? It's no big deal to us. We've got money, we're building a reputation. Plus, I like traveling around. And more than that…" He swallowed. "Ghosts were never my thing. Goddamn eerie. Give me a swampsquatch, or a giant carnivorous beaver any day."

"Giant carnivorous *what* now?" Lou giggled, which felt good, after all the boo-hooing.

"Never seen one? Not stuffed or anything? Oh, man, there are these beavers in Arkansas… that's how Millie ended up with us, you know. Sort of, at least. She hired us to hunt some with her, then decided to join up with us… her family all got munched one day while she was out chasing a shoat that had run off into the woods." Bo shivered. "She's never said much but that they gnawed right through the walls of her cabin. Didn't leave much to bury. Or to rebuild, for that matter. Her husband, her baby girl… gone."

"Jesus."

"I didn't mean to change the subject," said Bo.

Suddenly wishing to be alone, Lou stood, stretched her back, and grinned.

"Nah. It's late, and I'm hoarse from blubbering all over you. Isn't there some sort of early class I gotta go to tomorrow? Need to get my rest so I can jump around and touch my toes or whatever I'll be expected to do."

Bo stood as well, and embraced her again. "You know, if I'd realized you were counting on—"

She pulled away. "I wasn't counting on nothing," she lied. "I just didn't want to disappoint you if you assumed you had a job waiting for you. Seeing you cry once in my life is enough for me."

"Aw," he said. "Not me. You're kind of cute when you're all snot-nosed and whimpering."

"Gross."

Bo kissed her on the cheek. She pulled away, blushing, and yanked the bolo tie from her neck.

"Here," she said, thrusting it at him. She didn't want it anymore, didn't even want to see it. "I think… you should take this back."

Bo hesitated. "No, Lou… it's yours. I had it made specially for you."

"I remember," she snapped, but repented her temper when she saw the hurt in his eyes. "It's lucky, isn't it?" she said, more gently, pressing it into his palm. "Seems like you need it more than me right now. Keep it… until you get better. All right?"

"All right. Whatever you like."

"Yeah," she said. "Well… good night," she blurted, and did her best not to straight-up flee his room.

So that was that, she thought to herself, staring at the ceiling. All her expectations, all her plans, gone over the course of one conversation. The worst part was, she knew she should have seen it coming. Maybe not every little detail, but her whole dream—Bo coming home, them working together, maybe settling down, it all seemed so ridiculous now that she was really thinking about it. He'd never given her any indication any of that shit would ever happen, so why had she clung to the illusion for so long?

No use crying over spilled milk—or shattered dreams, for that matter. All she could do was resolve to stop letting her desire color her expectations so much. Reality was brutal enough, even when you didn't hold it up next to a fantasy.

It had been one hell of a night. The bellyache was just the capstone. Or was it? Realizing she'd been feeling kind of funny since before dinner even started, Lou hopped out of bed and relit the lantern. Her suspicions were confirmed. On top of everything else, she'd gotten her goddamn period.

Chapter Six

Lou had packed a few rags in with her clothes, but she could do nothing about the throbbing waves of aching pain that woke her sometime in the early morning—telling time was tough underground. When rolling around in bed curled into a ball got boring Lou got up, ran a comb through her hair, and decided to walk up to the exercise deck. She knew the mysterious gong would summon her when it was time for class, but she figured she might as well be outside as in, given she wasn't snoozing.

She questioned her decision when she stepped outside and the cold hit her like a slap to the face. It wasn't snowing anymore, but during the night several more inches had fallen. Lou shivered and fluffed up her scarf around her neck.

Clouds hid the rising sun; no birds called to one another as they had the day before. White drifts clung to every pine bough, but the boardwalk and deck were clear. There were a few snow-piles in unobtrusive locations; someone must have been out here at the very crack of dawn, shoveling away.

She wandered over toward the empty exercise deck, past the steaming hot spring and the iced-over deck chairs, until she reached the guardrail at the edge of the platform. Using her sleeve to clear away a patch of snow, she leaned on her elbows, chin in hand, and looked over the quiet valley. The trail that had been so clear yesterday when she arrived had disappeared, and the cows and goats were nowhere to be seen.

It was nice to think of nothing, to say nothing, after all the craziness the day before. She took in the beauty of the scenery and let her mind go blank, let Bo, his friends, Dr. Panacea, Shai, and everything else fall away.

Then another wave of cramps hit her, and Lou winced and put her hand over belly, hoping the warmth would soothe the muscles. It was too bad she couldn't take a dip without needing to do a lot of explaining as to why she'd introduced herself as Mr. Merriwether.

Something touched her shoulder. So lost in thought had she been that Lou yelped as she whirled—only to find Coriander standing there, wide-eyed, with both her hands over her mouth.

"Sorry!" she squealed. "I didn't mean to startle you."

"You didn't startle me," said Lou. "I mean, maybe a little, but no harm done."

"Good! Well, again, I apologize, but I was just so excited to see you!" Lou didn't know how anyone could be so chipper—ever, but especially at that time in the morning. "What are you doing out here so early?"

"Couldn't sleep. Say, want to come with me to get a bite to eat or a cup of coffee before whatever it is we're supposed to be doing this morning?"

Coriander giggled. "Breakfast is after class. Dr. Panacea says that exercising on an empty stomach allows the blood to flow more freely through the abdomen."

Lou groaned. Calisthenics class being required was bad enough, but withholding food? That was just *mean*.

"I know, it's terrible," said Coriander. "But trust me—after being here a few months, you'll get used to it."

"Months?" Lou wanted nothing more than to be away from this dump as quickly as possible.

"Oh, yes. I'm here for the duration. Nice to meet you, I'm Rapunzel," said Coriander, grabbing Lou's hand and shaking it. "Locked away until a prince rescues me. Or to be more specific, until my parents find some idiot willing to marry me, bad reputation and all. It shouldn't be too hard. There's lots of money in it for whoever signs on the dotted line."

Lou raised an eyebrow at Coriander. "What did you do, cause a scandal kissing a boy at a church social?"

"Oh, if I kissed boys it would thrill my parents to pieces," said Coriander, with another giggle. "They sent me here to cure me of my wickedness, you

know. Fiber and clean living to purge me of sin. I'm sure you know all about
that."

"Huh?" Lou was mildly baffled by Coriander's statement, but before she
could ask for clarification the door swung open again. It was the Rutherfords.

"Good morning," said Mrs. Rutherford cordially. Lou assumed the courtesy was due to Coriander. "Hope you both slept well?"

Right behind her were Mrs. Grosvenor and Mr. Magnusson. As the door
opened again, to reveal Mr. Dumpling and Bo, Lou heard the gong ringing
inside.

"Morning," Lou said to Bo as brightly as she could, after he limped up
alongside her.

"It sure is."

Lou couldn't tell if things between them were awkward or not, but there
was no time to worry about it. Miss Foxglove had just come outside, the
bleary-eyed Willoughbys trailing behind her, and was calling for them to
assemble in a circle so they could "warm up." She didn't mean going inside
for cocoa, unfortunately.

The next half-hour proved both hilarious and agonizing. Miss Foxglove
started them with a series of movements that had them jumping, running
in place, and all sorts of other incredibly silly activities, then made them
twist and bend into a bunch of bizarre poses. After this came jumping
jacks and toe-touches and some moves Lou had no words to describe. It
was not the sort of workout she would have thought would be suitable for
consumptives and the sickly. At least Miss Foxglove seemed a decent nurse
as well as instructor. She responded quickly to anyone's fatigue, suggested
alternate ways of completing sets when people faltered, and for every harsh
correction she gave some praise.

"Holy cats, I want a cigarette," said Lou to Bo when they took a short
break. Coriander hushed her quickly, but the damage had been done. Miss
Foxglove was staring at her, and she did not look pleased.

"Did you say *cigarette?"* she snapped.

"Yeah?"

"You have tobacco with you?" Miss Foxglove stomped over. The deck
rattled with the indignant force of her strides.

"Like, right now?" said Lou, confused. Bo laughed, and then started
coughing.

His wet hacking did not seem to concern Miss Foxglove. Lou stared after him, worried as he moved away from the group to ride out the attack, but Miss Foxglove was now all up in her face, scolding her in front of everyone.

"Despite what you might have heard, inhaling noxious fumes from burning plants is not at all good for the lungs or the heart," she said. She was slightly taller than Lou and loomed over her, waggling her finger. "Such substances are forbidden here!"

"I didn't—"

"Think, Mr. Merriwether! Even if you were to go off on your own to smoke, the clouds might drift into the faces of our other patients. All the good work of clean living and Elixir—undone! Literally *up in smoke!*"

"It's true," sniffed Mrs. Willoughby. "He was puffing on them the whole time we were traveling together. It was most unpleasant."

Miss Foxglove *tsk*ed. "After class I will escort you to your rooms. You will turn in your supplies at once!"

Lou had no intention whatsoever of turning over anything, but she was too preoccupied to protest. Bo was having a serious fit off to the side of the exercise area. The snow around where he was doubled over coughing was tinged with pink.

Miss Foxglove, upon realizing the recipient of her polemic was not really listening, snapped her fingers in front of Lou's face.

Lou swatted the woman's hand aside. "Quack at me later." She pointed at Bo. "Help him!"

"How dare you!" cried the sandy-haired fitness instructor. "I shall tell the doctor about this, mark my—"

"I don't give a shit what you tell the doc about me," said Lou as she crouched down beside Bo, "but you'll have to tell him why this man's died if you don't do your job and help him!"

"Calm yourself," said Miss Foxglove, and took a flask of the Elixir of Life out of her pocket. "Open your mouth," she instructed, and when Bo did so, she used a dropper to put some clear liquid on his tongue. He swallowed, and his coughing subsided almost immediately. Lou was amazed—and wondered what a straight dose of the water of life might do for him, given how powerful the diluted stuff was.

"I think he should see the doctor," said Lou, still anxious. "I'll take him—"

"He doesn't need to go to the doctor," said Miss Foxglove. "He needs to get back up and complete his morning exercises. As do you, Mr. Merriwether. Now stop this carrying-on and get into formation!"

Lou heard the murmuring behind her; knew she was attracting attention to herself, not quietly finding out information, but in that moment, she didn't give a shit. She knew she'd live to regret the words, but that only made speaking them all the sweeter.

"*Fuck* your formation."

The collective gasp made her pretty happy.

"Leave my class," barked Miss Foxglove. "Go—go and report to Dr. Panacea at once!"

"You really blew it," said Bo, under his breath. "I'm fine."

Lou stood and lazily dusted off her hands on her trousers. "Nothing would make me happier, Miss Foxglove," she said sweetly. "I'll see you this evening. Really looking forward to another one of these classes."

She left Miss Foxglove to sputter at her, striding across the deck with a swagger in her step, but really, Lou was feeling pretty low. She really, *really* didn't want to go see Dr. Panacea right now, but she couldn't refuse.

There was a bench carved into the rock just outside Dr. Panacea's office, its seat softened with a yellow cushion. Approaching the door, Lou raised her hand to knock, but she paused when she heard raised voices coming from within. Sounded like an argument, or at least an intense discussion. She put her ear to the wood, but couldn't hear anything through the wood. Deciding if she wasn't able eavesdrop, she might as well let the doctor know she was around, Lou rapped her knuckles on the door. The voices quieted and a moment later the door creaked open. Dr. Panacea stood there in his black suit, staring at her balefully.

"You're early," he said.

"Huh?"

Dr. Panacea crossed his arms. "As much as I abhor lateness, arriving before you are supposed to is just as rude, Mr. Merriwether."

"How can I be early?" protested Lou. "I just now got sent to your office for disrupting calisthenics class."

At first, Dr. Panacea didn't seem to know what to make of her statement, but then he chuckled. "My goodness. Whatever did you do to poor Miss Foxglove?"

"It's possible I got a little ratty with her. She seemed to take issue with me smoking."

Dr. Panacea stared at her, eyebrows raised. "As well she might. Well, please accept my apologies. It seems you are not early—you are right on time. But I must finish something first. Please, take a seat… I'll be with you in a moment."

He shut the door, and the conversation between him and the other person resumed. Lou still couldn't decipher much, so she plunked her bottom down on the bench—and realized with a start that it was time to decide exactly what she wanted to say to Dr. Panacea when she went in there. She'd been so distracted since her arrival she hadn't thought about which lie to cultivate—had fallen back on the old one, about being sick, as it seemed easiest. And yet, that might not be the best idea…

The way she saw it, she had two options. She could tell Dr. Panacea she was sick, and that was her reason for being at Fountain of Youth—the lie she had told Shai, and most everyone else—or she could tell him the lie she'd told Ned and Coyote, that she was interested in being a middleman, funneling cheap Chinese labor his way for personal profit.

The first option wasn't great. Shai had already called her on her bluff of being ill, and gotten her to "confess" in the process. In spite of that, she might be able to play it off to Dr. Panacea, feed him a line about being bashful in front of people who weren't doctors. Using the pretense of being sick might give her more time to explore the San, find the Chinese workers, see what they were up to, that sort of thing.

The second option might help to further her investigation more rapidly… but it would also put her in a much more vulnerable position. If Dr. Panacea didn't want a middleman—if he was hiding his recruiting of Chinese laborers in order to eat them, or work them until they died, then surely he wouldn't want her sniffing around, even if she claimed to be as unscrupulous as he regarding their welfare. She needed to be careful—if he viewed her as a threat, she couldn't think of much that would stop him from just snapping her neck in his office, or throwing her off a—

The door swung open. Lou got to her feet and took off her hat as Mrs. Panacea emerged, looking ethereal and lovely in a day-dress the color of sea foam. Lou felt disoriented, bemused by her own uncertainty. It was incredibly bizarre that she was unable to tell if this woman was Shai or not. Even identical twins had their differences, subtle as they were… in a fraternal pair, one would think it would be obvious.

"I'm sorry to keep you waiting," she said softly, calm and apparently unaffected by the disagreement she'd been having with her husband. "If you'll excuse me, I must go prepare to lead today's prayer meeting. It's this afternoon, at three, in the chapel. I do hope you'll come, Mr. Merriwether?"

"I'll see what I can do." Lou glanced over the woman's shoulder, feeling Dr. Panacea's eyes boring into her like a hand drill. "Might be busy, though. First real day here and all."

Mrs. Panacea inclined her head and disappeared down the winding hallway. Even her gait was different than Shai's.

Lou turned back to the doctor, who had regained his composure. He bowed to her.

"Come in, please. I'm eager to make your acquaintance. You've been making quite the impression here since your arrival."

"I have?" Lou stepped inside the doctor's office to find a cave three times the size of her private room, with a loftier ceiling, a deep, soft, but ugly rug on the floor, and rich mahogany furniture. Then she heard the doctor inhale twice quickly through his nostrils as she walked by, and it drove all thoughts of space or furnishings from her mind. He was *sniffing* her, and she turned on her heel to find him smiling pleasantly, if toothily, at her.

In that moment, pure panic hit her. Sweat broke out under her armpits and on her forehead, and she began to tremble. What had she been thinking, barging in to Dr. Panacea's office like it was no big deal? She'd been so steamed-up from her encounter with Miss Foxglove she hadn't thought anything through—hadn't, for example, stopped by her room to pick up any tools of her trade. And now she was alone with a goddamn vampire without even a vermilion-inked scroll in her pocket. She could die here, easily, if she said the wrong thing; hell, if the doc really wanted to make a party of it, and killed off Bo and his cronies, no one would even know where to find her bones.

"Welcome, Mr. Merriwether," said the doctor. "What do you say we go ahead with your intake appointment as we discuss your... conduct?"

"Sure." Her voice was too tremulous. She shouldn't be this nervous, she reminded herself.

Dr. Panacea looked at her expectantly. After a moment of them staring at one another awkwardly, he coughed delicately into his fist.

"To do your intake I must examine you, Mr. Merriwether. Please, shed your uniform down to your undergarments and get up on the table." He pointed at a long narrow bench covered in yellow leather.

It was time to make her decision—it was now or never. She made her choice. "Well, the thing is, I'm not really..." she began, but Dr. Panacea silenced her with a gesture.

"I am already aware you are female, Mr. Merriwether. Do not worry."

She froze, completely blindsided by this. The lie about acting as a middle-man had been right on the tip of her tongue, and now...

"Your reasons for concealing your sex do not concern me. I am a physician, and as such I am interested in the health of your body—whatever sort of body it might be."

Shai must have told him. *Of course* he'd told him—he'd told him everything. No reason he wouldn't have given his lover a more truthful account of his travels than his ill sister, if sister she was.

Lou felt abandoned, more even than she'd felt that morning after their heart-to-heart on the rock. Even after everything Shai had said and done, it hurt to know he'd betrayed *her* secret—that he'd betrayed her. After all his promises and sweet-talk, he'd sold her out to Dr. Panacea the first chance he'd gotten, body and soul. And if he'd told the doctor she was female, she had no way of knowing what else he had revealed—what the two of them had discussed, in bed, or over dinner, before she'd even arrived.

Perhaps Dr. Panacea thought she had come for the formula for the Elixir of Life. Perhaps he didn't, and was keeping an open mind. It was impossible to know what conclusions he'd drawn from the account Shai had given of those brief days spent in one another's company, whatever that account had been.

Fear claimed her, totally, completely. She was in over her head, had swum out of her depth, and had no idea what to say or do.

"I'm sorry if I alarmed you, Mr. Merriwether," said Dr. Panacea. "I didn't mean to be insensitive. It's just, men's and women's skeletons are different."

He had interpreted her fear as being that of someone caught in a lie. She decided to go with that for now, until she got a better handle on her emotions.

"Really?"

"Yes. The shoulders, the ribcage, the angle of the pelvis—all can be spotted by the trained anatomist," he continued, "which, of course, I am. As I said, it makes no difference to me. Now, may we continue?"

Lou didn't want to continue. She wanted to run out of there. To do so would call even more attention to herself, so she docilely shimmied out of her uniform, blushing furiously. She felt faint, and her armpits were now more than damp, sweat was running down her sides; to be so bare in front of this creature was terrifying and humiliating. Shai had been the only one to see her unclothed in years, and he'd had the decency not to act like such a creep about it.

She heaved herself up onto the bench, shivering. The warmth of the room had not prevented her from breaking out in gooseflesh.

"What seems to be the trouble?"

"My…" Lou faltered. If Shai had told Dr. Panacea she was a woman, surely he'd told the doctor she'd copped to not really being sick. Dr. Panacea must just be playing with her, a deadly game of charades, or maybe the gentle swats of a cat messing with a mouse before the final pounce. "Teeth," she said, saying the first thing that came to mind.

"Your… teeth?" She'd actually surprised him. She decided to run with it.

"Yeah. They bother me. A lot. And I'm too chicken to get 'em pulled."

"You're telling me you came all the way to Fountain of Youth for the sake of your teeth?"

"Why, is that strange? They're the only ones I'll ever have."

He still seemed puzzled. "I've just never had anyone… well… I suppose I might as well examine you, Mr. Merriwether, just on the off chance some other malady might be influencing your… *teeth*…"

"Whatever you think's best, Dr. P."

He began an examination similar to the ones Lou's mother performed on her patients. His cool fingers briefly prodded at the fresh pink scar tissue around her bullet wound, but he did not enquire about that injury, instead turning his attention to feeling her limbs and testing her reflexes while asking her about what dental treatments she had sought out before coming to Fountain of Youth. Lou invented some plausible-sounding quackery, and didn't think she was lying all that badly, but the doctor's eyebrow raises and occasional musical chuckles did not exactly indicate success. Still, he seemed to be taking her at face value for whatever reason.

"So what do you think, Doc?" asked Lou, after he made her lie on her back and pressed gently on her stomach.

"You seem to be in perfect health… other than your smoking, and your teeth, of course. Frankly, I'm amazed you came all the way out here just because they trouble you."

"You've no idea how bad it is, especially as I like to eat." Dr. Panacea seemed skeptical. "Plus, when Shai healed me up when I got shot, that Elixir of yours helped the bullet-wound, but it also made my teeth feel loads better. That's when I really decided it would be worth it to trek all the way out here."

"I beg your pardon." Dr. Panacea's voice sounded of distant thunder, the growl of some ferocious wild beast. "Are you saying you acquired that scar while traveling with my assistant?"

Lou was lost. It seemed bizarre that Shai had told Dr. Panacea that she was a woman, but not that they'd been rolled up on by road agents. "It wasn't a big deal. Shai knew just what to do. I tell you what, that assistant of yours is cooler'n an icehouse in January. Even when—"

"You're saying that Shai healed you after you were shot?"

Lou was having a difficult time understanding why Dr. Panacea was so upset. No—not upset… angry. She flinched when he spoke again. Knowing who he was, and what he was capable of, it made her understand Shai's fear a lot better.

"He healed me up, yeah. Considerate of him, but then again, I pretty much saved his life. See, he'd sliced up one of the bandits with his sword, but the other—"

"I don't care. I am asking whether Shai knew about you. Your… identity, I mean."

Lou finally understood. *Shai hadn't betrayed her.* He had kept his promise—kept her secret. Whatever else, he had been true to her in that regard. Dr. Panacea must have been telling the truth about male and female skeletons, or maybe that had been a big story and he'd just smelled her menstrual blood. That seemed possible, too, him being a vampire and all that. The problem was, what did it all mean? How was she to proceed? What was she supposed to say, or do, to get closer to either finding the missing Chinese, or sending this vampire where he belonged?

Oh, how she hated this detective work, the threads she was expected to tie together, the hints and clues she needed to process and respond to at a moment's notice! She vowed, if she survived, never to leave San Francisco again, and to turn any and all leads on this kind of monster over to people who actually knew what they were doing.

"I, uh, kinda got upset when it all went down," she stammered, realizing that she'd accidentally thrown Shai under the wagon, believing he'd done the same to her. "Don't tell too many people I'm a… you know? I made him swear to secrecy." Nothing she said seemed to mollify Dr. Panacea. "It's not his fault he didn't tell you once I showed up—if he even knows I'm here, right? Isn't he on the other side of the mountain, like you said?"

"Yes, and likely to stay there for the time being," said Dr. Panacea. He turned away from Lou and went over to his desk, where he sat down and began to write in a notebook. "Thank you for coming in Mr. Merriwether," he said without looking up. "I hope you find the duration of your stay pleasurable. I will come up with a treatment plan for your teeth as quickly as possible. Good afternoon."

It took Lou a moment to realize she'd been dismissed, but once she did, she high-tailed it the hell out of Dr. Panacea's office. Short of him actively trying to eat her sorry ass, she didn't know how her first encounter with the villain could have possibly gone worse.

Chapter Seven

Lou tried to keep from actually running back to her room; it was difficult to keep herself to a walk. She'd messed up, big time. No denying that. Not only had she concocted yet another ridiculous lie to keep track of, she'd gotten Shai into a heap of trouble, made herself stand out more rather than less to the most dangerous person at Fountain of Youth, and in the process gained exactly no new information on what was really going on.

More than anything she wished she had someone she could talk the whole thing over with. Bo would be the natural choice, but that was impossible. Thurlow had been right—Bo's job right now was getting better. He didn't need to be reminded at every moment of how those closest to him could sure use his help if only he were well.

Lou turned the key in her door and flung it open. She wished more than anything that she could ask her father for advice. He'd always known what to do, or at least how to think through a confusing problem. Maybe Bo and Vilhelm were right. Maybe she couldn't do this job on her own. Maybe she *did* need a partner.

And yet, her first attempt at asking for help had turned out pretty disastrously. She sat down on her bed, suddenly exhausted. No wonder—she was alone, matching her wits against an ancient monster who, to be perfectly honest, was much smarter than she was, and in spite of her being a psychopomp, was clearly more of a threat to her than she was to him.

"Mr. Merriwether?"

Lou didn't answer the voice on the opposite side of her door, or the hesitant knock.

"Mr. Merriwether, are you in there? It's me, Coriander!"

Bubbly debutantes were nothing Lou felt capable of handling, but as it turned out, she didn't have a choice. The door swung open and there was Coriander, looking fresh and lovely with her curly auburn hair braided and curled into a bun at the base of her neck. A few wisps had sprung loose, framing her face prettily.

Lou tried to school her face into calmness. "Hey Coriander," she said, "I—"

"I thought I heard your door slam. Why weren't you at breakfast? I saved you a seat!"

Given how few people were staying at the San right now that probably hadn't been too difficult. Lou elected not to voice that particular sentiment, taking the compliment in the spirit in which it had been intended.

"I had to go through the whole intake rigmarole with the doc," she said heavily. "Anyways, yeah, I appreciate you coming by, but…"

"What's wrong? Are you…" Coriander, instead of politely taking her leave, barged in and plunked her ample behind right down beside Lou's narrow one and took Lou's hands in hers. "You look so upset! Whatever he diagnosed you with, you'll be fine, I know it! I'm the only person here that the Elixir of Life hasn't helped, but that's because I'm not really sick. My parents claimed I was an hysteric during my intake, but really, it was just an excuse to have me locked up someplace less scandalous than an asylum. There's no cure for girls who like girls, of course."

Coriander's frankness shocked Lou out of her depression. "That's horrible!"

The girl turned pink and released Lou quickly. "Oh! I'm sorry, I thought you'd understand."

"What?" Coriander really looked unhappy. Lou couldn't figure out what she'd said to distress her.

"Just, last night, when Bo said that thing about you finally starting to like girls, I thought…"

"No, no," said Lou, realizing her error, "I'm sorry. I meant it's horrible your parents would bundle you off into the middle of nowhere over something like that!"

Coriander brightened. "Oh! Good. I know you can't tell about people, but the way you look at Bo, well. It wasn't hard to tell you like boys, Mr. Merriwether."

Lou cringed inwardly. Was she really so obvious? "Coriander," she said, "first of all, call me Lou. Secondly…"

"I won't tell Bo you have a crush on him if you don't want me to."

"He already knows."

"Good!"

"Not good. I don't have a snowball's chance with him." Lou smiled wearily. "I'm a girl… and you probably already know Bo's inclined elseways."

She enjoyed Coriander's wide-eyed bewilderment. After her failure to convince Shai and the doctor she'd been worried she was losing her edge.

"A girl?" asked Coriander. "Really? But you… did you—do you—" She bit her lip.

"I dress like this all the time, and let people see what they want. It's just easier."

"Is it?"

"Sometimes." She gave Coriander a look. "It's certainly easier for me to be 'Mr. Merriwether' *here.*"

"Of course!" Coriander giggled. "Don't worry. I love secrets, and I'm *very* good at keeping them."

"Keep being good at it."

"I will—which also means you can tell me what you were so upset about!"

Lou considered what it would mean to take this girl into her confidence. Could she be trusted? While it was true that Lou had rarely met anyone who seemed so genuine, Coriander was a very new acquaintance—even if she acted like they were old friends.

The real question was how Coriander would react to not only Lou's information about who the doctor was and what he was doing here… but to Lou herself. Millie had not been alone in her assessment that psychopomps were spooky. Nothing new there, but coming from a seasoned monster-hunter it had stung more than just anyone's discomfort with her profession. Would Coriander react the same way? Would she smell the sour reek of the grave on Lou and bolt for the sunshine?

Figuring that at this point, things couldn't actually get that much worse in terms of her investigation—or hell, her chances for getting out of the San alive—Lou opened her mouth to speak her mind.

Her stomach grumbled. Loud.

Coriander giggled. "Did you not eat?"

"No..."

"Well, then it's a good thing I came by. Mr. Haggard likes me, I can usually cajole him into giving me snacks when I'm hungry, even though technically it's not allowed." Coriander jumped to her feet and pulled Lou after. "Let's go! You'll feel better with some food in you, and then you can tell me all your troubles." She winked at Lou. "We'll have some *girl time!*"

Lou surprised herself with a giggle, and arm-in-arm she and Coriander headed up to the longhouse. Coriander chattered the whole way about everything, her family, the spice trade, growing up in Jamaica. Lou admired the girl's openness. She hadn't been nearly so confident at sixteen; indeed, when Coriander confessed her age, Lou was a little taken aback. She'd assumed Coriander was at ages with her, if not a little older.

In the kitchen at the back of the longhouse they found the sharp-faced Mr. Haggard skillfully carving up several big hunks of darkish meat. A cigarette was dangling from the corner of his mouth. He looked abashed when Coriander called to him, quickly stubbing out his cigarette and throwing a towel over the meat-bowl, but he relaxed when Coriander promised him she wouldn't tell about his contraband if she could bum a smoke and a late breakfast for her friend.

"How's about some cornbread?" he asked, ushering them into the pantry. He pushed a slab of dense cake into Lou's hands, which she accepted gratefully. It was good, if slightly stale. "And hmm... here, let me make you up a few things in this pail. Some cheese, and I have some of yesterday's lunch rolls if you ain't too picky? They ain't too hard."

"As long as they're not moldy," said Lou, through a mouthful of cornmeal.

"Some of last night's strawberries didn't get et, neither. That sound like enough?"

"I'm much obliged to you," said Lou. "Sounds delicious."

"Is anyone expected up here for a while?" asked Coriander, as she brazenly grabbed a pink-cheeked apple from a barrel.

"Nah, not for a few hours," said Mr. Haggard. "Why?"

"It's pretty enough I thought we could sit outside while Mr. Merriwether ate," she crunched, "but mostly I don't want anyone catching me smoking that cigarette you still owe me."

Coriander sure was a charmer. Lou admired the way the old codger actually seemed to enjoy doing her favors. Lickety-split he rolled up two cigarettes and pressed them into her hand. Then he gallantly escorted them back through the kitchen and out of the longhouse at close to a trot. Pushed along, Lou nearly stumbled over the slight lip of the trapdoor from whence Dr. Panacea and his bride had emerged the previous night, but she managed to hang onto the handle of her breakfast-pail.

"You two enjoy yourselves, now!" Mr. Haggard said, then slammed the door behind him. Lou heard the sound of a latch falling into place.

"Guess I won't be getting any seconds," she said. Coriander shrugged.

The early morning's grey skies had broken up into a bright blue expanse studded with great puffy white clouds. It was cold, but the sun on her face warmed her up just fine. Coriander suggested sitting under a tree close to the drop-off, and Lou hesitantly agreed. She situated herself well back from the edge.

"So what's going on?" asked Coriander.

Lou stalled by finishing off the cornbread. She was still uneasy about speaking freely in this place. Then again, a sunny cliff-face was probably the last place she needed to worry about being overheard by a vampire.

"All right. But you have to promise to hear me out. Reserve your judgment, I mean."

"Of course!"

Lou took a deep breath. "Do you know what a psychopomp is?"

"Oh, how dreadful!" Coriander looked so upset that Lou was gearing up to say she'd just been asking the question rhetorically when the girl smiled and apologized. "I'm sorry, I forgot to ask for a match. How am I going to smoke this? After herding us out, I don't think he'll look kindly upon me knocking."

"Oh." Lou reached into her pocket instinctively, but came up empty. "Sorry, left mine back in the room. Worried about Miss Foxglove confiscating them, you know?"

"It's fine, I'll sneak it later," said Coriander, tucking one cigarette behind her left ear and handing Lou the other. "Ooh, you know, it's a good thing actually. Later I'll show you my favorite spot to smoke, up on top of the barn. There's a water-barrel that makes it easy to scramble up, and the cliff above has a lip or something that hides you from snoops. I know that seems complicated, but you've no idea what zealots these people are! But anyways, so you were saying you're a psychopomp? That's so fascinating! What are ghosts really like? I've never met one. Do they talk? Can you hear them?"

"Uh, well, anyone can hear them," stammered Lou. "But you can't see them unless they want you to. Well, I mean, *I* can, but I have special tools."

"That's amazing!" Coriander looked so thrilled by all this Lou half-wondered if an asylum really would've been a better place for her. "I can't believe it! You're only three years older than me and every day you go into spooky old graveyards at the witching hour to dig up bodies and tell them to—"

"No, no, that's not what I do," interrupted Lou. "I mean, I go to graveyards pretty frequently, but not at midnight. Usually. And I don't dig up bodies. Well, okay, sometimes I have to. But mostly I deal with ghosts, and they always haunt the areas in which they die. Most people don't die in graveyards."

"No, I suppose not." Coriander looked mildly disappointed. "Can you raise the dead?"

"*No!*"

"Well, that's okay, you're still amazing! Are ghosts nice?"

Lou felt dizzy, and not just from the altitude. "Sometimes. Sometimes they can be real assholes, just like the people they used to be."

It took some time to answer all of Coriander's questions, but Lou didn't mind. It was actually pretty fun to discuss work with someone who seemed not only intrigued, but actually enthusiastic about her trade. It was also interesting to discover how little laypeople really knew about what she did for a living. Coriander had been under the impression that Lou's trade was more similar to Bo's than it really was.

"So people would hire you to banish a spirit, but you wouldn't take a job to kill a werewolf. Right?"

"Not unless it was an undead werewolf," said Lou. "And even so, that's still more the kind of thing Bo and his friends would do."

"I know! He told me all about it." Coriander looked wistful. "I wish I knew how to do something interesting, like you."

"It's interesting, but there's all kinds of risks. Stuff you wouldn't even think about. Possession… fevers from spirit-burn… but lots of psychopomps die early from mundane things you'd never even think about being a risk."

"Like what?"

Lou swallowed, then said softly, "Well, there's mercury poisoning. One of the raw materials lots of psychopomps use has quicksilver in it."

"I see." Coriander considered this. "I guess even if being a psychopomp isn't, I dunno, as *flashy* as being a monster-hunter with a big sword, you have to be brave to do it. It must be so difficult, emotionally I mean, being around death all the time."

"Not really," said Lou. "What's really hard is what normal people do. I'm used to death. Most folks aren't. Once the spirit has fled in whatever way it does, natural or with someone to help, then people have to figure out how to live without someone they love. How to clean up the things they left behind, deciding what they'll keep and what they'll get rid of. Navigating how to move forward, so that they don't feel like they're healing too quickly, but making sure they don't wallow." Lou shrugged, unable to meet Coriander's eyes. "Compared to that, banishing a spirit is easy."

"Easy, she says!"

"It's just a job. Anyone with the right training could do it."

"I mean, I'm sure building houses or railroads or whatever is just as dangerous and important and interesting on some level, but it's not nearly as... what's wrong?"

Lou had felt a chill at Coriander's exempli gratia. Here she was with someone who'd actually been living at the San for months, and instead of finding out if Coriander had seen or heard anything suspicious, she was up here gabbing with her like they were at a quilting bee.

"Nothing's wrong, I just wonder... have you seen any Chinese people around here? Other than me?"

"Yes," said Coriander. "Why?"

Lou's heart began to pound. *"Where?"*

"Well, I suppose I should say, I've seen them in passing. And not for a while." Coriander fell silent, and Lou almost prompted her before she saw there were tears welling in the girl's eyes.

"I'm sorry, it's just, the few times I saw them, I was with Mr. Gillis. You wouldn't know him, he... passed. Just before you arrived. He showed me the secret spot to smoke on top of the barn. Sometimes, late at night we'd skinny dip in the hot spring and then sneak down to smoke and gossip. He was such a nice man."

Given how thick Coriander's voice had become, Lou felt a little guilty that she cared less about honoring Mr. Gillis' memory than finding out what he and Coriander had seen. Thankfully she didn't have to ask again about what she really wanted to know.

"A few times—two certainly, but maybe three—and only very late at night, we saw groups of Chinese men being led up to the front door of the San—"

"Led by whom?"

"I've only seen him around the San a few times; until last night I never realized he was Mrs. Panacea's brother. He doesn't really interact with the guests, not like her. Speaking of which, she's leading a prayer meeting this afternoon I hear…" Coriander got a dreamy look in her eyes. "I'm so glad, it's been a few weeks since she's felt well enough to be social. Why do you ask? Is it important?"

"It's everything," said Lou. It looked like she had Coriander's attention again. "You said you could keep a secret, right? Well," she lowered her voice, just in case, "those men, they've been coming here… but they haven't been coming back. Their families are curious as to why, and so am I. That's why I'm here." Well, that and she suspected a vampire might be eating them— but Lou elected not to mention that part. Coriander was turning out to be an excellent confidant, but it seemed wiser to keep things between them on a need-to-know basis until she could confirm the girl was as good at retaining secrets as she was at soaking them up. "This morning, I wasn't upset about anything Dr. Panacea said to me about my health. I'm supposed to be investigating why the men you saw disappeared and I didn't get a single piece of information out of him. Even worse, I don't have any idea what I could have done differently, and I have no idea what to do next."

"Why not just ask him?"

"I considered it… but Dr. P didn't exactly take a shine to me. And anyways, in case something's going on that's, uh, you know, not quite right, I'd rather him not know that I'm actively curious about it."

"That makes sense," said Coriander thoughtfully. "And you're right, it does seem strange. For example, why only Chinese people?"

"That's the main reason I think something's really wrong," she explained. "Unless you've lived in a place with a big population, well… we're considered less than worthless to most people. Disposable. They'd rather we disappear—back to China, but any other way works just as well." She shrugged.

"Not everyone's like that, of course, but enough."

"I'd heard about anti-Chinese organizations and read some news articles in the papers, but I had no idea it was so awful."

"Yeah." It never failed to amaze Lou how people outside of California really had so little idea how rotten things were for your average Chinaman.

"Well, then." Coriander sat up straight. "The only thing to do is be proactive! Here's what we'll do—"

"Nuh-uh. I'm doing this on my own. I won't let you put yourself in danger."

"Are you sure you're not really a boy?" Coriander looked at her skeptically. "Really, there's no 'letting' here. I want to help! And frankly, you need it. You're too… innocent."

"Innocent?"

"You're clearly upstanding, honest, and—no offense—wholesome. You need someone devious and rotten to help you out. Someone like me."

"You do strike me as a hardened criminal of the first water."

"Save your sass for your mother. You said you didn't know what to do next." Coriander looked almost unbearably smug. "Well, *I* do."

"Oh yeah?"

"Yeah," said Coriander. "We'll go right to the source!"

"And what's the source?" As much as Lou didn't want to admit it, it was a great relief to have another person, especially one who thought so differently than she did, working on this problem alongside her.

It was looking as though she'd need to apologize to Vilhelm, too, when she got back. She did need a partner.

"Dr. Panacea, of course! But not the doctor himself." Coriander smiled. "His office."

"How's that?"

"If you want to find out something about someone, go through their stuff," said Coriander, like it was the most obvious thing in the world. "We'll sneak in when he's not around, and go through all his files and whatever else he has lying around."

Lou shook her head. "I dunno about that…"

"What don't you know?"

"I'm sure he locks it, for one."

"So what?" Coriander pulled a hairpin from her braid and waggled it at

Lou. "I can pick locks."

Coriander's logic was good, but her plan didn't sound wise at all. Lou was pretty sure it was a bad idea to irritate a vampire by pawing through his private records. Then again, he hadn't left her much choice.

"All right," she said at last. "Tomorrow, we'll—"

"Why tomorrow? Let's go now. You could have your answers before evening calisthenics!" Coriander seemed downright thrilled with the prospect of breaking into the doctor's office, her eyes were button-bright and she was almost quivering with desire. "I'll go and knock—you hang back—and if he's in, I'll pretend to need treatment for something. Lord knows I've stubbed my toes and barked my shins enough in those gloomy corridors! I usually have a bruise somewhere or other. But if he doesn't answer, then I'll get to work on the lock. If someone catches us... hmm, oh I know! You lie and say you lost something, and told me you thought you'd lost it during your intake, and I offered to let you in. I'll take the blame!"

"We'll see about that," said Lou, knowing that were they discovered she would not be following *that* part of the plan. "Let's just hope we don't get caught."

"Always have an explanation ready," said Coriander primly.

"All right already. Shall we?" Lou, nervous, stood and offered Coriander a hand up. She took it, batting her eyes at Lou.

"Why Mr. Merriwether, your chivalry is *so* appreciated! You know how weak we women are."

Flustered, Lou dropped Coriander's hand in alarm. "I'm sorry, I—"

Coriander poked her in the stomach. "You need to learn to relax!"

"I'll relax *after* we succeed with your crazy-ass plan."

"In your profession, aren't you always about to do something crazy?" Even Coriander's self-congratulatory smile was cute. "This should be easy as pie compared to raising the dead!"

Chapter Eight

Lou had never in her life made a pie, and she decided she never would if it was anything close to being as "easy" as picking a lock. She had to bite her tongue to keep herself from chiding Coriander, she knew the girl wasn't taking so long to open Dr. Panacea's door on purpose; indeed, she looked ready to fly to pieces over it. Lou transferred her workbag from her right hand to her left, and wiped her sweaty palm on her uniform.

"This is a lot harder than breaking the cabinet where Mother keeps her laudanum!" whispered Coriander. "But I think I've... almost—got it!"

There was a low click. Lou sighed, relieved, as Coriander turned the brass knob and slowly pushed open the door.

The room looked exactly the same as it had that morning: the desk, comfy chair, examination table, bookshelves, and rug were all just as Lou remembered them. The only change was the lack of a vampire checking her pulse. But just to be sure, Lou took out her skiameter—and almost dropped it.

There was definitely an undead presence in the room, somewhere at the back of the office. Her skiameter's needle quivered, pointing straight at the rock wall.

"So what can I do to help?" asked Coriander. "Gosh, what an enormous gun!"

"Shh," shhed Lou as she walked to the back of the room, LeMat in her hand. She had no idea if her vermilion-infused rounds would affect Dr.

Panacea, but it made her feel better to have the gun out and ready whenever all the hairs stood up on the back of her neck.

The strange thing was, there was no one in the office that Lou could see. Was there a ghost lurking here? Had Dr. Panacea killed someone in this very room? Remembering Millie's remark about vampires turning into bats, Lou tucked away her skiameter and pistol and retrieved her goggles. Maybe he could turn into mist, or something even less noticeable.

Fitting them over her eyes, she looked around at the wall and saw... nothing.

"What the hell," she murmured, scanning the stone several times.

"That's what I want to know!" opined Coriander. "What are you doing? I thought we were going to look through files or something. Why are you wearing that... thing? And inspecting that wall?"

Given that she had not told Coriander of possible undead complications during their mission, Lou knew she should not be so irritated with her, but even if Coriander didn't know about the potential for a vampire to be stalking around, that didn't excuse her volume. They were still breaking and entering.

"Force of habit," said Lou, still perplexed by her strange readings. "Go, I dunno, look through things that seem interesting."

"But I don't know what you're looking for! Lou, you're wasting time. We should do this as quickly as possible!"

Out of the mouths of babes. "You're right," she said, pushing the goggles up onto her forehead. No sense in staring at blank rock.

They began with Dr. Panacea's desk, the obvious choice, but a thorough search revealed nothing but a drawer with a few bottles of Elixir, personal files on clients past and present, and some purchasing orders for flour, cornmeal, and various sundries. Disappointed, Lou turned her attention to the bookshelves, but again found nothing. They held medical textbooks, which were either pristine or beyond well-used. None of them had so much as a bookplate with Dr. Panacea's name in the front; Lou wondered if he'd bought the lot to make his office look more legitimate. As she pondered this, Coriander searched the examination table to see if it had any secret compartments, but after perhaps twenty minutes they stopped looking around, more baffled and frustrated than they had been before they began.

"I was so certain this would be helpful, but there's absolutely nothing personal or interesting in this office," said Coriander, pushing a damp curl off her forehead. "Most professionals I know have *something* of their own around them even at work, a photograph or portrait of their wife, some recreational reading, a bottle of bourbon stashed in the desk. This is so bland it's suspicious!"

"I agree," said Lou. "The most unique thing in this office is that ugly rug." Their eyes locked.

"Let's flip it," said Lou.

"Just what I was going to say," said Coriander, grabbing a corner.

There it was. A trap door, with a handle right there, practically begging to be pulled on.

"Wait," said Lou, as Coriander reached for it. "Let me check something."

Lou took out her skiameter once more and tried to get a read on whether or not the undead presence was *below* them. Her goggles confirmed a faint glow emanating from under her feet. The range of her thumoscopic lenses was not infinite; whatever it was, it must be relatively close-by.

This just plain sucked. The likelihood of getting caught was going up by the second, and there was no real way to pretend she hadn't been snooping if she and Coriander were discovered after going down a trapdoor—and definitely not one hidden under a rug in a locked office. And if by chance they discovered Dr. Panacea down there... holy shit, what was she even thinking? What if that was actually him down there?

Then again, other than confronting him, there was no real way to get the information she came for. Unless the Chinese were hidden down in the bowels of the earth... Lou's heart skipped a beat. Maybe, just maybe, the ghost or whatever was attracting her skiameter was associated with the men who'd been lured here.

Whatever the case might be, it was up to her to do this, and she had to do it alone. She couldn't ask Coriander to let her in a second time; the girl was too green, and shouldn't even be here with her right now. Bo and his friends were unable or unwilling to help her. Asking Miss Foxglove or any of the other staff was just as risky as doing the legwork herself, when it came right down to it. It was either this or go home, and she wasn't ready to go home yet.

"What do you see? Tell me!" begged Coriander. "Is there a ghost?"

"I don't know," said Lou truthfully, "but there's something. You should head back, I'm going down." She glanced up and saw pure stubbornness looking back at her out of Coriander's face. "This is psychopomp business."

"I don't care," said Coriander. "I want to come! You never would have gotten in here without me in the first place. What if there's another lock?"

While Lou couldn't deny Coriander's point, the idea of taking an untrained, unarmed girl on what might turn out to be a vampire hunt seemed pretty irresponsible. Especially since the girl didn't even know it might be a vampire hunt, and Lou was still disinclined to mention that.

"There *might* be another lock, but there's *absolutely* something down there that should be more dead than it currently is," Lou argued, very conscious that she was hanging around debating things when she should be moving. "I can't guarantee you'll be safe."

"I know that!"

"I haven't told you everything going on here." Frustration was making her desperate. "This is dangerous stuff. I don't want to be responsible if something—"

"Please?"

Lou never thought she'd be a sucker for puppy-dog eyes, but Coriander's hopeful enthusiasm melted her resolve. That, and if the fool creature wanted to get herself killed, it was her own damn business—Lou's was doing her job, and the sooner she did it, the better.

"All right—only if you promise to run like hell if I tell you, okay?" Even this seemed questionable, but it was preferable to wasting more time.

"Sure!"

Coriander agreed far too quickly for Lou's comfort, but Lou had started training with her father younger than her, and with the same caveats. Then again, she'd known what she was getting into.

The trap door was heavy, but Lou got it open without too big a bang. An earthy, metallic smell wafted up. Lou eyed the stone stairs leading down into total blackness with distaste. There weren't many of those fungal wads illuminating the steps. They'd be nearly blind down there.

"Still feel like coming?"

"Of course!"

Lou kept her goggles on and her skiameter out as they started their descent, peering in every direction for signs of undeath, but saw nothing other than the faint glow she'd detected above. She kept them moving, and as they descended deeper into the dimness, she was increasingly grateful for Coriander's assistance. She could keep her skiameter in one hand and her revolver in the other, since Coriander had agreed to carry her bag. Even so, she knew she'd be fighting for two if it came down to it.

When they reached a landing, Lou paused to assess the situation. Two sets of stairs were before them, both still leading down. One did so dramatically; the other, more gradually. Her skiameter and thumoscopic goggles confirmed that the undead presence lay somewhere along the more gradual path. She was interested in the other set of stairs, however—it smelled like a pine forest down there. Odd.

"What's wrong?"

Coriander's voice echoed off the rock distressingly. Lou whirled around, about to murder the girl herself and leave her dead body to whatever was skulking around down here, but Coriander had realized her error and had clapped her hand over her own mouth.

"Sorry!" she whispered.

"I'm trying to figure out if we should follow whatever I'm seeing in my goggles, or go the other way," said Lou. "What do you think?"

Coriander shrugged. "We came down here because of whatever you're seeing, right?"

Fair enough. They could get lost in this warren; best to keep her focus.

Lou motioned for Coriander to follow as she herself followed the faint green light, an indistinct, hazy mass that befuddled her vision somewhat. She could see it, but it was not in front of her, and that played merry hell with her eyes.

Eventually the stairs leveled off into a smoother hallway much like those of the San above. The haze grew brighter, though it was still sort-of below her.

Lou shoved her goggles up onto her forehead for a moment, peering around with her naked eyes. It was too dark to make out much, so she resettled her goggles and, after taking a deep breath, continued to walk forward. It was uncomfortable, not being able to see well—and knowing what might just be looking out at her from the dark.

The toe of her boot thunked against something in front of her. She yelped.

"What? Is it something?" Coriander was right beside her, flailing around in the darkness.

"Shh," said Lou, feeling whatever it was in front of her. When her hands closed on a knob, she said, "it's just a door."

"Is it locked?"

"Nope," said Lou. Screwing up her courage, she opened the door—and was blinded by sunlight. Lou rubbed at her eyes with the back of her left hand, blinking until she could see again.

Before her was a cozy little balcony jutting out from the cliff-face, similar to the decks above but far smaller in scale. There were two chairs and a small table between them, but no other furniture. Beyond the balcony were distant, unfamiliar snow-capped peaks that sparkled in the sunlight. They must have gone under the San only to come out on the opposite side of the mountain.

"How interesting," said Coriander, as she followed Lou onto the deck proper. "Whatever do you think this is for? Not for patients… Dr. Panacea must use it." As she brushed away as much of the snow coating the little table as she could, she uncovered a small ashtray. She set Lou's bag down beside it.

"Oh yeah." Lou could easily imagine the doctor sitting out here at night, Shai beside him, smoking his hasheesh. Or with Eliana, bundled up for romantic stargazing. Or both?

Lou walked over to the guardrail and gazed out over the unspoiled terrain below. The forest was further below them on this side of the range, a dizzying drop into an unbroken expanse on every side. As far as the eye could see, thick black pines and willowy white aspens flowed up the sides of distant mountains.

"There's ghosts here?" Coriander peered out over the edge of the deck.

Lou, preoccupied, did not answer her. Something bothered her about this valley, but she couldn't quite put her finger on it.

The wind kicked up, and a sound reached her ears that made the hairs on her neck stand up again. It was a slow, moaning creak, and Lou could neither place the cause of the sound nor imagine what could be making it. Coriander heard it too. Holstering her gun Lou put a finger to her lips. The girl nodded. She looked worried—as well she might. Something strange was going on. Lou was used to this sort of business and even she was uncomfortable. She slid her goggles down over her eyes.

As in Dr. Panacea's office, nothing immediately registered with her enhanced vision. Then she looked down, wondering if the spectral element was still somehow below her.

It was—or rather, *they* were. But what really caught her notice were the two stout ropes tied around the opposing posts of the railing, that she needed no help to see. Whatever they held was swaying in the breeze; the ropes were making the sound. Lou was glad to have found a mundane source of the uncanny groaning, but she was curious as a cat about the undead glows. The shapes of the masses were… strange.

"I've gotta bring up whatever's swinging around down there," she murmured to Coriander. "Keep back, okay?"

"I can help," she insisted.

"I don't know what's down there," said Lou. "I'd rather you got the hell out of here entirely, but I know that's not going to happen, so just stay behind me. Please?"

Mutiny was written on Coriander's face as clearly as if someone had penned the word in ink, but that was just too bad. Lou turned away and reached her hand gingerly between the leftmost post and the baluster, getting her fingers around the rope a few inches below the knot. She pulled, and grunted. Whatever it was, it was heavy, though not heavy enough to be a corpse… unless it was a child. Lou briefly wondered if it was that kind of mentality that Millie had been referencing when she'd described Lou's job, and Lou herself, as spooky.

"What is it?" asked Coriander, as Lou slowly got to her feet, rope in hand, and began to haul up the whatever-it-was. When she had enough slack she switched to an overhand grip, looping the rope over the edge of the railing. Her palms began to protest almost immediately, but she kept at it.

When the back of a human head poked up over the side of the deck, Lou sighed, then frowned. Definitely a corpse, definitely an adult. How strange. When the shoulders below the head appeared, Lou saw it wasn't a small corpse, either. Why was it so light?

The body swung around when Lou yanked again, and when she saw who it was, she damn near lost her grip on the rope.

"It's Coyote!" cried Coriander. Given the matching rope around the rightmost post, there was little hope for Ned Clifford. So much for ensuring they came to no harm for helping her.

"It—*ungh*—was Coyote," corrected Lou, pulling again. He was waist-high above the deck now, and she rearranged her grip to begin dragging him over the railing. "It's just a body now. You okay? Ever seen a corpse before?"

"Lou," said Coriander, pointing. "I..."

"I know it's—"

"Lou, *look*," insisted Coriander, nearly pale as the snow at their feet.

Lou turned, and almost dropped the rope again. It was now evident why the body had been so light. Both of Coyote's legs had been cut off at the hip.

Chapter Nine

Ned's legs had also been removed, but neither had died from the amputations. After loosening the ropes looped around their necks and under their armpits, it was obvious that both of their throats had been slit with some sort of thin-bladed knife, wounds that spoke to who had likely done the killings.

Their leg-wounds bothered her more. Lou examined them after laying out both men on their backs on the snowy deck, poking at the frozen cuts for a while, an endeavor that finally conquered Coriander's cool, the girl retching over the edge of the railing for a spell. She decided the limbs had been severed with a saw.

As to *why* the two bodies had been divested of their legs, Lou did not know, and could not guess.

"I'm stumped," she said, and laughed hollowly. "Get it?"

Still green about the gills, Coriander did not even crack a smile. Lou understood. She was only joking around because she saw blame in Ned's and Coyote's open, frostbitten eyes; an indictment in the thin bloody lines that crossed both throats. Well, she deserved it. It seemed highly unlikely that these two men had committed some sort of execution-worthy offense on top of defying Shai's orders to keep Lou away from the San. Her lies about the welcome she would receive from the doc had lulled them sweetly into their final days. It was her fault they were dead.

"What are we going to do with them?" whispered Coriander.

"First, I'm going to exorcise them," replied Lou. "I owe them that. They're ripe as hell, just itching to wake up as geung si."

"I beg your pardon?"

"Ever heard of a zombie? Vampire?"

"Yes…"

"Geung si are somewhere in between the two."

Coriander did not seem to enjoy this exercise in imagination. She took a deep breath and nodded.

"How can I help?"

Lou admired the girl's pluck. She looked ready to puke again but still wanted to be useful.

"You can hand me things," said Lou. Reaching for her bag, she began to take out the items she would need for the procedure, her extractor, her bag of sticky rice, and her own version of a bone-saw. There was a door close by, but it was perhaps fifteen feet up the side of the mountain. She briefly considered attempting to scramble up there, as there seemed to be some decent handholds, but decided against it. "This is going to be sort of slap-dash, so don't think this is how I usually do things. I don't have everything I need for a pretty, proper nekuia."

Coriander nodded. "What can I get for you?"

"Nothing yet. First," Lou grunted, unwrapping her psuilver saw, "I gotta make a door."

She cut only a small portal, as there were no ghosts to corral, only spirit-matter to purge. Coriander was very quiet and attentive as she watched Lou work, perched on one of the deck chairs to keep out of the way, so as a reward Lou let her don the goggles and see what-all had been done. She gasped.

"What?"

"It's so black!" Coriander turned to look at Lou. Tears were welling up in the girl's wide eyes that blinked at her from behind blue glass.

"What's wrong?"

"Is heaven really so… dark?"

"That's not heaven, Coriander." She could have explained things a bit better. "It's just… well, it's the veil between our world and the spirit world." As to what the spirit world was like, Lou sure as shit didn't know. Heaven might well be that dark—if it even existed. Lou elected not to mention this. Her explanation had calmed Coriander substantially, so after taking back her goggles and changing out one blue lens for a pink, she began the exorcism proper.

What remained of Coyote's spirit was lurking in the blood vessels concentrated around the brain, a pulsing, pus-colored, pewter-flecked stain to Lou's eyes. It stubbornly refused to dislodge itself and circulate down to anywhere convenient, even when Lou poured sticky rice over his left shoulder in an attempt to coax it into the more accessible right common carotid artery. With a sigh, Lou collected the grains back into her pouch and rolled Coyote onto his stomach, carefully re-piling the rice over where the soul lurked so she could get at his external carotid. With a minimum of cussing Lou managed to plunge the psuilver needle of the extractor through the tough flesh of his neck and into the spirit-mass, and sucked it up into the barrel.

Sweaty despite the cold, Lou wiped her forehead and pushed her goggles up off her eyes. "Next, I squirt the whole thing into the door I made," she explained. "If you want to watch, grab my other thumoscopic lens from the case and hold it up to your eye."

Coriander did, hesitating only momentarily before kneeling in the snow next to what remained of Ned Clifford to get the best view possible. She gasped as the soul, cloudy and diaphanous as squid ink, spiraled away as Lou depressed the plunger.

"Neat, huh?" Lou winked at Coriander as she sat back on her heels. "Done and done."

Coriander nodded, returning Lou's smile—and then she screamed and fell into Lou's lap, writhing. The lens she had been holding so carefully between her delicate fingers flew out of her hand, spinning away over the edge of the deck.

"What the—"

"Get off!" screeched Coriander, shaking her left leg. "Oh God oh God get *off* me!"

Lou jumped to her feet. She hadn't been wrong—these two *had* been ripe and ready to become geung si.

Ned was awake, and clinging to Coriander's leg. His bony, bloodless fingers had wrapped around her left ankle, and his fingernails, longer in death and now green as bamboo leaves, were drawing blood where they poked into her flesh. Try as the girl might, tearing and pushing at his hand and kicking viciously at his head with her right foot, Coriander couldn't free herself. Her heel made contact with his jaw and his temple, but sadly, while her strikes looked powerful enough to knock a live man unconscious, the dead cared little for feats of physical strength.

Lou took a moment to shut the door into the mountain before pushing her goggles down over her eyes. Coriander's screams were shrill and would carry, and there was no telling if Lou would need to use her gun.

Ned's spirit was writhing and pulsing all through the veins in the hand that clung to Coriander. It hadn't festered enough to re-animate the whole of what was left of him, but it knew what it wanted—fresh, delicious qi.

"Help!" cried Coriander. "Lou!"

"Working on it," said Lou, pawing through her bag to find the thick yellow roll of vermilion-inked wards. She peeled one off and turned back as the legless geung si began groaning; the soul matter had slid upward into its neck.

Lou darted forward as the undead made a face-first lurch for Coriander's leg. It bit her above the ankle and began to worry at the muscle like a dog in its desperation to drink her blood.

Coriander had kept her head admirably, considering, but she was panicking now, thrashing around to get a better look at both Lou and the geung si, kicking wildly in her haste. As if her writhing wasn't making it difficult enough for Lou to find a clear place to stick the ward, one of Coriander's feet caught Lou in the jaw.

"Hold still!" snapped Lou, spitting blood and seeing stars, and with more force than she intended, smacked Coriander's hand away from where the girl pulled at the geung si's clutching fingers. Coriander cried out in pain, but Lou was able to slap the yellow strip onto the back of Ned's hand. The corpse froze immediately, teeth still embedded in the girl's flesh.

Coriander immediately began trying to open his jaws, wedging her fingers in between her leg and his mouth. Lou didn't bother telling her that her efforts were pointless. Vermilion immobilized the undead, for better or for worse. In silence she gently adjusted Coriander's body so she could turn Ned onto his back, and sprinkled some grains over the same artery she'd used for Coyote's exorcism. Only when the fragment of spirit coagulated in the shoulder of the body did Ned's teeth release. His head fell back onto the wooden deck with an unsettling thunk.

Lou extracted the angry spirit as quickly as she could. Coriander was bleeding heavily from the jagged bite-wound, and blood oozed from the marks Ned's fingernails had clawed in her calf and thigh. Lou knew too well how she must be feeling. When the undead bit, it chilled and sapped the energy of their victims much like spirit-burn. But unlike spirit-burn, the bites would turn rotten, and quickly.

With all possible haste Lou disposed of Ned's spiritual remains, but before shutting the door and stitching it closed, Lou set aside her syringe and took off her goggles. Coriander needed her attention first.

"Am I going to turn into a vampire?" wailed Coriander, looking desperately at Lou. Her face was grey and she looked like she might faint at any moment.

"No," replied Lou, as she rummaged through her bag. "You'll be fine, though you'll have to stay off that leg." She snorted. "We'll have to come up with an excuse good enough to get you out of Miss Foxglove's class but not so good it gets you sent to the doc. Any ideas?"

Coriander began to run through a list of reasons why she had to skip calisthenics, but Lou stopped listening when her fingers closed over the bottle of the Elixir of Life. She'd been looking for the pot of salve she'd started carrying after Vilhelm's lecture, what felt like years ago back in San Francisco; she'd forgotten she had the Elixir. Pleased, she unstoppered it and drizzled a little over Coriander's bite wound. The bleeding stopped immediately.

"Where did you get that?" asked Coriander, as she watched Lou. "Did you take it from Dr. Panacea's desk?"

"I got it in San Francisco, why?"

"They keep it under lock and key. No one has their own bottle here."

Knowing just how precious the stuff really was, this didn't surprise Lou. "Well, the Elixir healed it right up. I'm going to smear some salve on it now, but make sure you wash and bind it when you get back to your room. But don't worry. Ned didn't get much of your qi, so—"

"He didn't *what?*" Coriander's color was returning, as was her spiritedness, Lou was pleased to see.

"Qi. He was after your qi. Your… soul, spirit, something like that. Geung si feed on that, and they get it through your blood."

Coriander stared at Lou like one mesmerized. The information hadn't comforted her as Lou had expected.

"You'll be okay," added Lou, clarifying further. "Qi, like blood, regenerates; you make more if some is lost. You can lose it in all kinds of ways, some more fun than others. Anyways, sorry. I should have immobilized both of them before we began. I didn't think they'd turned ripe enough to attack while we were working. It was sloppy of me."

Coriander looked a little shocked, which Lou thought was perfectly normal. What wasn't normal, however, was what Coriander did next.

She threw her arms around Lou and kissed her on the cheek.

"Thank you for letting me come!" she cried. "Oh, Lou—do you think one day I could be a psychopomp like you? This is so… so… *fun!*"

Lou stared at her for a moment, amazed and impressed. "You've got the stomach for it, but if you really want to, you'll need to be a bit calmer the next time something grabs hold of you. Speaking of which, we should get out of here. No telling who—or what—heard us, making such a ruckus out here."

"But the Chinese—"

"First thing, take care of yourself," said Lou. She popped the pot of salve back into her satchel.

Coriander insisted she was fine to continue exploring, but when she hauled herself to her feet she stumbled and nearly fell. Her leg was wobbly and would not bear her weight, even after being treated.

"I want to keep on, too," said Lou, "but we need to get you to safety. To bed, really. For now, go sit just inside the door."

"What for?"

"Because I gotta make it look like we were never here."

It took a frustrating amount of time to tidy up. First, Lou pushed the ropes back over Ned and Coyote's heads and tossed them over the side of the deck. Next, she set to work stitching up the door she'd been forced to make. The cold had gotten into her fingers, so sewing up the edges was slow. After packing up her bag, she set to kicking the snow around as best she could to cover their prints. The clear skies gave her no hope of another snowfall before dark, so she took her time and tried to do a good job. In the end, her efforts weren't wholly invisible, but it looked fine if you weren't actively seeking signs of a disturbance.

Once they'd tottered back up the stairs, which took a long time with Coriander's leg, they were relieved to see the office looked the same as when they'd left. They closed the trap door and replaced the rug hastily, thanking their lucky stars that whatever errand the doctor was on, it was a lengthy one.

The only problem was they couldn't relock the door behind them. All they could do was hope that Dr. Panacea wouldn't notice anything amiss when he came back.

They headed back to Coriander's room, slowly because of her leg, but only when they got Coriander's door open and her bed was there, all made up and pretty, would she at last concede that she could use a nap. Lou left her to it and returned to her own room. She, too, was tired, and she had a lot to think about. Like what was down the other set of stairs—and what was so strange about that valley behind the San. It was still nagging at her.

She slung her bag on the bed, wondering if they'd missed lunch. Thinking was a lot more difficult on an empty stomach.

But hell, what *wasn't* difficult around here? Despite Shai's cautions, she had not fully comprehended how high the stakes would be up here at the San. She knew it was entirely possible that she could end up in the same state as Ned and Coyote, and frankly, that scared the shit out of her—as did the idea of Coriander, Bo, or anyone experiencing such an ignoble death. She'd already gotten Coriander injured. What else would she fuck up before this trip was over, one way or the other?

No use in harboring maudlin thoughts. She had to keep her head on straight, act smarter, if she wanted to do anything for the people she'd come to help. Like finding them, for starters.

Lou ruminated on her failures for a time, coming up with all sorts of schemes to run by Coriander in terms of getting her investigation back on track, but she must have dozed off, as the gong startled her when it rang. She picked sleep from the corners of her eyes, annoyed with herself. Naps always made her grumpy; she was in no mood for evening calisthenics. Before she even considered leaving her room, however, she needed to change her rag, so she hastily grabbed a fresh one. After changing it out, she rinsed her used one in the basin as best she could and darted out her door to knock on Coriander's.

Coriander didn't answer. Lou frowned, momentarily worried—and then realized none of her fellow patients were emerging from their rooms. That seemed strange. Maybe her ablutions had taken her longer than she'd realized.

"Lou?"

Bo was emerging from his room. He looked better than the last time she'd seen him, but his voice still sounded weak.

"Why aren't you at evening calisthenics?" he asked.

"I'm going now, same as you."

"That was the dinner bell." Bo sucked his teeth. "Be careful. Keep it up and you'll blow your cover, *Mulan.*"

"Shut up." Usually Lou hated it when Bo called her Mulan, but tonight it reminded her of old times and brought a smile to her lips. "I'm supposed to be sick, right? I was sick, that's all."

"Unlike everyone else?"

Lou shrugged. "It's all I got."

"Very convincing."

Lou sighed. "Maybe Miss Foxglove won't have noticed."

No such luck. Upon entering the longhouse, the fitness instructor glided over to Lou and took her back outside, where in low, angry tones, she reprimanded Lou for her failure to attend class, her behavior that morning, her skipping meals, and her general attitude about health and wellness. It was dark and windy outside, and the smell of food wafting their way was maddening, so Lou, hoping to get away from her as quickly as possible, nodded and tried to look contrite.

Miss Foxglove wasn't fooled.

"I'm very disappointed in you, Mr. Merriwether," she said.

Lou, tired of being yapped at, shrugged. "You and everyone else."

"I'm surprised you came all the way out here only to be rude to the staff and skip your treatments." Miss Foxglove looked rather like a mule when frowning. "It's almost like you aren't here to better your health."

Lou froze. It was just like Bo had said. Miss Foxglove was looking at her as if she expected some sort of confession. When it was obvious none would be forthcoming, the fitness instructor folded her arms across her chest and pursed her lips.

"Go in, then," she said. "But you should be aware, we do not lightly suffer frauds here at Fountain of Youth."

"No? What do you do with them?"

Unexpectedly, Miss Foxglove laughed as she breezed past Lou toward the door. "Why, we ask them to leave, Mr. Merriwether. What else would we do?"

Lou slid onto the bench beside Bo. It pained her to see that neither Bo, nor Coriander, nor Mr. Dumpling had eaten much of the starting course, but their dishes were already being cleared away. She could have cleaned their plates as well as her own, she was sure of it. She felt like she might be actually, literally starving to death.

"So," Bo wheezed, his voice as rough as a burlap sack, "what was that all about?"

"Aw, you know me. Always the teacher's pet."

Coriander tittered, blatantly eyeballing Miss Foxglove's backside as the woman strode back to the other table, where the Willoughbys, the Rutherfords, and the rest were deep in conversation.

"Lucky you," she said. "I wouldn't mind that at all."

Lou pulled a face. "Oh, Coriander!"

"Don't judge me," she said, winking at Lou. "I like 'em stern."

"Miss Gorey," said Mr. Dumpling reproachfully. "Your parents sent you here to cleanse unwholesome thoughts like those from your mind! Such wicked fantasies surely must hurt your chances of a full recovery."

"I don't want to recover," replied Coriander. "Boys are gross."

"Hey now," said Bo.

"Yeah," agreed Lou.

"You're both okay," she conceded, "but you're also not trying to woo me because you know I have a fortune. And good birthing hips."

"Both admirable things for a woman to possess," said Mr. Dumpling. "You should be proud to accept your role in life for what it is."

Coriander sighed.

When at last the main course was served, it didn't look so different from the previous night's fare. Instead of wilted greens there was steamed winter squash, and another small tin pan filled with stewed meat. Lou tucked in without hesitation, though Coriander and Mr. Dumpling chose to continue bickering.

Bo sniffed experimentally. "Don't look too bad tonight," he said, running a spoon around the edge, collecting gravy and grease. After licking the spoon, he said, "not bad at all."

Lou was happy to see Bo tucking into his meal. It was true, tonight's stew really was much better. The meat was still stringy, but it was tasty, and the sauce had been flavored with fresh thyme.

"All crudeness aside," said Mr. Dumpling, with a sharp look at Coriander, "you should be honored to be a woman, Miss Gorey! You are the bearer of life, the chalice into which God places the next generation. That is a woman's first duty, her primary role in marriage!"

"I don't think you really know so much about how babies are made if you think God places life in my chalice," quipped Coriander.

"My dear child!"

"Anyhow, Mr. Gillis would disagree with you, if he were still here. He believed in suffrage, equal rights for women, that sort of thing. I'll never forget the night we met… I had been trying to find a place to sneak off by myself for a bit, and gotten myself stuck in the crook of an aspen. He was out walking, and I called to him for help. He looked up at me, and he said, I shall never forget it, 'I admit I don't know much about *a woman's place,* my dear, but I certainly don't think it's in a tree.'" She sighed. "I was so glad it wasn't the doctor or any of the other staff who found me. I'm sure there would have been a scandal. Mr. Gillis, though, he never mentioned it again." Coriander looked sad for a moment, then brightened. "He was such a lovely person."

"If you say so," said Mr. Dumpling. "I found him rather negative. He hated it here. Hated the exercise, hated the uniforms, hated the lack of entertainments, hated the food," he said, ticking them off on his fingers one by one. "Though I suppose that's not so surprising in a gentleman farmer from Tennessee. Chicken at every meal and all that." Mr. Dumpling shuddered. "I hate to think of the state of that man's bowels."

"Well, that's lovely," said Coriander, at last tucking into her dinner. "I'm sure he'd be thrilled that his memory inspired such ruminations at the supper table. As for me, I was just thinking he'd have been overjoyed to have meat two nights in a row! I can't remember the last time that happened."

Lou paused, her spoon halfway to her mouth. Something about what Coriander had just said sent her mind whirling. She resumed eating, chewing thoughtfully. Shai, too, had commented upon the lack of meat at the San, and yet since she'd arrived it had been present… if not especially delicious. Perhaps Shai had come back early from the pens where they kept the beef and pork.

That was it. That valley, the one behind the mountain—that was supposed to be where they kept the stock! But from the doc's private deck there had been no sign of agriculture of any sort, and their view had been an open panorama with few blind spots.

Lou stopped chewing; swallowed. Why would they lie about such a thing? Perhaps they were hiding from the bears that they were hunting for the meat—the flesh on Mr. Haggard's butcher block had been more venison-colored than anything domesticated. Come to think of it, they hadn't been cuts she'd recognized from any animal…

All of a sudden Lou realized she had seen two shoes that day, so to speak, but failed to make a pair of them. Strange cuts of meat on the butcher's block; two bodies missing their legs. Lou's first night at the San, Bo had commented that Mr. Gillis had passed away the previous night, and there had been meat on the table. And of the same sort, indeterminate chunks in a dark stew. What had Shai said about the smokehouse back on his plantation with Lazarus?

Boy, she was a dummy. And now a cannibal. Probably. For a moment Lou thought she was going to spew, but she kept it down.

Lou felt a momentary despair as she wondered if the Chinese workers she sought were already dead and gone, served up for hungry San patients. Then again, that would be an incredibly bizarre scheme, especially considering Shai's comments about the San being under capacity… what with bribes, train fare, and the expense of shipping appropriate groceries from San Francisco through Cheyenne, it would be far less expensive to just purchase a few shoats and breed them. Farming meat that could be fed on slops was vastly more cost effective than importing humans—humans who might be missed. If the San patients were always dropping dead, and Shai could provide human blood in lean times, the Chinese must have been brought in for other purposes. But *what?* Maybe they were attempting to build a secret railroad spur to the San? And yet, she had seen no signs of blasting, heard no sounds of construction…

There *had* been that mangled body in the crate at Madame Cheung's. It must be that whatever Dr. Panacea had the men doing—wherever they were doing it—was very dangerous, something with a high casualty rate. And then what better to do with a corpse than dispose of it neatly, feeding it to the unsuspecting—especially when it saved you the money and bother of caring for livestock? Lou, queasy again, looked up from her plate, unable to bear the sight of her unfinished stew any longer. Coriander was staring at her intently.

"What's wrong?" she asked.

Lou reached for her cup of water. She took a long draught before answering. "The bodies," she said.

Coriander canted her head to the right. "What about them?"

"I don't want to talk about it now—not here. Just don't eat any more of that, okay?"

"Why not?"

"Yeah," agreed Bo, wolfing down another mouthful. "Ifs ashully goo f'onfe!"

Lou turned away from Bo's open-mouth chewing before she lost it once and for all, and glanced at Mr. Dumpling. She didn't necessarily want to let him into her confidence, but she did want him—and everyone else—to stop munching on Ned. Or Coyote.

What she needed was a distraction.

"After a meal that good, I need a smoke," announced Lou, so loudly that everyone at her table looked up at her like she had gone insane. She grinned at them and withdrew Coriander's cigarette from her pocket. Lighting it off the lantern in the center of the table, she inhaled deeply, and exhaled clouds of tobacco smoke, angling it away from Bo. She was trying to get Miss Foxglove's attention, not murder her friend.

Several things happened at once. Mr. Dumpling had gotten the worst of her smoke. Nose wrinkling, he waved his hand in front of his face so vigorously it wafted into Bo's face. Lou heard an indignant, feminine squawk from the other table as Bo began to cough violently. Cursing her luck, Lou muttered *sorry* as Bo doubled over in agony, unable to catch his breath, spattering the scrubbed pine of the tables with bright red sputum. Coriander was staring at her open-mouthed, completely horrified. Lou was unhappy, too, but determined to see it through she took a second drag when she felt the expected hand on her shoulder and snapped her head around and exhaled again, right in Miss Foxglove's face.

The fitness instructor made a show of fanning away the smoke and pretend-coughing, a series of staccato chuffing noises that sounded like a comic mockery of Bo's anguish. Distraction completed, Lou crushed out the cigarette into her unfinished bowl of stew.

"Sorry," said Lou. "Forgot about the rules."

"Your negligence may have seriously affected another patient, Mr. Meriwether!" scolded Miss Foxglove, who was rummaging in her pocket for something. Her urgent, angry tone took Lou aback; she sounded altogether like a different person than she had that morning. But when Miss Foxglove elbowed her aside and sat down next to Bo, Lou realized Bo's attack was far more serious than the one he'd had during calisthenics class. Miss Foxglove was having trouble keeping him still enough to dribble precious Elixir in his mouth.

"Lou," breathed Coriander, standing helplessly to the side. "What were you thinking?"

Lou knew exactly what she'd been thinking, but now wondered if it wouldn't have been better to just let him and everyone else eat their dinners and tell them after it had been people-meat. Bo was not recovering, even with the dose of Elixir. Miss Foxglove got another few drops into his mouth, and at last the medicine soothed his lungs. After taking several deep breaths, he fell limply into her wiry arms with a sigh, and closed his eyes.

"Bo?" asked Miss Foxglove. "Are you with us?"

"Yeah," he said. "I'm okay. Just tired."

"Let's get him back to his room," said Miss Foxglove, looking right into Lou's eyes. There was steel in her voice. Feeling helpless and ashamed, Lou nodded. Her throat was too tight for her to speak.

When Bo was ready they both got a shoulder under one of his armpits and helped him to his feet. Coriander limped before them, opening doors. As quickly as they could they hurried him through the biting air and back into the San.

He was shivering badly when they reached his room. Coriander retrieved Bo's key from the cord around his neck and got the door open, then hurried to light the lamp and turn down the covers on his bed.

Lou and Miss Foxglove got him under the blankets, clothes and all. After a few moments he stopped trembling. Lou was happy to see that, but knew she was in for it when Miss Foxglove turned her attention to her.

"So here's the thing," she began, but Miss Foxglove interrupted her.

"If you want to endanger your own health smoking those *things*, fine! But hurting other patients? I never heard of such cruelty!"

"It's not like that," said Lou, feeling smaller than a mouse.

Miss Foxglove shook her head. "I may not be able to claim Mr. Wong is family, but I am very fond of him. Please abjure future indiscretions of this nature. I would like to see him leave here one day."

It had not occurred to Lou that Miss Foxglove might have feelings about anything other than tobacco abstinence, and maybe the importance of lower back flexibility. She was also surprised about the fitness instructor's remark about Bo leaving. She'd assumed Miss Foxglove was in on whatever was happening at Fountain of Youth, but she seemed genuinely upset—and invested in the idea of patients recovering.

"I'm sorry," said Lou. "I was worried about him."

"He appeared to be fine before you blew smoke all over him!"

Lou looked at Miss Foxglove, and decided to trust her gut. "I was worried... about the food. That it might not be good—good for him, I mean."

"Why ever not?" asked Coriander. "It tasted fine."

Lou glanced at Bo. Weak and sweating and pale, he looked as though he were concentrating on breathing, as if respiration were some Herculean task that demanded his total concentration.

"Because," she began, but Miss Foxglove cut her off.

"Mr. Merriwether, I'm not sure what you know—or what you *think* you know—but the best thing you could possibly do right now is leave."

"Leave?"

"Yes, *leave*. Leave the San. Leave Colorado. Go back where you came from, and hope you are not followed."

Lou opened her mouth, but Miss Foxglove held up a hand.

"I don't want to hear any more about what you suspect is happening here. Speaking to me about it could be a very, very bad idea. As I said, I suggest you pack your things and go—tonight, if possible. Forget you ever came here, as I plan on forgetting we ever had this conversation." And with that, she swept out of the room.

Chapter Ten

"That was interesting," said Coriander. "Why would she tell you to leave? And what do you mean, the food isn't good for Bo? What about for me? And you? You were eating it."

"I was," said Lou, throwing herself into Bo's chair. "And then I realized…"

Lou sensed she was right about the whole situation, but that didn't make it any easier to say it aloud. Coriander was staring at her curiously, and even Bo had opened his eyes and was looking at her.

"It was Ned," she said. "Or Coyote. Their *legs,* Coriander. Think about it."

"What?" wheezed Bo.

"Don't be silly," said Coriander, though she didn't sound as certain or enthusiastic as usual. She sat down at the foot of Bo's bed. "Why would they do… that… when they have perfectly good animals to eat?"

"Have you seen any stock? Milch cows and nanny goats are too valuable to kill for meat, if they're producing—and anyways, that stew wasn't beef or goat, was it?"

"Well, no," said Coriander. "It tasted sort of… I don't know. But *really,* Lou! I know you work with the dead for a living, but you don't have to be so morbid! There's probably a perfectly good reason they chopped off Ned's and Coyote's legs."

"Can you," Bo took a deep breath, "explain what the hell you two are

290

talking about?"

"I just don't know," said Coriander, after they gave Bo an account of their afternoon. "It seems so… wrong! And why would Dr. P have sent his assistant to look after the stock if there aren't any stock? That just doesn't make sense!"

"We have no way of verifying if Dr. Panacea was telling the truth." Or if Shai was actually gone. Lou cocked her head as she gave Coriander her best imitation of the girl's smug smile. "I mean, answer me this: where does all this alleged stock *live?*"

"On the other side of the… *ohhhh,*" said Coriander. She turned pink, her realization rosy-fingered as it dawned. "Oh dear."

"Oh dear indeed," whispered Bo.

"But you know, it makes sense," Coriander said thoughtfully. "Before last night, the last time we had meat was right after Mr. Woodworth died, about a month and a half ago. Well, a proper plate of meat. Sometimes they crumble some sausage in with the lentils or what have you. But then Mr. Gillis died just before you arrived."

"It makes sense," said Bo. "Vampires can't just leave dead bodies lying around, it's suspicious and stupid. And Dr. Panacea isn't stupid—not if he's run a sanatorium incognito for this long."

Coriander cleared her throat. "I'm sorry—vampire?"

Lou winced. Right. She hadn't mentioned that yet. Whoops.

"You think Dr. Panacea's a vampire?" Coriander's eyes went wide when Lou nodded. "My goodness! They're not supposed to be common, I don't think. Not anymore. Right?"

"You know that thing I showed you? The skiameter?"

"Yes? Oh, I see. I suppose you of all people would know—and I don't think I've ever seen him in the sunlight, come to think of it. But the meat, I don't know! You're right, it's usually right after a death that we have it, but we've had meat other times, too."

"I suspect the Chinese we can't find might be involved in something dangerous," said Lou. "It might have been them. And hell, if a nanny goat gets too old to produce milk, you eat her, right?"

"Poor Mr. Gillis." Coriander raised a finger to her bow-lips, considering. "Though I suppose now he'll always be a part of me."

Coriander's ghastly remark made Bo laugh, and Lou was momentarily happy to see him amused—but too quickly his laughter turned into more of that scary coughing. Coriander rubbed Bo's back and tried to get him to sip from his cup of water, but he had trouble getting the fluid down.

"Wait a minute." Lou kicked herself for not thinking of her bottle of Elixir sooner, and ran to her room to retrieve it. She'd left her bag on her bed, so she just grabbed her whole satchel and sped back out the door, fumbling to locate the phial as she ran.

Bo was still coughing when she returned. She managed to get some in his mouth, then added more to the cup on his bedside table. Though not as severe as his supper-time fit, the phthisic attack had exhausted him. After he'd sipped maybe half of his water, he sighed weakly.

"I'll be all right," he wheezed. "Go on, go, I dunno, have some fun with Coriander. Smoke on top of the barn or something. Don't stay with me." He opened his eyes. "You hang out with the dead enough already."

"Stop that shit right now," said Lou, looking away. "I'll stay till you're asleep. Coriander—you understand, don't you?"

"Of course!"

Bo grimaced. "You want me to sleep with you staring at me?"

Lou fluffed the covers up around him unnecessarily. "All right. I'll leave the bottle of Elixir with you. Promise me you'll take some if you need it?"

Bo nodded and shut his eyes again. Lou sat beside him for a few moments. When the lines around his mouth relaxed and his breathing evened out she stood, and she and Coriander quietly set the room to rights. She scooted the chamber pot over so it would be more accessible for him, folded his scarf and put it on his wooden box, and then turned down the lantern so the room was bathed in the cool near-darkness of the fungus-lamp.

They tiptoed out the door, but before shutting it, Lou glanced back. Bo had turned over, and was now facing the wall. The covers were pulled up so high all she could see of him was the back of his head, and Lou almost walked back to look at his face one more time. She had an eerie feeling about leaving him.

"So what do you want to do now?" asked Coriander, as they walked down the hall. She was still favoring her injured leg; Lou wondered how she'd managed the calisthenics class. "I'm dying for a cigarette—and I'd like to hear more about—"

"Shh," said Lou shortly. "You know the gong? I dunno how we can hear it through all this rock, but it makes me not like to talk about that stuff inside, unless I have to."

"You're so smart!" marveled Coriander, stopping in her tracks. "I never would've thought of that."

"Not smart enough," said Lou. "I've fucked up pretty much everything since I started… whatever it is I'm doing here."

"Oh, please."

"You don't know," said Lou. "I've been an idiot, and I've—"

Coriander leaned in close, her lips almost touching Lou's ear. "Tomorrow," she breathed. "We'll figure something out!"

The feel of her breath made Lou shiver. She smiled at Coriander uncertainly. Her new friend's easy intimacy was new and pleasant, if sometimes startling, but Lou wasn't sure if she was interested in being more than friends.

"Coriander," she said, "you know, I, uh—"

Coriander rolled her eyes and poked Lou on the nose. "I told you I liked them *stern*, Lou. Not, well, whatever it is you are. Baffling, mostly!" She took Lou's arm as they walked toward her room. "It's just, I've never felt useful before, not really. I like working with you. You're so confident, and, well, more confident than patient, but you're somewhat patient too! And… I don't know. I mean, I'm annoyed with you for not telling me everything, but—close your mouth, I understand! And if you let me work with you again, I promise I won't demand more information than you're willing to give me, even if, privately I believe that a full disclosure would let me help out better."

"You're probably right."

They had reached Coriander's door. "So… see you tomorrow?" she asked.

Lou nodded. "Thanks," she said. "I need some… time."

"Of course," said Coriander. "Just promise me one thing."

"What?"

"That you won't spend the whole night grumping at yourself for not being perfect."

Lou finally smiled. Coriander had a way of bringing her out of dark moods. "All right. But only because you asked."

As she ambled back towards her room Lou found herself wondering what would it be like to work with someone like Coriander on a more permanent basis. Lou had never denied, to herself or to others, that she had her flaws; it was just that she felt she should learn to work with them rather than around them. But perhaps it would be easier—or differently challenging—to have someone around who balanced her.

Now she was sounding like her mother.

Maybe that wasn't such a bad thing.

Even her unfamiliar room and strange bed looked welcoming after the day she'd had. Lou couldn't wait to get under the covers, but as she moved to shut the door behind her, she paused. Giggling echoed down the corridor, high and playful. Wondering if Coriander had followed her, she waited… and heard the slapping of bare feet on stone coming down the hallway.

Lou froze. It was late, by San standards. Most doors, as she'd passed them, had had no light spilling from under them. And Coriander, the most likely candidate at the San to be running through the hallways barefoot and tittering, was still in no condition for a sprint.

Lou eased her door open a crack and listened hard. There was another burst of quiet laugher, this time deeper, and closer. Someone ran by, and a second person followed. On a whim, Lou released the doorknob and checked her skiameter. The needle pointed straight down the hallway.

Dr. Panacea was on the prowl, unless there were other undead here at Fountain of Youth, tee-heeing in the darkness under the earth. Lou sincerely hoped that would not prove to be the case, then decided it was time to do more than hope. She admired Coriander for her derring-do, didn't she? Even though she had just been musing on the idea of recruiting a partner, for now she would just have to settle for taking some pages from her friend's book.

Lou sensed how pissed Coriander would be when she found out about this little caper. But she was injured; speed and nimbleness were needed tonight. Coriander would just have to understand.

Poking her head out into the corridor, Lou caught sight of a slender figure in a white robe—Eliana, judging by the cinched waist and dark wavy hair—turning a corner. Lou took the time to buckle her shoulder holster, then gently shut her door behind her and took off after as quietly as she could, holding her workbag tight. She was annoyed. It pissed her off that Dr. Panacea and his wife were out playing grab-ass through the hallways while her oldest friend gasped and sweated alone in the darkness. The doctor might be a vampire but he didn't have to be such an asshole.

At the fork, her skiameter indicated to her that they had taken the left-hand stairs towards the deck. Eliana had been wearing a robe; they were probably heading outside to have a moonlit bath in the spring.

An idea came to Lou as she stole after the couple. This could be her chance to get some real answers. If they felt secure running around the San, they could hardly be anticipating an attack. If she played her cards right, she could bushwhack them before they knew what was happening. Eliana wasn't undead, which meant she could be more easily threatened. Lou might be able to take her hostage. Then she'd be in a position to bargain with the doctor for information. If he gave her any lip, she had her wards, and her special bullets were already loaded in her LeMat. She'd just have to take a chance on her vermilion-infused rounds working. If they didn't put him down, there was always the revolver's secondary, single-shot barrel was loaded with her nice big .60 ball—vampires might not have a pulse but they still had kneecaps, and blowing his off would probably slow him down enough for Lou to come up with a new plan.

Up the stone stairs she went in the glum light of the fungal sconces, the only sound other than her bootfalls the perpetual soft patter of water dripping onto rock. As she climbed, she opened her workbag and slipped on her goggles, then found her lens case with her fingertips. She flipped through the various pouches by touch, counting as she went, so she was irritated when she withdrew a blue lens.

Lou swore softly. She had forgotten Coriander had tossed one of her precious pink thumoscopic lenses over the edge of the deck when Ned attacked her. Ah, well. She replaced the wrong lens and withdrew one of the correct type. When she reached the outside door she paused to slide the pink lens into the left socket of her goggles, leaving the other clear.

Lou opened the door slowly and peeked out. The moon was very bright. She could see every detail of the deck, the copse of pines, and in the distance, the steam from the mineral spring. Through her goggle-lens she saw two faint but bright blobs bobbing in the distance. The two pairs of footprints visible in the thin dusting of opalescent snow on the wooden slats confirmed her skiameter's readings. Dr. Panacea and his bride were taking a swim.

Lou began to walk slowly toward the spring, gun in one hand, bag in the other, taking care to step into the footprints so no snow-crunch would give her presence away. She was nervous, sweating into her shirt despite the cold. The worried looks that Bo, Thurlow, and Millie had shared while discussing battling vampires kept running through her mind. There was still time to turn back, bide her time until… but until *what?* Until Bo got worse? Until she had Coriander underfoot?

No, risky as her plan might be, there was no way of taking down a vampire that *wasn't* risky, really. The longer she waited to act the more likely it was that her true motives for being at the San would be uncovered. Dr. Panacea was a lot of things, but he wasn't stupid—and she couldn't rely on her luck to keep holding.

As she drew closer to the spring, Lou was able to discern more about the spirits she saw through her lens. One was whole, a bright, human shadow the yellow-orange color of a campfire. The other… the outline was still human, but the crimson light was moving in swirling patterns, knotting and unknotting itself endlessly, chaotically. Lou had never seen vampirism this far progressed in a subject; it was actually fascinating.

The boardwalk and deck were only a foot or so off the ground here, so Lou stepped down, intending to cut over and to take advantage of the cover the pine-thicket provided. Unfortunately, the snow was untouched; it squeaked and crackled under her feet. As she crept carefully toward the small stand of evergreens her footfalls sounded horribly loud, but she saw no indication in the movements of her quarry to indicate they heard her.

A large bird screamed and took off from within the copse in a rush of wings and rustling boughs. Lou used the ruckus to make a break for it, bringing her behind the tree furthest from the spring. She set down her bag. Pistol in one hand, the other free, Lou took a deep breath and stuck her nose above the edge of the deck.

Dr. Panacea was casually naked, standing at the edge of the spring, apparently untroubled by the bitter night. His muscled body shone faintly, like the snow, and his languid motions were hypnotic, beautiful and precise. Lou had a hard time keeping in mind that he was a murderer and a villain. He was just so *likable*—his smile was genuine; his slight potbelly humanized him, as did his flopping genitals as he capered and posed for his companion.

Eliana was already in the spring. Looking at her profile, Lou was again confounded, wondering if she was Shai or not.

Dr. Panacea said something to her that Lou couldn't quite hear; in response, Eliana splashed forward in the water and gathered a handful of snow from the edge of the pool, quickly packing it into a snowball to lob at her husband. Lou's throat tightened a little, the scene reminded her of her last happy afternoon with Shai. But not entirely—her purpose in instigating the duel had been to avoid romance. When Eliana lobbed her missile at Dr. Panacea she leaped partially from the pool and Lou saw her small but distinctly feminine breasts, capped with light upturned nipples. They were as flawless as the rest of her.

The snowball hit Dr. Panacea on the jaw. He brushed it aside, hooting, "Beautifully done, m'dear!"

When he bent down to collect snow for a snowball of his own, his attention at his feet, Lou saw her opportunity. Eliana's back was to Lou; she was backing away from Dr. Panacea toward the edge of the spring closest to Lou. Before she could think herself out of it, Lou bounded onto the deck and bum rushed the spring, her gun extended and trained on Eliana.

Dr. Panacea straightened up as Lou dropped to her knees at the edge of the spring, her impact on the slippery, icy deck stinging her knees something fierce. For a moment she worried that she was actually going to slide into the water on top of Eliana, but even as the thought crossed her mind she reached down and hooked the startled young woman in a headlock, which served to steady her balance. Carefully, Lou pressed her gun to Eliana's temple.

"If you like her brains where they are, don't move a muscle," shouted Lou. She did not sound at all sure of herself, but she kept her weapon steady. "I'll kill her if you don't—" *don't what?* thought Lou frantically—"don't, uh, do as I say!"

Across the spring from them Dr. Panacea remained perfectly still, snowball cupped in the palm of his hand. He looked completely flabbergasted. Eliana struggled briefly.

"What the hell are you doing, Lou?" she asked through her teeth.

Lou froze. She sounded just like Shai.

"I'm taking you hostage," Lou announced.

"I can see that," she—maybe he—said. "Why?"

Lou looked right at Dr. Panacea. "I'm not sick, Doc. My teeth are *fine.* I came here to find out a few things that didn't seem quite right about this place."

"Shai told me you were an apothecary's brat." The doctor's voice was still calm and melodious. His lack of concern worried Lou. "Are you attempting to get the formula for the Elixir of Life, Mr. Merriwether? I'll give it to you, if you'll lower your weapon and stand down."

"There is no formula." Lou swallowed, cotton-mouthed. "Yeah—that's right, I know what's in the Elixir. But I didn't come for that. I came here after a bunch of Chinese fellas went missing, leaving behind their families and friends. I'm not leaving without my kinfolk, even if it's just their bones. So how's about I let your friend here put on her robe, and then we'll all head to wherever you're keeping them. Sound like a plan to you?"

Dr. Panacea's face showed no signs of emotion. His smile was bland, his posture bespoke nonchalance. Lou could feel his hatred, though, and she knew if she lost her concentration—or her grip on the gun—she was done for.

"You know a lot about my little sanatorium, don't you?" said Dr. Panacea, with a sharp glance down at Eliana. "What a shame. Now there's no way I'll let you live."

"Then say your goodbyes to your wife," said Lou, feeling a little ridiculous spouting dialogue straight from a yellowback novel. "Just don't you come any closer. I'd rather cozy up with a rattlesnake than get close to a vampire, so—"

There was only the barest flash of movement from the other side of the spring, and then something smashed into Lou's face, breaking her nose and knocking her clean off her feet. As she fell backwards, blind from pain and feeling her warm blood gushing down her cold face, her gun flew from her grasp. Then her head hit the edge of a deck chair, and her last conscious thought made her laugh before she blacked out entirely. Dr. Panacea had taken her down with a snowball. She was so fucked.

Chapter Eleven

Pain greeted Lou first as she oozed her way back to consciousness. Her nose burned like a fire and ached like a son of a bitch, but the sensations ebbed and flowed, almost as if she was being slapped repeatedly about her already-sore face.

As she became more aware of her surroundings it turned out that she was being slapped, sort of. More accurately, she was being bounced, and the motion was causing the side of her face to knock into something hard and unyielding.

When her vision sharpened a bit, Lou was baffled to behold an upside down pair of buttocks just above her nose—unblemished, beautiful buttocks. The muscles of the taut hemispheres were rippling; they belonged to someone who was walking quickly, and with each step her face was banging into that someone's back.

She had a pretty good idea of who might be naked and carrying her like a sack of potatoes. Rather than deal with that, Lou's mind elected to go blank again.

When next she became aware of herself it was much darker, and she was no longer in motion. Ivory buttocks and the small of a back still were taking up her field of vision. More awake this go-round, she recognized the feeling of an arm gripping her legs and a shoulder digging painfully into her guts.

She was in the lodge. The coals from the dinnertime fire had burned down low, but they cast enough light for her to see a little. There were voices, but it took her a few moments to focus enough to listen. She tried not to tense up or moan, figuring it would be better for her if her captors thought she remained unconscious.

"...didn't find out everything about her, now did you?" said Dr. Panacea. Lou could feel his words rumbling through his chest. "Or did you know all along she was after them?"

"I had no idea," said Shai. "She asked a few questions, but I had no notion they were her real goal. I would have done a lot more than try to talk her out of coming here if I'd known, of course."

"Of course," parroted Dr. Panacea. His voice had an edge sharper than a straight razor. "Nothing is 'of course' where this 'Mr. Merriwether' is concerned, apparently. Like that bag of... *things* she has. But I suppose you didn't know anything about that, either? Hmm?"

When Shai did not reply, Dr. Panacea sighed. "Get the door."

Lou heard a creak, and saw out of the corner of her eye a dark figure unlocking and then throwing open the trapdoor through which Eliana and Dr. Panacea had emerged during the welcome supper.

"I liked her," said Shai. "Is that such a crime? In another life we might have been friends."

"In another life maybe—but not this one."

"I know."

"Dearest," Dr. Panacea's voice softened, "it's not a crime that you liked her; what is criminal is that you *lied* for her. You've never lied for anyone before—or have you? I now must wonder that. And you told her to keep away from here. That worries me too." His tone had that keenness to it again. "I don't like to be worried. I have enough cares to occupy me without being suspicious of the one person I should be able to trust completely."

"Is it so easy for the seeds of doubt to take root in your heart?" Lou heard a rustling, then Shai's voice came from somewhere slightly lower than Lou's head. "She is nothing beside you—no, she could not even stand beside you! How could I care about someone so silly, so ignorant? So young?"

Lou heard the sound of a kiss. Dr. Panacea's rump tightened and he groaned so deeply Lou felt the tremors enter her body through his chest. Lou closed her eyes; she really didn't want to see Shai sucking Dr. Panacea's cock. Thankfully, the doctor put a stop to things pretty quickly.

"Not here," he said, more gently than before. "Not now."

After a pause and a slurp, Shai said, "Are you sure?"

"Perhaps after I interrogate her."

The descent down the stone stairs was yet another trial. Lou's abused face smarted with each jolt, but she was so eaten up with fear the pain actually helped her remain calm.

As they descended, their surroundings grew gradually brighter and colder; Lou thought she smelled snow and pine trees, and at last saw the glow of moonlight. Remembering the same smell wafting up from the staircase she and Coriander had not taken, Lou wondered just where on—or *under* the earth they were heading.

When they reached the bottom of the stairs it was undeniably easier for Lou to see, and so cold she could not help but shiver. She tried to look around as she was carried along level ground for a few yards, but before she could discern anything meaningful Lou had to shut her eyes. Shai, who had been walking behind the doctor, darted around in front of them. There was the sound of a key in a lock and then the low squeal of a hinge. When Dr. Panacea strode inside the doorway, darkness ate them again.

After the sound of the door shutting, Lou heard the scrape of a match. A dazzling flash accompanied by a sulfur odor preceded the room filling with bright light; a lantern had been lit. Lou screwed her eyes shut and willed them not to water.

"I know you're awake, Mr. Merriwether," said Dr. Panacea, as he slung Lou into a wooden chair. A cushion saved her tailbone as she came down hard. "You can stop pretending."

Squinting around, Lou saw she was in another office. It was styled similarly to the room where Dr. Panacea had examined her, but instead of looking clean and professional, this chamber was cluttered and lived-in. The floor was occupied by several crates of the Elixir of Life, just like the one in the cellar of Madame Cheung's, and a large desk off to one side was covered in stacks of paperwork. While this room was also lined with bookshelves, they were clogged with leather-bound tomes and paper manuscripts, some of which looked immemorially ancient. So this was why there was nothing personal in Dr. Panacea's office—it was all down here. She'd have to tell Coriander. If she survived.

"I'm not going to tie you up." Dr. Panacea's conversational tone frightened Lou more than if he'd sounded angry. "I think we should trust one another, don't you? That said, I will not be made a fool of. I'll kill you if you try to escape."

"Fair enough," she said. Her voice sounded flat and nasal from the broken nose. "I was out for a while though. You clocked me good with that snowball. Nifty trick, that. So, what'd I miss?"

"I know exactly when you rejoined us. Your heart rate increases when you're awake. Or distressed in some way." Dr. Panacea glanced over at his companion when he said this.

Lou took the opportunity to confirm that the third person in the room was Shai. It seemed to be him, but he was wearing a robe identical to the one she'd seen Eliana wearing earlier in the evening, and his hair fell about his shoulders in the same loose waves. But he was leaning casually against the desk, arms crossed, a pose Lou had seen him adopt many a time when they were traveling together. So maybe they were the same person, somehow.

Lou had mixed feelings about seeing him again, to say the goddamn least. She had missed his company, even after finding out she was better off without it. But she was also afraid of him. She kept searching his face for something, *anything* that would reassure her that she'd come out of this okay. She saw nothing.

"Observe how she looks at you, dearest." Dr. Panacea was still naked, still standing close where Lou was slouching in her chair. She tried to keep her eyes from his dangling genitals and was mostly successful, but she definitely flinched when he leaned forward to stroke her shaggy hair, running his icy fingernails over her scalp. "She wants so much to believe you'll help her—that you'll say something which will save her and end the nightmare." Dr. Panacea canted his head slightly, staring straight into Shai's eyes. "Is she correct?"

"She got here without my help," said Shai. "She can leave here without it. Or try, anyways."

"I'm sorry, Mr. Merriwether," said Dr. Panacea. "Your only potential advocate has abandoned you. How does that make you feel?"

Strangely enough, all Lou could think about was the faraway look on Shai's face when she had quoted the Li Po poem in the shadow of the front range, just before they had decided to take the Devil's Gulch road. He had not seemed really happy then, nor when he told her of the horrors he had endured during his lengthy existence. *In another life, we might have been friends.* How many times over the centuries had he said or thought those same words? How many times had he heard or known the inevitable response? The sheer scale of Shai's loneliness was staggering as Lou contemplated it.

Dr. Panacea's smile faltered momentarily as he watched Lou, and he walked over to the desk where Shai stood. He put his arm protectively around Shai's narrow shoulders, gripping him so tightly Shai winced.

"I think you may have bewitched her, my dear," he said.

Shai snaked his arm around the doctor's waist. "They say you catch more flies with honey, don't they?"

"And yet by your own admission you discouraged Mr. Merriwether from coming here." It seemed Shai's words had upset Dr. Panacea, rather than the reverse. "Shai has an uncanny ability to attract and compel," he said icily, turning to Lou. "I've never known anyone to resist his charms. And he has the same effect on men and women of every inclination. Don't you?"

Shai said nothing, but Dr. Panacea seemed to be expecting an answer. Thus an awkward silence descended upon the trio. Lou felt nauseated and unhappy. Much of her discomfort was concern for Shai. Despite his claims about the perfect harmony between himself and Dr. Panacea, they seemed pretty awful together. She decided to try and help Shai out. Perhaps, then, he would do the same for her.

"Shai didn't seduce me," said Lou, and, electing not to mention the night when he'd pressed his lips to hers and blown hot hasheesh-smoke deep into her lungs, lied a bit: "The only time he touched me was when I got shot—"

"Ah, yes! When you were *shot,*" drawled Dr. Panacea, tugging Shai even closer into his embrace. "If memory serves, that was when Shai first learned what you were. Well. Perhaps it's only fair to repay like with like."

Dr. Panacea's long white hand twitched. Shai's robe fell open, and there was one less mystery at Fountain of Youth.

"Isn't my little pet lovely? Please, look as long as you like, you have my permission. I rescued him, so he is mine to do with as I like." He touched Shai's cheek delicately. "I saved him from certain death at the hand of an unscrupulous alchemist who saw him as nothing more than a hermaphrodite—a virgin hermaphrodite, as Shai was at the time—a unique thing indeed... very precious, very powerful, if you know much about alchemy.

He was to be a sacrifice, a mere reagent. I saw him as more… but of course there's no need to dwell on the past. We got away didn't we, my beauty?" He came back to himself and looked at Lou. "So what do you think of your friend now?"

Lou had never disliked Dr. Panacea more than she did in that moment, and she refused to give him the satisfaction of ogling Shai's admittedly unique physiognomy. Instead, she kept her gaze on Shai's face, for he, too, had turned to see her reaction. She tried to say with her eyes that her opinion of him had not changed; that she saw him as only himself—Shai—not an oddity, not a freak; that she was sorry for being the reason he stood there, exposed, when he so clearly did not wish to be. For a brief moment, Lou thought she saw a flush coloring his cheeks; perceived the barest flicker of feeling in his beautiful eyes—but it was gone too quickly for her to decide if it was hurt or rage or gratitude, or something else entirely.

Dr. Panacea threw up his hands and laughed unpleasantly. Shai took the opportunity to cinch his robe tightly about himself.

"I can see why you fell for this one," said Dr. Panacea. His tone was nastier now, and Lou realized too late her actions had only made him angrier. "What was it, my dearest love? Did you see yourself in this little girl pretending to be a boy? Did she *move* you? Touch your soul? Did you think you could save her?" He looked at Shai keenly. "Or did you want to save yourself? Poetic, I'm sure."

"I cannot make you believe in my love," whispered Shai. "If nearly four hundred years of devoted service is not proof enough…"

Dr. Panacea shrugged. "I believe in your love, of course I do. Here, see—I had planned on dismissing you while I interrogated our guest, but I think, instead, I'll let you stay! As a reward! I shall even let you help. Why don't you go get the pliers while I begin?" He turned to face Lou. "My apologies for the delay, but now that we have everything out in the open, as it were, I'd like you to explain a few things to me. Sound good?"

All the ugliness was pissing her off, and being pissed off was helping her act brave. "Whatcha wanna know?"

Dr. Panacea's smile was wan as he idly scratched himself just above where his pubic hair began. Something caught under one of his fingernails; he ran his thumbnail under the ridge and flicked it away. "Let's start with something easy, shall we? Why did you arrange to meet Bo Wong here at

Fountain of Youth?"

"I didn't," said Lou. "It was just fate. God's honest."

"No need to swear," said Dr. Panacea. "I believe you."

"Then ask me something tougher. That was an easy one!"

"Something tougher?" Dr. Panacea stroked his mustache. "How did you come to find out that I had a group of Chinese trash in my employ?"

"*Employ?* You're paying them a wage? Shit, I'll just head on home then," said Lou. "I was all worried you were enslaving them. Or eating them. Or both, I guess."

Dr. Panacea sank down on his heels directly in front of her and smiled at her with a gentle, amused expression in his eyes. When he took her left hand in his she knew it would be useless to resist, so she didn't bother. He stroked her palm with the long white fingers of his free hand, and then applied just a bit more pressure to her middle finger, snapping it neatly at the second joint.

Lou screamed. She couldn't help it. Her shirt instantly grew clammy with sweat; it was cold in the office. She began to shiver.

His smile had never faltered. "And we were doing so well. You were telling the truth—yes, I can tell—so why sass me?"

"I—"

"Before you say another word, know that what I just did is nothing to what I'll do if you don't cooperate. Mr. Merriwether?" He snapped his fingers in front of her eyes until she nodded. "Shall we start again?"

"What was the question?" she gasped.

Dr. Panacea tutted at her. "Are you not afraid of me yet?" He broke her ring finger in the same place, then broke it again just where it met the hand. Lou retched and almost fell out of her chair, but Dr. Panacea caught her before she tumbled and settled her back into an upright posture. "Do I need to explain to you that I am a very dangerous person? I do not care if I hurt you. I actually enjoy it."

Lou looked over at Shai, who was hanging back from the proceedings. He had retrieved the aforementioned pair of pliers. She hoped the reddish stains on the load and fulcrum were just rust.

"How did you hear I was interested in employing Chinese workers?" Lou looked wildly up at Dr. Panacea, who was still entirely calm. "If you do not answer me, I will have Shai break your toes, one by one. He used to be quite good at it, though he's out of practice so no guarantees he won't mangle you worse than I would."

Lou took a deep breath to steady herself. She understood exactly what Dr. Panacea was up to; appreciated on just how many levels he was manipulating the situation. She decided to stick as closely to the truth as possible, to save herself—and to save Shai.

"It was just a rumor. Too many men went missing. People started to notice."

"But surely people must go away all the time?" said Dr. Panacea, stroking her hand again.

It occurred to Lou he was assessing the strength of his own plans as well as getting information.

"Chinatown's tiny, and it's a community where men and boys are valued. Boys especially, there aren't too many young folks in Chinatown. So when a bunch of them didn't come home, or write after claiming there was a call for workers in Cheyenne, people asked questions."

"Ah," said Dr. Panacea, considering. "That makes quite a bit of sense; I didn't think about that. Immigrant communities, of course. Well, well. You're proving your worth to me, Mr. Merriwether! Keep yourself safe by continuing to amuse me. So—after hearing about the missing men, you headed to Cheyenne to investigate? That seems… I don't even know how to describe it. Rash! Foolhardy! Maybe brave… I'm not sure. Perhaps just stupid. You had so little to go on!"

"Sometimes I surprise even myself," said Lou.

"She's lying," said Shai, and Lou's stomach tightened. She'd been so sure Shai was on her side, at least a little. "She knew who you were before she came here, and asked about you and the San the moment I said I was familiar with Estes Park. She claimed her doctor advised her to take Elixir of Life for her health problems."

Dr. Panacea touched Lou's index finger. She stiffened, but he did not put any further pressure on the digit. "How did you come by your knowledge of my Elixir?"

"It's real popular in San Francisco."

"Open your mouth," said Dr. Panacea.

Lou stared at him, silently aghast. She kept her lips firmly clamped together.

"Open your mouth," he ordered. "I want to see how ugly it is in there. Your mouth must be an ugly place, with all those lies inside it. Maybe that's what's wrong with your teeth, have you ever considered that?"

When Lou failed to immediately open her mouth, Dr. Panacea sighed. "Shai?"

When Shai stepped forward, pliers in hand, Lou parted her lips. Dr. Panacea immediately jammed his thumb and forefinger in her mouth, and yanked out her right incisor before she knew what was happening. Then he held it in front of her face. She dry-heaved at the sight of the pinkish root weeping blood, and her throat began to burn. She had never been in so much pain in her life, it was radiating from her hand and face running down her neck, up her arm, into her chest; it manifested in other places, too, like under her ribs, and the tops of her thighs. Maybe those were the "meridians" her mother had always talked about when discussing qi imbalances.

"I want you to look at this tooth," said Dr. Panacea, studying it as well. "I want you to imagine that all the ugly lies you've been telling were in this tooth. It wasn't your fault. It was your *tooth* that was lying. Now it's gone. I think all the lies came away with it. But what do you think? Did all the lies come away with your tooth?"

Lou nodded yes, and meant it with all her heart.

"I know that your tooth lied about buying my Elixir. We don't ship to California." Dr. Panacea sniffed her tooth, stuck his tongue out and tasted the root. Uttering a slight groaning sound as the tip of his tongue reddened with her blood, he stiffened, everywhere, and Shai ran to his side.

"No," Shai said, *"don't.* What if you can't stop, we still need to know—"

"I know what I'm doing," growled Dr. Panacea. "I don't need you to tell me my limits."

"I—"

"Let me be!" he roared, then turned back to Lou. "Excuse me. Let's try again—how did you come by that bottle of Elixir?"

"A friend had a whole pallet of bottles," she blubbed through a mouthful of blood. "Someone delivered them to her and I don't know more than that." Lou realized she was crying and hated herself for it, hated the sound of her nasal lisp, hated herself for not being stronger. "I swear I'm telling you the truth."

Dr. Panacea nodded, as if this made sense to him. "I recently received word that a store back east never received a crate of Elixir they'd ordered. It seems it went somewhere other than where it was supposed to. That is not your fault, of course. Apparently we have a security problem." He tossed away her tooth; it bounced on the carpet and rolled under the desk as he patted her thigh reassuringly. "I can't hold you accountable for that. It would be unfair."

Lou felt such overwhelming gratitude to the doctor for his fairness that she actually smiled. "Thank you," she said, and she meant it.

"You're very welcome," he said kindly.

Lou's feelings of relief faded away when he walked over to the desk where Shai hovered. "Still… there a few other small things I would like to know more about. You seem intelligent enough to put the clues together with my little sanatorium and the missing workers," he said, "which explains your presence here—but only to a point. This, however, I find less comprehensible." He trailed off, and Lou saw something she had not earlier perceived: her leather satchel was sitting open on his desk. Lou sat up a little straighter at the sight, but she fell back as her ruined hand throbbed and her vision clouded. "I cannot even begin to ascertain the purpose of some of these items. Like this…" He had pulled out her mechanical bee. "I wonder what on earth it could be for," he said, holding it in his palm. His left hand hovered above the winding key, delicately wrought in the shape of insect wings—and cranked it several times. A buzzing filled the room. Dr. Panacea shouted and dropped the construct on the carpet, clapping his hands to his ears.

"Lazarus?" Shai was beside his lover. He looked at Lou accusingly. "What did you do?"

"Leave me!" he slurred. "Don't touch me!"

The doctor hadn't wound the bee much. It quickly ground to a halt, and once the sound stopped, he straightened, his face full of rage.

"What is that thing?" he snarled.

Lou didn't know how to answer this, but before she came up with a viable explanation that was not her actual profession, Dr. Panacea gestured at his companion.

"Shai," he said.

Shai stepped forward, pliers in hand, and Lou lost her shit. For some reason the idea of Shai being the one hurting her was more frightening; she tried to make a run for the door, but after leaping to her feet with all the power left in her she felt herself falling over, her legs betraying her at the crucial moment, her eyes going blurry with flashing colored blackness. Her face struck the carpet, and she blacked out again.

When she awoke, Dr. Panacea was straddling her chest, his testicles smushed forward against her breastbone. He was very heavy. It was not lost on her that he now held the pliers.

"Ah," he said. "Hello again."

"Please," whispered Lou.

Dr. Panacea flicked open the pliers, only to close them on the bit of cartilage between Lou's nostrils. He applied only slight pressure but it was enough to make Lou's eyes seep. It occurred to her that she had never once been actually terrified before this very moment.

"I'm going to let you in on a little secret," he said, holding the pliers perfectly still. "You're not tough, Mr. Merriwether. What on earth were you thinking, trying to take my dearest Shai hostage? And attempting to bargain with me? Lest you harbor any illusions about yourself, that wasn't a brave act. You just had no idea what you were getting yourself into. You have no idea how powerful I am—no, not even now. If you want to know strength, toughness, look at Shai. Now there is strength. Look at him. Look over at him now."

Lou rolled her eyes to the right, saw Shai standing calmly at the desk once again, her bag at his side.

"Shai is strong. He does what needs doing. He survives—does quite a bit better than surviving, actually. Yes, I think I can say that without flattering myself. But you... you are impetuous and stupid. That is not strength." Dr. Panacea yawned. "I could have made you tell me everything I wanted to know without laying a finger on you. It was just more fun for me this way. The only problem with being perfect and immortal is that it gets dull sometimes..."

Dr. Panacea tightened the pliers on Lou's broken nose. She squealed. Tears were freely running down her face now, it took everything she had not to try to squirm away from him.

"You are going to tell me what on earth you do with those awful trinkets," said Dr. Panacea. "If I sense even the slightest dissembling, I will pull your nose out, and make you uglier than you already are—no small task. Do you understand me?" He waited until Lou grunted something like a yes. "Shai, do you think she understands me?"

"I do," said Shai.

"Hmm," said Dr. Panacea. "I'm not sure. Maybe I should pull out your nose right now. What do you think, Mr. Merriwether?"

Someone pounded on the door. "Dr. P!"

Dr. Panacea turned around to bark, "Not now!"

"Dr. P! It's Miss Foxglove!" Her voice was muffled by the wood. "It's urgent."

"Get the door," said Dr. Panacea. Shai moved to open it. It had been unlocked the entire time.

Lou, in spite of her situation, was impressed by how easily Miss Foxglove took in the scene before her. She looked at Shai, standing there, disheveled and in his bathrobe, then at Dr. Panacea, naked and squatting over a body. Only when she recognized Lou did Miss Foxglove's face betray any emotion, but it quickly disappeared.

"What is it?" asked Dr. Panacea impatiently. "I'm very busy."

"Yes, I can see that," said Miss Foxglove, "but Tom Hill's just arrived."

Dr. Panacea sat up straight, grinding his tailbone into Lou's guts. She whimpered.

"Does he have it?"

"Yes."

Dr. Panacea immediately released the pressure on the pliers and cast them aside, then got to his feet and commenced rubbing his hands together in excitement. "Did you see it?" he asked.

"I didn't inspect it, no. I left that to you."

"Did you let him leave?"

"No. He was belligerent and demanding upon arriving, so I gave him supper and a bottle, and locked him in the chapel."

"Good girl." He kissed Miss Foxglove on the cheek, then turned and gathered Shai into his arms. Lou watched all this from the floor, unsure if she should sit up or remind the doctor that she was in the room at all. "My dearest—we are so *close,* can't you taste it?" He spun Shai around in some sort of fancy dance move. "I must go to Tom, I must—" He looked down at Lou. "Ah," he said. "Yes. I'm afraid I must delay our discussion, Mr.

Merriwether. In the meantime..."

Dr. Panacea thought for a moment, and then his face lit up in the purest expression of joy Lou had ever seen.

"Shai, I'm going to consult with Tom, so I need you to do something for me. I think we should give Mr. Merriwether here what she's been wanting for quite some time."

"I don't quite follow," said Shai.

"Her kinsmen, of course!" cried Dr. Panacea, nearly capering with the need to be gone and attending to whatever it was the man called Tom Hill had brought. "Put her in with the Chinamen! That will keep her safely out of the way." Then Dr. Panacea grew serious. "This is your chance for you to show me how contrite you are," he said softly, looking deep into Shai's eyes. "I'll ask her later about how you treat her now. Just remember that."

Shai opened his mouth, looking as though he wanted to say something, but he shut it again, and nodded.

"Good, good," said Dr. Panacea, his mood restored. "Let's go, Miss Fox-glove, let us away. Join us soon, my love!"

Lou did not move as Dr. Panacea followed Miss Foxglove out the door. As it shut behind them she heard him musing on whether to get dressed, but did not hear his decision. Then she looked up at Shai, who stood over her.

"Get up," he said.

"Shai—"

"*Get up!*"

Lou got unsteadily to her feet. "Your boyfriend sucks," she lisped.

Shai snorted. "I'm sorry you feel that way, but I suppose it's understand-able."

"Come on, Shai," begged Lou, as he opened the door, indicating Lou should go ahead of him. "Can't we talk about this?"

She stepped into the dark, snow-smelling space they'd walked through to get to the office door, then allowed herself to be led deeper into wherever they were.

"Shai, come on," whispered Lou. "Let me go. Let us all go! Heck, you could come with us, we could all get away from this place—you, me, any Chinese you've got hanging around here, all of us! It could be fun, right? We had fun on the road, didn't we, Shai? We could again, if only you'll just..."

Lou trailed off. Shai was looking back at her quizzically, his face angular and harsh in the light of the kerosene lantern.

"Why would I want to run away? With you, or with anyone else?"

"Because..." Lou didn't know how to explain something so obvious, but Shai picked up on what she couldn't articulate.

"Lou, I'm not a slave. I could leave if I wished it—could have left many times over. I like it here."

"Why?"

"You're really very innocent, Lou. Perhaps it's because you have never loved, nor been loved by anyone, that you have trouble understanding the simple fact that I love Lazarus and he loves me." He shrugged. "What can I say? He's the right kind of sinner."

Lou had heard of having bad taste in men, but this seemed a little extreme. Regardless, she believed the Shai who had whispered his life story to her in the moonlight on a rock by a burbling stream had been just as real as this cruel, uncaring Shai. She believed he hadn't been lying when he'd said he cared for her.

"Shai, come on. Didn't you say I was, you know, the only human you've ever really liked? Then help me!"

"Of course I'm going to help you. Don't be silly." Shai had dropped his voice to match her whisper. He'd stopped walking.

She felt weak with relief. "I knew it," she said. "I knew I could trust you. I mean, all that stuff about rescuing you, and you belonging to him... you don't buy that, of course you don't. You see through it, right?"

"See through what?"

"You yourself said you can't make more Elixir of Life, but you're selling, sometimes giving it away. A plan your precious Lazarus came up with, to hear you tell it! So what happens when you run out? What happens to *you*, when... what are you doing?"

Shai, who was looking more pissed off than Lou had ever seen anyone look, had produced a key from somewhere, and unlocked a door made of metal bars. It looked like it might lead into a jail cell. He opened it with his free hand.

"You made a mistake, Lou, believing in me. I'm a monster, just like him."

"No, Shai, you're not. You're just a person, like me or anyone else. I don't care what anyone's told you. You're just like me and I'm just like you."

"No, you're not." He sighed. "You couldn't possibly understand."

"Try me."

"Maybe some other time. At present, I'm not at liberty to discuss the matter further. The time has come for me to help you." He smiled, that brilliant, beautiful smile. "I'm going to help you solve the mystery you've traveled so far to unearth."

Then he pushed Lou away from him and into the cell. She stumbled. Unknown arms grabbed her and kept her from falling.

"Make her feel welcome, boys," called Shai.

Then he blew out the lantern. Metal clanged against metal as he slammed the door, and his footsteps retreated into the blackness.

Chapter Twelve

Whoever had Lou in his arms tightened his grip around her waist.
"Don't worry, I've got you."

It took Lou a moment to realize the voice had spoken in Toisanese.

"Careful—please—my hand," she replied in kind, grateful for the assistance. Her legs were shaking and she was feeling pretty goddamn lightheaded. "He broke some of my fingers. It hurts."

"Which hand?"

"Left," she said. After he had adjusted his hold on her, she asked, "Who are you?"

"My name is Leung Kwan," he answered. "Come over here, it's warmer by the stove."

Lou looked in the direction he was guiding her, and saw a reddish glow several yards away. She took a second halting step forward, then froze. She had not registered that there were other voices, and close-by, until that moment.

"Was that Shai?" someone was asking, also in Chinese.

"Who are we supposed to welcome? I couldn't see with the glare!"

"Is it a girl?" asked another.

"Hard to say," said a third.

Lou kept hearing Dr. Panacea whispering *you're not strong, you're not tough* in the back of her mind. Nearly every day of her life she'd heard insults about being Chinese, or being ugly, or being whatever else, but those words had gotten to her worse than anything. He was right—after all, here she was, locked up with the very people she was supposed to be rescuing.

But now was not the time for misery, despair, or fear. Now was the time to introduce herself to the people she'd been trying to find.

"My name is Lou Merriwether," said Lou, addressing the largely unseen crowd. "My mother is Ailien Merriwether, she's an apothecary in San Francisco. Her shop is just off Stockton Street. My father was Archibald Merriwether, a psychopomp and professor at Loxias College." Lou took a breath. "I came here to find out what happened to all of you. Your families are missing you."

Her eyes had adjusted to the low light. She'd guessed correctly when she'd thought she'd smelled snow and pine trees and winter air. She was in a cell in the back of a large cave, perhaps even larger than the Great Hall. Outside, she could see the miles of unbroken moonlit forest and snowcapped peaks she had seen earlier in the day. Or, perhaps, yesterday. She had no idea what o'clock it was.

As her vision continued to improve, she saw that along the edges of the cave were dark, lumpy, indistinct shapes; closer to her was a small potbellied stove, and clustered behind it, maybe two dozen men. She swooned briefly in Wen's arms, acutely aware of the cold, and the agony that was her face and left hand.

"Steady," he said. "Let's get her closer to the stove, she's hurt."

Lou was grateful to be ushered closer to the heat-source, but she felt more warmed by their reception. As one they rose, a wave of sound and motion, all welcoming her among them, most of them keeping a respectful distance.

The closer she got, the better she could just what the hell was happening in this cell. The men had been manacled together by the ankles, and she could just make out the points where the links had been bolted to the cave wall. Most had the gaunt, rangy look of a team of men accustomed to working hard on not a lot to eat. Several had injuries that she knew could have easily been healed up with the Elixir of Life.

"Did you say she was hurt?"

"What about our families?"

"They broke her hand," said Kwan. "I don't know what else."

"Move over, let her sit down!"

"They broke her *hand?*"

Lou's tongue found the socket where her tooth should be, felt the throbbing in her nose.

"Her face is bloody, too!"

"Are you surprised?"

A man stepped forward. He was lean and muscular, like Kwan.

"It's likely my fault you're here," he said. "I'm sorry."

"No… I got myself into this mess. Trust me."

His face fell. Intrigued, Lou asked why he felt it was his fault.

"I managed to send out a… message," he said. "I thought perhaps you'd received it."

"A message?" Maybe he meant the body in the crate. "Is your mother called Heung-kam?" She could not remember the face of the body she'd seen in the basement at Madame Cheung's well enough to see if this man held any resemblance.

"Yes! My name's Gan-bou, my brother Tai died in an accident. I decided…" He caught himself, and looked around. "I, ah…"

Of course Gan-bou was reluctant to speak. These men had likely long since abandoned whispering anything private to one another in the darkness.

"I think he's off doing something right now—the vampire, I mean," she said. "You can wait until it's sunup to tell me if you want, though. I don't think any of us are going anywhere anytime soon."

"Vampire? He is a demon!"

She'd used the Toisanese. "A different sort of vampire than…" She paused. "You were worried about your brother succumbing to geung si possession."

"I know enough to know there was cause to worry. The letter was from my cousin, they let me keep it when I came here. I never thought I'd be more grateful for the stamps than for the letter, though. Or for spraining my ankle. They reassigned me to pack up bottles of the doctor's medicine for shipping. I was able to put Tai's body in a box and re-address the label without anyone noticing. I made room for him by throwing a flat of bottles over the edge of the cliff so they'd never notice." He smiled. "My mother always said learning to read and write English would come in handy one day. She was right."

Yes, it would have been a real coup d'état... if only it had reached some-one other than her. Instead of saying what she thought, however, Lou said, "Your plan worked. He's at rest now."

Gan-bou frowned. *"Now?"*

"Yes," she said wearily. "You were right to be worried, but in the end I helped him. I'm a psychopomp. I took over my father's business."

The silence following this was profound and respectful. Lou, angry at herself for her words and angry at them for their awe, wanted to disillusion them as quickly as possible.

"I meant to help you, too—all of you. But I failed."

"Not yet you haven't," said Kwan. "Surely when your friends notice you're gone..."

"Friends?" Lou was not at all sure anyone she knew would stage a rescue. Hell, they wouldn't even know where to look.

"You..." Kwan took a moment to compose himself. "Did you come here alone?"

"Of course she didn't," said Gan-bou, with a dismissive wave of his hand.

"No, he's right," said Lou. "I did."

"What?" Gan-bou was dismayed. *"Why?* What was your plan?"

"Well I didn't exactly know what I was in for, did I?" snapped Lou, then she willed her face to relax. It hurt to snarl.

"My brother was turning, wasn't he? That wasn't a clue that something odd was happening?"

"No," said Lou flatly, trying to keep her face impassive. "I see it all the time in Chinatown. Geung si possession can be caused by anything traumatic. Murder, yes, supernatural goings-on, okay—but once I found a case in a man who'd died at his job, but how he'd hated his job! The rage turned his corpse sour. Spiritually." Lou scooted closer to the stove, held up her hands. The warmth helped the ache. "So please forgive me for not assuming when I encountered your brother without a note or context or anything that he had come from a corrupt health spa run by an immortal blood-drinking fiend."

Though not the most perceptive person, Lou could sense that no one was particularly happy to hear that their hoped-for rescuer was a busted-up nineteen-year-old girl. She tried not to listen to the disappointed murmurs at her back. Instead, she contemplated what she was going to do next.

Nothing came to mind.

"Wait," said someone. "Maybe she *can* help."

Lou turned, saw that one of the mob of workers wore a crafty expression.

"The foreman," he whispered. "She's not chained up, right? So in the morning, when he comes out of his room, she can wait by the door, and when he opens it, she can hit him! Then…"

"Then?" Lou and everyone else waited, intrigued.

"And then he'll be… we can hold him hostage. Right?"

Someone groaned. "That's a terrible plan, Hak-fu!"

"It really is," agreed Gan-bou. "When the doctor comes down and finds us holding him hostage, he'll, what? Bargain with us for the man's safe return? He doesn't care about the foreman, or any of us. You know this."

"Remember So," said another man, from behind Lou.

After a few moments of awkward silence, Lou asked, "What happened to…?"

"He was the last to try anything," said Kwan slowly. "The doctor, when he found out…"

"Don't," said someone. *"Please."*

Gan-bou shrugged. "Now he is dead."

"Yeah," added another man. "And don't forget, Dr. Panacea told us, once the dragon is finished, that he'd let us go…"

"You believe that?"

"The dragon?" asked Lou. "I'm sorry?"

"Go to the door and look up," said Gan-bou.

Lou did so, but in the darkness, through the bars of the cell, Lou could make out only an enormous, serpentine shape hanging from the ceiling, far above the center of the cave.

"What is it?" she whispered.

"It's a train," said Kwan. "A flying train. A flying train needs no track. The bears cannot object, and the doctor will become a very rich man."

"How does it fly?"

"It doesn't," said Gan-bou. "Not yet. They have been waiting for something to make it fly, a special bone from a real tianlung, from China. He says it is the final piece." Gan-bou shrugged. "I cannot say if it will work. He says it will, because we have made the train a perfect reproduction."

"A bone…"

Lou thought back to a certain rainy afternoon in San Francisco; remembered the way Vilhelm's *Chronicle* crinkled as he flipped the pages, recalled the smell of steaming tea and fresh jam tarts. It was all coming together. Well, sort of.

Dr. Panacea must have sent the aforementioned Tom Hill, whose name Lou now recalled Griff Evans mentioning, to steal this bone from the Academy of Sciences—and, probably, replace it with a fake to avert suspicion. After all, the paper had said nothing had been stolen…

Even with a few good theories to work with, Lou was still plenty confused, not the least by how some bone would make a train fly. She wanted to ask more questions, but the sound of a door banging open silenced her, as did a sudden brightness that blazed somewhere above them, to their right.

It was Dr. Panacea. He was walking down the stairs that they must have all earlier come down, holding a torch over his head to light his way. The light pooled around him but illuminated little else. He was wearing his usual costume: black frock coat and trousers, white shirt, bolo tie. His hair was unbound and swept back from his temples. He was smiling. His teeth glinted in the light.

Just behind him was Shai, looking especially winsome in fawn-colored trousers, a pale blue shirt with a cream waistcoat, and khaki serge jacket. His sword was buckled around his waist and he carried a lantern. Unlike the doctor, he was trying to light the way for two other men, who each carried one end of a large canvas-swathed package. The bone Gan-bou had mentioned, probably. One of the men, the one gingerly stepping backwards down the steps, Lou thought she'd seen around the San. The other was a stranger. Tom Hill, maybe.

"Carefully, carefully," cautioned the doctor cheerfully as he ran ahead of them, fleet-footed as a nymph. After reaching the floor of the cave, he ran up to a door in the far left wall and pounded on it repeatedly with his fist. He struck it with such force Lou wondered if he would break it. She suspected the wood would crack before his hand.

After the assault on the door the doctor took a turn about the perimeter of the cavern. There were many torches set into iron brackets, and the cave gradually grew brighter as Dr. Panacea lit them off his own. The indistinct shapes at the edges of the cavern turned out to be piles of equipment and machinery, drills and sledgehammers and other items Lou could not identify. She saw, too, that she had been right about her estimate regarding how many men were captive in the cage or cell where they were, and that the cave was even larger than she'd suspected. She could also better see what hung above her.

It really was a dragon. Or, at least, a beautifully wrought, lifelike reproduction of one. Its metal scales glinted ebony and red in the torchlight, and though firmly secured by chains threaded through eyebolts driven into the ceiling, it seemed already in flight. Its legs were drawn in tightly to its body, but its claws were extended. The horselike head, capped with curling horns, was angled back in a joyful attitude, mouth open, tongue lolling; the eel-like tail curved away in an S-shape, feathery scales capping the tip. Lou didn't believe it would ever fly, even with some sort of special bone, but as a sculpture it was one of the most magnificent works of art she had ever seen.

"Zebulon!" Dr. Panacea was shouting and pounding on that door again, startling Lou out of her amazement. "Out of bed, slug!"

The door finally creaked open, and a youngish, sandy-haired man in a dirty union suit stumbled out. He was shoeless, and his erection strained against the front of his nightclothes.

"What time is it?" he yawned.

"Time to make the dragon fly," said Dr. Panacea.

At this, Zebulon perked up. He rubbed at his cock unconsciously with the heel of his palm and said, "It's here?"

"Yes, and we've hours yet till dawn!" Dr. Panacea pointed at where Shai and the other two men were just navigating the last few steps. "There, there it is! Look! If you get this scum up and working quick enough, maybe we can make the test run before sunup!"

"Even if we don't, I can—"

"No! I want to be here to see if something goes wrong."

Zebulon's enthusiasm seemed to wane. "Goes wrong? What do—you said it would be safe…"

Dr. Panacea backhanded the young man across the mouth. Zebulon dropped like a stone to the cavern floor, landing hard on his ass. He stared balefully up at the doctor, wiping away the thin trickle of blood that oozed from his lip as Dr. Panacea scolded him, waggling his finger at the young man like a teacher lecturing a naughty student.

"*You* came to *me,* coughing your lungs out, about to die. Didn't you?"

"I did, but—"

Dr. Panacea *tsk*ed. "So ungrateful. Perhaps I should start charging you for the very valuable medicine you take daily? It's not worth keeping you alive if you won't work."

"But…"

"But what? Will you do the job for which I hired you, or not?"

"I will," mumbled Zebulon. "I just, I… I'm sorry."

"Don't tell me how sorry you are," said Dr. Panacea, "show me! Get them to set up a block and tackle, we'll lift it that way. Have a crew get up on the back of the infernal thing to open the case and get it secured. *Now!*" Then he turned, and hurried over to where Shai awaited him.

That Zebulon immediately leaped to his feet did not come as a surprise to Lou. Dr. Panacea had that effect on people. But when he began jabbering in a mixture of English and Toisanese at the workers, his proficiency with the language took her aback.

At Zebulon's instruction everyone stood up, shuffling away from one another until they stood in two lines with about two feet of chain separating each from each. While the workers readied themselves, Zebulon retreated to his room, emerging moments later with his trousers on and shrugging into his suspenders.

Lou had edged to the back of the group by the time Zebulon withdrew a key from his pocket, unlocked the cell and began methodically unlocking the chains that bound the men to the wall. Lou noted that even after being released to walk about the cave freely, the workers were all still hobbled by chain fetters. For all his arrogance, the doctor was a cautious slave-master.

"What's this?" asked Zebulon, when he noticed Lou. She had been standing a bit behind the line of workers, hoping to remain unnoticed for as long as possible. "Who are you? How'd you get down here?"

"I," Lou swallowed, "uh, the doctor…"

"Oh yes, Mr. Merriwether." Dr. Panacea was beside the confused Zebulon all of a sudden. "What to do with you…" He mused on this until he noticed no one was assisting the two men that still flanked the package. "What's this? I told you to get them working! I want that thing secured and ready!" Dr. Panacea turned to Lou. "Stay out of the way or I'll kill you. I'd rather be curious for eternity regarding you and your inscrutable schemes than let you interfere with this operation, so don't think I'm just playing games. Do you understand me?"

Lou nodded. She didn't say so, but she was already well aware that the doctor didn't "play games" where his interests were concerned. As she stepped away from the throng, Gan-bou caught her eye and gave her an encouraging smile, but she saw the defeat and disappointment in his eyes. She'd failed them all.

A half-dozen workers, all laden with various tools and blankets, climbed up the rope ladder that spilled over the back of the dragon and down to the ground. Once at the top, they began doing something with the head of the metal beast, but down on the ground Lou couldn't see exactly what. All she knew was that the men on the ground were rigging a pulley system using one of the eyebolts in the ceiling as the hook.

She was more curious about the bone. Even wrapped up thickly in canvas she could tell it must be crescent-shaped, perhaps six feet from end to end and eighteen inches thick at the center. Dr. Panacea kept trotting over to gaze down at it, rubbing his hands together in excitement. The rest of the time he walked among the busy laborers, snapping at Zebulon.

Even with all the activity the two men who had brought down the package looked bored. The one Lou recognized—she recalled he had been a waiter up at the lodge—sat down on his heels and rolled a cigarette. When she caught her first whiff of smoke she couldn't help inching closer to him. The smell of shag was irresistible. She didn't get too close, however; Shai waited nearby, and Lou had no desire to sidle up alongside of him.

The other man remained standing. He was annoyed, that was obvious enough, though by what Lou could not fathom. He sighed, turned to Shai, and said something. Lou was still too far away to hear what it was, but Shai shrugged, gestured at the doctor, and replied.

Dr. Panacea noticed the movement, and strode over to the three men. After a few brief words, the squatting, smoking man stood and headed toward the stairs. This just aggravated the standing man more.

"I want to get paid," he said, loud enough for everyone to hear. The room went very still.

Dr. Panacea smiled thinly. "And here I thought you'd want to see what your efforts have enabled, Tom."

It was clear from the doctor's tone that if Tom hadn't cared before, he should begin, and quickly. He nodded numbly, looking slightly shaken. Dr. Panacea patted him on the shoulder.

"Good man," he said, and glided off again towards Zebulon.

When Gan-bou and the rest had readied the block and tackle it was time to do whatever was so important it necessitated waking up everyone in the middle of the night. Torn between fear and curiosity, Lou kept back from the group, wondering if at any point Dr. Panacea and Shai would both be so distracted she could make a break for it. Perhaps she could sneak off and… and *what,* she wondered glumly. Abandon everyone? Come back with a bunch of invalids as backup?

"Have them bring it here!" called the doctor.

Shai looked up and caught Lou's eye. He waved her over. So much for their forgetting about her. Lou really didn't want to go anywhere near any of them, but she wanted less to find out what Shai—or the doctor—would do to her if she didn't hurry.

"You look awful." Shai, much calmer than he'd been when they'd parted, spoke in the manner of one remarking upon the weather. "I can't imagine you're feeling very good, either."

He was right. Lou felt like pure hell—but neither because of her wounds nor the biting cold of the cave. Until that moment, she had not been close enough to Shai to observe what he wore strapped across his chest and under his arm; drawing nearer, she recognized her beloved shoulder holster—and her LeMat revolver.

It gleamed at her. Lou's hand itched to hold it, to feel the smoothness of the wood, the heaviness of the gunmetal, the beautiful balance of the weapon. She wanted it back in her possession more than she'd ever wanted anything, but she didn't want to give Shai the satisfaction of letting him see her upset. Surely he had put it on to provoke her, so she decided to play it cool.

First thing was not staring at the gun; now was not the time to try to get it back. Shai had a sword and a firearm, and the man to Shai's right was armed, too. Zebulon was too far away for her to feel confident she could shoot all three before Dr. Panacea was on her, which would be quickly.

The only reason she even entertained the notion of trying anything so foolhardy as wresting her gun from Shai was that the mechanical bee had affected the doctor so potently. Likely Shai had not had cause to fire the weapon, which meant she had ten chances to do some good, even if it resulted in her death. If she could plug the Doc with the .60 vermilion-infused ball, she could manage to eliminate the rest with the remaining rounds while they were scrambling to find out why their ears hurt and the room was filled with smoke.

Eliminate. She realized with a start that she was seriously contemplating killing a bunch of people. Even though she knew she had to, it didn't sit well with her.

"Cat got your tongue?" Shai said softly.

"Nah. Just never been one to speak unless spoken to."

"Oh yes; you've always been the very picture of decorum." He glanced skyward at the dragon-train. "So, what do you think now about black-guarding my lover?"

Lou was truly lost. "What?"

"The train. That's always been the big picture, here. Once we get it running, once we get it patented we'll buy a manufactory, and get a production line going. The orders will likely exceed our capacity to produce them. Railroads will be in business again, and then once the military hears about this, we won't need to sell Elixir anymore. We'll be wealthy enough."

"Oh, well, at least you're not leaving anything up to chance," said Lou. "Has either of you ever considered just, you know, getting a *job?*"

Shai scowled at her. "Shut up and get the lantern, and don't do anything stupid."

Lou nodded, but was already busy considering doing any number of stupid things. Feeling the weight of the lantern in her hand, she wondered if she could smash it across the back of Shai's skull and make a grab for her gun. The idea disgusted her; the glass would shatter and splash ignited kerosene all over his body, and he would likely die from the impact or the burns. Even after everything Shai had done to her, she didn't know if she could force herself to commit such a brutal act. She'd only ever killed one person, and while it might be poetic, in a dime novel sort of way, for her second murder to be the man who'd been the reason she'd committed the first, she had no great love of poetry.

Dr. Panacea was hollering at them to hurry over to where he stood, so Lou obeyed without coming to a decision. Shai and Tom were out of swinging range, anyways, so after them she went, but she made damn sure to hang back a bit from the action.

"Set it down. Gently—gently!" cried the doctor. "Now get out of my way, let me…" He crouched down and began to unwrap the package. Shai dropped to his knees beside him, and at last Lou could see this bone that was such a big fucking deal.

It was a large, crescent-shaped piece of ivory. That was it. Lou wasn't sure what she'd been expecting, but not this. She was baffled. What the hell was going on? How would this make the train fly?

"It's beautiful," sighed the doctor happily. "Now—"

"I'm real glad you like it," interrupted Tom. "Any chance you could pay me now? Safe delivery and all that? Had to lay low for too long in San Francisco, paying out of pocket for lodgings and food, watching out for the law."

"You did no such thing," said Dr. Panacea affably as he delicately ran his fingers over the top edge of the bone. "You were drunk and idle, and think you can defraud me by claiming more difficulties than you experienced."

Tom fidgeted. "I, uh, thought they'd be watching the trains."

"Watching the trains? You were supposed to switch out this real chimu for the fake I gave you so that no one at the Academy would be, as you said, *watching the trains.*" Dr. Panacea still seemed amused rather than annoyed. "You should have been here weeks ago."

"I was careful, sue me for it why don'tcha." Tom shrugged. "Come on, if it's all the same to you, I'd rather be on my way."

Dr. Panacea ignored him. "Look, my dearest darling," he said to Shai, "it must have bumped its head and survived, there's a healed-over mark on the bone just here."

"I want to get paid." Tom's hand was on the pistol at his waist.

Dr. Panacea noticed, too, and he stood. Lou sensed some bad things were about to happen to Tom, if she was any judge.

"Tom," said Dr. Panacea calmly. "I am busy. When I'm finished, I—"

Tom picked something off the corner of his left nostril. "I don't like you," he said, examining the yellowish lump on his fingernail. "And I don't like this. Why won't you pay me and let me go? It'll take you five minutes, maybe less."

"All right, you win," said the doctor, after a tense pause. "Come along with me."

Dr. Panacea slung his arm around Tom's shoulders conspiratorially. Tom looked uncomfortable with this. He stopped smiling and tried to wrest himself away, but before he could, the doctor reached his hand around and tore out the man's throat with his fingers. Lou almost dropped her lantern but managed to keep her grip, even when Dr. Panacea took the handful of flesh and blood and larynx, and, jamming it into his mouth, chewed thoughtfully.

What had been Tom fell to the ground, face smashing into the floor. A puddle spread out from the ruined body, but Dr. Panacea kicked the corpse over onto its back and crouched down beside it. After taking a few long, guzzling draughts where little spurts of blood yet pumped through severed arteries, he sat back on his heels and sighed happily, brilliant red stains spreading across his shirt. Then he cocked his head, noticing Tom's holster rig, a beautiful customized black leather affair with silver buckles and stamped patterns scrolling down the holster and around the belt. After taking another long drink from Tom, he unbuckled the belt and then secured it around his own waist craning his neck to admire himself. The effect was indeed impressive with his black suit, stained shirt notwithstanding. With a satisfied look on his face, he stood and wiped his mouth on his sleeve. The cuff of his shirt was already saturated, and it left a smear.

"Someone hang him up to drain," he said to Zebulon.

Zebulon commanded one of the workers to do what the doctor ordered. The task fell to Kwan. Reluctantly, he picked up Tom's left leg and began to drag him to where two metal rings had been driven into the cavern wall. A stained bucket and a step stool sat close-by, off to the side.

Kwan grunted as he stepped up, lifting the whole body by its left leg to jam one foot and then the other through the rings. Lou was impressed by his strength even as she pitied him having to do such a grisly task.

After the body had been secured, Kwan trotted back to the group, leaving the corpse to drizzle steaming blood into the wooden bucket. The steady *plat-plat* made Lou feel sick. She tried to ignore it.

"You know, if everything works with this train, I may just eat one of those idiots upstairs to celebrate," said Dr. Panacea thoughtfully, as he glanced from Kwan to the men securing the curved wedge of bone for its eventual hoisting. "They'll certainly be iron-rich with all this meat in their diet recently. I've been spoiling them."

"Someone will notice," said Shai. "It's too soon after Mr. Gillis."

"My little killjoy," said Dr. Panacea affectionately, with a gentle pinch of Shai's cheek. "Always here to keep me in line. Well, perhaps—though you've claimed the same at every stage of this operation, and the only person who came looking was *that,*" he said, nodding in Lou's direction. "Hardly a serious threat. When will you learn to relax? We've sent out letters for every patient who's died here, and no one's even come to collect their remains."

"Hey, Doc," said Zebulon. "I think we're just about..."

"All right, all right," said Dr. Panacea. "Don't hang around making announcements, lift it up there already! The night's not getting any darker."

"Let's go, boys! Go on, but take it slow," cried Zebulon, in Toisanese.

The ivory crescent began to rise. Dr. Panacea watched intently. His back was to Lou, as was Shai's. They stood together in front of her, and as it rose higher and higher, Dr. Panacea stretched out his hand to take Shai's in his. He squeezed it, and smiled tenderly at his lover. Shai raised Dr. Panacea's hand to his lips and kissed the knuckles.

Lou refused to let this sweetness affect her. She had to deal with Shai; she needed to get her gun back. Then, she might be able to save her kinsmen—and herself. This was the perfect opportunity to enact her earlier plan of bashing in Shai's head with the lantern, but her reluctance to kill held her back. She asked herself if Shai left her any alternative and knew he hadn't. He could have helped her escape—he could have prevented Dr. Panacea's interrogation. He could have done a lot of things. That had been his choice, and, thus this was hers.

She inhaled, tightened her grip on the handle, cocked her wrist.

Dr. Panacea turned around to look at her.

"What on earth is making your heart race so?" he asked, eyeing her up and down. Lou felt ashamed at her relief at being caught. "Are you so moved by this sight? You *are* Chinese, I suppose... a sentimental race..."

"We are," said Lou, not bothering to keep her skepticism out of her voice. "I'm curious, though, what makes that bone so special? Gan-bou said—"

"Who?"

"One of the workers. We were chatting, and he said you had a notion this bone would somehow make that giant thing into a trackless train?"

Dr. Panacea's lips twitched into a smile very similar to Shai's distinctive smirk. "You are a spirited thing. I wonder if I'm losing my edge. How are you not afraid of me?"

"Well, you know. Curiosity always gets the better of me. How else would I end up here?"

"It's in!" called Gan-bou, from atop the dragon's head. He waved his hands to try to get everyone's attention. "Bolted in place and everything! Fits perfectly, everything's ready!"

"We're ready," translated Zebulon. Dr. Panacea looked from his foreman to Gan-bou, and nodded.

"Get yourself up and in, Zeb," he said, and turned to Lou as Zebulon began to climb the rope ladder. "You, too."

"I can't." Lou shrugged. "My hand."

"What? Oh, I'll carry you up with me. No, keep that lantern, Mr. Merriwether. Shall we?"

"Wait, what?" asked Lou. She took a step backwards. "What do you mean? I…"

"Your coolie friend was right," said Dr. Panacea. "This is indeed a flying train. But I'm not sure it's safe, so we need to send someone on the test flight. Zebulon will be driving it, but *you*, Mr. Merriwether—you'll have the honor of being the very first passenger."

Chapter Thirteen

Lou felt keenly the indignity of once again being slung over Dr. Panacea's shoulder, but she felt the vertigo more.

As the ground beneath her receded, Lou closed her eyes. There was nothing she wanted to see. The swinging motion of Dr. Panacea's climbing was nauseating, and it didn't help that he was carrying her over his left shoulder with his left arm encircling her waist. That was the one still tacky with Tom's blood. She felt the wetness of it against her skin, it seeped from his sleeve through her shirt, and as Dr. Panacea's body was cool to the touch, she was shivering before they were halfway up the ladder.

"You're heavier than you look," commented Dr. Panacea, as he set her on the dragon's back and leapt up lightly alongside her.

Lou was too busy trying not to vomit to respond. As the doctor helped Shai up, she scooted herself away from the edge and as far from both men as she could, retreating down the dragon-train's body. The metal scales were even colder than the doctor's skin.

Out of the corner of her eye, Lou saw Dr. Panacea adjusting his new holster. He seemed quite pleased by its lavish appearance.

"Lovely, isn't it? So well crafted!"

"Very stylish," said Shai, but his tone said *is this really the time to talk about this?* "It hangs well on your hips."

"Much less, shall we say, *rustic* than your piece, eh, m'dear? Though less 'stopping power,' as they say." He chuckled. "Good thing for you to have, while you stay up here and keep this lot in line."

"I'd like to come down with you…"

"I won't have them left unsupervised."

"What is it you think they're going to do?"

Dr. Panacea frowned. "Your trusting nature is the most ridiculous thing about you, and that's saying something," he said. Shai seemed to shrink a little at his words. "It bespeaks to your inability to consider the world with appropriate perspective. You think we have cowed these people into submission. I know we have crushed them until all they can feel is hatred and fear. Given the chance they would destroy us, this train, everything we've worked for. I will not give them any such opportunity, not here at my moment of triumph."

"But—"

"I will not waste further time discussing this. Stay out here and watch them. With your gun out."

My gun, thought Lou.

Shai hesitated, then shrugged his acquiescence. "Whatever you desire."

"That's my pet," said Dr. Panacea. He picked up the lantern and snapped his fingers in Lou's direction, beckoning to her like a dog. "You—come with me."

Lou kept her gaze on her boots as she slowly got to her feet and followed the doctor with careful, halting steps. The back of the dragon wasn't particularly narrow, she guessed six or seven men could safely stand abreast across it, but she was not thrilled by the sight of cave walls sloping down from where she stood coupled with the vibrations from everyone stomping around. Also, the black and silver scales of the dragon overlapped, creating a landscape of little ridges, and she really didn't want to trip.

Gan-bou and the rest were up near the head of the dragon, talking animatedly where they crouched. Lou couldn't meet their eyes as she made her way to the trapdoor where Dr. Panacea awaited her. She had failed them, and now, perhaps, she would die. She still didn't believe this thing could fly; real dragon bone or not, the train must weigh tons.

"Follow me, pumpkin," said Dr. Panacea, as she reached his side. Then he jumped down through the open hatch into the dragon's belly.

"I'd suggest using the ladder," added Shai, from just behind Lou's left ear.

Lou startled; she hadn't realized he was right behind her.

Now that Dr. Panacea was inside, she saw a series of bronze rungs glinting in the light of the lantern he'd taken down with him. Climbing down one-handed would be tricky, but Lou didn't trust herself to jump the distance and not break an ankle. She sat down on the edge and swung herself around, clinging to the ladder with her right hand. To balance herself, she hooked her left wrist around the vertical part of the ladder, wondering if she could make it down like that.

"It's not too many steps," said Shai. "You'll be all right."

Lou glanced up at him, incredulous. "Thanks for the moral support."

"Any time." Shai leaned in close. "Oh, and Lou? In case you hadn't realized it yet... you *really* fucked up."

As she began to climb down the ladder, Lou felt tired. Not necessarily physically, though she was exhausted from lack of sleep and physical pain; she was more tired of Shai's betrayals, of Dr. Panacea's hammy villainy, of being dragged from pillar to post. But mostly she was tired of messing up, of being completely unable to help herself—or anyone else.

Her stomach yawed when her foot went down a bit too far, seeking another rung and not finding one. Looking down, she saw there was a gap, and so she jumped free and landed unsteadily. A carpet cushioned her from the impact.

As distinctly Chinese as the exterior of the train had been, by the glow of Dr. Panacea's lantern she could see the dragon was pure American opulence inside. Her first impression of the interior was a blur of crimson and gold, but as she looked closer she saw just how exquisitely detailed the traveling compartment was. There were a dozen or so rows of winged love seats, all upholstered in scarlet velvet, and installed at angles that would allow travelers to face one another, and each pair of seats had its own small mahogany table set between them, outfitted with a caddy that secured four cups and a soda syphon. At the back of the compartment she saw there was a brass pump sink, as well as a door with PRIVATE written on a black plaque in scrolling gold letters. Scarlet curtains with gold fringe framed the small, smoked-glass windows.

It was fancier than a first-class train carriage, fancier than most whorehouse parlors, which seemed to Lou to have been the inspiration for the aesthetic. She said as much, and Dr. Panacea shrugged.

"Perhaps it is a bit ostentatious," he admitted, "but that is what Americans want, I've found. New money, the lot of you, and it shows."

"I still don't get it," said Lou. "This is nifty, but—"

"Tonight the Transcontinental will become obsolete, and you call that *nifty?* Mr. Merriwether, tonight the iron horse will be put out to pasture, for you stand within the belly of the first iron dragon. It will revolutionize travel as we know it!"

"Isn't that what nifty means?"

"It is more than nifty!" Dr. Panacea took a deep breath and said, in a calmer tone, "It is the culmination of years of planning, hard work, and more money than you could possibly imagine! This model is just to show off to potential investors, of course, take them for little rides in style, that sort of thing. When I get enough funding—when I patent this—just think of the applications! Travel, yes, and delivering the post more reliably… I assume after word gets out the U.S. government will be commissioning an entire fleet, as this machine will be far superior to their current aeronautical technology. Even this small of a train will carry more people than their largest hot air balloon, and it will be able to do far more than reconnaissance if I'm correct in my estimations. I'm hoping my invention might even be of interest to the remainder of the Confederacy, if they can pay me enough I might consider helping them, too… I assume they'll be especially interested as this machine requires neither coal nor lumber to run, and that was such a problem with their trains during the war…"

"It needs bones, though. Where are you going to get all the bones?"

"At this point there are many unknowns," said Dr. Panacea casually, "as regards both manufacturing and the nature of the machine itself. I don't even know how fast it can go! We installed a brake, of course…" Dr. Panacea, distracted, looked behind him into the cab, located in what, from the outside, would be the dragon's head.

Lou turned too, and saw through the open cab-door a chamber vastly less elegant than the carriage. It was cluttered with a dizzying selection of levers and metal boxes of varying heights, which in turn housed dials, gauges, and buttons. Zebulon was in there, looking harried and nervous, fiddling with things and occasionally mopping his brow. Some of the light from his lantern spilled out of the large glass windshield at the very front of the cab, and Lou could see the dragon's jaws with their pointy metal teeth above and below the edges of the pane. She couldn't quite ascertain what Zebulon was trying to accomplish with his meddling, as it just seemed to her like he was just touching parts of the array in a daze, but she allowed perhaps he had some purpose she couldn't appreciate.

"Zebulon!" Dr. Panacea walked inside the cab. Lou followed him, not particularly interested in standing by herself in the dark car. "Can we begin?"

"Soon," he said distractedly, doing something with a large lever. "A few of the controls were sticking, but I'll have gotten everything working, I think, after I finish up oiling this, so—"

"Yes, yes," interrupted the doctor, withdrawing a large silver pocket watch from his waistcoat to check the time. Lou's heart did a somersault; for a moment she wondered if he'd "acquired" her skiameter in the same way Shai had "acquired" her gun rig. When she saw the timepiece was far nicer than hers, as well as being actually a watch, she relaxed. "Let's put some speed into it, shall we? It's past four in the morning, and I want this test run completed before dawn."

"I'm going as fast as I…" Zebulon paused. "Yes, sir. I think we're just about ready to test the connection."

Lou, half-bored despite the hustle and bustle, navigated her way through the cab up to the windshield. She cupped her hands around her eyes so she could take in the view, and saw the cave mouth, and the forest beyond. The sky had not yet begun to lighten.

"Her again?" Zebulon sounded pissed. "Why is *she* allowed in here?"

"Oh, that's right," said Dr. Panacea. "I never introduced you two properly. Zebulon, meet Mr. Lou Merriwether. She came here to Fountain of Youth looking for our workforce, as it turns out. It seems, tragically, all their letters home have gone astray." Dr. Panacea allowed himself another evil chuckle. "She's quite the little spitfire, so I'm keeping her close to my chest. Earlier in the night she tried to take on Shai and myself with only a revolver—"

"It was a LeMat," said Lou, over her shoulder. When she looked back out over the landscape, she was absurdly pleased to see her hands and the tip of her nose had left smudge marks on the glass.

"Indeed," said Dr. Panacea, cocking his left eyebrow. "Well, even so, it didn't work out too well, now did it?" When Lou did not reply, he continued. "Her presence is valuable to me. I've decided she'll ride in the coach during the inaugural voyage, so she can report back on a passenger's experience. And if something goes wrong, I won't have lost any valuable members of my workforce."

Zebulon looked hurt by this, but said only, "Whatever you think's best."

"What I think is best is for you to focus on getting everything running!"

Zebulon cringed. "It's already ready already. The chimu's installed but the train'll start to move immediately once the lever's engaged. Should I go tell them to get down?"

"Them?"

"The workers?"

Dr. Panacea furrowed his brow in confusion. "Get down where?"

"Down… somewhere, right?" said Zebulon, just as puzzled. "Either inside, or down on the ground?"

"No. I want them on-hand for any emergencies."

"So they should come inside?"

"There's plenty of chains. Tell them to hang on tight."

Zebulon looked skeptical, but Dr. Panacea's face darkened when he opened his mouth to protest. With a shrug, Zebulon headed toward the ladder in the carriage.

"Tell me, Mr. Merriwether," Dr. Panacea said, as Zebulon climbed upwards toward the roof, "have you repented yet?"

Lou frowned. "Repented?"

The doctor shook his head. "Don't you realize that if you had succeeded in your pathetic efforts to thwart me that you would have been single-handedly responsible for one of the biggest setbacks to industrial progress since… well, since perhaps the ursine-imposed moratorium that made my invention necessary?"

"Sophocles never wrote such a tragedy."

"Mr. Merriwether, your nonchalance marks you as a backwards thinker, not that I had any doubt of that. But you must have observed how so much of what makes this nation great has ground to a halt ever since the end of the war? American expansion, American industry? Even my own humble endeavor, this sanatorium, which I founded to help the sick and vulnerable…"

Lou snorted, but Dr. Panacea was too taken with his lecture to heed her.

"I thought the remote location would *benefit* my patients, not hinder their ability to reach these hallowed, healing halls. When they chose Cheyenne for the crossing, I knew flying transportation was the only solution to my problem if I wanted more than the most modest of success for my venture here."

Lou looked around at the heavy furniture, the gilded fixtures, the machinery in the cab. "And you really think this thing'll fly?"

"I know it will. Are you worried it shan't?"

"How could it? It doesn't even have *wings*. You gotta excuse me, but I'm not bright. I really don't see how some bone will—"

"Some bone! My dear Mr. Merriwether, how are you so ignorant of your own people?"

"Am I a dragon? Gee, all this time I thought I was just a person."

Dr. Panacea rolled his eyes. "This a real skull-bone from *Sinicadraco tumidus,* more commonly known as the tianlung, or common Chinese dragon. They are able to fly—without hollow bones, without wings—due to the bone that fits above the dragon's skull proper, the chimu. Have you never read Wang Fu?"

"No, I pretty much stick with yellowbacks."

"That does explain quite a bit about you," said Dr. Panacea. "Well, then. Wang Fu identified the chimu, the 'big lump' as he put it, atop a dragon's head. Without a chimu, he said, the dragon could not ascend to the sky. Other natural philosophers confirmed this, but every text on dragon biology, including Mr. Fu's, cautioned readers that the chimu only worked within a real dragon. But after extensive research I decided to gamble on the chimu working if I built an artificial dragon that had every significant aspect of the real one. Much of Chinese numerology is actually based off of the biology of *Sinicadraco tumidus,* did you know that? So my dragon has the nine animal resemblances, one hundred and seventeen scales—eighty-one yang and thirty-six yin, of course—et cetera. This construct, like its living counterparts, hangs between heaven and earth!"

Lou, despite herself, was intrigued. "I still don't get how that'll make the damn thing fly."

"It doesn't matter if you understand," said Dr. Panacea shortly. "Suffice it to say, the chimu is the linchpin of dragonflight, and whatever essential properties the chimu possesses, it continues to work after death, as is evident when dragons die whilst airborne. They continue to fly. That is why I propose—and shall be proven correct tonight—the chimu will work under artificial, but precise biologically similar circumstances." He smiled. "You must admit the perfection of my plan even if you despise me for it. It was the simplest thing in the world."

"Seems pretty complex to me."

"Does it? All it required was a thorough understanding of both the natural world and human psychology. Knowing that vermin are never missed I lured your precious workers here to blast out this cave and then do the work of assembling the component parts—which I simply commissioned from foundries and manufactories all over the nation. Who would put all the clues together? Not even a Chinese detective actively investigating me, as it turns out. The sole weakness was needing to employ someone like that idiot Tom, but even that turned out all right in the end." He smiled. "Well, not for him, but for me, and that's what matters."

Had Dr. Panacea managed all of this legitimately—without tricking his workforce into dangerous slavery, for example—Lou herself would have hailed him as one of the greatest inventors of all time. As it was, her opinion of him had simply changed from "horrible, unethical, murderous monster" to *"brilliant,* horrible, unethical, murderous monster."

"Once Zebulon creates a connection by engaging the mechanism that will bring the chimu into contact with the rest of the construct, the train should—theoretically—begin to hover and move forward." Dr. Panacea looked over his shoulder. "Where *is* Zebulon?"

He fell silent. Voices drifted down from atop the dragon. Some sort of discussion was occurring.

"Oh, what now," muttered the doctor. He headed for the ladder, and called up, "What's going on?"

"Just working out how best to keep everyone safely onboard," said Shai. He jumped down as the doctor had done, landing in a crouch and then straightening up. Zebulon followed after, clambering down the rungs. "I think we're ready! I'm so very excited, my love! Do you—"

"Why are you down here?" asked the doctor, giving Shai the hard-eye. "I don't want those coolies up there unsupervised."

Shai took a step back. "I didn't want to get thrown off..."

"I see," snapped the doctor. "Fine. If you're more concerned for your own skin than our mutual safety, then by all means stay."

"Dearest, it's not like that," said Shai nervously. He glanced over at Lou, who couldn't help giving him a smug look that clearly said *I told you so*. Shai looked away, face reddening.

She'd made her point. It was cold comfort, but as that was all she was like to get that night, she clung to it. If she got the chance, she'd hammer everything home by mentioning to Shai that while explaining his intentions Dr. Panacea hadn't once mentioned shutting down his sanatorium—indeed, he seemed hopeful to increase the numbers of patients, thereby further depleting Shai's supply of Elixir. If that didn't open his eyes she'd just give him up as a lost cause.

As Shai and Dr. Panacea continued to bicker, Lou turned away to watch Zebulon wind and wind what looked like some sort of generator, using both hands to turn the brass crank. A soft humming filled the cab, and the air began to feel heavy and prickly. Zebulon was sweating from the effort, but he did not let up. His eyes were fixed on some sort of gauge, which was gradually inching toward full.

"I think that's enough," said Dr. Panacea. Apparently tired of scolding Shai, he had wandered into the cab to look over Zebulon's shoulder. "Why don't you engage the mechanism?"

"Yes, sir," said Zebulon, after mopping his brow with an already-saturated handkerchief.

The lever in question was located away from the other controls, standing off to the side and jutting up from the floor perpendicularly. As he pushed the lever downwards with all his bodyweight Lou heard a great squealing above her head, the sound of metal sliding against metal. Next there came a thump of something falling into place, and instantly, the entire dragon shot forward at incredible speed.

Hardly expecting such a sudden jolt—really, she hadn't expected it to work at all—Lou had failed to properly brace herself. She lost her footing, and without thinking tried to arrest her fall with her left hand, slamming her broken fingers into the floor.

When the worst of the pain had passed and she was able to think and act again, Dr. Panacea seemed to have forgotten his quarrel with Shai. The happy couple were doing a silly, joyful jig in the cab of the train while Zebulon used another array of levers to angle the carriage to the left and then to the right.

"The controls are all working!" he said happily.

As she got to her feet Lou realized they were not moving forward. The train was straining against the chains which had formerly held it aloft; restrained by heavy iron cable, it quivered in midair.

It was an actual goddamn miracle. A flying train. Just the same, Lou was less thrilled by this accomplishment than the rest her companions. She hoped the men on the roof hadn't lost their footing, as she had.

"Now let's see if the attitude controls work," said Zebulon, mostly to himself.

The sensation of slowly dropping in space sent Lou's stomach reeling. So restrained, slowing meant the dragon sank slightly. When Zebulon eased up off of the control, it rose again.

"What do you think, Doc?" he asked. "Do you want to get everything ready for the test fli—"

The squealing of tearing metal interrupted him. All faces turned upwards in dreadful unison, and they heard the sounds of shouted Toisanese and the pounding of feet shuffling quickly along the roof.

Lou heard an unsettling groan, and then a pop.

The train lost all power.

With no forward momentum to hold it aloft, the dragon-train was only a pendulum of steel and wood and metal and bone. It swung backwards, Lou's guts lurched again as she again lost her footing, and this time everyone joined her on the floor. As they arced backwards and up, Lou winced at the sound of groaning chains and then metal crumpling against stone. The tail had hit the ceiling. Then they started to move forward again, slower this time.

Dr. Panacea was up first, on his feet even as the train continued to swing. The nose of the beast bumped the ceiling at the apogee of the arc, sending the doctor careening into a wall, but he kept his balance.

"What the hell was that?" he shouted, as he raced back into the passenger coach. Lou followed after only to stop at the edge of the carriage proper. Apparently the ornaments and luxuries had not been designed to withstand impacts of that intensity, the carpet was covered with the shattered remains of tumblers, soda siphons, and other detritus.

"Glad I wasn't up top," remarked Shai, pushing past her and climbing the ladder to the roof.

The comment did not exactly soothe Dr. Panacea, so without further comment Shai pushed open the trapdoor and scrambled out. Moments later, he poked his head back down.

"We lost five," he said.

"Scales?"

"No—men."

"But what of the train?" asked Dr. Panacea. "How's the nose? The tail?"

"The tail's looking bad, I have no idea if it'll affect flight." Shai puffed out his cheeks as he sighed. "The nose doesn't look great, but seems structurally undamaged."

"I want to see," said the doctor.

Five men, thought Lou, despairing. She turned back to the cab and saw Zebulon battling the lever that adjusted the chimu's position. It was stuck, and he was yanking on it with a level of frustration and violence Lou did not normally associate with fine mechanical tinkering. As Zebulon threw up his hands in exasperation, Dr. Panacea climbed back down, less stormy-faced than Lou had anticipated.

"I called up a few more to help," he said to Zebulon. "It looks like one of the chimu's bracing mechanisms snapped and it's stuck out of position. We had a replacement part, so once they get it installed, we should still be able to make the test flight before sun-up."

"Sounds good, boss," said Zebulon, leaving off with the lever.

"What sounds good to me is you getting this cab cleaned up. Fix anything that wants fixing, I still want to test this thing—"

He was interrupted by the distant boom of a shotgun, and then Lou swore she heard her own gun fire twice.

Shai dropped down into the carriage again. He looked furious.

"What's going on?" Dr. Panacea left the cab to join Shai by the ladder.

Shai shot Lou a dirty look. "You're needed up-top, my love. *Now.*"

Chapter Fourteen

Dr. Panacea swore when he peered out the window of the train carriage. "How did they know to come down here?" he demanded.

"I don't know," answered Shai impatiently. "They just rushed down the stairs from your office. The one with the shotgun would have got me if I hadn't ducked. This pop-gun doesn't have the range to hit them. It's become a situation; that Wong fellow's there, and he's talking with the workers."

Lou ran to the window to see as Dr. Panacea fled up the ladder. Bo had come for her! And hadn't Millie trained a shotgun on her when she visited them? But how had they known to come?

Then she felt an arm catch her around her neck, choking her, and her concerns became somewhat more immediate.

"Hold up!" cried Zebulon, right in Lou's ear. She tried to twist away from his grip, throwing elbows and kicks behind her, but after one impact he grunted and applied just enough pressure to her windpipe to quiet her down.

Shai was halfway up the ladder, but he stopped climbing and surveyed Zebulon coolly. "What?"

"Don't leave me alone with her! You think she won't try something when you're gone? *I* would, and *she's* crazy."

"What do you want me to do?"

"Gimme your gun! You've got a sword!"

Shai hesitated. Another shotgun blast sounded below. He shot a nasty smile at Lou and unbuckled her holster, chucking the entire rig at Zebulon before shimmying up the ladder. Zebulon caught it in his free hand.

Lou, despite her current lack of air, was thrilled. Her gun—within her reach! But before she could try to wrest herself from Zebulon's iron grip she heard, then felt, a crack on the back of her head that sent her spiraling into darkness and pain.

"Run up on the Doc and Shai with a dang pea-shooter," she heard Zebulon muttering over her somewhere.

Lou's vision swam when she opened her eyes, so she kept still, trying to pull herself together. She thanked her lucky stars—all of them, they were right there, dancing in front of her eyes—that Zeb's angle with the butt of her gun must not have been right for him to knock her out entirely, just rough her up real bad. Regardless, she couldn't just lie around and let Bo and his friends risk their lives for her sake. Getting her gun back was crucial; with it, perhaps she could shoot the doctor while he was distracted.

She still didn't know if vermilion would work on him, but it was better than nothing—and her gun was right there, sticking out of the back of Zebulon's pants as he again fiddled with the controls. He'd thrown her holster off to the side.

He obviously thought he'd knocked her out, he was ignoring her entirely. That was good, but she had to keep him from noticing she was awake while still moving—and quickly. Her shoulder had come down on some broken glass and several pieces were cutting her. Slowly she inched away from the worst of the shards. As she did so, she angled herself to watch him more easily. He was gathering up his tools that had spilled everywhere during the crash.

She tried to assess Zebulon's movements, figure out when she should make her move, but pain was a constant distraction. The back of her head was throbbing from the blow and the inside of her mouth hurt with distracting insistence. And if that wasn't bad enough, her hand was swelling something fierce from all the broken fingers. Nothing fatal, but it added up to a hell of a lot of awful.

Zebulon had his back to her, pumping grease from an oilcan into and around the seized-up lever, rattling it occasionally to work the fluid into the joints. It seemed as good a chance as any so once he really set to, Lou took a deep breath and quietly slid her ass up the wall to get to her feet as slowly as possible. The world wobbled and she almost puked from the dizziness and disorientation, so she took some long slow breaths to steady herself.

Zebulon hadn't seen her yet, but he would as soon as he turned around. Her peril increased by the moment. Focusing all her attention on the Chinese coin winking at her from the grip of her LeMat, Lou ran at him, screaming like a berserker. Zebulon jumped, startled, and dropped the oilcan, but before he could get his hand around the revolver's grip Lou had crashed into him, using her shoulder as a battering ram to the guts.

The force of her strike sent them both reeling into one of the many control boxes, the sharp edge of which caught Zebulon in the back. He cried out as they fell together, limbs entangled, but Lou got her right arm free while he was still trying to figure which way was up and clocked him as hard as she could in his left eye. Zebulon howled and tried to kick her, but he missed. She socked him again, this time hitting him in the jaw, right below his ear. She heard a satisfying clack of teeth meeting teeth, and then he went still.

Rolling him over, she wrested her LeMat from the waistband of his pants. Her hand might be tingling from the punches, but it felt wonderful to hold her gun again. After gingerly buckling on her shoulder holster, Lou felt ready to do what needed doing.

She heard the sounds of battle when she emerged into the fresher air above the carriage. Inside the train she had only heard the occasional shotgun blast; out here, clashing metal and shouting reached her ears, and the smell of blood and gunpowder filled her nose. Before she looked down, she glanced at the three workers still doing whatever they were doing to the dragon's head. She immediately noticed that Gan-bou was not among them. Trying not to think about having to tell Heung-kam both her boys had died, she peeked carefully over the edge.

Thurlow had organized a handful of workers into a kind of militia to battle Dr. Panacea, and they were doing as good a job as could be expected. Thurlow was swinging on the doctor with a pair of long-handled war-hammers, and the rest of the men dodged and wove in and around the massive man as he recovered from each of his heavy, wide-swinging blows, striking at the doctor with repurposed mallets, hand-saws, and various other tools. Unfortunately, none of their blows seemed to affect him; in fact, Dr. Panacea looked like he was having a good time. More cat and mouse games, Lou realized, her stomach sinking into her boots.

Closer to the center of the cave Shai's saber was glinting in the torchlight. In between dodging blasts from Millie's shotgun he struck quickly but with precision at five or six more uniformed workers—and Bo, who was wielding his beloved sword. Shai's agility bordered on supernatural, but they were holding their own against him. The workers had fanned out to encircle Shai, striking at his elbows and knees with their more makeshift weapons as he focused on Bo, meeting him blow for blow, feint for feint.

The problem was, even with so many striking at Shai at once, it still didn't seem like a fair fight. It was obvious that if not for his posse Bo would have been in serious trouble. He was struggling to keep up with Shai's speed and control, and kept taking small sips from a bottle of Elixir of Life whenever he got the chance. This sight in particular inspired Lou to take a deep breath and sling herself over the edge of the dragon so she could climb down the swaying rope-ladder, busted up hand, possible concussion, vertigo and all.

"Hey!" called someone above her, before she was too far down. Two of the workers were peering down at her. "She's escaping! You—girl! Come back!"

"Like hell," grunted Lou, trying to put as much distance between herself and the men as possible. A few of their number clearly still believed Dr. Panacea would let them go if they worked hard to complete their jobs. Soon they'd find out... one way or another.

"Let her be," said the other. "Let's get back to work."

Feeling a strange motion shuddering along the rope ladder, Lou looked up. She despaired to see the first man sawing away at one of the lines with some sort of tool.

"He'll kill us if we let her go!"

Lou privately agreed with him, but didn't express an opinion. She was most of the way down, and figured it would be safer to jump in case the bastard above her managed to cut through. Steeling herself, she kicked her feet free and let go with her good hand; after a dizzying, harrowing drop, Lou bit back a noise somewhere between a groan and a whimper when she landed hard on her feet. The heel of her boot slipped, and her left ankle twisted underneath her when she landed, sending waves of agony up her leg.

Through the powder-haze from Millie's shotgun Lou saw there were several bodies strewn about the floor, all Chinese, but if they had fallen from the train or died slightly more recently, Lou could not tell. Not that it particularly mattered right now. Her concern was with the living. Mostly.

Bo and his troupe were still battling Shai. Lou scanned beyond them for Dr. Panacea. Not only was he outside the functional range of her gun, he had darted away from Thurlow and his companions and was right behind Bo from where she stood.

Millie was off to the left and in the back of the cave, firing on Shai whenever he backed away from the group enough for her to chance a shot. The blasts were deafening when they came, and she was clearly having a hard time hitting such a nimble target while avoiding shooting everyone else in all the confusion. But as Lou began to limp around the clusterfuck surrounding Shai, one of Millie's potshots must have grazed Shai's shoulder. He cried out and fell back momentarily.

Dr. Panacea's hearing must have been as astonishing as the rest of his abilities, for at the sound of his lover's pain he whirled around, snarling in anger, and loped straight for Millie. In moments he was on top of her, smacking the shotgun out of her grip with one hand and grabbing her face with the other. She didn't have time to scream before he crushed her skull with his fingers like he was crumpling a wad of paper. Lou, shocked, began to limp towards the ugly scene. She had to put a stop to this if she could.

Throwing Millie's broken body carelessly aside, Dr. Panacea wheeled around to face Thurlow, who had chased after the doctor with his three remaining compatriots. Thurlow struck out first, swinging hastily at Dr. Panacea's face with one of his hammers. To Lou's joy, he walloped Dr. Panacea in the right temple, and for a beautiful moment the big man had the vampire flying through the air, flailing. Dr. Panacea hit the wall of the cave with a sickening smack, but somehow clung there with his fingers. Without missing a beat he swung his legs up above his head like they were clock-hands pointing to noon, braced himself against the wall of the cavern, and after gathering himself into an upside-down crouch, launched himself through the air straight at Thurlow.

Lou glanced toward Bo, Shai, and the rest as she limped closer and closer to the doctor on her unsteady legs. She wanted to give that group a wide berth, in case any of her rounds went wide. As she drew nearer she began to set up potential shots in her mind—only to hear Bo call out in Chinese for his troops to retreat.

Time seemed to slow when one of the men failed to move as quickly as the rest. He bumped into Bo, and they both momentarily lost their footing. Shai took the opportunity to strike down with his saber, clipping Bo's ear. Bo clapped his hand to his head with a shout as Shai mockingly saluted him with his sword before renewing his advances.

Upon seeing Bo's bloody wound and Shai's ruthless, wide-sweeping attacks, one of the men panicked and bolted; Lou was just coming around the rear of the group and tried to get out of the fleeing man's way but he blindly collided with her, knocking into her hurt hand. She stumbled on her twisted ankle but then Bo was there, grabbing her around the waist and steadying her.

"Watch it, will you? I'm trying to rescue you," he said as she blushed furiously in spite of everything. Blood was running down the side of his face but he was grinning at her. Before Lou could stutter a reply, he took a slug from the bottle he still gripped in his other hand, and turned again to face Shai.

Shai had not been idle, his sword rising for a strike; Bo's gim met steel with steel as Lou ducked down and crab-scuttled aside, wincing with each step. Once she was out of range she stood again, but only seconds later she heard the unmistakable tinkle of glass breaking. Bo must have dropped his medicine, but Lou didn't turn to confirm her suspicions. The doctor was at last in firing range.

Dr. Panacea had done something to Thurlow, the larger man was on the ground and the doctor was smiling down at him, Tom Hill's gun trained on him as Thurlow tried to scoot himself away from the doctor, his enormous feet and hands slapping the stone in his haste. The front of his shirt and pants were reddening with blood, and his war-hammers lay abandoned, several feet beyond his reach.

One of Thurlow's remaining companions was tugging on his shirt, trying to help get him away from the doctor; the other two stepped between the vampire and his prey, their weapons poised to strike. The first swung with a sledgehammer, but Dr. Panacea swatted it out of the way and with a second swipe of his arm he knocked the man aside into a pile of machinery. The poor fellow did not get back up again.

Black and white and red all over, just like the joke, the doctor aimed and shot the second of his assailants in the guts, tossed the gun aside, and poked his fingers into the man's stomach before he had time to lift his crowbar. Dr. Panacea's strike ripped through cloth and flesh, and when he drew back his hand, it was coated with slimy viscera and he was holding the bullet between his thumb and forefinger. The doctor sucked the shot free of blood as he began his final advance on Thurlow and the other man.

Lou saw all this blurrily out of the corner of her eye as she used the heel of her broken hand to force the lever that switched the LeMat's action to the sixteen-gauge smoothbore barrel. The lone .60 round packed a helluva lot more wallop than the smaller bullets, as well as much more undead-immobilizing vermilion. She just hoped Shai's firing the gun twice hadn't shaken the ball *too* loose.

Only one way to find out. Lou leveled the revolver and took aim at Dr. Panacea's heart.

She took her time setting up the shot, as Dr. Panacea's attention was fixed solely on the men he slowly stalked, but just as she fired she heard Bo begin to cough. As a spume of blood erupted from somewhere around Dr. Panacea's liver, Lou spun around to see Bo on his back, writhing on the floor in a severe tussive fit. Only the small battalion of Chinese were preventing Shai from hacking her best friend to pieces, but it was clear they couldn't hold him back for long. The men were all brave and strong, but Shai had centuries of experience—and had not spent the last however many months locked in a freezing cell and forced to work under extreme conditions.

"Lou!" she heard Thurlow shout. "Shoot him again!"

Startled, Lou turned and saw Dr. Panacea spinning around wildly, trying to get a look at his side like a cat after its own tail. As he turned his back to Lou, she saw a wet stain on the back of his black frock coat.

Feeling truly hopeful for the first time, and trying not to pay attention to the pathetic sounds of Bo trying to catch his breath behind her, she worked the lever on her gun back to fire the remaining revolver rounds.

She again aimed with care, but the first shot went wide. Her vision was still fuzzy from Zebulon's blow to her head, but her second shot struck the doctor in the body; the third, his right arm. She let out a whoop of triumph and instantly regretted it. Dr. Panacea went totally rigid, and, realizing that she was the source of his distress, came at her—but his movements were comparatively sluggish and clumsy. The bullets had slowed him down! Lou got off one more round before retreating, but when she took a step backwards she tripped over the body of a fallen Chinese worker.

"What on earth do you have in that gun of yours?" slurred Dr. Panacea as he stepped up to loom over her, swaying and heavy-lidded.

"They're laced with vermilion," answered Lou, flat on her back. She smiled as she leveled her gun again. "You think you're big and bad, but at the end of the day you're just another undead—and a sight trashier than most."

She fired on him, not point-blank but damn close to it. The bullet struck Dr. Panacea in the neck. Cold blood spattered across her face as the wound fountained. Dr. Panacea clapped his hand to the hole with a scream, falling to his knees with a sickening sound like a block of ice shattering on stone. Lou shot him a final time in the heart, but her triumph at seeing the vampire laid low was cut short when someone grabbed her by the hair.

"You *bitch*," said Shai in her ear, and she felt his blade at her throat. "And after everything I did for you!"

Lou hurled herself backwards into Shai, swinging her legs around and up in a desperate attempt to save her neck. Her back spasmed but one foot made contact with the elbow of Shai's knife-hand; the blade swung away and instead of slicing her jugular it raked her across her face from chin to forehead. She lost her grip on her gun as she screamed, it skittered away over the stone and she rolled away, instinctively clawing at her face. But she was alive, and Shai was no longer attacking her. Wiping blood from her burning eyes she looked around to see what the bastard would try next—but Shai's concern had shifted.

"Oh, my dearest, oh Lazarus!" Shai was babbling as he knelt beside Dr. Panacea, frantically trying to plug the gushing holes in the doctor's neck and chest with his palms. "I didn't realize—just look what she did to you, we have to get out of here and—"

"I'm fine," growled the doctor drunkenly, swatting Shai away, "just let me at her!" But when he got unsteadily to his feet he immediately collapsed onto Shai, pale as a ghost.

"You're not fine." Shai, wild-eyed and covered in Dr. Panacea's blood, commenced dragging his lover toward the train. The doctor must have been feeling pretty awful; he allowed himself to be pulled away as Shai said, "Another day! There will be another day! That's what you've always told me, isn't it?"

The seven or so remaining workers mobbed the pair as they fled, striking at them with crowbar and fist and whatever else they had. Lou went for her gun to try to finish them off, but by the time she retrieved it, Dr. Panacea and Shai had emerged from the horde, having done something that put Kwan on his knees, vomiting, and another man on his back, shuddering as he bled out. Most of the workers fell back upon seeing their companions so casually dispatched, so the only thing in the couple's way was an emaciated figure, lying on his back, gasping alone in the smoky dimness.

Shai limped past Bo and began to holler and gesture at the Chinese workers still atop the train until one of the poor saps threw down a rope. Shai immediately began to climb, but Dr. Panacea paused before following after his lover.

With awful, deliberate slowness, the doctor turned to look at Lou. He blew her kiss. Then he brought his foot down on Bo's abdomen, stomping him hard on the solar plexus and grinding his foot against her friend's snapping ribs. Only then did he begin to haul himself overhand up the rope to where Shai already waited atop the hanging train.

By the time Lou reached him, Bo was bleeding freely from the mouth, and moaning when he wasn't coughing. She smelled bile and shit and blood, and was only vaguely aware of what was happening around her:

Bodies falling like stones from the train to splatter on the floor below,

Thurlow bleeding all over her when he joined her at Bo's side,

Shai on the top of the train, stomping the chimu into position,

The dragon shuddering to life above their heads,

Dr. Panacea running about, tearing away the thick chains that tethered the train to the ceiling with his hands,

And Bo talking to her, his voice fainter than a whisper.

"Damn, Lou. You look rough," he wheezed. "But I think I win. I'm dying."

"You're not dying," protested Lou, not sure why she was lying to him. "You'll be okay, we'll get some Elixir, we'll get—"

"No," said Bo. "Lou, you have to help me. Elixir can't fix this, it couldn't even stop me coughing. I'm crushed to a pulp. Miss Foxglove—"

"Miss Foxglove?" Lou didn't understand, but Bo was coughing again, and it seemed like he might never stop.

"She said your bag was in the office," said Thurlow, looking at Lou as if she was the Lord Jesus himself, about to perform some kind of goddamn miracle. Lou had to turn away from his gaze when he asked, "Do you have something to help him in there?"

"No," said Lou. "No, I—"

Bo took Lou's hand, squeezed it, and managed to cough out, "You do have something that will help." His brown eyes met her green ones, and that was when she understood what he was saying.

"No, Bo, listen…"

He whispered, *"Please."*

"What's going on?" asked Thurlow. "What are you going to do?"

Lou was momentarily sidetracked when the dragon shot out of the cave and into the night sky. As it arced upward she briefly caught sight of Dr. Panacea on the roof, pulling himself along on his belly towards the trap-door, his fingers finding purchase in the crevices between scales and the moorings where the chains had hooked into the back of the dragon.

Lou didn't care about them anymore. She turned back to the crumpled body of her best and oldest friend. To do what Bo asked of her… she had sworn she never would, said over and over that it was wrong and terrible; that no one in his right mind would ever request such a thing. But those vows, that reasoning, all of it had come before being asked for help by someone she loved. Lou didn't know if what he desired was right, or if it was best, but she knew it was what he wanted—and she would give it to him.

Chapter Fifteen

Lou hardly realized she was stumbling towards Dr. Panacea's office until she was nearly at the door. The enormity of Bo's request weighed on her with every step she took, wholly occupying her fevered mind as she limped as quickly as possible—until she heard an unmistakable giggle from inside the chamber.

"Try pulling the books off the shelves," said Miss Foxglove absently, as Lou pitched against the doorframe. The fitness instructor was sitting in Dr. Panacea's chair, rifling through his desk-drawers, pulling out thick file-folders and sorting them into stacks. The whole office was a mess; they had clearly been doing whatever they were doing for some time.

"All of them?" Coriander began working on the bookcase farthest to the left of the office, grabbing several tomes at once and then looking around for a clear patch to put them. Eventually she set them on a crate of Elixir bottles.

"I've looked everywhere else," said Miss Foxglove. "It's got to be here somewhere."

"Where's my bag?" gasped Lou, trying to keep herself from sliding down the wall.

"Lou?" Coriander turned around. "Oh, Lou! I knew you'd—oh my God! Lou!"

Miss Foxglove had looked up from her efforts at the desk and was also staring at Lou, wide-eyed.

"I need my bag," repeated Lou. "Do you know where it is, or not? Thurlow said you'd…"

Miss Foxglove nodded and bent down behind the desk. "It's here. But Mr. Merriwether, first, let me—"

"Later. There's something," Lou swallowed, tasted her own blood, "I gotta do. Fast."

"First thing, take care of yourself," scolded Coriander as she ran over to where Miss Foxglove was rummaging around on her hands and knees. Lou felt the sudden urge to lunge forward and slap the girl across her foolish face. How dare she lecture her in a moment like this!

"Just look at you!" said Coriander, as she joined Miss Foxglove on the floor. "Vivien, where's the—"

Lou hobbled toward the desk, wincing with each step. If they weren't going to give her the bag, she'd just fucking take it. There wasn't time to mess around. Every moment Bo was in pain was one more than she wanted him to endure.

Miss Foxglove sat up, Lou's workbag in her hand, but as Lou reached for it, Miss Foxglove grabbed her wrist.

"Wait," she said.

"No!" cried Lou, as she jerked her hand away, finally losing it. "You don't have any idea what I need to do, or why, so just hand it over!"

"Whatever you're doing, you'll do it better healed." Coriander popped up from behind the desk, a large Mason jar with a few inches of golden liquid sloshing in the bottom gripped in one hand, a miniature pewter ladle in the other. "Look! We found the undiluted Elixir! From what Vivien tells me, it'll get you right as rain in no time."

Lou regretted her earlier impulse to strike Coriander. Once again, the girl had proven to be surprisingly insightful. And she just might have saved a life, too…

"Bo's dying," said Lou. "He needs help, fast. I was going to—it doesn't matter. Come with me!" She saw Coriander open her mouth to argue and held up her hand. "I promise, after we see to him and anyone else who needs it more I'll fix myself up. Okay?"

"Take care not to die," said Miss Foxglove, turning back to her files. "I need to talk to you."

Too anxious to snap back at Miss Foxglove, Lou snatched up her bag, lest Bo move beyond even the power of the Elixir of Life, and headed out into the cave proper. Coriander followed behind her, Elixir in hand.

"What on earth happened to your face?" asked Coriander. Lou noted the girl was no longer limping—had she sampled the Elixir, too?

"Everything that possibly could," said Lou, through gritted teeth.

"Oh my God!"

Coriander was looking over the carnage, aghast, as well she might be. The living numbered far fewer than the dead, and in some cases, they weren't much better off. The cave reeked of death and metal, and the cries of the wounded were gut-wrenching in their misery.

"I should have helped," said Coriander softly. "I wanted to, but Vivien said I'd be in the way, and helping her would—"

"You're helping now," said Lou firmly.

They had reached Bo and Thurlow. Bo looked unconscious, or close to it; Thurlow as though he'd aged ten years as he slouched on his knees, helplessly holding Bo's hand in his. When Lou sat beside them, her hurt ankle stretched out, Thurlow looked at her with an expression of loathing and horror.

"He says you're gonna…"

Lou cut him off. "Coriander has the Elixir of Life. The real stuff."

"No," moaned Bo. "Please, I'm a goner, just…"

Thurlow looked poised to start arguing with Bo, but Lou took the jar from Coriander and unscrewed the lid, drew out a ladleful, and trickled a little into Bo's mouth as he spoke. He swallowed reflexively. Opening his eyes wider, he looked at Lou in wonder.

"More," she said, and gave him the rest. He drank willingly, sucking down the remaining pale liquid from the spoon.

After he finished swallowing, his head fell back against the stone floor with an unsettling crack, but when Lou and Thurlow nearly busted their own skulls against one another in their haste to check on him, they found that he was merely sleeping. His breath was coming now in long, steady pulls, stronger than she'd seen him since she arrived. Before their very eyes his swollen abdomen shrank under his torn shirt and turned the yellowish-green hue of a healing bruise, then that color melted away into unblemished umber. Lou wondered if the water would also help what would probably turn out to be a terrible knot on the back of his head, too.

"Holy shit," said Thurlow.

"Now you!" said Coriander, gently shaking Lou's shoulder. "Come on, down the hatch! I promise if you pass out I'll dole some out to everyone else who needs it."

Lou saw the wisdom of this. "All right," she said slowly, suddenly acutely aware of the itchy blood dribbling down her gashed face. "But if I do pass out, promise me you'll get everyone ready to get out of here and away from the San as quick as possible. We have no idea if Dr. Panacea will come back, or when. We should put as much distance between ourselves and this place as soon as we can." She lifted the ladle to her lips, then lowered it again. "And do you know how to load a gun? My LeMat should be reloaded from the sack of bullets, the reddish ones. They're the ones that work on undead."

"I promise," said Coriander, the girl's eyes darting around everywhere but Lou's face.

"And—"

"Lou!"

With a final glance at Bo, Lou took the water in the silver ladle in one big gulp—and knew no more.

***

When Lou awoke she was in her bed, in the room she had been assigned upon arriving at Fountain of Youth. The fungal light, which she had previously found dim and irritating, was soothing to her eyes.

What a night. Lou took a few moments to marvel at the simple fact that she had survived, then sobered at the thought of all who hadn't. Gan-bou, Millie, and so many whose names she'd never even had the time to find out. She wondered how Kwan fared, and all the other survivors.

Lou was startled out of her grim pondering by a prodigious snore. She groggily peered around and saw Coriander snoozing in a chair with her feet propped up on another. Her head was lolling onto her shoulder and drool was sliding down her cheek. The sight cheered Lou. The normality of it was beautiful to behold.

Trying not to wake her friend, Lou hauled herself out of bed and dressed quietly in her own clothes, eschewing the San uniform. She was glad to see there was clean water in the basin, she wanted to wash her face and rinse out her mouth. She lit the kerosene lamp, keeping the flame low, and held it up to her reflection in the mirror.

She gasped. The deep slash of a scar that ran from below her left ear, across her nose, to her right temple might look like she got it years before, but was obviously much more recent.

"Lou?" Coriander yawned behind her. "You're awa—oh."

Lou turned around. "How's Bo?" she demanded.

Coriander's bleary dismay was not immediately reassuring.

"He's fine," she said, though her tone said he wasn't. "Thurlow's with him, looking after him. He'll just have to, you know."

"No, I don't," said Lou harshly. "If I've got a healed-over cut deep as a canyon and a nose that still looks like a Cornish bare-knuckle boxer's, then how is he?"

"He can walk with a cane. There's some pain, though. I guess some of his ribs healed funny."

"Shit," said Lou, and sat down heavily on her bed. She looked at her left hand and flexed the fingers—they were bent at all kinds of angles, but they were working. And entirely pain-free. Well, goody for her.

"After we saw your nose heal… like that… we figured out to use the Elixir only on people with pretty minor injuries, or those who wouldn't survive without immediate care. But Miss Foxglove, she has a little first aid training, so everyone else got patched up pretty well and then we hit them with the Elixir."

Lou stared helplessly at her knees. She felt numb, beyond the point of having opinions about her own actions. Had she done the right thing? She felt like she'd yet again fucked everything up. Maybe she should just get used to it.

"He's not coughing anymore," said Coriander, sitting down beside Lou on the bed.

"Oh," said Lou. "Good."

"And I did what you asked—Vivien's put everyone to work packing so we can get moving as soon as possible."

"Vivien, huh?"

Coriander blushed, surprising Lou. "She was more than happy to help, she seems nervous about something, I don't know what. Anyways, I got your things and mine packed up before I fell asleep. It was maybe six in the morning once we got done healing everyone down in the cave and getting them back up to the San proper. I'm not sure what time it is now. You and Bo slept for hours but someone's supposed to come by and knock when it's time to go."

"What about the dead?"

"What about them?" Coriander's eyes widened. "Of course! You'll want to do all those things that you do. Can I help?"

"Maybe. Are they burying the bodies, or are we taking them back with us?"

"They're not going to bury them. Whoever was able is building boxes so we can take them all back to Chinatown with us. Is that... usual?"

"Definitely," said Lou, remembering another time when she'd rushed into a situation, fist in a ball and gun blazing, only to lose lives she should have saved. Maybe one day she'd learn to think before she acted. "It's probable their families will want to send them back to China for burial. Falling leaves coming to rest at the roots, you know." Lou gestured vaguely at where she thought outside might be. "Out here in the wilds, there's no one around to tend their graves. But I—we, if you like—can definitely help them out, though if we want to, we should get down there."

"Vivien will know where they've set up..."

Miss Foxglove had installed herself up in Dr. Panacea's official office, so they headed that way. As they walked, Coriander explained how Bo, Thurlow, and Millie had come to find out about Lou's situation, as well as what she had been doing with Miss Foxglove when Lou found them digging through his things.

"Vivien woke me after she left Dr. P and the man who'd come in from San Francisco. She knew you and I were friends and wasn't sure what to do. She told me a little of what was happening to you—you poor thing!—and that's when I suggested contacting Bo's friends. Vivien didn't know they hunted monsters for a living. She thought it was ever so funny! So we woke Bo. He was so anxious to save you, but so sick, so while Vivien rode down to the camp with him to get them I took her keys and got into the supply closet to get him all the Elixir of Life I could stuff in a sack. Then we headed down to see what was what, and, well, you know the rest."

"Do I?"

"Oh, I suppose not. Well, I've never even slapped someone before, not even my mother—which required much restraint on my part, I'll have you know—so I stuck with Vivien. She wanted to get everything she could out of Dr. Panacea's office, and said it was safe enough because even if he won—not that she was hoping for that, of course—she could claim she was just trying to protect his interests. Everyone who works here has sort of criminal record, you know; Dr. Panacea had huge files on all of them so they wouldn't ever be able to run off and tell about what was really happening here. It's too bad for them, really."

"Who?"

"The staff. Vivien says she'll make back all of her out-of-pocket expenses just with the bounties alone! But don't mention that, right now she says she's holding their files in, uh, *escrow,* or something, at least until we get down. Oh, and what was I telling you about Vivien... ah, that she said if you defeated the doctor, well then she'd have everything she needed for her investigation, and lots of the Elixir to boot!" Coriander paused to take several quick, deep breaths before continuing—Lou suspected the girl had to remind herself to do so, lest she faint from lack of air. "In the end, she found plenty of very interesting plans and schematics and letters and whatnot, but we only found that small jar of the Elixir. And we looked everywhere!"

Lou was impressed. Miss Foxglove was kind of a beast. Too bad Lou hadn't confided in her. Things might have gone a lot better for her, and for everyone else.

Too bad for Shai, too—that was probably the last of his Elixir of Life. She wondered what on earth would happen to him without the substance that made him so useful to his companion.

He'd made his choice... but just the same, she wished he'd made a different one. *In another life, we might have been friends...* how she wished she'd been able to help him see they could have been friends in this life, too. She reckoned she'd never met anyone who needed one more.

"So what was Miss Foxglove investigating? Dr. Panacea?" asked Lou. She would think on Shai when she had more time, she was sure of it.

"She came here looking for a job after getting a tip that Mr. Rutherford had fled here. I guess he cheated someone badly, some business deal, I don't have the whole story, it's not really that important. Vivien was only pretending to be a fitness instructor. She was in, what did she call it, *deep cover,* but when she found out about everything else going on here it was pretty much the investigation of the century! She's a Pinkerton agent, and has been for years. Can you imagine? How exciting!"

Lou wasn't so sure "exciting" was the word she would use to describe that particular piece of information, but Coriander seemed downright thrilled so she tried to muster some enthusiasm.

"So've you kissed her yet?"

"Well," said Coriander, blushing prettily, "wouldn't you?"

Lou bit back the *"hell* no" itching to escape her mouth, and instead patted Coriander on the back. "Maybe you can butter her up for me, so she won't stab me in the back and bury me in a shallow grave for telling her to fuck off in front of everyone."

"Vivien wouldn't do that!"

Lou had her doubts as to whether Coriander's theory held water, given that "Vivien" had sat idly by, calmly eating people while her employer murdered them for who knew how long, but they had just entered the Great Hall and Lou's protest died on her lips. The door was standing open, and she could see the deep blue of a beautiful, clear night sky beyond the stone and wood of the San—but having slept an entire day was not what shocked Lou.

Miss Foxglove was standing in the center of the hall, surrounded by three bears. She was speaking and gesturing animatedly, and Lou got the impression that she was pretty frustrated.

"We are packing up and leaving with all due haste," she said. "I assure you, I am fully aware of the bargain you struck with the previous owner of this establishment, but we must see to our dead and pack and—"

The largest of the bears, a boar with a shining ebony coat and a red sash decorated with what Lou recognized as those new-fangled military "medals of honor" slung over one shoulder, waved away Miss Foxglove's protests with a heavy paw. "Twenty-four hours was what the contract stipulated," he grumbled. "It has been that long since Dr. Panacea departed—"

"No it hasn't!"

"Shai said—"

"Shai *lied!"* Miss Foxglove took a deep breath to compose herself before speaking again. "They left sometime in the very early morning today.

Please," she begged, "the situation here has been rather… difficult, given everything. You must give us a little more time!"

"Or what?"

Lou didn't like the bear's casual, amused attitude one bit. She wondered how many of his kind lived in the surrounding forest, and if they had already rallied to take the San by force should it prove necessary.

"Please just let us stay until dawn," pleaded Miss Foxglove. "You know why."

"Slippery slope," said one of the other bears. He had a white patch on his bottom, it flashed brightly as he shifted from leg to leg. "We don't negotiate with humans. Give you a paw, and you'll take the arm."

Lou felt this was a fair enough point, but she decided to intervene before Miss Foxglove lost it. She already looked about ready to pull her hair out.

"Hey now, folks," said Lou, stepping forward, though Coriander pulled at her arm, trying to prevent her from getting involved, "sorry to interrupt, but I couldn't help but overhear. You having some sort of problem?"

Miss Foxglove shot her a frazzled look. "The San property was leased from the bears, and the terms of the agreement stated if the doctor left the premises for longer than twenty-four hours, we—"

"Twenty-four *consecutive* hours *without prior notice,*" said Sash.

Lou nodded. "Everyone has to vacate, should that be the case?"

"Yes," said Sash. "It has now been, according to the doctor's very reliable word, twenty-four hours, so…"

Lou nodded, and began to rummage through her workbag. She took out her tobacco pouch and matches, and rolled up a lumpy cigarette—it would take some time to relearn the perfect technique, what with her newly crooked fingers. Her activity seemed to interest the bears, as she thought it might. She offered the cigarette to Sash.

"Fancy a smoke?"

"That's friendly," he said. "Thanks."

He looked even happier when Lou struck a match and lit it for him.

"My pleasure," said Lou, as he exhaled. "Can I oblige anyone else?"

White Patch was also interested in a cigarette, so Lou rolled him one, too. The third, a lighter-furred, smaller bear—maybe a sow, maybe a young one, Lou couldn't tell—was apparently abstaining.

"That's nice," said Sash, taking another long drag. "Hard to get good tobacco out here."

"I heard as much, when I was chatting with Victoria," said Lou, rolling one for herself now. "Do you know Victoria? She's the attaché for the Utah and Wyoming Territories. Met her on my way out here. Real nice sow. Classy."

White Patch looked at Lou askance. "You know Victoria?" he asked.

"Well, you know how it is, on trains…" Lou briefly wondered if, indeed, he did, but continued anyways. "She was telling me that folks—human folks—have been shameful about contract law and the treaties with the bears and all that. You know, doing whatever they please while you hole up to hibernate and such." Lou noted with pleasure Miss Foxglove's mouth was hanging slightly open. "Victoria said she kept awake all winter just to make sure the same didn't happen this year. Can you imagine? I get cranky after one sleepless night!"

"What's your point?" said White Patch, nonplussed.

"Just that we're not doing that," said Lou, addressing herself to Sash, who seemed slightly less hostile. "See, the whole reason I'm here is that a bunch of people like me—I'm Chinese, you know—have been used and abused by your man Dr. Panacea. Maybe you heard something about it. It doesn't really matter except that I know we're all looking to get the hell out of here quick as possible. But 'possible,' well, what with all the bodies we gotta prep for transport and everything else besides, it might take a little more time. Trust me, I want to get out of here. I'm homesick. You know when I met Victoria? When she was passing through Cheyenne, I don't know how long ago. And before that, I'd never been out of California. Imagine that!"

White Patch still seemed underwhelmed, but Sash looked interested.

Sash had finished his cigarette; he flicked the butt onto the floor with an enormous brown claw and stamped it out. "Regardless, you are in violation of the terms of the prior agreement. I suggest you take what you can and go. There are fewer of you than there are of us, I assure you, and we have the law on our side. Really, you ought to be grateful we don't bring everyone up here and slaughter you all. We would be well within our rights."

"That's—" began Miss Foxglove, but Lou shot her a look and she shut her mouth. A goddamn welcome change of pace, that.

"Well," Lou said with a sigh, "There's no way we can get out of here yet. So yeah, what I'm saying is if you're gonna kill us, I'd sure appreciate it if you'd amble down to Estes and telegraph my mother in San Francisco? I didn't have time to tell her that I'd invited Victoria to stay with us if she ever came to town. I'd really hate to have her show up and not get a proper welcome. My Ma doesn't like unexpected guests and might be less than welcoming without a head's up. I'd hate that."

"You offered Victoria hospitality?" Sash looked over at White Patch. "Buckrump, we can't—"

"You believe her?" The bear with the white patch looked incredulous. "She could be making it up!"

"I have her card," offered Lou, bending down to look through her bag once again. "Pink, smells like perfume. Ah, here it is." Lou handed it to the silent, smallest bear, who handed it to Sash.

Sash shook his hairy head. He looked like he was on the fence about the whole issue at this point. "They're only asking to stay until dawn," he said at last. Lou tried to hide her glee with a puff on her cigarette. "I say we let them."

"Percival!" cried Buckrump.

"But," said Percival, looking hard at Lou, "if anyone lingers behind, and we find them…"

"That's nothing to me," said Lou. "I'll be gone, and anyone who stays would be in violation of our new verbal agreement. I'd have nothing to say about it other than it serves 'em right."

"Clementine?" asked Sash.

The light-furred bear shrugged. "You were the ones who dragged me out of my den for this," she said. "I never cared about it."

"Sows," said Buckrump, disgusted.

"I know, but what can you do?" said Lou, imitating Clementine's shrug. "Anyone want another cigarette? I'd be happy to roll you a few, but I should get to work on what I got to do before I can leave."

"I'll take another," said Percival. "Thanks."

"I'm going home," said Clementine. She dropped to all fours, and loped away through the front door. After one final unhappy look at Percival, Buckrump followed her.

Lou handed the bear another cigarette, but begged his pardon for not sticking around while he smoked it. He said he was aching for his den anyways, and so took his leave after she lit it for him.

"That was fun," said Lou, feeling pretty goddamn slick as she turned to Coriander and Miss Foxglove, who still looked a little dazed. "How're you, Miss Foxglove? You come through that okay?"

"I'm…" Miss Foxglove swallowed, then smiled. "Thank you, Mr. Merriwether. I'm in your debt. We all are, actually."

"Well, I already know how you can pay me back, but don't you worry about it right now," said Lou. "I need to get moving—Coriander said folks were building boxes for the dead? I'd like to see the coffins in case there are any problems I need to take care of before we get on the road. Whereabouts should I go?"

Miss Foxglove looked deeply unsettled by her speech, and for once, the reaction amused Lou.

"Lou's a psychopomp," said Coriander helpfully, when Miss Foxglove didn't immediately reply. "She wants to make sure no one comes back as a… *geeoohngseeh.*" She turned to Lou. "Right?"

Close enough. "Yep. And it'll be a sight easier if I don't have to pry up a bunch of nailed-down coffin-lids."

"Oh." Miss Foxglove nodded vaguely. "Of course. Actually, I told them to head down to the stables. There's a small lumberyard close to there, I thought they might find most of what they needed pretty easily."

"Great. Well, while I'm gone, I wonder…"

"Yes?"

"Could yoou find me some vittles? I'm famished."

"After all you've done, I'll cook you a feast with my own hands."

"Shucks, it wasn't nothing," said Lou, as they headed upward. "I like bears. Oh, and Miss Foxglove?"

"Call me Vivien."

"Well, Vivien… I'm sorry I cussed you out."

Miss Foxglove looked amused. "I deserved it," she said. "Go and do what you must. Later, when we're out of here, I still have some matters I'd like to discuss with you." Coriander and Miss Foxglove were making eyes at one another, so Lou decided to leave them be, heading out the front door and breaking into a trot down the hill toward the stables once she was outside.

Lou nodded and headed out the front door, breaking into a trot down the hill toward the stables once she was outside. She was eager to set-to with those who might be in need of her skills—and anxious to be gone from the

San on time. It seemed unlikely she could broker yet another extension of the deal with Percival and Buckrump. She did, however, slow her pace when she heard Coriander cry, "Lou! Hey, Lou! Wait up!" and the patter of feet behind her. Lou had no idea how much she'd have to do once she got to the makeshift funeral parlor. Some help might be nice.

Chapter Sixteen

By the time Lou and Coriander arrived at the stables, Kwan and two other men, a skinny fellow called Cheung and Yan-chiu, a short stocky kid, had just about finished building the necessary boxes. Lou thanked them for their time, and begged their pardon when it turned out five of the dead men had need of her talents, as did Millie's corpse. They agreed to wait before nailing any boxes shut, but due to time constraints they'd begin situating the corpses for transport as she worked.

"So we're going to exorcise them, like with Ned and Coyote?" asked Coriander, as Lou crouched down next to the body showing the most signs of early geung si possession.

Lou pushed her goggles up on her forehead, shaking her head. "Actually, the opposite." She'd been thinking about traditional Chinese psychopompery after explaining to Coriander the importance of sending bodies back for burial in China, specifically old-fashioned Taoist practices of transporting bodies back to their hometowns. "I'm going to turn them all into geung si. Temporarily."

"What?" Coriander sounded a little panicked. Her first experience with qi-vampires had been pretty traumatic. *"Why?"*

"Because geung si possession halts physical putrefaction." Lou looked up at Coriander. "These corpses won't get any easier on the nose over the course of a few weeks on the road, if you take my meaning. So I'm going to inoculate each of them with a little of the spiritual corruption that's beginning in a few of the bodies and put a ward on them so they won't wake up while we're traveling. Then, when we're back in San Francisco, I'll cleanse them for whatever sort of burial their families want. Easy."

Coriander's eyes were wide with surprise. "And that's… okay?"

"Okay?" Lou realized Coriander was speaking of matters moral. "Yep, there's even an expression for it in Chinese, 'Seung Sai gon si.' It literally means 'driving corpses to Seung Sai,' because so many of the men in that area left home to work and had to be returned home if they passed on while away. Families would hire Taoist priests to bring the bodies back—either like how I'm doing it, so they weren't rotten when they got home, or in other ways… like letting them re-animate enough to walk or hop along to their…" Coriander was looking nervously at the corpses, as if one might hop up right now. Lou decided to let it go. "In any case, this method seems best to me right now." She shrugged. "Honestly, I might be more hesitant to do this with non-Chinese, as it's definitely unusual in other populations, but given the circumstances…"

Coriander still seemed doubtful, but there was no time to argue about it—Lou just reassured Coriander that none of the bodies were currently in a position to wake and attack her, and then set to work. This inspired Coriander to lend a hand, and they worked together on preparing the corpses for the journey ahead. It wasn't a big job, but Lou appreciated having an assistant. Once she'd extracted sufficient corrupted soul-matter with her extractor, Coriander held shirt-collars or sleeves aside to give Lou access to convenient veins, which, given the volume of bodies and Lou's newly wonky left hand, sped the process along considerably.

It was not lost on Lou that she was more able to help these men now that they were dead than when they were alive. That didn't sit entirely well with her… but she was who she was. If this was all she could do for them, she would do it properly, as her father had taught her.

As she gently encouraged the kind of spiritual possession that she usually weeded out while carefully affixing wards to the corpse's foreheads to keep it under control, Lou wondered just what her father would think of her if he could see her now—if he would be proud of her successes, or if he would struggle to find something kind to say in the wake of her various failures. It was difficult to say. He had always been gentle to his family, but also dedicated to professional excellence. Letting a vampire escape was hardly a great example of professional excellence.

Then again, neither was letting her focus slip when performing her duties. In the end, Lou knew that whatever his opinion might have been she'd done her best, and would try to do better in the future. Come to think on it, that was all anyone could ever do.

Silently apologizing to her father's memory for her many shortcomings, Lou turned her thoughts back to the job at hand. When she came to Millie, not knowing what the woman would have wanted, she preserved her in the same way as the rest of the bodies, figuring Thurlow would have further insight when they had the time to talk it over. As she did so, she whispered a hoarse thank-you to the body as well as another apology; she had no words to express her guilt over having, through her foolishness, caused the death of the woman who'd warned her away from tangling with a vampire in the first place.

"I think that's it," she said in Toisanese to the three men who had been standing around, waiting for her to finish her business. "Thank you all for your patience."

"Thank *you*," said Kwan.

Lou felt her cheeks go warm. "I only wish I could have…" she swallowed. "I'm sorry, Kwan. When you said what you said about me coming alone… you know, when I decided to come out here I didn't know about Dr. Panacea. I just thought—"

"The only reason any of us are going home is because of you," interrupted Cheung.

"We'd better get them loaded up and secured," said Yan-chiu, glancing at the sky. He seemed less willing than Kwan or Cheung to engage with Lou. "She said we had to be gone by dawn, right?"

"Do you need help?" Lou very much wanted to check the big cave below the San for any lingering undead presence, but given the limited number of hours left to them, she thought it would be rude to leave the men to get themselves ready to travel as well as load the bodies.

"We'll be fine," said Cheung. "Go, do whatever else you need to."

"Care to help me out in a different way?" asked Lou, as she and Coriander headed back up to the San, making their way carefully along the path. The moon was long down, and while the stars were bright that night, it was still very dark.

"Of course!"

"Go get me that snack Vivien promised me? I want to check out the dragon cavern for any ghosts, but after that, I want to eat something before I blow away in this mountain wind. I can't imagine it's long before we need to get on the road."

With Coriander seeing to the more mundane parts of leaving the San, Lou was free to once again make her way under the earth and push a handful of lingering spirits into death. Unusually, all of them were eager to pass through the door. Lou chalked that up to plain old common sense. Nobody, not even a ghost, would want to spend any more time than they had to in that awful cave.

After packing all her materials back into her bag, Lou stood, stretched, and—noting the color of the sky beyond the cave mouth—trotted back towards the stairs. In her haste, her toe hit something small that skittered across the floor. Curious, she inspected the object and found Shai's knife, still crusty with her blood. For a moment, she considered throwing it out into the wilderness beyond… but then decided to keep it. Something about carrying the knife of the villain who slashed her face appealed to her—and she figured Shai would be annoyed by the loss of the blade if he and Dr. Panacea came back to collect their things. He'd be more than annoyed by the loss of his other treasured possession that she was planning on taking back with her to San Francisco, but that was just too damn bad.

When everyone finally gathered at the stables, the sky was definitely lighter in the east. They needed to be on their way—gone, really. Thankfully, most everyone was there already by the time Lou was gobbling down the sandwiches Coriander had brought for her, including the person she'd been most and least eager to see. But when she noticed Bo limping along, keeping close to Thurlow, she didn't know what to say, so she headed towards one of the wagons full of luggage and idled over loading her portmanteau and other bags.

"There you are," she heard Bo say from behind her, as she tucked away the last of her effects. "I haven't seen you since…"

Lou took her time adjusting her last bag, shy about meeting Bo's gaze. She felt some amount of comfort when she turned around, noting that even in the dim torchlight he looked much healthier than he had the whole time they'd been at the San. His cheeks were fuller and she no longer smelled the disturbing, rotten odor on his breath when he spoke. Despite this, however, his movements were careful and slow, as if he was attempting to avoid pain. She had no idea if he would live his whole life like that or not. Had she done him a favor, saving his life? It was an unsettling question, and one she knew she'd never have the courage to ask him.

"Sorry I didn't come by," she said at last. "I had some things to do. You know, dead-folks stuff. I know you think it's boring, so I didn't ask you to help."

He was smiling at her, though there was definite sadness in his expression. "Oh, was that the reason? Or is it that you have yourself a new assistant? She's cute. Sure you don't like girls?"

"Aw, go to hell."

"One day," he said, his voice studiously neutral. Lou flushed. She'd held out hope that all the crying and carrying on and admitting her feelings to him wouldn't affect their friendship. Maybe it hadn't, but saving his life surely had.

"Look," she mumbled, wondering if she could clear the air—but as she spoke, Bo stage-coughed into his hand, *ahem*. She let him speak.

"I guess... I wanted to say that I'm glad we're all headed back down to Estes together. Should be fun times."

"But?" she said, feeling the word hanging in the air when he paused.

"But after that... we'll be staying while you head on. Jack and Cait were gonna stop by the Fish Creek camp before heading all the way to the San in case I got better before they got back." He shrugged. "Griff might not like it, but Thurlow and I may have recently come into possession of a few, let's call them *unclaimed items of value*. I figure even with his opinions, Griff won't turn down an antique silver candlestick as payment for a few weeks of staying in a cabin."

"Just give me a goddamn letter that I can take home to your ma," said Lou. "She's probably worried sick about you."

"Of course," he said. "And speaking of things to take home..." Bo took Lou's hand and dropped her bolo tie into her palm, closing her fingers over the leather and metal. "You said I only had to keep this until I got better. Well, I'm better."

"Bo, no..."

He kept his hand closed over hers. "It'll make me happy, knowing you're wearing it, okay?" That smile! It always melted her. Lou felt her resolve weakening. "Anyways, no matter what you say, you need the luck more than me. Walking a path alone... that's tough."

Lou thought about all the times Imre had insinuated how much he'd like a job at the Merriwether Agency. "Maybe I won't be, much longer."

"Good."

Bo let her go, and hobbled away back toward where Thurlow waited for him. Lou stared after him, feeling sadder and happier than she had in a long time. She uncurled her fingers, and after a moment, she looped the tie around her neck and settled it into place. The familiar tension felt even better than before.

The sun was just cresting the ridge when they began their trek down the mountain and across the pastureland. Nobody had been left behind to the mercy of the bears, not even Mr. Magnusson, who had been surreptitiously dosed with a slug of the straight Elixir of Life and was now the picture of health. Turned out he was real nice... at least, it seemed like it. He was still pretty quiet, what with not speaking much English. But now that he was recovered he stayed as far away as possible from the Willoughbys, which earned him high marks with Lou at least.

Also with them were the San's staff. Speaking to Lou's opinion that Miss Foxglove was a scary hardass, the former fitness instructor had chained together several of Dr. Panacea's employees who'd attempted to escape in the confusion, and then tied their fetters to her saddle. They lurched unsteadily behind her on foot, looking sullen and disheartened as their temporarily free associates kept their eyes down and feet moving to avoid being treated in a similar manner. Lou had mixed feelings regarding this, but wasn't inclined to cross a Pinkerton agent over it.

It was a beautiful morning. The mist turned the dawnlight a hazy pink-yellow, hooves and feet crunched musically through the melting snow and ice, and a gentle wind that Miss Foxglove told them was called the "Chinook" gusted over them as it made the trees bend and rustle. Finches and jays trilled as they dived and dipped on the breeze, disappearing and reappearing as hawks circled above them, riding the drafts.

But the pastoral beauty wasn't the only reason Lou was watching the skies that morning. That Shai and Dr. Panacea might swoop down upon them at any moment worried her, but, as she mentioned to her companions, that would be more of a concern after the sun went down. Her remark was met with sullen, unenthusiastic silence, but Lou felt it was better for everyone to be aware of the reality of their situation. Just because they were away from the San didn't mean they were safe. No one seemed to want to think about that, though, so she hadn't yet mentioned that they'd be eating only cold meals until they reached Estes Park. From above, any amount of firelight and smoke would give away their position.

Mr. Rutherford distracted her from her thoughts when he whined, "Can't we take just a quick break?"

He was walking in front of Miss Foxglove, who cut a fine figure on her horse, dressed stylishly in a hunter-green split skirt and a fitted scarlet riding coat embellished with gold buttons and braid. Given how impressive she looked, Lou could finally agree with Coriander's insistence that the woman wasn't nine kinds of heinous. Physically, at least—she kept her anger and resentment over the Pinkerton agent's casually being a party to murder, cannibalism, slavery, and whatever else to herself, for Coriander's sake and her own continued health. Thus it was really more for her own peace than Miss Foxglove's when she decided to lead Speckled Betty closer and reprimand the annoying fellow; it had been his third request in under two hours.

"We're not stopping yet," said Lou loudly, hoping to embarrass the man into silence, "so lemme give you some advice, walking's a lot easier when you hush up your mouth. And trust me, you're going to want your breath. Look at that next hill, it's a doozy! But keep your chin up, at least you have dinner to look forward to."

"I do?" Mr. Rutherford's sweat-slick face shone up at Lou.

"Sure!" Lou grinned. "Hard tack, some of the San's cheese, and ice cold river water. Just the stuff after a hard day of hiking. Aren't you excited?"

"I like your style," said Miss Foxglove, as Mr. Rutherford trotted ahead, looking miserable. "I wonder if you might be interested in a proposition?"

Lou was immediately suspicious. Goddamn Pinkertons. Goddamn Miss Foxglove! "Interested? You need a psychopomp for something?"

"No; I have need of someone sensible. I plan on bringing the Rutherfords back to Chicago via Cheyenne, on the Transcontinental." Mr. Rutherford's back straightened when he heard his name mentioned. "I'm going to need to keep a close eye on them, they've slipped through many fingers before. Coriander's volunteered to keep watch, too, but another reliable pair of eyes would be most welcome."

"I'd be happy to help you bring them to Cheyenne," she said. "How much are you paying me for my time?"

Miss Foxglove smiled. "You'd claim more of a reward than the Elixir of Life?"

Lou glanced momentarily at a well-padded saddlebag hanging off Speck-led Betty. She wasn't ashamed for having claimed the remaining undiluted Elixir as her reward for helping Miss Foxglove with the bears, not one bit. She didn't plan on using it for herself—she just figured it would be safer in her hands than in anyone else's. And she figured her mother would be pretty damn pleased to be able to take a look at a medicine like that. Any-ways, they'd distributed the remaining commercial Elixir of Life to whoever wanted some, so she didn't feel *too* bad about taking the real stuff for herself.

"But afterwards, after we get to Cheyenne, I mean..." said Miss Foxglove, trailing off.

"Yeah? What about it?"

"I assume you'll be going back west? No way to keep your help all the way to Chicago?"

"Even if I didn't have my business waiting, I'd be disinclined. I'm not much of a traveler."

"And yet you came out here? By yourself?"

"Yeah, yeah, I realized a while ago that wasn't the best plan. I'd be dead now, if not for you, and for Bo and everyone else..." she added. Then she shut her mouth. She did not want to talk more about the matter.

"I am very sorry for everything you and your friends endured," said Miss Foxglove. "I wish I could have done more, but I assure you that my finding the files on these criminals, and immediately securing them, will make our journey away from here much safer."

"Oh, is that all you took?" Lou winked at Miss Foxglove, not expecting a response. She did not receive one. Instead, she got a job offer.

"Lou... what I'm about to say is nothing you don't know. You're fool-hardy and slightly insane, but those are qualities prized by my agency. If you ever get tired of the dead, there are several living people I know who would be interested in employing you. I'll give you my card before we part ways. Look me up. I can probably get you some steady work."

Lou was taken aback—Lou Merriwether, a lowdown dirty Pink? But she thanked Miss Foxglove nonetheless, and offered her a place to stay in San Francisco if she ended up out there for some reason.

"Other than investigating me, I mean," added Lou. "If that's your angle, I can't have you in my house. It's where I keep all my secrets."

"Of course," said Miss Foxglove. "Wouldn't dream of it."

Something occurred to Lou. "Have you thought about offering Coriander that job you were mentioning?"

"Coriander?" Miss Foxglove tilted her head, peering skeptically at the auburn-haired girl. She was the lone person who had not left her uniform behind, claiming it was more comfortable to hike in than anything else she had in her wardrobe, and was somehow managing to look radiant though she was already stained and muddied from the road. As she walked along with Kwan, Cheung, and Yan-chiu, Lou occasionally caught snippets of their conversation; Coriander was apparently attempting to learn a little Chinese. "I appreciate your sense of loyalty, but she's hardly of the same caliber as you are."

"You're wrong," said Lou, with more heat than she intended. "Really wrong. Coriander is brave, smart, confident, and enthusiastic. So think on it. I bet she'd enjoy working with you before she goes home to her family, and all that."

Miss Foxglove looked thoughtful. "Perhaps you're right. I'll mention it."

After that, for the rest of the day Lou kept mostly to herself. Part of her reticence was due to exhaustion, but she was also feeling a bit low about the prospect of Coriander's heading east with Miss Foxglove. Though working as a Pinkerton would surely be right up Coriander's alley, Lou knew she'd miss her.

It was funny, she'd always considered herself self-sufficient… but it was a little lonely, watching Bo and Thurlow leaning against one another as they rode in the wagon, just as it was later on, after they'd made camp, when Miss Foxglove and Coriander begged Lou to keep an eye on the Rutherfords so they could sneak off into the forest for a "quick nature walk." Not that Lou liked Coriander *that* way… not really. It was the companionship she envied.

Oh well, she thought, as she accepted two chunks of stale bread and a lump of cheese from Kwan. Once she was back in San Francisco she'd ask Imre if he'd consider staying on at the Agency, part time perhaps, so it wouldn't interfere with his studies. She felt little hope about them getting on as well as she had with Coriander, but maybe in time.

"Lou Merriwether!"

Lou almost dropped her bread. She'd been lost in thought, staring at where the San's patients were huddled together under blankets in lieu of a fire. Coriander was standing over her in the moonlight, hands on her hips. She looked deeply pissed off.

"What'd I do?"

"So you know you did something," said Coriander matter-of-factly.

"Huh?"

"Vivien says you thought I'd like to do a spell as a Pinkerton before I head back home!"

"Yeah?"

"Did you think to ask *me* about that?" Coriander tossed her hair. "What makes you think I even want to go home?"

"I just assumed you would," said Lou. "I've been homesick as hell since I left San Francisco, and you've been gone even longer'n me."

The girl's expression softened. "Well, fine. But what makes you think I'd want a job as a Pinkerton?"

Lou was still very confused. "You've said a bunch of times how much you've enjoyed working with me... and you and Miss Foxglove seem to have a good thing going. Right? So it just seemed friendly-like, to put your name in the hat."

"You are so dense sometimes." Coriander plunked down beside Lou on the log where she'd been sitting. "I think you missed my whole point. I've enjoyed working with *you.*"

"Yeah?"

"Yes! So what's wrong? Am I terrible or something?"

"Terrible at what?"

Coriander sighed. "At psychopomp... things."

"Psychopompery." Lou grinned at her. "No. Actually, you're a natural. Need to toughen up a bit, but—"

"Well?"

"Well what?" Lou could not for the life of her figure out what Coriander was after. "Tell me what you're saying to me. I'm having one of those dense moments you were talking about."

"If I'm a natural, what... do you just not like me? Why else would you get someone else to offer me a job instead of offering me one yourself?"

It took Lou a few moments to parse this, but when she did, she smiled so wide she felt her lip crack. "Are you saying... Coriander, San Francisco's a long way from New York. I just never thought you'd want to... it's dangerous work, and you don't even know the half of it. And I'm sorry to say when it's not dangerous, it's actually pretty dull. You sure?"

"Am I sure I'd rather work with you than go home and get married off to some lummox only interested in my money?" Coriander *tsk*ed at her. "Yes, Lou. Try asking people what they want sometime. It's a great way to figure out their thoughts and feelings!"

Lou snorted. "Fair enough. Well, Coriander Gorey, how's about you and I chat about what it really means to be a psychopomp. No, I'm serious—I want you to understand the full scope of things." Her father had made sure she began her training with her eyes open, about the dangers of ghosts, and possession, and the risk of mercury poisoning from vermilion. She'd do Coriander the same courtesy. "Then, if it all still sounds good to you... well, then I'd be real pleased if you'd come and brighten up the Merriwether Agency. Sound good?"

Coriander giggled and nodded. "Better than I can possibly express!"

"That's saying something," said Lou, handing Coriander her half-smoked cigarette. "You know, your parents are probably going to hire Miss Foxglove to kill me if they ever find out where you are."

Coriander thought about this for a moment.

"True," she admitted, after taking a long drag on Lou's cigarette. "But if they do, at least I'll know how to appease your ghost."

Acknowledgments

I finished the first draft of *Vermilion* in the summer of 2010. Five years, countless revisions, and two titles later, the book is in your hands. I would like to thank the people who helped it get there: my agent Cameron McClure and my publisher Ross Lockhart, my husband John and my best friends Jesse Bullington and Raechel Dumas, my mother, my father, Gina Guadagnino, Brad Deutsch, Selena Chambers, Erin Stocks, J. T. Glover, Mary Hu, Sally Harding, Guy Tanzer, and Shaolin Hung Mei Kung Fu. I would also like to thank Elmer Choy and his parents for their assistance with the Cantonese in the novel, Doug Wicklund for helping a gun-ignorant writer with the puzzle of period firearm accuracy, the staff at the Chinese Historical Society of America in San Francisco for running such a wonderful museum, and scholars Iris Chang, Wendy Rouse Jorae, and Robert Eric Barde for their illuminating research on the (real) history of San Francisco's Chinatown. I have inevitably left off many other names that should be honored here; my apologies for that, but please know I am truly grateful for your assistance. I will conclude by thanking Ricky Lau, Sammo Hung, Lam Ching-ying, and everyone else involved with *Mr. Vampire,* the wonderful 1985 film that first introduced me to geung si and Taoist necromancy. If you haven't seen it, find a copy. You're in for a treat.

Language Note

Lou Merriwether, her mother Ailien, and the other ethnically Chinese characters in *Vermilion* are largely of Toisanese descent. Toisan, formerly Xinning, and called Taishan in Mandarin, and Hoisan by native speakers, is one of the five counties in Guangdong Province (formerly called Canton, in English). During the California Gold Rush and subsequent periods of Chinese immigration to America, a large proportion of Chinese immigrants were Toisanese, so naturally their language became the lingua franca of San Francisco's Chinatown, and among the laborers working on the Transcontinental Railroad.

Though sometimes called Yue Cantonese, Toisanese is its own language, distinct from Cantonese. Unfortunately, being in general less accessible to an outsider like me, who neither speaks nor reads any form of Chinese, Toisanese proved too tricky to consistently and effectively Romanize. For this reason, on the advice of a native speaker, a language scholar, and the good people at the Chinese Historical Society of America in San Francisco, I have used Cantonese in the various instances where Chinese words appear in this novel—save for when Mandarin terms were vastly more familiar (such as qi).

Learning about the history of Chinese immigration to San Francisco was one of my favorite parts of researching *Vermilion*, but research is fundamentally humbling. I have tried my best to be accurate and respectful, but I know too well that sometimes one's best is not good enough. All this to say, I apologize for any errors in *Vermilion*, and I hope in spite of any inaccuracies it proved an enjoyable read.

TITLES AVAILABLE FROM WORD HORDE

Tales of Jack the Ripper
an anthology edited by Ross E. Lockhart

We Leave Together
a Dogsland novel by J. M. McDermott

*The Children of Old Leech: A Tribute to the
Carnivorous Cosmos of Laird Barron*
an anthology edited by Ross E. Lockhart and Justin Steele

Vermilion
a novel by Molly Tanzer

Giallo Fantastique
an anthology edited by Ross E. Lockhart

Mr. Suicide (July 2015)
a novel by Nicole Cushing

Cthulhu Fhtagn! (August 2015)
an anthology edited by Ross E. Lockhart

Painted Monsters (October 2015)
a collection by Orrin Grey

Ask for Word Horde books by name at your favorite bookseller.

Or order online at www.WordHorde.com

About the Author

Molly Tanzer is the Sydney J. Bounds and Wonderland Book Award-nominated author of *A Pretty Mouth* (Lazy Fascist, 2012), *Rumbullion and Other Liminal Libations* (Egaeus, 2013), this novel, and *The Pleasure Merchant,* forthcoming from Lazy Fascist in the fall of 2015. She lives in Boulder, Colorado, with her husband and a very bad cat. When not writing, she enjoys mixing cocktails, hiking in the Rocky Mountains, experimenting with Korean cooking, and (as of recently) training for triathlons. She tweets @molly_the_tanz, and blogs—infrequently—at http://mollytanzer.com.